FOLKTALES OF *Greece*

 *Folktales*
OF THE WORLD

GENERAL EDITOR : RICHARD M. DORSON

FOLKTALES OF
Greece

EDITED BY
Georgios A. Megas

TRANSLATED BY HELEN COLACLIDES

FOREWORD BY
Richard M. Dorson

THE UNIVERSITY OF CHICAGO PRESS

Chicago and London

GR
170
M39

International Standard Book Number 0-226-51785-3
Library of Congress Catalog Card Number 75-107224
The University of Chicago Press, Chicago 60637
The University of Chicago Press, Ltd., London
© 1970 by The University of Chicago
Published 1970
Printed in the United States of America

Contents

Foreword

For twenty-five hundred years the folklore of Greece has woven its spell over the Western world. Surely the proud myths of ancient and illustrious Hellas must conceal some message of majestic import for lowly mortals. Plato dallied with the myths, and lesser contemporaries—Apollodorus and Hyginus—began the practice of assembling them that has continued to our own day with the latest handbook of Robert Graves. The tales of the Olympian gods and heroes regale readers of each new generation and intrigue each new school of mythologists. Since the present volume consists of folktales collected from modern Greek storytellers, we should like here to consider the relation of folklore to mythology, two terms widely and loosely used and abused.

Modern Greek folklore scholars have understandably shown zeal in pursuing possible ties between the peasant tales of today and the myths of antiquity. The close links between nationalism and the study of folklore can be observed in one country after another, but nowhere has this connection been more ardently and spectacularly advocated than in Greece. Emerging as a nation-state in 1821 after over twenty centuries of eclipse under the Roman, Byzantine, and Turkish empires, the new Greece strenuously sought to build bridges back to Homer and Herodotus, Socrates and Plato, Aeschylus and Sophocles. Could Greek culture and the Greek spirit have survived the long centuries of foreign domination? Some scholars emphatically said no. The German historian Jacob P. Fallmerayer in 1827 (*Geschichte des Kaisertums Trapezunt*) contended that Greek country folk of the nineteenth century contained not a drop of blood that coursed through the veins of Athenians, Spartans, and Thebans in the days of Pericles. Slavic peoples had inundated and washed away all elements of classical Greek civilization.

Then in the twentieth century the Nazis repeated the charge during their occupation of Greece, in order to woo the Bulgarians. Alfred Rosenberg in *Der Mythus des 20. Jahrhunderts* (1936) asserted the Levantine basis of contemporary Greek society.

Greek scholar-patriots vigorously rebutted these declarations, and found in folklore one of their main resources. They sought to demonstrate that the folk beliefs, folktales, folksongs on the lips of Greek peasants harked back to the golden age of Greek mythology. The founder of folklore studies in Greece, Nicholas Polites (1852–1921) advanced the thesis of continuity between ancient and modern Greeks on the basis of extensive field and library researches. His published works, all in Greek and often running to several volumes per title, covered proverbs, traditions, folksongs, peasant life, and *Various Studies on Folklore* (3 volumes, 1920–30), described as "a real treasury of unused and unstudied [in England and America] material on modern Greek folklore."[1] Polites introduced the term *Laographia* in 1884 as a Greek equivalent to "folklore," and helped found the Folklore Society of Greece in 1908.

His foremost disciple, Stilpon Kyriakides (1887–1964), who held the chair of Ancient Greek Religion and Greek Folklore at the University of Salonica from 1926 to 1958, further developed his master's theme in over four hundred publications on dialects, folk traditions, and cultural history.

One lengthy essay in particular expresses the Greek nationalist view. In 1946, following the German occupation and ideological assault on Greek claims to antiquity, Kyriakides published in rebuttal "The Language and Folk Culture of Modern Greece." Here he brings to synthesis four strands of nineteenth- and twentieth-century cultural nationalism so often intertwined: history, language, literature, and folklore. European peoples who conceived of themselves as separate and special cherished the idea of

[1] Al. N. Oikonomides, Foreword to John C. Lawson, *Modern Greek Folklore and Ancient Greek Religion* (New York: University Books, 1964), p. xiv.

a mother tongue preserving an olden lore while cradling a new literature that in turn centered on indigenous heroes. If there existed a true and pure spirit in the modern world inheriting the glory that was classical Greece, it would be found, contended Kyriakides, in the living speech, beliefs, legends, and poetry of the village people.

Kyriakides set out to show the relations of the moderns to the ancients. First turning his attention to language, he retraced the long and bitter battle over the composition of a modern Greek script. One faction known as purists favored a basis in the ancient written language, and supported "katharevousa," while another championed the current spoken language of the people, the "demotic." A compromise group aimed to restore corrupted demotic words and forms to their true archaic sense, rather than replacing them with new idioms, but instead of healing the breach it added a third warring school to the controversy. "The conflict was reduced to a mockery because the archaists called the demotic language vulgar, semibarbaric and solecistic; the demoticists called the language of the archaists macaronic." [2] University and church supported the archaists or purists while the state slowly relented toward the demoticists, but with violent shifts of policy; demotic books were thrown out in 1920 when King Constantine and the royalists regained power, and reintroduced in the revolution of 1922. The archaists held tenaciously to their unrealistic position because of their overriding urge to link up with the ancients. Some of their number called the demotic school antinationalists serving foreign propagandists such as pan-Slavic Russians and German linguists. The division extended into literature, with poetry seeking expression in the demotic and prose keeping to the archaic. The situation in Greece differs from the analogous language battles in other countries, say Finland or Norway or Ireland, where the folk speech in its dialect forms ap-

[2] Stilpon P. Kyriakides, "The Language and Folk Culture of Modern Greece," in *Two Studies on Modern Greek Folklore,* tr. Robert A. Georges and Aristotle A. Katranides (Thessaloniki: Institute for Balkan Studies, 1968), p. 22. For comments on the language battle by an American sociologist, see Irwin T. Sanders, *Rainbow in the Rock, the People of Rural Greece* (Cambridge, Mass.: Harvard University Press, 1962), pp. 255–57.

pealed strongly to the nationalists, who appreciated the tongue of the people all the more for preserving the traditions of the people. But the Greeks already possessed a classical language and literature filled with mythology. Where the Finns wished to throw off the Swedish, the Norwegians the Danish, the Irish the English language yokes, the Greeks faced the problem of reclaiming a hallowed heritage after a gap of twenty-five centuries. Actually the demoticists and the archaists were both striving for a national language. The question dividing them was whether this new written language could best be represented by the vulgar or the classical mode.

In logical sequence Kyriakides next considered "folk culture." Now he spoke of social customs, folk beliefs, and the material culture of food, shelter, and clothing—the tripartite divisions of the European ethnological folklorist—and in each he found continuities with antiquity. Grain was holy in the time of Pericles, protected by Demeter; it strengthened fraternal bonds, and Priam's son Lykaon asked Achilles to spare him because together they had eaten the grain of Demeter. Likewise the modern villager respected bread as magical, with power to drive away evil spirits; he regarded the dropping or stepping on a piece of bread as sinful. Wedding customs with their elaborate ritual seem little changed in the villages of the twentieth century from those described in the pages of Hesiod and Pausanias. Peasant folk religion perpetuated the old polytheism of Mount Olympus.

To underscore his point, Kyriakides emphasized the harmonious coexistence of Christianity of the Eastern Church with pagan concepts. Country people worship the Virgin Mary and the saints much as their forebears worshiped the gods and heroes of old, and even attributed supernatural powers to their icons. Legends of the saints echo myths of the gods. In a tale still told, the Prophet Elijah was a sailor weary of the sea who walked with an oar on his shoulder to a place where people would mistake it for a shovel. He reached a mountain top, settled, and there he is worshiped. In the Odyssey, Tiresias tells this story to Odysseus, saying he should sacrifice to Lord Poseidon at the ultimate spot. Kyriakides did not report the version known at the present time to Greek sailors, who link the episode to their patron saint, Nicholas. Maine lobstermen tell a purely secular and bawdy form, a witness to its circulation over the centuries among the international fraternity of seafarers.[3]

Kyriakides pushed other continuities. The seductive Nereids (*neraides*) of hill and stream descend from the classical nymphs. Hades as an underground abode of the dead lingers on in laments for the departed (*moirdojia*), and Charon is easily recognizable as Charos, a demon of death, or his Christian equivalent in the Archangel Michael. The holy feasts of the church correspond to pagan holidays, and even incorporate certain pagan rites, such as masquerades during the Twelve Days of Christmas that recall the Dionysiac revels. When he turns to "Folk Poetry," Kyriakides sets down some eloquent texts in the so-called Akritic cycle, revolving around Basil Digenes Akrites and Byzantine border guards of the eighth century A.D. One song in which a mother kills her child and serves it cooked to her husband reminds him of the painful myth of Procne and Tereus in which Procne kills her son Itys and gives his boiled flesh to her husband Tereus, king of Thrace, who has cut out her tongue so that she cannot reveal his seduction of Philomela; the gods change them all into birds.[4] On the whole Kyriakides presses his claim less for folksong than for folk legend, although he believes that the shorter narrative songs popular today derive from the orchestral tragedies of the ancients.

The parallels assembled by Kyriakides were not in themselves novel. A work in English had appeared as early as 1910 by John C. Lawson, *Modern Greek Folklore and Ancient Greek Religion, A Study in Survivals,* wholly devoted to the same cause although operating from a different premise. Lawson was much influenced by Polites' *Study of the Life of the Modern Greeks* (2 volumes,

[3] Kyriakides, p. 259; Richard M. Dorson, *Buying the Wind* (Chicago: University of Chicago Press, 1964), pp. 38–39; Sanders, *Rainbow in the Rock,* p. 35; Robert A. Georges, "Addenda to Dorson's 'The Sailor Who Went Inland'," *Journal of American Folklore* 69 (1966): 373–74.

[4] Robert Graves, *The Greek Myths,* 2 vols. (Baltimore, Md.: Penguin Books, 1966), 1:165–66. Graves believes the myth to derive from a misrepresentation of wall paintings. The motif of a father eating his child cooked by his wife appears in Type 720, *My Mother Slew Me; My Father Ate Me* (Motif G61).

1871–74) and Bernhard Schmidt's *Das Volksleben der Neu-griechen und das hellenische Altertum* (1871), but he belonged intellectually to the English school of anthropological folklorists, and was himself a Cambridge University scholar. His subtitle indicated plainly enough his assumptions—those of survivalism, after the manner of Lang and Hartland, and what more glorious field laboratory in which to test the doctrine of survivals than modern Greece! But the folk traditions he uncovered in abundance on his rambles did not, as with Polites and Kyriakides, reflect a continuous artistic vitality of three thousand years so much as the remnants and fossils of a primitive and savage system. As classical mythology, in the theory of Andrew Lang, itself incorporated the ideas of a barbarous past, so did modern folklore exhibit the once accepted ideas of animism and human sacrifice in a still more advanced state of decay. The real quest of the Victorian folklorists was the mind of the prehistoric savage, and their conception of folklore was superstition still accepted by peasants. In an introductory section titled, suggestively, "The Survival of Ancient Tradition," Lawson clearly stated this frame of reference: "If then I can show that among the Greek folk of to-day there still survive in full vigor such examples of primaeval superstition as the belief in 'the evil eye' and the practice of magic, I shall have established at least an antecedent probability that there may exist also vestiges of the religious beliefs and practices of the historical era." And later he declares that a modern tale, "straight from the peasant's lips" in the same form it had been told by countless generations of peasants, could contain more authentically primitive matter than a literary version from classical times.[5]

Lawson distinguished between survivals of ancient, Hellenic, and pagan traditions. By ancient survivals, harking back to the childhood of man, he understood animistic and magical beliefs and practices, and found them in numerous evidences of the evil eye, so prevalent in the thought of contemporary Greeks (even to second generation immigrants in the United States); in wax, lead, and clay images fashioned in the likeness of one's enemies to injure them; in secret recipes for inducing love. In speaking of

[5] Lawson, *Modern Greek Folklore*, pp. 9, 77.

Hellenic tradition, Lawson rejected the Fallmerayer thesis that modern Greeks were Slavonic, asserting that, irrespective of their lineage, they were Hellenic in their sense of local patriotism, their hospitality, their delight in festival. These qualities overrode the difference in physical type between the handsome people south of the Peloponnese and the mongrel people of the mainland. By pagan tradition Lawson alluded to polytheistic concepts blending with Christianity, in much the manner noted by Kyriakides and indeed by every observer of the Greek scene for the past century. Lawson too expressed his astonishment at the proliferation of saints' miracles and faith-cures and the peasants' familiarity with supernatural beings of the mountains and sea.

The English doctrine of survivals has waned, but the spirit of nationalism in Greece, as elsewhere, has waxed, and by a fitting logic Lawson's study reappeared in an American edition in 1964 with a new foreword by a Greek classical scholar, Al. N. Oikonomides, who annexes Lawson's work to the cause of Greek national folklore. After hailing *Modern Greek Folklore and Ancient Greek Religion* as a "classic in its field . . . even more rewarding now than when first published," Oikonomides explains how it contributed to studies already under way in his own country.

> The science of folklore and the new independent nation of modern Greece were born almost simultaneously; the term folklore was not officially minted until 1846 when Greece had already had its new constitution for three years. . . . The only method which the new state could use to prove its ties with ancient Greece was the very same procedure followed by German scholars in connecting their nation with the ancient Germans This was the study of the survival of influences or memories of antiquity in modern traditions, folktales, songs and customs. Thus, the study of folklore became a nationwide project and a number of studies and collections of folk-literature were published in Greece together with the first modern Greek publication of the ancient authors, for both were deemed equally important.[6]

[6] Oikonomides, p. vii.

No more explicit statement could be made relating the study of folklore to the stirrings of nationalism. The inspiration of Jacob Grimm's *Deutsche Mythologie* for Greek scholars, alluded to by Oikonomides, applies also to Lawson, for Grimm's seminal work exerted enormous influence on the English folklorists, and was indeed translated into English as *Teutonic Mythology*. Yet a key difference separates the English from the Greek method; Oikonomides talks of survivals from antiquity, where Lawson and the "great team" of English folklorists spoke of survivals from savagery. The English were not concerned with forging links from peasants back to illustrious Hellenes but with demonstrating the long uphill route from barbarians to illustrious Victorians.

In emphasizing the unity of Greek and English folklorists, Oikonomides was on strong ground in one matter, the relevance of field investigations to historical research. He praised Jane Harrison, Frazer, and the overlooked author-compilers of *Greek Folk Poesy*, Lucy Garnett and John Stuart Stuart-Glennie, as precursors to Lawson in recognizing that modern data could illuminate ancient history. Folklorists had expanded the narrow horizons of classicists who examined only vase paintings, statues, choral dramas, and epic poems from twenty centuries and more in the past. Hats off to these English philhellenes! But in the final analysis the native Greek alone could appreciate and improve on their fieldwork. Oikonomides here introduces a personal and mystical note. "Truly and fully to understand the great value of Lawson's book, one must really be born in Greece and hear from his childhood the thousands of stories of dragons, nymphs and vampires related by 'eye-witnesses' to this day, not only in the backwoods of Greece, but in the very center of Athens where folk traditions seem to be strengthened every day despite the arrival of jets from abroad and the erection of a Hilton Hotel."[7] He knew of ten survivals of pagan cult practices, thinly Christianized, within a mile of the Agora below the Acropolis. He had seen icons in old Athens churches that annually received gold, silver, and precious stones weighing hundreds of pounds in return for their miracles and cures. He once witnessed the sacrifice on the steps of a church of a flower-wreathed bull, but like Pausanias before him,

[7] Ibid., p. ix.

would vouchsafe no further details, out of respect to the vow of
secrecy exacted by the priest. He had heard of a sailboat captain
who in a storm threw overboard the icon of the Virgin Mary
that had failed him, and called on Saint Nicholas, the Christian
Poseidon, with success, for shortly the sea grew calm. His own
boyhood friend had been spanked by his mother for sleeping in
his back yard under a tree inhabited by an evil spirit. Experiences
and observations such as these bound the Greek intellectual to
the folk, and made him thrill to his long-rooted heritage.[8]

Here indeed is the voice of the Greek folk nationalist. But to
test his thesis we will have to look at more detached observers.

Greek mythology is a bequest to all Western civilization. The
gods and goddesses and demigods and heroes of Mount Olympus, Athens, Sparta, Thebes, Corinth are as familiar to Europeans and Americans, through countless literary and juvenile retell-
ings of their adventures, as any pantheon of their own, and probably more so. Lacking an indigenous mythology, and brought up
on the Homeric myths, Americans in the 1920s and '30s eagerly
embraced a supposed set of home-grown superheroes led by Paul
Bunyan, but they proved to be fabrications, and the storybook of
Greek mythical tales still makes its annual reappearance. Rival
mythologies seem alien or incomprehensible, and in the standard
series of volumes titled Mythology of All Races, only the names
of the Greek protagonists are household words in the West. Mythology is a much older concept than folklore, going back to the
Greek *muthos,* while the science of folklore, and the word "folklore," only emerged in the nineteenth century. At the present
day, scholars of Greek mythology have depended increasingly on
the approach of the folklorist, and some have come to perceive
that mythological literature belongs under the umbrella of folklore traditions.

Interpretations of mythology began with the Greek philoso-
phers and have never ceased. What meant these fantastical accounts of Zeus and Hera quarreling on Mount Olympus, of Pro-

[8] A number of similar extant folk beliefs and saints' legends held by an
emigrant Greek family in the United States are given in Richard M. Dorson, "Tales of a Greek-American Family on Tape," *Fabula,* 1 (1957):
114-43.

metheus the fire-bringer, tortured on the Caucasian mountains, of Perseus cutting off Medusa's head, of the labors of Herakles and of Theseus, of Oedipus who unwittingly slew his father Laius and married his mother Iocaste, of Jason and the Argonauts questing for the golden ram's fleece from Colchis, of the siege of Troy and the wanderings of Odysseus? On only one point have the commentators agreed over the centuries, that the accounts are not to be taken at face value. The ancient Greeks themselves contributed two theories that long endured in renewed formulations: the allegorical, which viewed the gods and heroes as emblems of moral principles (Herakles was wisdom, and the monsters he slew were human passions); and the euhemeristic, named for Euhemerus (c. 330–c. 260 B.C.), who conceived of the gods as famous men and myth as fancified history (Zeus was born and died on Crete and once ruled the known world). Christian theologians, from the early church fathers to the late medieval schoolmen and the Protestant reformers, had their say about the myths they had displaced. Some, like Augustine, used euhemerism to reduce pagan mythology to chronicles. Others conceded that the meritorious elements of Greek religion had been plagiarized from Judaism. As late as 1858 England's prime minister Gladstone favored one version of this thesis, preferring degeneration to plagiarism, in his *Studies on Homer and the Homeric Age*. In the doctrine of Condescension, churchmen adopted a more charitable position, seeing paganlike practices among the Jews as a spiritual stepping-stone to higher revelation.

Philology, anthropology, and psychology brought new analyses to bear on the cherished themes. Celestial mythologists trained in Sanskrit philology explained the comparable deities of ancient India and Greece as solar and lunar figures (Zeus was the sky, like his Indic counterpart Dyaus). Anthropological folklorists recognized in Greek myths survivals of barbaric customs. In three long volumes Sidney Hartland unraveled *The Legend of Perseus* (1894–96) as a tissue of savage ideas (Medusa is a maleficent witch possessed of a death-dealing evil eye). The Cambridge school of anthropology, including such eminent names as James G. Frazer, A. B. Cook, F. M. Cornford, Jane Harrison, Jesse Weston, Gilbert Murray, and Lord Raglan, understood the

Greek myths to originate in narrative accompaniments to dramatic fertility rituals. Psychoanalytically-minded mythologists found Freudian symbols and Jungian archetypes, according to their preference, in the mass of myths. While the number of myth cycles known to Western scholars has greatly broadened in the twentieth century, thanks to numerous ethnologists in the field, the familiar Greek pantheon still remains a favorite object of myth explication, the more so since ethnologists have plied their trade eagerly in modern Greece.[9]

These elaborate interpretations, greatly as they differ, share a conception of the myths as a fixed and representative body of narratives open to exegesis that will disclose the hidden thoughts of the narratives' possessors. Folklorists see myths as relatively fluid, variable, and migratory, like all oral traditions, and thus imperfect reflectors of the cultural ethos of a vanished people.

In the present century the mythologist has gradually yielded to the comparative folklorist. While monistic theorists still have their say—Joseph Campbell is a Jungian mythologist on a grand scale—the writings of such progressive classical scholars as William Halliday, James Alexander Ker Thomson, Martin Nilsson, Rhys Carpenter, and Joseph Fontenrose—two Englishmen, a Swede, and two Americans respectively—show clearly enough the new perspective.

Halliday eschewed the term myth in the titles of two discursive volumes, *Greek and Roman Folklore* (1927) and *Indo-European Folktales and Greek Legend* (1933). A professor of ancient history, Halliday belonged to the English Folk-Lore Society after the heyday of the survivalists, and although not a fieldworker himself, he guided another folklore-minded classicist, Richard M. Dawkins, who became a highly successful collector of modern

[9] Brief résumés of the history of mythological theory can be found in Richard Chase, *The Quest for Myth* (Baton Rouge: Louisiana State University Press, 1949), chap. 1, "Traditional Views of Myth," pp. 1–6; Stanley Edgar Hyman, "The Ritual View of Myth and the Mythic," in *Myth, A Symposium,* ed. T. A. Sebeok (Bloomington, Ind.: Indiana University Press, 1958), pp. 84–94; H. J. Rose, *A Handbook of Greek Mythology* (New York: E. P. Dutton and Co., 1959), "Introduction: History of Mythology," pp. 1–16.

Greek folktales. In the years after the Great War, when Lang's evolutionism had fallen to rest along with Müller's solarism, Halliday looked at Greek myths dispassionately and found them operating in another sphere from folklore. He thus challenged the continuity thesis of Lawson. "It is perhaps remarkable that constant as has been its influence upon the sophisticated literature of Europe, the higher classical mythology and literature has exercised very little direct influence upon folktale."[10] Rather it was the reverse; folktales had fed the myths. Halliday thus drew the line between the literary and the spoken, or the mythological and the folk, channels of tradition, in ancient Greece as well as in modern Europe. Unlike the myths of the intellectuals, stories told by the common folk in antiquity were never assembled, but they were directly available to the mythmakers.

Writing before the Motif-Index and Type-Index were available, Halliday resorted to the Grimms' collection of Märchen as the touchstone to determine the presence of traditional tale elements in the myths. He saw variants of the incident in Grimm 20, "The Brave Little Tailor," whereby a hero tricks magical persons of low intelligence into fighting with each other—a favorite ploy of Jack the Giant Killer—in the myth of Cadmus (Kadmos), who slays a dragon guarding the Spring of Ares, god of war. At Athene's command, Cadmus sows the soil with the dragon's teeth, which sprout into armed soldiers; he throws a stone among them, and they fall to quarreling and slay each other—a motif repeated in the saga of the Argonauts and told of Jason.[11] Where Fontenrose, pursuing the combat myth, fastens on Cadmus struggle with the dragon, Halliday, alert for Märchen, eyes the aftermath.

An act of rejuvenation links the myth of Medea and Aeson with Grimm 81, "Merry Andrew." In the fairy tale, Saint Peter restores a king's daughter to life after dismembering her corpse

[10] William R. Halliday, *Greek and Roman Folklore* (New York: Longmans, Green and Co., 1927), p. 147, n. 1; and p. 85.

[11] Graves, 1: 196 (Cadmus), and 2: 238 (Jason); *The Grimms' German Folk Tales,* tr. Francis P. Magoun and Alexander H. Krappe (Carbondale, Ill.: Southern Illinois University Press, 1960), pp. 83–84; Motif K1082.1, "Missile thrown among enemy causes them to fight one another."

and boiling the bones. The Greek episode is not fully analogous. When the Argonauts return to Thessaly, Medea persuades two of Pelias's daughters to carve up their father in anticipation of a similar return to life. This is deception, not magic, but in another version Medea does truly restore Aeson to life, then tricks Pelias into undergoing the same treatment, from which she omits the necessary spells.[12] Resuscitation learned from a snake unites a myth of Polyeidus with the Märchen "The Snake's Three Leaves" (Grimm 16). Polyeidus is locked in a tomb in the palace of Minor with the body of Glaucus, son of Minos, who had drowned himself by sticking his head in a great honey jar. Minos will not release Polyeidus until he revives Glaucus. In the gloom Polyeidus sees and slays a snake, then watches while another snake lays a magic herb on its dead fellow and revives him. Polyeidus applies the herb to Glaucus, who starts up. The feat is also told of Tylo and Ptolemy. In the Grimm tale, a young king similarly immured in a tomb brings his dead wife back to life in an identical manner.[13]

The daring act of confining Death, and so stopping mortality in the world for a time, unites a mythical and a household tale. In the Iliad, Homer tells of Sisyphus tricking Hades into demonstrating the use of handcuffs and locking them on him, thereby keeping people, even beheaded ones, from dying, until Ares, worried about his wars, set Hades free. In Grimm 82, "Gambling Jack," the title hero maneuvers Death into climbing a tree from which no one can descend without his leave, according to a favor granted him by Our Lord.[14]

Still another possible correspondence between Greek myth and European Märchen is seen in the worldwide motif of the magic flight. Halliday cites Andrew Lang and Martin Nilsson on the appearance of this motif in the flight of Jason and Medea and in Grimm 79, "The Nixie." In the folktale, sometimes called "The

---

[12] Graves, 2: 251–53; *Grimms'*, pp. 294–95; Motif E30, "Resuscitation by arrangement of members."

[13] Graves, 1: 304–5; *Grimms'*, pp. 64–67; Motif E64.18, "Resuscitation by leaf."

[14] Graves, 1: 217; *Grimms'*, pp. 300–301; Motif 2111.2, Death magically bound to tree."

Devil's Daughter," fleeing lovers or children delay a pursuing parent or demon by dropping toilet articles, which grow into formidable barriers. In the myth, Medea causes her father Aeëtes, chasing her by sea, to stop and gather the pieces of her small brother Apsyrtus, whom she has cut up and thrown overboard piecemeal. To Halliday this device seems an excessive rationalization of the Märchen magic.[15] He prefers to indicate the close motif of the transformation flight as connecting the Grimm tales 51 "Foundling Bird" and 56 "Lover Roland" to Zeus's elopement with Aegina. To elude Aegina's father Asopus, Zeus turns Aegina into an island (since bearing that name) and himself into a stone. In "Foundling Bird" two children escaping a witch change themselves successively into a rosebush and a rose, a church and a chandelier, and a pond and a duck; in "Lover Roland" the lovers avoid a wicked stepmother by transforming themselves into a lake and a duck, and a flower and a fiddler. Halliday's correlation is indeed the more accurate.[16]

Yet other myth-Märchen relationships suggested by Halliday are confirmed by our present knowledge. He perceives in the myth of Daedalus—the famous smith who becomes jealous of the craft of his nephew Talos when Talos invents a saw from a serpent's jawbone, or a fish's spine, and pushes him off the roof of Athene's temple—the folktale of the sorcerer and his apprentice.[17] The classical account of Aëdon, who in envy of her sister Niobe's twelve children tries to kill the eldest and by mistake kills her own child Itylus, does indeed connote the incident of the stupid ogre who is led to kill his own offspring when the intended victim shifts nightclothes or places in bed.[18] And again

[15] Motif D672, "Obstacle Flight. Fugitives throw objects behind them which magically become obstacles in pursuer's path"; Graves, 2: 241; Halliday, *Greek and Roman Folklore*, pp. 93–94.

[16] Motif D671, "Transformation flight. Fugitives transform themselves in order to escape detection by pursuers"; Graves, 1: 212.

[17] Halliday, *Greek and Roman Folklore*, p. 94, citing two articles in Folk-Lore by W. Crooke and F. W. Hasluck; Graves, 1: 311–12; Grimm 68 "The Swindler and His Master"; Type 325, *The Magician and his Pupil*.

[18] Halliday, *Greek and Roman Folklore*, p. 94; Graves, 2: 27; Type 1119, *The Ogre Kills his Own Children* (Motif K1611), citing variants of Grimm 15, "Haensel and Gretel."

Halliday identifies the ruse of Odysseus blinding Polyphemus as a folktale episode to which Homer helped himself.[19]

The only "complete folktale" Halliday finds in classical sources is the romance of Cupid and Psyche, which Apuleius in *The Golden Ass* places in the mouth of a drunken old woman in a bandits' cave. Though set forth in literary dress, Halliday sees it clearly as a variant of Grimm 88, "The Singing, Hopping Lark," an elaborate Märchen revolving around an enchanted prince in lion's form finally unspelled by his bride after a series of magical adventures. The Cupid and Psyche story is thoroughly Grecian in its cast of Olympian and Underworld characters, but it does hinge on a love affair, freighted with magical episodes, between a mortal maiden and an invisible god.[20]

Turning from Märchen, Halliday comments perceptively on two less prestigious classes of folk narratives, ghost stories and noodle tales. Unpleasant ghosts were popular in the fifth century B.C., or at least the populace believed that black-faced shades of departed heroes emerged at night from their tombs and paralyzed unwary passers-by. Pausanias sees a picture of the ghost of Temesa, driven into the sea by a celebrated athlete, Euthymus, who rescued and married a girl abducted by Temesa. The hideous ghost is clad in a wolfskin. Nilsson too speaks of the prevalence of these ghost legends.

Drolls, or humorous anecdotes of simpletons, also circulated in antiquity. Athenians mocked the dull-witted Boeotian "pigs," just as modern Greeks poke fun at the islanders of Chios. Proverbial sayings ridiculed dullards named Morichus, Praxilla, Meletius, and Margites; the last-named would not make love to his wife for fear that she would protest to her mother. A surviving joke-book, *The Jests of Hierocles and Philagrius,* supports Halliday's

---

[19] Halliday, *Greek and Roman Folklore,* p. 98; Graves, 2: 355–57; Type 1137, *The Ogre Blinded* (Polyphemus); Richard M. Dorson, Foreword to *Folktales of Ireland,* ed. and tr. Sean O'Sullivan (Chicago: University of Chicago Press, 1966), p. xii, quoting Jeremiah Curtin, *Myths and Folk-Lore of Ireland.*

[20] Lucius Apuleius, *The Transformations of Lucius, otherwise known as The Golden Ass,* tr. Robert Graves (Harmondsworth, Middlesex: Penguin Books, 1951), "Cupid and Psyche," chs. 7–9; Type 425C, *Beauty and the Beast* (to which Grimm 88 is linked).

contention about the popularity of jokes among the ancients. One cycle deals with the absent-minded "pedant," prototype of today's university professor. Nearly drowning on his first immersion in the sea, the pedant swears he will never go near the water until he has learned how to swim. Calling on a lampmaker, he is asked what size lamp he wishes. Oh, large enough for eight men, he replies. A whole series of jests revolves around the discomfiture of ruptured people, a theme of jokelore now vanished from our midst. But other drolleries of our time are found among the Hellenes, such as the attempt of a simple farmer to teach his horse how to live without eating, by reducing his feed in half each day. But just as the horse is learning this regime, he dies.[21]

In the volume of essays on *Indo-European Folk-Tales and Greek Legend* (1933), originally delivered as lectures, Halliday again rejected the term mythology in favor of the concepts preferred by modern folklorists. "What is generally called Greek mythology consists of a comparatively small number of cosmological myths and a large store of legends," he states matter-of-factly.[22] Common sense prevails throughout his discussions of the relations of myth, fairy tale, and legend; of the diffusion of Indo-European folktales; of correspondences between Indian and Greek stories; of the rationalizing nature of Greek legend, exemplified in the tale of Procne and Philomela, who were transformed into a nightingale and a swallow (discussed by Kyriakides, "Language and Folk Culture . . . ," p. 5), and in the adventures of Perseus.

The reader is hardly aware that Halliday is treating the hallowed stuff of Greek mythology. Halliday speaks continually of folk processes that cause tales to travel across continents, take on local coloring, shift from Märchen to legend, or rise from a local to a pan-Hellenic legend, and he concludes that it is "very unsafe to deduce a ritual fact from a legend." Unlike the nationalists, he recognizes that the fables and folktale elements present in Greek

---

[21] *The Jests of Hierocles and Philagrius,* newly translated from the Greek by Charles Clinch Bubb (Cleveland: the Rowfant Club, 1920); Type 1682, *The Groom Teaches His Horse to Live without Food. It Dies.*

[22] Halliday, *Indo-European Folk-Tales and Greek Legend* (Cambridge: Cambridge University Press, 1933), p. 42.

legends have entered from outside Greece, particularly from the Levant. Miraculous elements tend to be rationalized, so that marriage tests take the form of athletic events. Legends do not stem from immemorial antiquity, and, except when written down, are always fluid. Folk memory will preserve only one or two momentous and striking events, such as the siege of Troy, and will muddle the order and chronology of all else. Halliday fully appreciates that historical and apocryphal episodes gather around eminent personalities, whether Argive warriors or Oxford and Cambridge dons. He knows the extravagant theories of mythology, propounded from the time of the ancient Greeks themselves down to modern pundits, and he smiles at "weather specialists, anthropologists and natural historians."

In their place he puts the theory of comparative folklore. At the core of the great myths lie elements and fragments of the intercontinental store of Indo-European Märchen. His chapter "Perseus, the Gorgon Slayer" applies this thesis to a specific myth. Save for Odysseus, no ancient Greek hero so clearly depends on the motifs of popular fictions, Halliday declares, and he points to one instance after another of fairy-tale formulas: supernatural helpers, magical objects, bogey creatures, marvelous insemination. Halliday thoroughly revises Hartland's exhaustive dissection of the Perseus legend as a tissue of primitive beliefs. Instead he sees a fairy tale, rationalized into historical tradition to suit the Greek taste. Hartland erred in emphasizing Perseus' rescue of Andromeda, chained naked to a rock as a sacrifice to a sea-monster, rather than his slaying of the Gorgon—and Halliday here anticipates the reading of Fontenrose in *Python,* a learned book about dragon slayers.

The conclusions that Halliday reaches in these studies are modest but convincing. A few whole folktales and many scattered incidents—what we now call types and motifs—circulated in the same form in classical times and in modern Europe. But he did not press for continuity from ancient to contemporary Greece, and saw external influences, from Oriental storytelling, medieval literary collections, and diffusion both east and west in the Persian empire, affecting the Greek repertoire over the centuries. Writing before the development of the method of motif-analysis, which surely proves his thesis, he yet unerringly seized on the common features in the narratives of Hellenic bards and European peasants. The one point we might add is that continuity within Greece, or any land, is more likely for local demoniac legend than for perambulating Märchen.

In *The Art of the Logos* (1935), James A. K. Thomson concentrates on the use of traditional narrative by Herodotus, and offers some excellent commentary on storytelling in ancient Greece. Thomson recognizes that Herodotus, even though an historian, provides the touchstone for the popular fictions of the Hellenic world. The folklorist customarily looks for a collection of tales, like the *Panchatantra* or the *Arabian Nights* or the *Decameron,* and finding none, perforce turns to the collection of myths made by Apollodorus and Hyginus in ancient Greece or to Ovid's *Metamorphoses* in Roman times. Herodotus opened his pages to every supernatural explanation known to the people for events of the Persian Wars, just as Thucydides closed his ears to any such wonders in chronicling the Peloponnesian Wars. Thomson rightly sees the twice-told tales assimilated in Herodotus's history as fitting into an "organic whole," whereas the great story collections remain disunited compendiums.

Thomson prefers "logos" to "muthos" as the term most appropriate for the oral prose traditions of early Greece. Originally both words meant "what is said," with no distinction inferred between truth and falsehood. Homer used "muthos" in this sense. Plato employed the two terms synonymously. Not till Pindar did "muthos," and consequently myth, come to acquire a distinctive currency. By speaking of the "logos," and of Herodotus as the master of logopoeic style, Thomson avoids all the confusing nuances of myth, and deals with folk narratives as a class that subsumes the myth. His distinctions are ingenious: a myth is an unconscious fiction in the field of religion, a legend is an unconscious fiction in the field of history, a Märchen is an unconscious fiction in the field of custom or ordinary life. Since legend is usually thought to be a truthful account—as indeed is myth on the supermortal plane—some might boggle at this definition, but legend does indeed contain its elements of unreality, perceived by

the outsider. As Thomson says, a popular tradition could contain
a series of facts in proper historical order, but it never does. He
recognizes, as does Fontenrose, that these arbitrarily separated
forms glide into each other. Herodotus himself presented variants
of the same tale. But the "logos" reflected the spirit of its people
in always seeking historical anchorage; hence myth and legend
are more commonly found among the Greeks than Märchen or
"pseudos," the conscious fiction. Thomson makes this point
shrewdly:

> Now it is a marked characteristic of the Greek popular tale
> —the more interesting because it is not characteristic of the
> *conte populaire* in general—that it eschews anonymity. It
> does not like to say 'A certain king'; it likes to say 'Croesus'
> or 'Cyrus'.[23]

An historian could well be attracted by floating fictions or sem-
ifictions if they wore the guise of sober truth, and if, like Herodotus and certain other followers of Clio, he savored the personal
anecdote and graphic incident to make more intimate the chroni-
cle of large-scale happenings. Thomson extracts a number of the
logoi inserted in the history of *The Persian Wars,* prints the texts
in English translation, and discusses their traditional qualities.
Having no international legend index at his disposal, nor even
the Motif-Index (not completed until 1936), Thomson was com-
pelled to rely on his own familiarity with variant texts to spot the
legend masquerading as history. So in the episode "How Zopyros
came to Babylon" he recognizes the "story of the patriot who
mutilates himself and deserts to the enemy with a lying tale
which lures them to destruction," a story that "appears over and
over again, sometimes with precisely the same details as in Herodotus, among the fabulous and legendary lore of the East and
even of Western countries." [24] Odysseus, and Sinon in Virgil's
Aeneid, perform the same trick. Thomson then proceeds to give
historical reasons why this adventure could not have befallen Zopyros.

[23] James Alexander Ker Thomson, *The Art of the Logos* (London:
George Allen and Unwin Ltd., 1935), p. 61.
[24] Thomson, p. 94; Motif K2357, "Disguise to enter enemy's camp
(castle)."

Another historical legend that Thomson unmasks is told as "The Wife of Candaules." A bodyguard of King Candaules named Gyges is ordered by the queen to gaze upon her naked, and then to kill the king and take her, or suffer death for having looked upon her; he takes the first option. Thomson juxtaposes a variant from Plato, in which a magic ring renders Gyges invisible as he seduces the queen and kills the king. Other traditional motifs to which Thomson calls attention are the warning dream that afflicts Xerxes before his ill-fated expedition into Greece; the concealment of the babe whose death has been commanded by a prophecy-fearing king (told of Cyrus and Cypselus in Herodotus, and also of Romulus, Moses, and Sargon the First); the children reared in isolation to determine what words they will utter; the treasure of Rhampsinitus, one of the oldest known Märchen, going back to Egypt; and the eating of his son's flesh by Harpagus, at a dinner given him by Astyages, angered at his failure to kill Cyrus.[25]

Where he does not find complete analogues, Thomson detects historical distortions and structural patterns that betray the logos. In "The Founding of Cyrene" he apprehends an urban genealogy as fabulous as any legend of an individual hero, for "Cyrene was as much interested in its origin as Philadelphia or Boston," but of course farther removed from its beginnings. The annals imputed to an oracle were actually fashioned by a storyteller from elements at hand. The wicked stepmother plays a role in the founding of Cyrene.[26]

It is greatly to Thomson's credit that he appreciates the social setting of the logos and discusses the act of storytelling as well as the content of the text. Only in recent years have folklorists come to stress context along with text and to recognize that each delivery of an oral narrative is a unique occasion, equally involving audience and teller. Thomson devotes a whole section to "The

[25] Thomson, pp. 87–90, 152–56, 158–61, 183–85, 56–57, 161. The respective motifs and types are D1076, "Magic ring"; D1813.1.2, "Dream warns king of error in judgment"; K515.1, "Children hidden to avoid their execution (death)"; J2260, "Absurd scientific theories"; Type 950, *Rhampsinitus;* Type 1119, *The Ogre Kills His Own Children* (see note 18).

[26] Thomson, pp. 44–49; Motif S31, "Cruel stepmother."

Art of the Story Teller" and underscores the fact that the folk narrator must adapt his style and repertoire to the psychology of the audience. The logos is a joint product of the teller and of his listeners, who demanded stories that purported to contain lessons of history and that demonstrated the value of prudence. Mere entertainment was not enough. Thomson also shrewdly points out that skilled writers, like Herodotus and Mark Twain, do not reproduce the spoken word and oral tale literally, but rather the *effect* of the spoken word.

The storyteller's art and the historian's craft necessarily conflict. On the vexed question of the trustworthiness of oral traditional history, Thomson states unequivocally that "whatever has been long sunk in the enchanted waters of the popular imagination does not so much gather incrustations as suffer a sea change."[27] A scholar cannot peel extraneous matter off the logos as if it were a barnacle to find the residue pure history.

The Persian Wars pivots on the tragedy of the Great King, Xerxes, the theme indeed of a drama by Aeschylus. This is popular history, says Thomson, and not scientific history. The folktales, the logoi imbedded in the history, reflect attitudes of the people, as in "The Ring of Polycrates," a legend conveying the moral, prevalent still among the Greeks, that excessive admiration of one's person or goods invites danger; the flatterer may possess an evil eye. Because Polycrates conquers and prospers, he takes the advice of his friend, the Egyptian king Amatis, to rid himself of a prized possession, and casts into the sea his most precious ring, that others will not envy him. But a fisherman gives a fat fish to Polycrates as a gift, and in its belly is the ring. Amatis then sorrowfully severs his friendship with the too lucky Polycrates, who meets a horrible death by crucifixion. "That story . . . belongs not to history, but to folklore. . . . It is a tale of the people made in the spirit of the people; its philosophy of life is the popular philosophy."[28] Herodotus is not an historian so much as an Homeric artist, weaving the logoi into a prose narrative of epic proportions and tragic unity.

[27] Thomson, p. 96.
[28] Ibid., p. 131; Type 736A, *Ring of Polycrates.*

Martin P. Nilsson's vivid study *Greek Folk Religion,* as it is titled in its 1961 paperback edition, was called *Greek Popular Religion* in its hardback edition of 1940, and the title change is itself a victory for the folklore approach. For Nilsson is discussing the religious notions and observances in ancient and contemporary times of Greek peasant folk, who, he believes, share the folklore of northern Europeans. He concentrates on the farmer and herdsman of the backcountry rather than the famous personalities of the cities, and he deals with minor deities and demons in place of the celebrated high gods. When he does briefly turn to urban centers, it is to show how artisans, like the potters of Corinth, feared and sought to neutralize such destructive creatures as Sabaktes, Syntrips, Smaragos, who cracked and splintered their pots.

With the feeling for the peasant's daily round acquired from his own life in rural Sweden, and with his knowledge of published folk materials, Nilsson reconstructs a new picture of ancient Greece. In place of the high civilization reflected through mythology, literature, and art, he portrays the culture of the countryside with its blend of the sacred and the secular. Religious rite and folk custom coexist, great gods and local heroes are equally reverenced. One comes to see that "superstition and a belief in magic and witchcraft were very common and widespread in the heyday of the classical age." [29] The guidance of oracles and omens, the insurance from garden rituals and house cults, the fears of underworld punishments and monsters above ground governed the lives of Plato's contemporaries. Nilsson realizes that literature ignored routine living and that mythology often followed a grander course than popular belief; hence he depends heavily on comparative folklore to flesh out the bare bones of folk life in Hellas. Thus in combing the *Works and Days* of Hesiod, himself a peasant from Boeotia, Nilsson extracts proverbial wisdom, rules of conduct and purity to placate gods and demons, lists of lucky and unlucky days, and superstitious codes of behavior, which are all "well known from modern folklore." Taboos in Hesiod warn a worshiper not to cut his nails at a sacrificial meal, a boy not to sit on an object not permittted to be moved, a man

[29] Martin P. Nilsson, *Greek Folk Religion* (New York: Harper Torchbooks, 1961), p. 115.

not to bathe in a woman's bath. Elsewhere Nilsson recognizes as
common in European folklore such phenomena reported in ancient Greece as river spirits appearing in the shape of bulls; the
half-human half-bestial qualities of centaurs; the May bough that
symbolizes fertility and renewal; the weather-changing spells of
magicians; the prophecies of seers; snakes conceived of as house
guardians.[30]

Turning aside from the hallowed myths, Nilsson gives recognition to the role of ghost stories in the ancient world. Often they
attached themselves to heroes. Athenians feared to meet Orestes
at night because he would thrash and strip them. Boeotians
chained the statue of Actaeon to a rock, on an oracle's advice, to
prevent his pillaging their fields. In general, peasants venerated
heroes at their gravesites, strewn over the countryside. Hecate became the goddess of witchcraft attended on dark nights by ghosts
and barking dogs. Old and young were alarmed by grotesque
specters, such as the Empousa, described by Aristophanes as a
chameleonlike creature, now a dog, now a snake, now a wild animal, now a fair maiden. These bloodsucking *lamia,* and the more
attractive nymphs, live on where the gods are forgotten. Horrors
and torments of the underworld, based on the idea of retributive
justice, permeated the folk mind far more thoroughly than the
records of mythology suggest.

Nilsson pointedly distinguishes between the mythological and
the folk conceptions of heroes. Heracles was a conventional mythical hero who averted supernatural evil by slaying monsters,
ghosts (like Antaeus) and Death itself. Theseus was a local hero,
protecting the peaceful arts of an agricultural society against robbers and highwaymen. Heroes were closer to the people than the
mighty gods, and it was natural enough that they would merge
into the medieval cults of saints. Peasants attributed miraculous
powers to the relics of heroes and saints alike.

Unlike other classical scholars utilizing folklore, Nilsson chose
not to concentrate on the folktale, and much of his success lies in
detecting more pervasive kinds of popular tradition. Matters that
interest him are the leaden tablets bearing curses placed in tombs
by the kin of the deceased; homely, mundane questions about

[30] Ibid., pp. 105, 11–12, 38–40, 112, 124, 71.

daily problems posed to oracles, and oracular verses that circulated orally; seasonal rites and weather magic important to husbandmen. Yet he does refer too to folk narratives and seeks to relate them to peasant life, mentioning a comic story told by herdsmen about Hermes as a babe stealing Apollo's oxen; like Thomson, he cites the "Ring of Polycrates" legend in Herodotus to illustrate folk religious belief, in this case the Greek idea of *baskania,* that the too fortunate person will receive excessive praise which brings harm.

One wishes that Nilsson had offered some specific references in place of his general allusions to "modern folklore." Once he spoke from his own knowledge of a Swedish farmer who set milk before house snakes as a propitiatory offering. Still there is no doubt that Nilsson has convincingly demonstrated the presence of folklore elements in the worldview of Greek farmers and artisans in the fifth and fourth centuries B.C. *Greek Folk Religion* presents a much needed balance to the overweighted emphasis on the Greek high gods.

Another striking instance of a classical scholar employing the resources of folklore to illuminate heavily worked materials is *Folk Tale, Fiction, and Saga in the Homeric Epics* (1946), glowingly written in lecture form by Rhys Carpenter. The talk here is not at all of mythology but of concerns central to folklore: Märchen plots and motifs, the historical residue in oral legends, the technique of oral epic, parallel themes in the great heroic cycles. Addressing himself to the much mooted "Homeric question," Carpenter seeks to ascertain the ingredients, date of composition, and authorship of the Iliad and the Odyssey, and he comes up with bold answers. He avers that the Iliad was composed about 700 B.C., the Odyssey between 640 and 620 B.C., and that two different poets stitched together the epics, for the Iliad is basically saga and the Odyssey is basically a transmuted folktale, both decked out with fictional scenes and extended characterization.

These celebrated epics, then, are elaborations of folk narrative. Carpenter begins directly with a discussion of oral literature and its overwhelming dominance over written literature in man's history. This overture leads him into folklore questions such as the distinction between fully literate, partly literate, and wholly illiterate peoples, whose oral traditions increase in complexity as their dependence on print declines. Surprisingly, Carpenter casts his vote for the alignment of classical Greece with literate western Europe and places the Märchen at the bottom of the hierarchy of oral narrative forms, rather than with the well developed oral epic tradition of eastern Europe and the Middle East. He of course knows and praises the work of Milman Parry with the south Slavic epic, and he fully accepts the oralness of the Homeric poems, but he links Homer to fairy tale and saga, not to independent heroic epics. It is with the Märchen of the brothers Grimm that the great epic stories find their brethren—and Carpenter mentions in the same breath the talented peasant woman who regaled Jacob and Wilhelm Grimm, Frau Viehmannin, with "the makers of Iliad and Odyssey." Aware of the Greek tendency to rationalize away the marvelous and to humanize the monstrous, Carpenter ferrets out Märchen devices and stereotypes tucked inside the bardic tales, which themselves drew upon a lengthy oral tradition preceding Mycenaean Greece. The whole episode of the witch Circe who imprisons Odysseus's companions and at length is overcome by the hero, suggests to Carpenter the adventure of Hänsel and Gretel, capped by the witch's recognition of her conqueror through a prophecy. "Whence came this gratuitous touch of folklore unless out of the great universal tradition of folk tale, to which Homer must have had access?"[31] So too in the Iliad does Märchen lore appear in the talking steed, the dread spear, the impregnable armor, the fiery halo that accompany Achilles.

But it is the parallelism between Odysseus and other mighty heroes of epic and saga, Beowulf and Grettir and Roland, and their joint indebtedness to the folktale of the Bearson, that particularly excites Carpenter. He weaves a tenuous web uniting the Getan tribal cult of Salmoxis, a deified bear whose rites were described by Herodotus, with modern European peasant festivals, the groundhog weather forecast brought to colonial America by

---

[31] Rhys Carpenter, *Folk Tale, Fiction and Saga in the Homeric Epics* (Berkeley and Los Angeles: University of California Press, 1946), p. 20.

German immigrants, and the Bearson story exhaustively studied by Friedrich Panzer. Carpenter reads into the cult and tale of the mighty Bearson an allegory of a struggle between a mighty hero (Odysseus, Beowulf) and an ogre (Circe, Grendel), who is death personified. Bearson overpowers the demon and then follows him to the underworld, where he finds treasure, rescues a princess, and marries her after his return—hindered by his faithless companions—to the upper world: ". . . the parallel between Bearson and Odyssey is undeniable and unchallengeable." [32] Alike, they tell a story—conjectures Carpenter—of death casting its fatal shadow over the living, and of a hope for life beyond death. One thinks of the Python struggle between god and dragon that Fontenrose traces in other grooves of Greek myth.

Odysseus is also related, in Carpenter's view, to another folktale, "The Man Who Disappeared," best known in literary versions as Rip Van Winkle, but attested as true in a series of documents that can only be migratory legends. In some of these texts the missing man reappears after six weeks, the conventional period for the bear's hibernation. And Herodotus provides a clue to link the Man Who Disappeared with bear hunters and bear worshippers.

Even the Iliad, converted into saga purporting to be history, may rest on a folktale base. Carpenter finds "enough basic resemblance to folktale to leave us wondering whether some popular story, known to the Greeks but no longer familiar to us, may not have inspired the narrative and motivated the action." [33] He also offers an alternate hypothesis, that the Iliad arises out of an actual sea invasion the Greeks undertook in an enemy country, but incorporates many floating incidents of Märchen and Sagen.

It is not the validity of Carpenter's arguments that concerns us but rather the method and the concepts he employs, which are those of the folklorist. As he himself says, there are no final proofs in comparative folklore. Yet the persuasiveness and novelty of his reasoning have reopened the whole Homeric question. The classicist does not deal, he rightly observes, with the story-within-the-story linkage in the structure of the Odyssey, which

[32] Ibid., p. 152.
[33] Ibid., p. 76.

substitutes a series of variant popular tales for a continuous narrative. Carpenter is no dilettante in folklore. His statement about the lack of an adequate English term for what we loosely call folktale, and about our necessary reliance on the German Märchen for certain kinds of magical plots and incidents, could not be improved. It is only regrettable that he did not include the motifs of Stith Thompson, just available at the time of his lecture, in his Märchen references.

The relations of Achilles and Odysseus to other celebrated heroes of epic, saga, and romance have of course been frequently noted, as in the Heroic Age view of literary history presented by the Chadwicks, or the myth-ritual thesis of Lord Raglan. Strong men everywhere display certain similarities in their feats. Carpenter, however, has worked outward to these resemblances from the heart of classical Greek epic literature, steering a moderate course between the Scylla of extreme diffusion and the Charybdis of extreme polygenesis. Not all is Märchen, nor saga, nor fiction, but something of each enters into the finished epics.

In *Python, A Study of Delphic Myth and Its Origins* (1959), Joseph Fontenrose begins with one famous episode of Greek mythology, the combat between Apollo and the dragon Python at the oracle of Delphi, and brilliantly traces its recurrence through Greek, Near Eastern, and even Far Eastern mythic narratives. As other mythologists before him, Fontenrose recognizes the similarity in a number of tales of gods and heroes slaying monsters and serpents, but where they perceived mythic representations of the sun conquering darkness, or a ritual sacrifice to ensure fertility, or a sublimated sexual act, he examines the source materials from the point of view of the comparative folklorist and reaches quite different conclusions about the origin, dispersion, and ultimate meaning of the combat myth. Fontenrose sees the Apollo-Python and Zeus-Typhon combats, as well as the conflicts with dread creatures of other heroes, such as Herakles and Perseus, and the similar combats known in Mesopotamia, Egypt, India, even China and Japan—but not in the Americas—all as genetically related offshoots of one great central myth, a conflict between Cosmos and Chaos. The god-champion stands for light and order, the dragon-demon for darkness and disorder. All this Fontenrose works out with clarity, learning, and ingenuity.

The terms and concepts he uses are those of the practicing folklorist. Myth is a traditional story attached to a cult. In the history of man, legends probably came first, as primeval hunters told graphic accounts of tussles with mighty beasts and robbers. Embroidered still further and rendered fanciful, the legends passed into folktales. When national religions and their deities emerged, the reservoir of legend and folktale could be siphoned into myth. Fontenrose here has reversed the process conjectured by the Grimms, who conceived of Märchen as the degenerate fragments of myths. All three of these basic forms of traditional narrative—and Fontenrose emphasized that he was writing about such narratives—were oral. Here was the point so little understood by mythologists: myths like any other species of folk narrative lived by word of mouth. Hence they were subject to continual and chameleonlike variation. (Fontenrose cleverly distinguishes between *variant,* when names are changed but the plot stays the same, and *version,* when details change.) But pre-Christian myths can no longer be heard and recorded, as can secular legends and folktales. Accordingly the classical mythologist must treat his sources in literature and art as imperfect and secondary fragments of full-bodied oral recitals, to which authors, painters, and sculptors had constant access. "Scholars have tended to neglect the oral transmission of myths," Fontenrose remarks in quiet understatement.[34] By comparing closely the pieces of myth preserved in ancient literature, and observing how analogous elements shift and recombine, in the manner of all oral folklore, the scholar can fathom the complete myth.

The particular technique employed by the folklorist to identify the component parts of folk narratives is motif analysis, for which Fontenrose quite properly substitutes theme analysis. *Motifs* in the Stith Thompson index apply labels to characters and incidents in folk literature, but in the combat myth these labels are often interchangeable; hence they can be better covered by

[34] Joseph Fontenrose, *Python: A Study of Delphic Myth and Its Origins* (Berkeley and Los Angeles: University of California Press, 1959), p. 5.

more inclusive *themes*. The enemy that the champion fights may be a dragon, snake, lion, boar, vulture, or other animal, or a mixture of human and bestial features, but all are manifestations of the same theme, "The Enemy had extraordinary appearance and properties." In the Motif Index, each variant would be classified under the respective animal. Fontenrose's table of "Themes of the Combat Myth" is another kind of folklore index, tailored to a specific family of narratives. Yet he still provides a motif index in an appendix.

Throughout his compendious work, Fontenrose indicates the insensible gliding of one story element into other variants and versions until, when the whole, vast mythic cycle is unraveled, a Hegelian synthesis has merged god into demon, savior into destroyer, life into death and rebirth. These continuous variations lie at the heart of the folklore process, as Fontenrose well understands. "Giant and dragon interchange as opponents of god or hero in folklore." Typhon "was dragon, giant and monster in one, good evidence in himself of the folkloristic identity of every kind of ogre. . . . Spectres, bogeys, and demons . . . are forms of the dragoness and dragon who fought the gods' champion. . . . The infernal boatman is a powerful demon who may in folklore become the lord of death himself." Then there are the Hegelian blends: "The hero-ghosts were very likely to be malignant; . . . the Titans are the descendants (folkloristically speaking) of the rebel gods. . . . The dying fertility god . . . may become champion or victim or the enemy himself . . . Chaos demoness, earth goddess, and mother goddess are alike spirits of fertility"; Herakles "occupies every point in the religio-mythical spectrum from mortal hero through demigod and chthonian deity to Olympian god. . . . The hero-gods of the displaced peoples tended to become cast in the role of dragon or brigand"; the voyage of the Argonauts is actually a descent to the underworld, and the Argo's pilot is truly Charon. Fontenrose will make a bolder leap beyond text analogies and see Hitler as a modern counterpart of the dragon, and the divine combat as a Freudian drama between life and death instincts.[35]

[35] Ibid., pp. 56, 70, 145, 478, 119, 243, 254, 257, 321, 424, 478–85.

In his attitude toward the controversial question of myth origins, Fontenrose again takes a folklorist's position. The myth does not initially accompany and explain the rite, but emerges from a previous stock of narrative traditions and fastens onto a cult or rite in need of a colorful genesis. Such a proposition is anathema to the devout believers in ritual origins of myth, whose most strenuous advocate in the United States is Stanley Edgar Hyman. The exchange between Hyman and Fontenrose, following Hyman's review of *Python*, illustrates crisply the rigidity of the ritualists and the flexibility of the folk mythologist. To Hyman's charge that he has treated myths as "distorted trivial history," Fontenrose answers that migrations, raids, invasions are deadly serious business to tribal peoples, and that men who conceive animistically of the seasons would most likely envision a real combat in the struggle between winter and summer.[36]

All these appliers of the folklore method to the classical Greek sources had perforce to speculate on likenesses between ancient texts of oral epics preserved in writing and modern texts of folktales collected in Greece and elsewhere. For who in the twentieth century could invoke the aid of the gods to wing back into the charmed era of the Hellenes and tape-record their heroic lays? Yet two imaginative scholars, Milman Parry and Albert Lord, did the next best thing: they examined with meticulous care a living oral epic tradition close to Greece, and then reexamined the Iliad and the Odyssey in the light of their personal observation and interrogation of Yugoslav bards. In a brilliant collaboration, Lord the Slavicist and field folklorist continued the work of Parry, the classicist who died in 1935 at the age of thirty-two when he had just set out to write a revolutionary book about epics. Lord produced this book, *The Singer of Tales*, in 1960. Instead of comparing the texts of folklore, Lord compared the performances of folklore, in this case the singing of long heroic poems by Serbian *guslars* accompanying themselves on their national musical instrument, the one-stringed fiddle known as the

[36] Stanley Edgar Hyman, review of *Python*, in *Carleton Miscellany*, I (1960): 124–27; Fontenrose, "Some Observations on Hyman's Review of *Python*," ibid. 2 (1961): 122–25.

gusle. Did the author of the Iliad and the Odyssey sing and com-
pose in a similar manner?

Lord believes he did, and marshals his evidence according to
formulaic and thematic patterns that depend, in the Homeric as
in the Yugoslav poems, on the techniques of oral composition.
The epic singers are totally oral bards—not passive transmitters
but active arrangers of traditional materials. Marginal shadings
between an oral and a written epic form do not exist; the poet
works either within an oral tradition or at his writing desk. The
oral poet knows and cares about no fixed text, and the Iliad and
Odyssey as we have them are variants in a fluid medium. Lord
renders his judgments with the authority of the experienced field
observer—for instance, when he dismisses the idea that Homer
performed at a festival, this being an unlikely if not impossible
milieu for a lengthy recital.

The foregoing works belong to no particular school but they
have in common the approach of the folklorist rather than the
mythologist to the body of Greek myths. Halliday pointed out
correspondences between episodes in the myths and in modern
Märchen and inferred that they came from a common source.
Thomson showed the role of popular story in the artistic history
of Herodotus, and Carpenter revealed the debts of the composers
of the Iliad and the Odyssey to saga and Märchen. Nilsson uncovered the broad base of folk belief beneath the formal religion
of the ancients. Fontenrose traced one recurrent majestic theme,
the dragon slayer, through the classical sources to illustrate the
variety, in unity, of a folk legend. Lord separates the Homeric
epics from other sources—Herodotus, Hesiod, Pausanias, the
Attic dramatists, friezes, paintings, and sculptures—in calling attention to the special character of oral bardic composition. Still,
the themes and motifs of narrative folklore forms flow freely
back and forth between epic, legend, fairy tale, and ballad, and
all are permeated with folk belief. In the light of these studies,
Greek mythology can be understood as a literary and artistic revi-
sion of oral folk traditions that floated freely in Homer's day and
are floating still today. The continuity is not from classical myth
to present folktale within Greece, but from a European body of

folklore that existed then and exists now, always in flux yet remarkably pertinacious, which nourished the myths.

Georgios A. Megas, editor of the present volume, continues the exemplary tradition of Greek folklore scholarship initiated by Polites, his "unforgettable teacher," and Kyriakides. Born in northern Thrace in 1893, he attended the universities of Athens, Leipzig, and Berlin, taking his doctorate at the University of Athens in 1925. He has served as director of the Folklore Archives at the Academy of Athens, 1936–55, professor of folklore at the University of Athens, 1947–61, and honorary director and professor in both positions to the present time; editor of *Laographia,* 1952 to the present; president of the Greek Folklore Society, 1960 to the present. Besides being the central figure today in Greek folklore studies, Professor Megas has also represented his country in international folklore organizations, and played host to the Fourth International Congress of the International Society for Folk Narrative Research held in Athens, September 1–6, 1964—a spirited gathering highlighted by a tour to Delphi and an open-air performance of Euripides' *Alcestis.* Megas edited a fat volume of the papers delivered at the congress.[37]

His own writings span three major areas of Greek folklore: traditional house types (in Thessaly, the Dodecanese, and the Balkans); festivals and saints' days of the calendar year; and folktales. Throughout his versatile work Megas remains faithful to the principle of continuity. In *The Greek House* (1951) he has contended that "the survival of the ancient building types in all their variety and vitality in modern Greece . . . proves their continuity also during the Middle Ages, so that the tradition in Greek soil remains continuous and unbroken from the most ancient times up to today."[38] Megas tells us how he gradually enlarged his field researches in the Didymoteichon from folk-reli-

---

[37] *IV International Congress for Folk Narrative Research in Athens, Lectures and Reports,* ed. Georgios A. Megas (Athens, 1965). Cf. *International Congress for Folk Narrative Research of Kiel and Copenhagen* (Berlin, 1961), pp. 109–205, for a paper by Megas on Greece as a distinct folktale region.

[38] George A. Megas, *The Greek House, Its Evolution and Its Relation*

gious beliefs and habits to peasant houses and the problems of
construction, space arrangement, stabling of cattle, and storage of
cereals, in relation to conditions of climate, soil, biology, and history. From the house structure as a whole he turned to the specific details of roof, hearth, storeroom, oven, loom. "Thus in spite
of the many technical difficulties I had to overcome, I found that
the study of popular dwellings was the most interesting and fasci-
nating, and at the same time, the least explored part of my folklore researches."[39] Far from divorcing spiritual and material
folklore, Megas sees them as forming congruent parts of popular
civilization, calling forth the practical energies, traditional values,
and aesthetic sensibilities of the "man of the people." With this
view he places himself in the advance guard of contemporary
folklore scholarship.

In his *Greek Calendar Customs* (1958), Professor Megas provides a rich feast of the interrelated lore that comes to synthesis in
Greek religious folk festivals. Saints' miracles, traditional carni-
vals, popular demonology, seasonal rituals, folk musical and
dance performances are all woven into the tapestry of calendrical
folklore. And the author is ever quick to point out threads of
continuity. He speaks of the May day celebration at Zagori in
Epirus, where shepherd girls play the game "Zapheiri." A youth
selected as the May Boy lies on the grass as if dead and is decked
with flowers and green boughs. The girls encircle him and sing a
poetic lament, likening him to a fallen cypress and bidding him
rise, now that spring has come. The boy does arise, and all dance
across the meadow. Megas sees here a derivation of the ancient
festival of Adonis. "This is but one among many proofs of the
unbroken continuity of Greek tradition."[40] Other examples are
duly given, as in the ceremony of Anastenaria. Dancing members
of the cult gather by the sacred springs of Saint Constantine on
May 2. A procession headed by musicians carrying special musical instruments marches to the church, obtains the icons of Saint

---

to the Houses of the Other Balkan Peoples (Athens: Series of Publications of the Ministry of Reconstruction, no. 37), pp. 52–53.

[39] Ibid., p. 2.

[40] Megas, *Greek Calendar Customs* (Athens: Press and Information
Department, Prime Minister's Office, 1958), p. 119.

Constantine and Saint Helena, proceeds to the village square, and the participants begin dancing around a great fire. The dancers sigh; hence the name of their cult, from *anastenazo*, "to sigh." Gradually the pace quickens, aided by wine and spirits, and the impassioned dancers walk barefoot across the live coals. The sacred bull, black, three years old, unbroken and ungelded, is ritually sacrificed in the church courtyard by the chief Anastenaris. For eight days the dancing, procession, and all-night church services continue, while new cult members are initiated. Megas believes that the Anastenaria descends from the Dionysiac orgies, which took place in the same area of eastern Thrace and were marked by the same wild frenzy induced by thundering music and the glow of torches lighting the nocturnal mountainsides.[41]

In his third specialty, the folktale, Megas has again made large contributions. He prepared in 1965 a volume of Greek folktales, *Griechische Volksmärchen,* for the authoritative German series, *Die Märchen der Weltliteratur,* and another in 1968, *Greece-Germany,* for a bilingual text series, *Begegnung der Völker in Märchen (Folktale: The Peoples' Meeting-Place).* In addition he has written studies of special tales and tale themes, such as his monograph on the beardless man in modern Greek folktales. Professor Megas has for a number of years been cataloguing an index of some 20,000 Greek folktales by type and variant according to the Aarne-Thompson system. The present selection of tales is drawn in good part from his own splendid archives. In folktales, as in other genres, Megas perceives continuities between the Greeks of today and of antiquity. He quotes, in the Introduction that follows, the English and German scholars Dawkins and von der Leyen in support of continuity, and he has written on modern oral Greek parallels to Aesop's fables, saying that while all ancient tales do not survive nowadays, those that do are found in fuller forms than their counterparts in early sources.[42] On the

[41] Ibid., pp. 142–46.

[42] Megas, "Some Oral Greek Parallels to Aesop's Fables," in *Humaniora: Essays in Literature, Folklore, Bibliography Honoring Archer Taylor on his Seventieth Birthday* (Locust Valley, New York: J. J. Augustin, 1960), pp. 195–207.

moot question of continuity, let the reader judge for himself as he peruses the orally told tales presented by the master of Greek folklore explorations.[43]

Richard M. Dorson

[43] For assistance in the editing of this manuscript I am particularly grateful to Yvonne Milspaw.

Introduction

Even today, from the provinces and islands of Greece, folktales and folk narratives are brought to us by collectors of folklore material. This is proof that the folktale still exists in Greece. But it no longer has the vigor that in former times made the storyteller a distinguished personage in village society. Those were the times —no more than sixty or seventy years ago—when the people themselves had their own literary movement and cultural aspirations, when renowned storytellers would tell assembled listeners their tales of wonder.

We have a description from the collector Adamantios Adamantiou, dating from the close of the last century, of this aspect of the life of the people as it was on the island of Tinos, in the Cyclades. "Each with his lantern, they would all go to the evening session, whither the village storyteller would be summoned, and listen to the tale with religious attention." The manner of telling, the appearance and technique of the storytellers, the facility with which they strung together the incidents and delivered the tale, are described by Adamantiou at length. "The moment I hear you, master," a storyteller told him, "I get a story! Well, if it's short, I stick on a bit and make it long." Along with the versatility and skill in composition of the popular narrator goes the charm of narration, a talent innate in the people. "The tale differs," says Adamantiou, "when you have them tell it to you and when they tell it among themselves. 'You see, when you tell the tale, you put the accents in as well . . . it's got accents . . . it's fine, with the accents in.'" We are thus afforded a graphic account of the art whereby the popular narrator consciously elaborates the aesthetic aspect of the story and gives both pleasure and contentment to his audience. Only when one is a member of the popular narrator's audience at an evening session is it possible to feel what popular narrative is in substance: what the folktale, what the legend, what the religious tale and the droll, what the moral tale and the anecdote. Here it can be sensed whether story-teller and listeners look on a story as true or false, as credible or not; and the chances are that questions of popular storytelling technique disputed among scholars will be solved. When the eyes of the listeners are seen to glow with suspense and amazement at the adventures of the hero, when the old woman storyteller is seen to wipe from her eye a tear prompted by the sorrows of the heroine, how can there by any doubt that the people believe in what is narrated to them? It is another matter, of course, when at the close of the tale the storyteller delivers the cadence, "Nei-ther was I there, nor need you believe it." This is not one of the customary jests that are found at the conclusion, but it suggests the imaginative fabric of the tale.

Today things have changed, even in Greece. The folktale con-tinues to survive, but not with the brilliance that once graced it in village society; the environment in which it once lived a whole and natural life is met with only rarely.

There is no doubt that the tales belong to the most ancient and widely propagated cultural heritage of mankind.

The ancient Greeks could not have done without their folk-tales, being, as they were, a people blessed with a vigorous and well-trained imagination. It is true that the folktale had no place in the rich literature of the Greeks, but there is no lack of evi-dence that "old crones' tales," as they were called, did exist then. These evidences were collected by Johannes Bolte, of revered memory.[1] Furthermore, we have knowledge of the ancient Greek folktales through the myths of the ancient heroes. The ancient Greeks believed their myths to be the earliest history of their peo-ple. But apart from their conjectured historical origins, the myths of the heroes were steeped in folk narrative. "As for the stories, charming, but of no known origin," says Wilamowitz, "and to which no credit is given in the myths, the Greeks chose heroes to

[1] Johannes Bolte, *Zeugnisse zur Geschichte der Märchen* (Helsinki, 1921).

be protagonists in these. We must therefore not allow ourselves to be led astray by the heroic names and the subsequent poetic and geographical embellishments." [2] Just as Alexander the Great became, in the beliefs and in the narratives of the Eastern peoples, a folktale hero, so must have Perseus, the founder of Mycenae, and other heroes of the Mycenaean world: Bellerophon, Jason, Peleus, Meleager, Atalanta, Oedipus, Melampus, Polyeidus, heroes of a world which, as perusal of the Mycenaean script has proved, was Greek in character. Replete with folktale elements that were not always random but were frequently put together to form the biography of a folktale hero, these myths take us back to the middle of the second millennium. Thus, Greece must be considered one of the most ancient cradles of the folktale, at least to the same degree as was Egypt and the other countries of the eastern Mediterranean. It is still incumbent upon specialists to seek out those folktales which are at the basis of the myths of Oedipus, Melampus, Atalanta, Alcestes, and other heroes of the Mycenaean age.

Later, in their migrations to all parts of the Mediterranean and Euxine coast, the Greeks influenced the popular culture of the European peoples, and, as we know, folk narrative followed in the wake of culture. There is no doubt that in the Alexandrian era, as the Greeks advanced eastward as far as India, the treasury of Greek narrative was enriched by tales from the East. The same is true for the Byzantine period of Greek history, which saw incursions of peoples from all directions into Greek territory.

Indeed, there has always been a rich store of genuine popular narrative handed down, in all its vigor, from generation to generation, narrative preserved by the people so faithfully that newly acquired material is assimilated with the old.

During the long years of the Turkish occupation (1453–1821), the Greek people lived an intensely national life, preserving in pure form its national and popular traditions. In a Greece enslaved and struggling to free herself, matters of popular culture were the exclusive concern of the Greek men of letters.

[2] Ulrich von Wilamowitz-Möllendorff, *Die griechische Heldensage,* I (Berlin, 1925), p. 59.

During that time, the life and intellectual heritage of the Greek people was attracting the interest of foreign visitors and scholars, among whom two in particular stand out: the French scholar Claude Fauriel, and the Austrian consul Johann Georg von Hahn. To the former we are indebted for the first edition (1824) of Greek demotic songs, and to the latter, for the first collection and edition of Greek folktales (1864). Hahn began his collection in 1848 while in Ioannina, in the province of Epirus, and continued it in Syros, in the Cyclades, whither he had been transferred. His collection *Griechische und Albanische Märchen* contains 101 Greek tales, of which 66 are from Epirus and 35 from the island, and 13 Albanian tales, of which 9 were transcribed from Albanian-speaking Greeks of Northern Epirus and of the small island of Poros in the Saronican Gulf. There are also many variants of the tales noted by Hahn in the appended notes. By a happy chance, the Greek texts of Hahn's collection came into the hands of the Danish classical scholar, Jean Pio, and are now in the Manuscripts Section of the National Library of Athens. From this material Pio was able to publish, in Copenhagen, in 1879, 30 tales, to which another 17 tales (11 from Astypalaea and 6 from Upper Syros) were added from this same collection.

After Hahn we must recall the work of Bernhard Schmidt, whose *Griechische Märchen, Sagen, und Volkslieder* was published in 1877. He had already begun his collection in Zante, before Hahn's appeared. However, whereas Hahn's enthusiasm was that of the student of folk narrative or of comparative mythology, what motivated Schmidt was, as he says himself, "the classical scholar's desire to find out whether, and in what measure, traces of Greek mythology survive in the Greek folktales of today." Accordingly, he made it a rule to write down only those tales that were orally narrated to him. Thus, his collection, though smaller (25 tales) is richer in its references to antiquity than Hahn's.

The appearance of these two collections aroused the interest of scholarly Greeks. They desired not only to acquaint themselves with the narratives of their own people but also to assemble specimens of the popular tongue and to study modern Greek dialects in genuine popular texts, such as are provided by the folktale.

Learned societies were at that time being founded for the study of the language and literature of the people, and folktales are found in the periodical publications of these societies such as the *Neo-Greek Miscellany* (1870–74), the *Greek Literary Society, Bulletin of the Historical and Ethnological Society of Greece* (1883–1910), and *Star of Pontus* (1884). Popular narratives also appear in the *Cypriot Writings* of A. Sakellariou (1868), the *History and Statistics of Trebizond,* by Savas Ioannides (1870), and the *Salmian Writings* of E. Stamatiades (1881–87). Foreign scholars of more recent times, Paul Kretschmer in Lesbos, Karl Dieterich in the Dodecanese, and Richard M. Dawkins in Cappadocia and Pontus, have not only collected tales but enriched them with learned notes.

A new period in the work of collecting tales began in Greece with the foundation of the Greek Folklore Society by Nicholas G. Polites in 1909. The Society's publication, *Laographia,* which to date comprises 21 volumes (each numbering 36 to 42 pages) contains a quantity of popular stories, legends, and droll tales, most of which are accompanied by critical notes. The systematic classifying of folktale collections in general from all parts of Greece has been in process since 1918, when the government of Greece founded the Folklore Archives, which were entrusted to the Academy of Athens in 1927. More has been added to the treasury of popular narrative through the Athens University Folklore Seminar.

In this way the number of published and unpublished variants of Greek folktales has now reached 21,000.

Scholarly research on Greek folktales began with Hahn's large edition. In his introduction, as well as in the notes to his collection, Hahn made a scientific examination of the texts he had assembled, compared them with tales in the other collections of that time, and was finally able to sort them into forty types. His notions on history and theory may seem out-of-date to us today, but, taken one by one, they contain much that is useful and interesting. In particular, the conclusion reached by Hahn that the store of neo-Greek tales in its inner substance belongs to the family of the European folktale had special importance for its time.

Special mention must be made here of the British philologist and archaeologist, Richard M. Dawkins (1871–1955). Dawkins made extensive tours of Pontus and Cappadocia with the purpose of studying the dialects of those regions. He consequently wrote down much linguistic material that had come to him orally from the people before making up his mind to become a specialist in folk-narrative research. This is why he deputed the work on the folktales in his first book, *Modern Greek in Asia Minor,* to a classicist, William R. Halliday, who graced it with a scholarly commentary. Later, Dawkins's studies were to provide a superb contribution to knowledge of the Greek folktale.

Profoundly conversant with Greek dialects, he also brought out, besides his renowned collections of Cappadocian tales, the *Forty-Five Stories from the Dodecanese* (Cambridge, 1950), enriched with very important critical and interpretive notes. Toward the end of his life he shouldered the task of selecting and translating Greek folktales, his aim being to make the modern Greek tale accessible to a wider circle of scholars. For his two volumes, *Modern Greek Folk Tales* and *More Greek Folk Tales* (Oxford, 1953 and 1955), he assembled 110 tales from divers Greek collections. "The object of this book," he says in the introduction to the first, "is to pick out the specifically Greek form of each story; what von Sydow has called its Greek oikotype." This should then serve "to reflect the character and ways of thought of the people who tell them and like listening to them." Dawkins added a table of variants and a commentary on the texts. Of especial interest is the extensive foreword Dawkins wrote for the first book of texts, in which he attempted, by comparing the folk narrative of neighboring peoples (particularly the Turks, whose language he knew as well as he did Greek), to define the type, aspect, and character of the Greek folktale.

". . . I would say," he wrote, "that the characteristic of the best of the Greek stories is that they have in the background that spirit of lively curiosity which marks the Greek genius. . . . I see the greatest merit of Greek folktales . . . in this faculty for displaying truths of human nature behind the literal narrative. . . . In their folktales we have, it seems, an art product of a people naturally progressive and active but with no means of making progress."

Nor did Dawkins leave untouched the question of the connection of these stories with the folktales of ancient Greece, of which, as he says, we have, unfortunately, very few. He quotes Halliday on certain instances "where stories told by ancient Greeks are identical in plot with modern folktales, but there are not very many." He winds up the discussion of the matter as follows: "These folktales of today do suggest one very real inheritance from the ancient world, and that is the character of the Greeks themselves . . . This Greek character is one that we may or may not like or admire, but it is as evident in their folktales as it is in all the products of the Greek imagination." [3]

In this, Dawkins appears to agree with the *Altmeister* of folk-narrative study, Friedrich von der Leyen, who, bearing in mind the narrative charm of the Greek folktales, says, "These narrators have exceptional aptitude in the telling of tales. Can it be that this is a survival of the ancient Greek skill in recounting and narrating?" Although he, too, considers the question of the ancient Greek folktale as ineluctable, he believes that "the ancient folktales, in their bubbling, flashing vitality, and with their joy in reality, might have been something like the folktale of modern Greece." [4]

It is not therefore surprising that figures of the supernatural world who in the modern folktales appear to the hero, now to give him aid, now to pursue him, belong to ancient Greek demonology with the same, or only slightly changed, names: the Fates and Chance, Nereids and Gorgons, Lamias and Stringlas (vampires and harpies), *Drakoe* and *Drakaenes* (ogres and ogresses), Master Sun (Kyr Helios), Charon, and so on. As in the history of the Greek folktale, these references to ancient mythology and religion are mingled with spirits from the East.

Something should be said here of these figures of Greek folk narrative:

1. It is a custom of the Greek people, on the third night after the birth of a child, to tidy the mother's room and lay the table with bread and honey for the entertainment of the *Moerae*, the

[3] Richard M. Dawkins, *Modern Greek Folktales* (Oxford, 1953), pp. xxvi–xxxiv.
[4] Friedrich von der Leyen, *Die Welt der Märchen*, 2 vols. (Düsseldorf, 1954), pp. 95, 102.

three old women who come to decree the fate of the newborn child.

Whatever happens, then, in life and in reality, will be given its place in the folktale. The myth of the birth of Meleager is found, even today, in the initial portion of the tales about chance: there is always someone in the newborn child's room who pretends to be asleep but is really attending to what the three Fates, speaking one after the other, are saying about the child's future.

This belief in the existence and power of the Fates, extending still further to their mission and function, does not restrict itself to the birth of the hero but is also shown in what happens after and in the adventures that come his way. Usually the Fates preside at critical moments, either giving useful advice to the hero or helping him in some manner. For example, in our tale 38, the Fates make themselves useful to the poor girl who, by her conduct, has made the unsmiling fate (the Atropos of antiquity) laugh. Again in our tale "Brother and Sister" the beings who shower gifts on the poor but gracious girl for the hospitality she has shown them are the three Fates (instead of the dwarfs or the Christ of the foreign variants). In the Tale of *The Three Old Women Helpers"* (Type 501) the poor girl receives aid from the Fates (instead of from the three witches in foreign variants) for an impossible amount of weaving.

2. Another regular figure of the modern Greek folktale is the Nereid (Neraida). By the name *Neraides* (Nereids) must be understood the ancient nymphs in their entirety. These correspond to the *Feen* or "Swan Maiden" of foreign mythology. Their whole existence consists of dance and play in the clear waters of the ravine. While they are bathing, having left their veils on the banks of the water, the hero, hidden in the foliage nearby, seizes the veil of the youngest nymph so that she cannot escape and is obliged to follow him home. There she becomes his wife and bears him a most beautiful child, like the Thetis of Achilles. But her thoughts ever turn on how to recapture her veil, until at last she is able to do this. Then she goes into her exotic dance and soon vanishes, to return to her companions. At this point in the tale there begins the husband's adventurous search for his vanished supernatural spouse (Type 400, *The Man on a Quest for his Lost Wife*).

3. A further demoniac figure that lives at the bottom of the sea and recalls the *Enalios,* or sea-demon, of antiquity is the *Gorgona,* a beautiful woman, fish from the waist down. When the unlucky fisherman casts his nets and sighs to think he has no child to comfort him, a *Gorgona* suddenly comes out of the sea and gives him the means (an apple) whereby his wife may have a son. But when twelve years have passed, he must give up his son to the *Gorgona.* The queen of the *Gorgones* is *Kyra Thalassa* (Dame Sea, Mother Sea), who, like Amphitrite, has her palaces in the depths of the sea (see no. 30); here, Mother Sea brings up the boy who has been offered up to her and intends him to be the husband of one of her daughters.

On the other hand, the *Lamia* or vampire ogress, who also lives in a watery element such as a well or water hole, is, like the *Empousa* of ancient myth, a devourer of human flesh, as is the *Stringla* or witch.

4. The imaginary figure who most often appears in the magical and heroic tales of Greece as a supernatural adversary of the hero is the *Drakos,* the counterpart of whom, in English folktales, is the ogre or dragon. The name *Drakos* comes from *drakontas* or dragon, but the figure appears in purely human form. It is of immense size and strength and of terrifying appearance: it can catapult great rocks and carry whole trees on its shoulders. It is not indomitable, however, as its powers of comprehension are very small. The *Drakoe* live in the mountains and wildernesses, in caves or else in castles and palaces that they themselves have built, usually in bands of forty brothers. Their mother, the *Drakaena* or ogress, waits every evening for them to come home from the hunt and lift down from over the fire the cauldron with the forty handles. Their main occupation is hunting out, seizing, and pillaging the fortunes of men, so that they end by amassing boundless wealth. Most frequently they abduct beautiful maidens. The features of the *Drakoe* in their entirety characterize them as mountain demons, and they appear to have taken the place of similar demons of antiquity—the Centaurs, Cyclops, and others.

5. Another creature of the demoniac order that is also inimical to the hero is the *Arapis,* or Blackamoor, literally, "Arab." He is represented as an enormous Negro. The Blackamoor originates in the East, indeed in Turkey, where the same part is played in

the national folktales by the huge Negro as in the folktales of
Greece. The Turks, in their turn, adopted the Blackamoor out of
the Arabian folktales, in which he not infrequently appears as an
evil demon.

6. One of the most important and peculiar figures in the Greek
folktale is the *Spanos,* the baldchin, who typifies the cunning
man. *Spanos* is the term for one who has very little hair or none
at all on his chin and upper lip. But what makes an adverse im-
pression on the ordinary man is not so much the lack of beard as
the lack of moustache, for the habit of shaving the beard is of
very old standing among the Greeks, clergy excepted. In the view
not only of our villagers but, up to fifty years ago, of the town
dwellers as well, the moustache was considered to be a necessary
appendage of a man's appearance and something that would un-
mistakably distinguish a man from a woman; it was thus a special mark of masculinity. The lack of a moustache, then, would
relegate a baldchin, in the minds of the people, to the ranks of
womankind and justify his being treated with scorn. Thus, as a
man must beware of the lame, the maimed, or the crookbacked,
so must he also beware of the baldchin. We must add to these
the redbeard and the woman with hair on her lip, who are
equally looked on as "evil souls."

The people's attitude toward these persons is evident in many
Greek popular sayings such as "bald of chin and unclean," and
"God preserve thee from the redbeard and the baldchin." In the
tales, the figure of the unfeeling villain is typified with dramatic
distinctness in the person of the baldchin, as in "The King's Godson and the Baldchin" (no. 39), in which the hero is sent,
through the false witness of his treacherous companion, the baldchin, to bring back the Beauty of the World to the King (Type
531, *Ferdinand the True and Ferdinand the False*). Cunning is
certainly an outstanding trait of the baldchin, but he will be out-
done by one of greater cunning and it is usual for the case to go
against him. The fundamental idea on which the story is built is
the popular concept that "the crafty fox ends with all four paws
trapped" or "God loves the thief, but He loves the householder,
too." So it happens that our protagonist is beaten in the lying contest by the youngest of three brothers (no. 69). By virtue of his

unreasoning boldness he appears as the slayer of the ogre (no. 57).

7. In conclusion, we must mention a female imaginary figure of the Greek folktale, called the *Pentamorphe,* Five-times Fair, or *Omorphe tou Kosmou,* Beauty of the World. She is a distinctive personage, being the daughter of an ogress (no. 22), or else a maiden of outstanding beauty held captive by ogres. It seems that she, like Helen of antiquity, is the most beautiful woman in the world, and the hero sets out to win her. The adventures that make up the threads of which the tales are woven emanate from this concept of the ideal of beauty guarded by ogres or lions in a distant land. She sets her suitors difficult questions to solve or else she herself is able to enter into contest with the hero, running like the Atalanta of antiquity and wrestling (no. 21) with him, always threatening that, should he lose the contest he will also lose his head. Kretschmer is of the opinion that the Beauty of the World, who is also found in Turkish, Kurd, Albanian, and Italian tales, is of Eastern origin (*Neugriechische Märchen*). But the figure of the Amazon is not wanting in ancient Greek so much as in Byzantine and Modern Greek mythology.

My selection has been drawn from the following sources:

1. The journal *Laographia,* vols. 1–20 (1909–62): 20 texts.

2. The collection *Greek Folk Tales* (in Greek), edited by G. A. Megas, series 1, 3rd edition, 1962; series 2, 1962 (the majority of these tales were taken from the MSS of the Folklore Archives of the Academy of Athens): 39 texts.

3. Other published collections: 6 texts.

4. Unpublished material in the Folklore Archives, and from compilations made at Athens University Folklore seminars (under my own supervision): 10 texts;

5. *Paradoseis (Legends),* edited by N. G. Polites (Athens, 1901): 7 texts. Helen Colaclides has endeavored to render the Greek texts as literally as possible into English, for which my thanks are due. My deep gratitude goes to Professor Richard M. Dorson for including the *Folktales of Greece* in his series *Folktales of the World.*

G. A. MEGAS

Part I
Animal Tales

·1· The Fox and the Wolf Go a-Fishing

· ONCE UPON A TIME there was a wolf and a fox.

The wolf said to the fox, "Good friend, are you of a mind to go with me today and steal a lamb which we can share between us?"

"I am," said the fox.

So they went to the sheep pen and stole a lamb.

Then the fox said, "What good is one lamb to us? Let's go fishing and eat our catch."

"Very well, then," said the wolf, "but what shall we do for a rod and line?"

"Here's what we shall do," said the fox. "You are the strong one, so you take that big pot for a float while I take this big pumpkin; when we've done fishing, we'll go out and eat. As for the lamb, we'll hide it among the rushes. What do you say?"

"Very well," said the wolf.

So they hid the lamb. The fox tied the pot around the wolf's neck, and the dry pumpkin to his own waist, and together they went down to the sea.

They went in and began to fish.

Soon the wolf cried, "I've caught a fish, shall I keep it?"

"No," answered the fox, "it's too small. What could we do with it? The bigger fish are farther in."

The wolf kept crying out that he had caught a fish, and the fox kept answering "No," until the pot filled with water, and the wolf went under and was drowned. Then the fox came out of the water and went back to the place where they had hidden the lamb. He took it to his lair and ate it all by himself.

·2· The Nun Vixen

· THERE WAS ONCE a vixen who had nothing to eat, so she took it into her head to go to the nunnery and become a nun.

On the way she met a rooster, who asked her, "Whither away, Dame Maria?"

"To the nunnery," she said. "I'll never eat meat again, nor oil, but only dry bread and onion."

"Shall I come, too?" he said to her.

"If you like," said she. "Do I have to tie you to my apron strings?"

So the rooster went along with her.

Farther on, she met some pigeons, and when they saw her they flew off. But she said to them, "Don't go, don't go, I've done with all that, and I'm on my way to the nunnery. I shall never eat meat or oil again, only dry bread and onion."

"Shall I come, Dame Maria?" asked the largest pigeon.

"The rooster is coming, so you may as well come, too," she said. "Or do I have to tie you to my apron strings?"

The pigeon went along, too.

Farther on, they met a flock of skylarks. When they saw the vixen, they flew away.

"Don't go," the vixen said to them. "I'm done with my old ways. I'm on my way to the nunnery, and I shan't eat meat again, or oil, but only dry bread and onion."

"Shall I come, too?" asked the largest.

"Well, the others are coming, so you may as well come too. Must I tie you to my apron strings?"

After they had walked a long way, they came to a cave, and there the vixen said to them, "Come in here, now, and make your confessions, for we have to cross seas and rivers, and dear knows if we'll live till we get to the nunnery. Rooster, I'll hear you first!"

"What have I done, Dame Maria?" the rooster asked her.

"What have you done?" said the vixen. "When you raise your voice at midnight, you wake the married people; sometimes you sing out too early, and the wagoners are deceived and come out on the street and the thieves run them down!"

Then the vixen sat down and ate the rooster.

"Your turn, pigeon, I'll hear you confess."

"What have I done, Dame Maria?" said the pigeon to her.

"What have you done?" said the vixen. "When the people sow their seeds to raise crops, you go and dig them up and eat them!"

She ate the pigeon as well. Then she called the skylark. "Now I'll hear your confession, skylark."

"What have I done, Dame Maria?" the skylark asked her.

"What have you done? When you stole the king's crown you put it on your own head!"

"No, I did not, Dame Maria," the skylark told her, "and I have witnesses to prove it."

"All right, then, get them!" she said.

So the skylark went out and perched in a wild pear tree, when who should pass below but a hunter who raised his gun and took aim, ready to shoot the skylark.

"Don't shoot me," said the skylark to the hunter, "and I'll do you a good turn. Let me show you where there's a vixen hiding."

So the skylark took the hunter along with him and, as he went in by the entrance of the cave, he called:

"Kindly step outside, Dame Maria, I've brought you witnesses."

"Have you indeed? And wouldn't your witnesses care to come in here?" said the vixen.

"No, they don't want to come in. May it please your honor to step outside!" the skylark said to her.

So the hunter took aim at the entrance to the cave, and as the vixen came out, he fired, and down she went.

As she lay dying, the vixen said to the skylark, "I wish you joy of the witnesses you brought me."

·3· *Lion, Wolf, and Fox*

• MANY, MANY YEARS AGO, when the world began, all the animals met together to choose a king. They all agreed that the most courageous among them was the lion, which made it most fitting that he should be their king. So they put a crown on the lion's head, and lo! he was King.

Many years later, the lion fell ill and lay on his couch. All the animals went to visit their King on his sickbed.

One day, the wolf—a white wolf, mark you!—was on his way

to visit the King. As he went along, he found the fox on the same road.

"Fox," said he, "will you come with me to visit our King (may he live for ever!)? He is sick."

"Oh, you go, if you've a mind," answered the fox. "Is he so much better than I, that I should go on my belly to him? Let him go on his belly to me, say I."

The wolf made no reply to the fox. Indeed, he was glad to be going to the lion, so he could tell him, "The fox said such-and-such," and so get into the lion's favor. He went on his way in the best of spirits.

But the fox crept along behind him to see what he would tell the lion.

When he came to the lion's lair, the wolf went in and settled on his haunches beside the lion. The fox hid behind a curtain, and heard what passed between them.

After a while, the lion said to the fox, "The fox surely must have little respect for us, never to say, 'The King is sick. I'll go and see how he does.'"

Said the wolf to the lion, "O King, live for ever! On my way here, I saw the fox, and I said, 'Come with me to the King (may he live for ever),' and the fox said, 'Not I! Is he better than I am?'"

At this, the lion said, "Just let him fall into my hands! I'll set him to rights."

At that very moment, the fox came in and bowed to the King.

"Fox," said he, "how is it that you have never come nigh me till now?"

"Ah but, O King," said the fox, "if you but knew where I was till now! It came to my ears that you were sick, and so I set about asking where a good doctor could be found, and I was told there is a famous doctor in Baghdad. So I set off for Baghdad, for it was my dearest wish to bring him here to cure you. But he said to me, 'There is no need for me to come, for I know what ails your King. I will tell you what physic to give him. As soon as you come nigh him, do thus: cut up a wolf—not just any wolf but a white wolf!—and wrap your King in its skin. If you fail in this, your King will die.' I did not tarry, but came here within the hour."

The wolf sat there, dumbfounded. The lion immediately gave orders for the wolf to be cut up. The lion then wrapped himself in the skin and was cured.

Then said the lion, "Oh, that son of a dog, the wolf! The fox sought to do me nothing but good, but the wolf strove all he could to do him harm."

·4· Fox and Stork

• ONCE A STORK asked a fox to dinner.

So he fetched a pitcher of milk, stood it on a stone, put in his beak, and drank the milk. When he pulled out his beak to breathe air, a few drops of milk dripped off, which the fox licked up.

When the stork had drunk well of the milk, he said to the fox, "Have you drunk your milk, brother? Have you had your fill?"

"I have," said the fox, "and I want you to be my guest tomorrow, and eat with me."

And, just as they had said, they met next day, very early, in a rocky place. The fox, in his turn, brought a pitcher of milk. He took it to a flagstone and beat it on the flat surface, it broke, and the milk ran out over the stone. The fox fell to and licked it up, while the stork beat his beak on the stone to no avail.

Then the fox asked, "Well, brother, have you drunk your milk? Had your fill?"

"Ah, brother, you put one over on me!"

"I only gave you back, brother, as good as you gave me."

·5· Rooster, Fox, and Dog

• ONCE UPON A TIME, a rooster and a dog became friends and went everywhere together. One day they set off for a village, but, on the way, night fell as they were in the forest.

"Now," said the dog, "where shall we spend the night?"

"I," said the rooster, "shall get up on a branch, and you look for a place here below where you can creep in and sleep."

The dog looked, found a hollow, and got in. The rooster flew up above.

At dawn the rooster began to call, "Cock-a-doodle-doo!"

A fox who happened to be near heard, went up to him and said, "Good day, rooster!"

"Good day, Dame Molly," he said.

"Why here, rooster? Wouldn't you rather have put up at my house?"

"We were overtaken by night, Dame Molly. I have another with me, a friend who is fat and couldn't go any farther, so we stayed here."

"Well, then, where is your friend, the other one?" said the fox, thinking it was another fat rooster.

"Here he is," said the rooster, "down here."

The fox went forward to look, the dog flew out, and the fox changed her mind and fled.

•6• *Ten Years the She-Fox,*
Eleven the Wee Fox

• ONCE, a vixen and her cub were crouching outside their lair, half dead with hunger and cold. All at once the vixen began to rub her two forelegs together, as brisk as brisk, and go "Oo! Oo! Oo! Ow! Ow! Ow!"

"What's the matter, mother?" asked the cub.

"I'm too hot, my child."

"How can you be?"

"Don't you see the fire the shepherds have lit?"

The fox cub looked and saw the fire, far away on the mountain. He said nothing, but a while later he lifted one leg and rubbed his ear, as brisk as brisk, and cried, "Ouch! Ouch! Ouch!"

"What's the matter, my child?" the vixen asked him.

"What else, mother," answered the cub, "but the fire that is too hot for you threw out a spark and burned my ear."

The vixen turned, looked him in the eye, and said, "Well done, my child, you outdo me in cunning. The saying is right that goes, 'If ten years is the she-fox, eleven is the wee fox!'"

·7· The Fox in the Pit

• ONE DAY, the fox was prowling about in the forest in search of food. It grew dark, and he still had not had so much as a bite, for nothing at all had come his way.

In the trees the birds were still a-fluttering and a-twittering. The sound of them caused the fox almost to burst with vexation at his own plight. Now he walked, now he stood still. He watched and watched them; he licked his lips. He cudgeled his brains as to how he could catch one. But there was nothing he could do.

As he walked about and watched them, he said to himself, "Surely God cannot know His own business! Else, why should he have made me like this, to walk about the earth and never find aught to eat? If He had made me a bird, would I have suffered like this? Would that bird over there, and this one up here, and the she-raven with the voice that startles me every now and then, have been safe from a fellow like me?"

All at once, while he was turning this over in his mind, he found himself at the bottom of a pit. Whereupon, he said, "A good thing there's no water in here; I'd have drowned before I knew it. To think I didn't care for the way God made me, and was wishing He'd made me a bird to fly in the sky!"

·8· Hedgehog and Fox

• ONCE, when both rain and hail were falling, a hedgehog who had strayed in the wild wood could not find a place to burrow to get out of the hail. After a while, he found a foxhole and tried to get inside, but the fox, who was inside, would not let him in. The hedgehog pleaded with the fox, saying that if he would let him put only his head into the hole, it would not matter if the rest of him remained outside. He begged so hard that the fox at last consented, but the hedgehog, little by little, got himself right in, and, once there, pressed close to the fox, raised his prickles, and pricked her. The fox could do nothing but withdraw to the very edge, while the hedgehog began to fill the hole entirely. Thus he contrived, little by little, to drive the fox out of the hole, while he stayed on in it as lord and master.

·9· *Wolf, Fox, and Ass*

• THERE WAS ONCE an ass, plump and well fed, grazing in a meadow. A fox saw him, and the sight gave him an appetite. He went to the wolf. "Come and see this ass, wolf. You've never seen the like before for eating."

The wolf went and looked, and his mouth began to water.

"I'll tell you what we'll do, Wolf," said the fox.

"What? You're the one with the brains."

"We'll buy a boat and load it with olives; then we'll take the ass on as a sailor, and when we get out to sea, we'll eat him. Come on now, you see about getting a boat, and I'll get the ass."

The wolf bought the boat (this is only a story!) and loaded it with olives. The fox got the ass, took him down to the seashore and onto the boat.

When they got out to sea, the fox said, "Very good! We're under way now, but who can say if we'll get there alive? So, for good or evil, let's make our confessions."

The wolf became father confessor, and heard the fox first. "What are your sins, good fox?"

"I've eaten hens a-many and as many wild creatures—hares, rabbits—as I could catch by the throat."

"That's not much of a confession, Foxy. Worms, that's what you've eaten. Now it's your turn to confess me."

"Well then, what are *your* sins?"

"I've eaten sheep a-many, goats a-many, cows, and such, a-many."

"Pooh, that's nothing—just worms."

Then the wolf said to the ass, "Come on, Ass boy, tell us what your sins are."

"As for me," said the ass, "once when I was loaded with lettuce I turned around and ate a leaf because I fancied it."

"Oh, Ass," cried the other two, in the same breath, "you ate the lettuce leaf with no oil or vinegar e'er a sip? We wonder how, as yet, we haven't drowned on this trip. Your sin is a grievous one, and we must eat you."

"Mercy!"

"No, we must eat you."

"All right," said the ass. "Only, when he died, my father gave me a paper that I have in my shoe here. Come on, Goodman Wolf, and read it, so that I can see what he wrote me before I am eaten."

He lifted his hind leg, but when the wolf went to read it, he gave him a kick in the teeth that shot him out into the sea. Seeing this, the fox jumped into the sea to escape, but the two were drowned, and so the boat and the load of olives were left to the ass.

· 10 · Man, Snake, and Fox

• ONCE A POOR MAN was coming from the fields. On the way, he came upon two children who were about to kill a snake. He gave the children a ten lepton piece, picked up the snake, took it home, and said to his wife,

"Today, wife, I did a good deed: I saved this snake from some children who were going to kill it. Bring the stiffening from inside your headcloth, and let's put the snake in that."

He put it in the stiffening, and when he got up next morning, he fed it. The snake grew bigger in time, and was soon all but too big for the stiffening.

One morning when the man went as usual to feed it, it leapt out of the stiffening, coiled itself round the man's neck, and would have choked him, but the poor man began to wail, "Think what you're doing! I saved your life, and now you'd choke me."

Then the man thought of a way out.

"Come on," said he, "and let's go have a judgment on it. Whatever the judgment is, so let it be."

The snake consented, and they set out to find a judge. On they went until they found a flock of sheep.

"Come," said the man, "deliver us judgment."

"Judgment on what?" said the sheep.

"Well, here you are," said he, "I found this snake when it was but a little one, and some boys were going to kill it. I saved it, took it home and brought it up, but now it wants to choke me."

"Well, so it ought," said the sheep. "So are we kept: we bear young, and our lambs are slaughtered; our milk is drunk, and our fleece shorn; then, on top of that, we are killed, too, and eaten."

"Wait a bit," said the man. "Let's go somewhere else for a judgment." So they went on, and found a herd of oxen.

"Come," said the man, "deliver us judgment."

"Judgment on what?" said the oxen.

So the man sat down, and told them the same as he had the sheep.

"Well, so it ought to choke you," said the oxen, "for us, too, you keep. You put the yoke on us and then, after all that, you kill us off and eat us."

"Here," said the man, "we've had no sense out of them, either. Let's go elsewhere." So they went on, and found a fox.

Again the man sat down, and told the whole story, and, in the telling, he dropped hints to the fox that, if he saved him from the snake, he would give him a fair quantity of birds as a gift.

The crafty fox saw this at once. So he turned, and said to the man, "You say that this big snake lived in the stiffening you're carrying in your hands, but I can't make it out. I'd never believe," said the fox, "that such a big snake could get into a little bit of stiffening like that. Just unwind yourself from that man's neck, and let's see if you can get into this. Then I'll say what I think."

So the snake uncoiled itself, and got into the stiffening, but left its head out.

Said the fox, "In with your head, in with it!"

So the snake curled up smaller, and got its head in, too. Quick as a wink, the man put on the cover, and they stoned it to death.

"Well," said the fox, "now that I've saved you, go and get me my reward."

"Never you fear," said the man, "for the favor you've done me, I'll bring you a laying hen and her chicks as well."

When the man got home he said, "Well, wife, Fox saved my life, so let's take him the laying hen and chicks."

"Oh, sit down a while, husband, and rest yourself, while I catch her and put her in a sack."

Now the wife got a sack and in it she put their bitch dog and her pups.

Then the man came out, and thinking the fowl and chicks were inside the sack, picked it up and went off. As he drew near the fox, he called out to him, "Hey, master Fox, come and get the laying hen and chicks I've brought you."

"Well," said the fox, "untie the sack, and I'll catch them one by one."

So the man opened the sack, the bitch dog flew out, and catching the fox by the tail, bit it right off. Away went the fox, without a tail.

When he had run a long way and made sure that no one was after him, he climbed up on a high bridge, and bewailing his own plight, said,

"Look you, Fox, your father wasn't a judge, nor was your mother, neither was your granddad public prosecutor, so what business had you to go delivering judgments?"

· 11 · Cat, Lion, and Man

· THERE WAS ONCE a cat who went out for a walk on the mountain. All at once she saw a lion in her path. She moved to one side, and waited to see what the lion would do. The lion went up to her, sniffed at her, and then said to her, "You seem to be of our kind, but you are very small."

And the cat answered, "You'd be, too, if you had to live cheek-by-jowl with Man."

"How's that?" asked the lion. "What is Man? Is he so big and fierce? Where is he? I want to see."

To this the cat said, "Come with me, and I'll show him to you."

The lion made no objection; so off they went. As they walked along the mountain path, they beheld a man cutting wood.

The cat said to the lion, "There he is. That's Man."

They moved closer. The lion bade the man good day, and said, "Are you Man?"

"I am," said he.

"I have heard that you are very strong; so I've come to wrestle."

"So be it, let's wrestle. But, first, help me split this wood, I've already done half—and then we'll wrestle."

"That will I do."

"As you are so obliging, put your paws in here, where it's split, and I will finish it off."

The lion put in his paws, and the man released first one side of the wood that he had been holding, and then the other side, so that the lion's paws were caught fast in the wood. Then the man picked up a thick stick and began to rain down blows on the lion, "Take that! And that! And there's one to make you tingle! And one to make you ache!"

He was half dead by the time the man was done.

Then the man pulled the wood apart, and freed the paws of the lion, who lay down like a dog. The man hoisted the wood on his back, picked up his axe, and went off home.

When the man had gone, the cat, who had been hiding, came out, went up to the lion, and asked him if he had recovered.

"And what did you think of Man?"

"Well," the lion answered, "if I were in your shoes, I'd make myself smaller still!"

•12• *The Old Woodcutter and the Lion*

• THERE WAS ONCE an old man, as poor as he could be, who had many children to keep. Every day he would take his donkey to

the forest and chop wood with his hatchet, here a blow, there a
blow, everywhere he could a blow.

One day, a lion crossed his path, and said, "Why don't you sit
down, old one, and rest yourself? I'll cut your wood so that you
can load your beast with it, sell it, and get your children a bite to
eat."

And so it was done. The old man sat down and rested himself,
while the lion cut the wood. Then the old man loaded his donkey and went on his way.

Some days later the old man went to the forest again, and the
lion said to him, "Old one, bring your beast every day, and I'll
load it with wood for you."

After many such days it befell one day that it was fearfully
hot. The lion grew tired cutting wood, and said, "Sit down, old
one, under yon olive tree, where it's nice and cool, and I'll come
and lay my head on your knees to rest."

He laid his head on the old man's knees, and asked, "Am I
handsome, Daddy?"

"You are indeed, my son."

"Am I hardy?"

"That you are, Son Lion!"

"And young and sprightly, too?"

"That, too."

"Why, see what a fine fellow I am! I have all the graces."

"You have all the virtues, but you have a bad fault, too—your
breath stinks!"

At this, the lion got up, loaded the wood on the donkey, and
said to the old man, "Come now, pick up your chopper, and
strike me on the back of the neck."

"Oh, I could never do that to you, my son! Strike a creature
who has done so much for me!"

"But I wish it," said the lion.

So the old man hit him with his chopper on the back of the
neck, and opened a wound two fingers deep.

The old man continued to go to the forest every day, and the
lion, wounded though he was, cut wood, which the old man
loaded onto his beast.

When some time had gone by, the lion said to the old man,

"The back of my neck, old one, how does it look to you now?"

"Altogether mended, my son," said the old man to him.

"My wound has healed," he answered, "but what you said about my breath stinking has stayed in my heart. So hasten and leave this place, and never come again, or I'll eat you up."

And that is why it is said:

> *Knives flash like day,*
> *But harsh words will stay.*

·*13*· *Why the Dog Chases the Hare*

• ONCE A DOG and a hare became partners, and went to the sea to swim. When they came to the shore, the hare said to his new partner, the dog, "Will you take off your socks, partner, and see if they fit me?"

"Whatever you say, partner."

So he took them off. Then the hare said to the dog, "Now, I'll walk a little way, and you watch me, partner, to see if I get along all right." And when he had gone a ways, he said, "Chase me, partner, and catch me if you can!"

But how was he to catch him now? And ever since, the dog has gone barefoot while the hare has worn socks. And that is why the dog now has it in for the hare, and whenever he sees him, chases him.

·*14*· *Ox and Ass*

• IT HAPPENED ONCE that the ox and the ass fell to chatting in the stable. The one asked the other how life was treating him.

"Well, Ox, how goes the world with you?"

"Why, Ass, I find this life a sore trial. It's nothing but whip cuts all day long, working in the fields."

"Poor fellow! I can tell you a way out of that."

"If you can, I'll be greatly beholden to you."

"All you need do is pretend to be sick."

So the ox did as the ass had bidden. That night he refused to eat his hay or drink his water.

"Why, something ails our ox," said the master. "What's to be done? We'll harness the ass tomorrow."

So the ass was taken out and harnessed to the plow, and all day long it was cuts from the whip and blows from the stick with nary the time to so much as breathe. The ass came home late, ready to drop from weariness.

"So how went the day with you, Ass?"

"Oh, very well indeed! But guess what I heard the master say?"

"What did he say, friend Ass?"

"I heard him say he'd kill you off before you died a bag of skin and bones!"

On hearing this the ox recovered at once. He ate and drank, and went out to work the very next day.

And thus it was that the ass escaped the plow.

·*15*· *Ass and Camel*

• ONCE AN ASS and a camel became friends and would go out grazing together. One day, the two of them went into a garden and began to eat the cabbages. As they were eating, the ass said, "Friend, I have a mind to sing."

"Oh, don't do that, friend!" said the camel. "The gardener will come and flay us alive."

The ass did as he was minded. He began to bray, and the gardener heard him, seized a stick, and came. When he saw the gardener, the ass found a gap in the fence, and got out, but the camel stayed where he was, and got the beating of his life. Then he got out, too, and went to meet the ass.

"Oh, friend, what have you done to me?" he said to the ass.

Along the road, they came to a big river. On the other bank, they could see, were some thorn bushes. The camel said, "Shall we cross over and eat the thorns?"

"Well, friend, you can cross over, but I can't."

"I'll kneel down," said the camel. "You climb on my back, and we'll cross."

The camel knelt, and the ass got up on his back. The camel walked into the river up to the middle. Then the camel said, "Friend, I've a mind to dance."

"Oh, don't do that, friend. You'll throw me into the river, and drown me."

"No, I must dance."

So the camel began to dance, the ass fell into the river, and went under. The ass was drowned, the story is ended.

· 16 · *The Mouse and his Daughter*

• THERE WAS ONCE a mouse who had a very pretty daughter. He wanted to marry her off, but not to a mouse. One day as he stood in thought, he saw the sun shining. "Ah!" he said to himself, "there's a groom fit for my little girl." And, without more ado, he was off to the sun's palace.

"Sun, will you take my daughter to wife? I could not bring myself to give her to anyone else but you, so strong and handsome as you are."

"Oh, dear me," said the sun, trying to get himself out of this situation, "I'm not the strongest thing as you think I am. Take those clouds over there—if they pass over me, I grow dark and can do nothing at all about it. Try them, you're sure to strike it lucky."

What could the unhappy mouse do, but get up and go over to the clouds? But he had no luck there, either.

"You see the North Wind?" the clouds said to him. "When he blows, we are scattered all over the place, and can't put ourselves together again. Try the North Wind."

Then the mouse fetched his daughter and took her with him to the North Wind, and told him why he had come.

"I should be happy, my dear mouse, to take your pretty daughter, but I don't happen to be what you take me for. Try that tower over there. You see it? If I blew for forty years, I'd never blow it down."

To cut a long story short, he went to the tower, and made the same proposal. Whereupon, the tower turned, and said to him, "Mouse, mouse, do you hear a sort of groaning inside my walls? What do you suppose it is? Those bold beasts, the mice, are eating me up and all but throwing me over. There's none in the world bolder or stronger than mice, whatever anyone may say."

So the mouse did the sensible thing, and gave his daughter to a bold and handsome young fellow of a mouse.

· *17* · *Owl and Partridge*

· ONE DAY, all the birds met together and agreed to send their little ones to school to learn their letters. They found a teacher and gave him the job. He opened the school, took in the little ones, and wrote down their names in his register.

Some days later, some of the pupils went to school without knowing their lessons. Consequently, the teacher would not let them go home to their midday meal. Among the pupils who were punished was the owl's child.

When the owl saw that her baby did not come out of school with the other children at midday, she took some bread to him at the school. Then said the partridge to the owl,

"Pray you, neighbor, take some food for my child, too, for I have too much to do to go."

"Willingly, neighbor," said the owl, "but I don't know which your child is."

"Oh, as to that," said the partridge, "he's very easy to find. My child is the prettiest in the school."

The owl went to the school. She asked the teacher if she might give the bread to her child, and he consented. Then the teacher allowed her to see all the little ones. She looked at them hard, but could not find the partridge's child. She went back to the partridge, and, handing her the piece of bread, said, "What was I to do? I searched for an hour, but I could not find your baby, because, in all the school, there is no prettier child than my own!"

18 · Crab and Snake

• ONCE UPON A TIME, a snake went down to the seashore and, meeting a crab, said to him, "Crab, my dear fellow, I should like to make a sea-friend of you, someone I could come down and have a bite of sea food with, and my sea-friend, if he liked, could come to my hole, and taste a little tender greenery. So what do you say? Shall we exchange hospitality?"

So the crab gave it some thought, and, when he had thought, "Very well," said he.

So they shook hands on it and straightway sat down and ate. The crab served different sea foods, shrimps and seaweed.

When the meal was over, the snake was in high spirits, and with many a "Good for you, sea-friend!" and a "Good old sea-friend!" he wrapped himself round the unhappy crab.

The crab was somewhat bothered, and he said to the snake, "You hold me too tight, land-friend."

"But I like you, sea-friend," said the snake to him. And after a while he again said, "Good old sea-friend," and held him all the closer.

"But you're holding me too tight, land-friend. I'll burst!"

And the snake, who had made his plans, said, "But what can I do, sea-friend, when I'm so fond of you?"

"And I like you, land-friend," answered the crab, but he saw that things were not going well. The snake coiled tighter and tighter, and would not let go.

In a while, the snake was holding him so close that the crab grew desperate and turned around and dug his claws into the snake's neck. Then the snake let go, and stretched himself out to his full length in the crab's hole.

So then the crab said, "There, now we're all right! Straight out does it, land-friend, no coils to choke me with!"

19 · Shepherd and Snake

• ONCE A SHEPHERD was grazing his sheep when he saw a snake come out of a hole and begin to circle around the sheep. When the shepherd saw it, he put out a little milk in a dish for it, and the snake drank it up.

The next day he again put out a little milk in the dish and placed it near the hole and said, "Come out, little snake, and drink your nice drop of milk."

The snake came out, and drank. When the shepherd went to get the dish, he found a gold piece beside it, and he was glad.

At noon, he again placed some milk beside the hole, and the snake came out and drank it, and again it left him a gold piece.

And that evening he put out some more milk for it and called to it, and it came out and drank. So the shepherd and the snake became friends; he took it milk three times a day, and it left him three gold pieces a day. In the end the shepherd became gentry, and made up his mind to go on a pilgrimage to the Holy Tomb. He left orders for his wife to give the snake its milk every morning, noon, and night, and he set off for the Holy Tomb.

The shepherd's wife gave the snake milk every day.

Now the shepherd had a young son, about five or six years old. One day, as he was wandering among the sheep, playing with them and stroking them, the snake, too, was creeping about among the sheep. The child did not see it, and trod on its tail, and, as there were nails on his clogs, he cut off the snake's tail. It threshed about with pain, and bit the child, poisoning him with its bite, so that he died and was buried. At noon, milk was placed beside the hole for the snake, but it did not come out to drink. And, that evening, more was put out, but as the first was found untouched, no more milk was set out, and the snake was never again seen to come out in the enclosure.

After six months had gone by, the shepherd returned from the Holy Tomb, and when he did not see his child, he asked, "Where is our child?"

"Our child was bitten by the snake, and died," said his wife.

The shepherd said nothing, but he put some milk in a dish, put it by the snake's hole, and said, "Come out, my little snake, and drink your nice drop of milk."

Then the snake called from inside, "Alas! shepherd. Whenever you remember your dead child, and whenever I turn around and see my shorn tail, what friendship can there be between us?"

And so the shepherd and the snake were never friends again.

Part II
Wonder Tales

The Monk

· ONCE UPON A TIME there were a King and Queen who had three sons. The King loved the two elder sons because they loved arms and were good hunters, and he had it in mind to make these two heirs to his kingdom. The youngest he did not love because he did not care for arms, but busied himself all day with papers and books; thus he was called "the Monk."

Now the Queen did not care for the elder sons, but loved the youngest, and whatever papers and books he needed, or however many teachers, she saw to it that he had them.

Meanwhile the King's eyes were hurting him, but none of the doctors who saw him were able to cure him, so that at last he went blind. One doctor alone among them said that the King's eyes might be cured if he were to send for a certain kind of earth that was to be found in a distant kingdom.

As soon as the doctor's opinion came to the ears of the two elder sons of the King, they decided to go and fetch some of this earth and asked permission of their father. Even though he did not believe in the doctor's words, the King, wishing to recover his sight, gave permission to his sons and ordered his council to make royal preparations and give to his sons one hundred soldiers and gold pieces for their expenses, for this place was a four months' journey away.

So, when all was ready, the two princes set forth. When the Monk heard of this, he bade his mother go to his father and seek permission for him to go too.

The Queen began to try to persuade him to give up this notion, saying that the place was very far away, that the King would not give him permission, and that he would not be able to catch up with his brothers. But the Monk insisted and told her that his brothers would not be able to do anything, but that he himself, knowing from the documents he had read where the kingdom was, would bring the earth to heal the King's eyes. Then the Queen ran to the King and told him this.

The King at first grew angry and refused permission for the Monk, saying, "I shall indeed be blessed by fate if I wait for the

Monk to bring me physic. As his elder brothers are going, there is
no need for him to go too."

But, after much pleading by the Queen, he gave his consent,
and said, "Oh, let him go. He may take the old horse and a serving man, and go on his way."

The Queen went and told her son, the Monk, of this. He
began on the instant to make ready, and set forth the next day.
On the way, wherever he went, he asked for his brothers, to see
if they had come that way or not. Four days had he been on the
road with his serving man when he caught up with them.

When they saw him, his brothers were taken aback at first,
and asked him what he was seeking.

"Whatever it is you seek yourselves," said the Monk.

"What do *you* know and what have *you* heard?" asked the
eldest. "God help our father if he expects you to make him
whole."

"Well, I'll have a try," said the Monk.

At these words the second brother turned and said to the eldest, "You seem to think the Monk knows nothing; but with all
the books he has read, he knows where the kingdom is and how
many months away. He'll show us the road."

"You say well," said the eldest. "Let's take him with us." And
so they continued on their way.

They had been on the road for two months when, by asking
here and there, they arrived at a place where three roads met.
They stood there wondering which road to take, for beyond this
point no one knew the road.

Then the Monk came into the middle and said, "My beloved
brothers, these three roads all lead to the kingdom where we
wish to go, but as they are so frightful, no one has ever traveled
them nor knows them. On the road on the right there blows a
great wind, which for twenty days will lift a man up high, and if
he does not fall from his horse and gets to the other end, he is
safe; otherwise he is lost. The middle road, again, belches smoke
and fire, and a man must roast in this fire twenty days until he
gets to the other end. And this road on the left is such that men
go on and never turn back. I have seen no other road marked on
the maps, or, if there is one, it seems the learned have not heard
of it. Now you," he turned and said to his brothers, "take which-

ever road you will, and whichever one you leave for me I'll take myself."

Then his two elder brothers pondered, and the eldest took the road to the right, the middle brother took the middle road, and the left-hand road was left to the Monk.

When they had chosen the roads, the Monk went on, "All well and good, we now know which road each of us will take. But on the return journey, we shall not know which of us has returned and which has not. So let us leave a sign here, where the three roads meet."

"You're right," said the others. "Let us each place a ring under a stone."

So when each had left a ring, each went on his way. The elder brothers each took half of the servants, and the Monk went on alone.

The eldest kept going for ten days and was lost in the country because there were no townships or villages there. When he came to the place where the wind was blowing and it began to lift him and his servants higher and higher into the air, he grew afraid and turned back. He went to where the rings had been left, took his own, and went on to a nearby town. He put up at an inn and settled down to wait for his brothers.

The second, too, went on for ten days, but when he saw the fire and burning heat, and it began to singe his face, he too was afraid and turned back. He went and lifted the stone and when he saw only two rings, he understood that the eldest brother had turned back and that only the Monk was left. He took his ring and went to the town where he found his brother.

That evening, both sat down together and considered what they would do. They said, "Even if we don't wait for the Monk, how can we go to our father without the physic, and what are we to say to him? And supposing the Monk comes afterward and brings the physic and cures our father's eyes? Then *we* should appear worthless and *he* worthy!"

So they ended by deciding to stay.

Let us now leave them and come to the Monk. After separating from his brothers, he took the road to the left and went on alone for ten days and ten nights, through the mire, meeting neither man nor winged creature. At the end of this road, he dismounted and tethered his horse so that it could eat the grass, while he laid himself down to sleep.

When he awoke, he set himself to consider by what means he could delude the *drakoe* [ogres] and a great and ferocious beast that lay on the upper road, so he might pass on toward that kingdom, for, according to the documents he had read, whoever chanced to pass that way was devoured by the *drakoe* and the wild beast.

The *drakoe* were one hundred and twenty in number and lived in three palaces which were one day's journey distant from, one another. At each one, forty *drakoe* lived with their mother. They were all cousins because their mothers were three sisters who had been born of the great beast that dwelt farther down the road, but they had run away, and so were safe. Every time the beast gave birth, it turned round and ate its young.

At last the Monk thought of a plot. He knew from books that, many years before, the *drakoe* of the first palace had lost their youngest brother. So he decided to appear to the *drakaena* [ogress] and tell her that he was her lost youngest son, and if she should ask why he was so small, he would tell her that he had been caught by men and set to do heavy work, and that was why he had grown smaller instead of larger.

When he had thought this out, the Monk got on his horse and went on his way. The next day, he drew near to the first palace, and at noon, when the *drakoe* were not there (for they go out in the morning and return in the evening), he went and found the *drakaena* on her own. He got off his horse, left it in a place, and went to the palace.

The *drakaena* was very fierce and made up her mind to eat the Monk, but he told her that he was her lost son. When she asked him why he was so small, he told her that men had set him to work, and that was why he was small and had not grown.

The *drakaena* believed him and took him in her arms and kissed him. Then she brought him a meal and, when it grew dark, she hid him so that the *drakoe* would not eat him.

It was not long before the *drakoe* came in, all thirty-nine of them, and sat down in a great hall to enjoy themselves. Then their mother went to them and bade them be glad for their lost brother had been found. On hearing this, they all got to their feet and asked their mother to let them see him. She said to them, "Sit down and I'll bring him to you, but don't you lay a hand on him."

"Very well," they said, and so their mother went and brought him to them.

But when they saw him, they said, "Get away, he's not our brother! Our brother was never so small. He's a man!"

"No," said their mother, "it's he. Only, while those cursed men had him, they set him to labor, and that is why he is so small."

The *drakoe* were convinced by their mother's words and they all welcomed him with joy and embraced him. One picked him up in his fist and raised him high, another hid him in his pocket, and still others questioned him; so he told them how he had been caught by men and in what manner he had got away and escaped.

The Monk stayed there three days and had a good time. The fourth day he told the mother that he wished to go and see his cousins, and asked her to give him a letter that they might not harm him.

She gave him such a letter, and he at once set out and went to the *drakaena,* his aunt, and the *drakoe,* his cousins, and was made very welcome. He stayed there one day and then he got a letter from his aunt and went on to the other aunt. He saw the *drakoe* there and stayed a few days.

One day the Monk made as if he did not know, and asked his cousins to tell him what there was on the slopes farther on. They told him that there was a tall mountain and by that mountain was a great sea. Between the mountain and the sea there was only one road, and on this road stood a great and terrible wild beast. It was so big that its head touched the sky and its belly wanted only a little to touch the earth and it straddled the road so that no one could get by. When it was hungry, this beast ate of the peaks of the mountains and, when thirsty, drank of the sea.

"And even we," said the *drakoe,* "fear lest the beast should eat us, even though it is our grandsire."

Then said the Monk, "As it is our grandsire, I will go myself and see it, and kill it, if I can."

"It can't be done," said the *drakoe;* "we will not let you."

"I shall go," said the Monk. "I shall kill it, so that you too may go safely by there, without fear."

After much more of this they at last said he could go, and the next day he got on his horse and set forth. He took with him a big iron spit and an arrow.

He rode all one day, and near evening he caught sight of the beast. Then he waited until it grew a little darker and then, step by step, he came closer to the beast and, passing beneath it, he raised the iron and made a breach in its belly. At the same time, he threw the arrow and made a hole in it. Then he whipped up his horse and rode away speedily.

As soon as it felt it had been hit, the beast began to turn its neck here and there to find out whomever it was that had made a hole in its belly, but it could find no one, for whenever it lowered its neck, the Monk ran and hid.

Then blood began to run from its belly like a river until the sea ran red. In its rage the beast would have uprooted the mountain, and as it grew weaker and began to falter and fall one would have thought it was Noah's Flood happening again. Every time it bellowed, the mountain shook from top to bottom and the sea boiled and the waters rose high and there was a loud noise of thunder. (Never may such a thing happen here; may you neither see nor hear it.)

Next morning, at daybreak, the Monk was on his way and twenty days later he reached the country where the healing earth was to be found. There he discovered the people all asleep, for in this place, the people spent six months asleep and six months awake.

This the Monk knew from books, but he did not know how long they had been under sleep. This only did he perceive: they had succumbed to this sleep by day, for as he went through the country he saw the workshops open and the people asleep. One carried a pair of scales, another a rule, a third bearing a load still stood in the street, while yet another was holding some bread. And to cut a long story short, whatever each man had been doing when sleep overcame him, so had he stayed.

All this the Monk saw as he walked about, until at last he came out on a wide street and found the palace. Its doors were open, and eight soldiers, four on each side, stood with their rifles, sound asleep. He went in and found still more people asleep and so came into the courtyard.

The courtyard was big and full of trees. On one side stood the palace, so goodly that anyone might think he had got into paradise. Before the palace was a great, tall cypress tree, encircled by an iron fence. On the inside of this was the earth that cured the eyes.

The Monk got off his horse, tied it to the fence, took up his saddlebag, and got inside the fence. Then he dug with his knife and picked up some earth and put it in his saddlebag.

When he had done what he had to do, he went into the palace and found the King still sitting on a throne, asleep in the royal apparel and the royal crown. Next to him stood an officer holding a golden fly whisk. When he had taken a good look at him, he went and took his watch and his fly whisk.

Then he went into the next room. There he found the Queen, also sitting on a throne, with a woman standing beside her holding a fly whisk. He took her watch, too, and fly whisk. Then he opened another room and found a girl, sitting like the Queen, and enough like her to be her daughter. He took her watch and fly whisk, too. Coming out of there, he went into another room and there found yet another maiden sitting, just like the first. He took her watch and fly whisk, too.

He left this place, too, and went into another chamber where he found a maiden who was like a princess, too, but so very pretty that the very moment the Monk saw her, he was like one frozen. She lit up the whole room with her beauty.

At the sight of such beauty, the idea at once came into his head of making the maiden his wife. But how could he, when she was asleep? Then he went up to her, and took her watch, her fly whisk, and her embroidered kerchief; then he took off his ring, with his name written on it, and put it on the girl's hand. He took her ring in turn and put it on his own hand, and then he bent and kissed her with all his heart on both her cheeks, and behold! two roses fell. He bent and picked them up and, thus alone, he ended his betrothal ceremony and told himself that when the maiden awoke and saw the ring, she would come and find him.

When he had been all around the palace, he went out, got on

his horse, and rode away. To cut a long story short, he went on for some days and came to the place where he had slain the beast, and once more came to the *drakoe*. As soon as they saw him, they were very glad and asked him what he had been doing, and when he told them he had killed the beast, they were amazed.

He stayed there one day, and set out next day for the other *drakoe*. There he said the same, and at last he came to those *drakoe* whom he had called brothers. Here he stayed three days and considered in what manner he could escape without the *drakoe* becoming aware of it.

At about midday, when the *drakoe* were away from home, the Monk told the mother *drakaena* that he was out of sorts and wanted to walk outside for a while. The *drakaena* gave him leave, and he mounted his horse and set off at a gallop to put a distance between himself and the *drakoe*. Only when he came to the bog did his pace slacken.

By that night he had gone a fair way through the bog when he came to a place where he sank in deep and could not get out. Suddenly, as he was struggling and fighting to get out, one of the roses fell from his hat, and on the instant the whole bog disappeared and became dry. Then he spurred on his horse afresh. When they returned home that evening and heard from their mother that their brother had gone and not returned, the *drakoe* at last realized that he was a man and straightway set out to capture him before he could get to the bog, for they could not get across the mire.

All night long the *drakoe* hunted him, and next day they all but caught him. Then the Monk said to himself, "I'll throw down the other rose. It may save me." And no sooner did he throw it than the watery mud came back again and he was saved. On and on he went till at last he came to the stone where the rings had been hidden. He lifted it, but found only his own beneath it. He knew that his brothers must have gone back with nothing. The Monk took back his ring and went to the town nearby to spend the night. When he arose next morning, he asked the innkeeper if two young men had not passed that way about two months before.

"I did see two such," said the innkeeper. "They stayed at this
very inn. Each one had fifty soldiers and seemed to be a prince,
but after staying here a longish while, they had no money left
and so they dismissed their soldiers and, in the end, were obliged
to sell their horses and whatever else they had, and go to work—
God help them!—for their bread, one at a baker's and the other
at a cook's."

On hearing this, the Monk got up without a word and went to
the baker's where he found out the one brother; then he went to
the cook's, where he found out the other brother, and he said to
them, "See to it that you find two good horses to take you back
home."

"We know," they said, "of a place where there are two good
horses, but they are very dear."

"So much the better," said the Monk. "Buy them."

Then they went and bought back the very horses that they had
sold. The Monk counted out the amount they had agreed to give,
and told them to make themselves ready and to get his own
horse ready so they might set forth. On the road, the brothers
asked the Monk where he had found the earth, but having his
suspicions he would say nothing. Lest they should rob him of the
earth, he put it in a saddlebag on one flank, and put different
earth in the bag on the other flank, and gave them some of that.
And the saddlebag with the good earth in it never left his side.

They went on for two months until they drew near to their
homeland. Then the two brothers conspired to kill the Monk.
There was a dry well they knew of close by, and they agreed to
go on ahead and light a fire as if they were about to eat, and,
over the mouth of the well, to lay a rug for the Monk to sit on so
that he would fall into the well. And, just as they had plotted,
one went on ahead, and when the others reached the dry well,
they dismounted, and the Monk, carrying his saddlebag, went to
sit on the rug. No sooner did he step on it than the hapless
young man fell in.

Then the two brothers got on their horses and went back to
their country. They gave the earth they had to the King, and he
put it on his eyes, but they were not cured. And the King said
that the doctors were liars. The two brothers, seeing that the

earth was of no use, perceived that the Monk had tricked them, but it availed them nothing to say so. Their mother asked them what had become of their brother, and they answered that they did not know where he could be.

Now let us come back to the Monk. He was two days in the well with never a bite to eat. His face was all bruised by the knocks of his fall. There was nothing he could do all day but cry out, but no one heard him.

The third day it happened that a shepherd took his sheep to that place to graze. All at once it seemed to him he heard a cry; so he went to the well, bent over, and saw a man at the bottom. He took off his waist rope, threw it to him, the Monk caught it, and he pulled him out.

Once saved, the Monk gave the shepherd a gift, and, by walking all night, came to his homeland. He entered the palace in secret and went straight to the Queen. As soon as she saw him she hugged and kissed him and asked him why he had been so long. He told her about his journey, but about the manner whereby he had got the earth he told her nothing, for he had a suspicion that, woman as she was, she might tell. He asked her only to take a little of the earth and put it on the King's eyes.

She took a little of the earth and went to the King to put it on his eyes. The King, at the outset, would not hear a word about the Monk and the earth he had brought. But, through the Queen's many entreaties, he gave in and put the earth on his eyes, and on the instant the sight came back into them!

Then the King believed that it was the Monk who had done him this good. But, when they saw this, the elder brothers went to the King and told him that the Monk had robbed them of the good earth and put the useless earth in its place. Then the King was again angry and would not even set eyes on the Monk. The Monk suffered all this with patience, and hoped that one day the truth would come to light.

Now let us leave the Monk and the others, and come to the kingdom that had slept for six months. When the six months had passed, the people awoke and set about their toil. But the King, Queen, and Princesses, when they awoke and saw that

their watches and fly whisks were gone, were amazed and wondered who had come and taken them, for they imagined that
even if a stranger had been there, he would have fallen asleep.

They made a great to-do over it, and most of all the youngest
Princess, who found the ring on her finger. She saw, too, that the
cypress had been dug about, and it came to her mind that this
was the work of a certain prince whose father's eyes were ailing
and who had come to take the earth. So she sought her father's
permission to go and find this prince.

Her elder sisters also asked to go along with her, until the
King saw whether he liked it or not, there was nothing for him
to do but to grant them permission. With them he sent two of
his loyal sages to watch over them, and a number of soldiers to
guard them. And so, the next day, they put on men's clothing
and set off by a road where there was neither fire nor wind nor
drakoe nor wild beasts nor sidetracks.

They traveled through many kingdoms, asking if there had
been a blind king there six months before, but nothing could
they discover until they came to the kingdom where the Monk
was. There they asked, and were told that the King had been
blind, but his sons had cured him with soil they had brought
from a distant kingdom. Then they rose and went to the King,
saying that they wished to speak with him.

The King received them graciously, and asked them what their
will was.

So then the youngest spoke for them, and said, "We have
heard how your eyes were ailing and how you were cured by a
certain physic. As our father's eyes are likewise ailing, we have
come here to beg you to tell us where this physic is to be found,
so that we may have some, too."

Then the King answered her, "That same physic is a certain
kind of earth which my sons brought to me. But how and where
it is to be found I do not know. But I shall now send for them to
tell you."

And straightway he gave the order, and his two elder sons
came, and he asked them from what place they had brought the
earth. They told what had happened and what they had seen up

to the place where the three roads met, but then they said they had taken a road of fire and wind, had got the earth, and returned home.

"We can make nothing out of these words, and it seems that they did not go or else do not wish to tell us," said the youngest Princess.

Then the King bethought himself of the Monk, and likewise ordered him to come before him, asking him where he had got the earth. No sooner had the Monk entered than he recognized the strangers and began to tell how he had been to the kingdom and got the earth, and how his brothers had thrown him into the well, and how he had been saved. In the end, he brought out the watches and the fly whisks and showed them. Then he sorted them out, and said to the strangers, "Look you, this watch and fly whisk are your father's, and these are your mother's. You three are not men, but girls. This watch and fly whisk are yours" (giving them to the eldest), "these are yours" (and he gave them to the second), "and these are yours" (and he gave them to the youngest). Then he said, "That ring you are wearing is mine, and the one I am wearing is yours. This kerchief is yours."

Then the youngest said to the King, "Behold, your youngest son was there. I am the daughter of the King of that place, and these are my sisters. It was to find out who came and put the ring on my hand that I have been searching all this while. Now I know that it is your son; him do I want to be my husband, and I beg you to give him to me by your leave and with all your will."

Then the King asked the Monk if he wanted her for his wife, and the Monk consented. Thereupon the King gave the order for great rejoicing. There was nothing too good for the Monk, so much did he love him. And his elder sons, who had done so much to the Monk, and told nothing but lies, he put in prison and would have had them hanged, but the Monk would not let him and pleaded with him to forgive them.

To please him, the King gave the order for them to be released from prison. And, afterward, he made his will and left his throne to the Monk. And to crown it all, there were great royal festivities that lasted a full month.

I was present, too, sirs,
And wore my bright red trews, sirs,
      Eating lentils off the skewer, sirs.
And as much as a skewer through lentils can thrust,
So much in my story may you also trust.

· 21 · *The Twin Brothers*

• THERE WAS ONCE a fisherman who had no sons. One day, an old woman came by, saw the fisherman's wife, and said to her, "What can your goods profit you, if you have no sons?"

"It is God's will, good dame!" answered the fisherman's wife.

"It is not God's will, my child," the old woman told her, "it is your husband's, for if he caught the golden fish, you would have sons. When he comes home this evening, you must tell your husband to go and catch it, if you wish to have sons. And you must cut it into six pieces: you yourself eat one piece and let your husband eat one, and you'll have two sons; let the bitch-dog eat one piece, and she'll bear two puppies; let the mare eat one piece, and she'll bear two foals; put one on the threshold of one door and one on the other, and two cypress trees will grow."

That evening when her husband came, she told him all that had happened, and he went and caught the fish, and they did with it as the old woman had bidden. In time they had two sons, so like each other there was no telling them apart. The dog bore two puppies very like each other, and the mare two foals very alike, and on the threshold grew two cypress trees. When they grew up, the lads did not want to stay at home however great the comfort, but they wanted to go and win a name for themselves. Their father would not let them go, for they were all he had; so he said for the one to go first, and when he came back, the other could go.

So one of the twins took one of the twin horses and one of the twin dogs, and set off, saying to his brother, "For as long as the two cypress trees are green, think of me as living, but if one withers, set out to look for me."

He went on and on, a long way from home, and at last drew up at an old woman's house. That evening he said to the old woman, "Whose is the house above this one?"

And the old woman told him, "That is the palace of the Beauty of the Country."

"I have come," the lad told her, "to win her."

"Many have come to win her, my son, and no one has been able to do so," the old woman told him, "and they have had their heads cut off and put on iron spikes, as you can plainly see."

Then said the lad to her, "I shall go and tell her I've come to win her, even though my head be cut off."

Now the lad could play the lute, and very well, too. He played it that evening and the Beauty of the Country heard him.

Next day, the Beauty of the Country said to the old woman, "Old woman, who is it you have in your house that plays the lute so well?"

"A young man is here from foreign parts," said the old woman, "and it was he."

"Tell him I wish to meet him."

So the lad went to the Beauty of the Country, and she asked him what country he was from and told him that she was very taken with his playing of the lute and would like to marry him.

"That," said the lad, "is what I, too, have come for."

"Go and tell my father," she told him, "that you want me for your wife, and come and tell me what he says to you."

The lad went to the King and told him that he wanted his daughter for his wife. And the King told him, "If you are worthy, do what I tell you and do it well, otherwise, I'll have your head. There's a tree stump in my field so big that two ropes cannot go round it; if you can fell it with one blow with your sword, I'll give you my daughter to wed; if not, I'll have your head."

The boy got up and went to the old woman's house in sorrow, for the next day he might have his head cut off. That evening he did not play the lute, as he was wont to play every evening, but sat thinking how he would fell the tree stump that was so big.

When the Beauty did not hear the lute, she cried to him,

"Why don't you play the lute this evening, but instead sit there thinking?"

So the boy told her what her father had said.

"Is that what troubles you? Play a brisk tune on your lute to cheer us, and tomorrow morning come to me here."

The lad played the lute all evening and they made merry; next morning, at daybreak, the Beauty gave him a hair from her head and told him to tie it round his sword and he would fell the tree stump.

The lad went to where the tree stump was and felled it with one stroke of his sword.

But her father said to him, "I have yet another task for you to do and I will give you my daughter to wed. Mount a horse and travel the road for three hours, carrying in your hand two pots full of water; if not a drop is spilled, I'll give you my daughter to wed. If not, I'll have your head."

Again the lad went in sorrow to the old woman's house and did not play the lute. Again the Beauty called him, and said, "Why aren't you playing the lute?"

Then he told her what her father had said. And she said to him, "Never grieve over that, but play the lute, and tomorrow morning come to me here."

The next morning, the Beauty gave him her ring and told him to put it in the water and the water would freeze and not spill. Then the lad did as she had bidden, and the water did not spill.

And as it had not spilled, her father said to him, "I have one word yet to say to you, and then no more. I have a blackamoor; tomorrow you will fight him, and if you win you may take my daughter."

Then the lad went joyfully to the old woman's house and made merry. The Beauty called him, and said, "You seem happy tonight. What did my father tell you to make you happy?"

And the lad said to her, "He told me to fight tomorrow with a blackamoor, and I hope to win, for, as he is a man, a man, too, am I."

"That is the worst of all," the Beauty told him, "for I am the blackamoor; they give me a drink and I turn into a blackamoor.

Tomorrow, you must go to the market and buy twelve buffalo skins to put on your horse; take this kerchief and when I fall on you, show it to me, so that I may remember and not kill you. Also, you must try to strike my horse between the brows, for in killing my horse, you may conquer me."

The lad went to the market and bought the buffalo skins and put them on his horse, and he and the blackamoor came out to fight. When they had fought, and eleven of the skins had been pierced through, the blackamoor made ready to kill the lad, but the lad struck the blackamoor's horse on the brow, and the horse falling lifeless, the blackamoor was beaten and the lad won.

And her father told him, "Now you have done that too, I will make you my son-in-law."

Said the lad to him, "I have a certain duty that I must now do, but in forty days, I will come and fetch her."

The lad set out for another country, and he went on till he came to another old woman's house. That evening, when they had eaten their bread, the lad asked this old woman for water.

"I have none," the old woman told him. "Only once a year do we get water here, for it is kept by a *stoecheio* [spirit]. Every year, we give him a maiden to devour, and he lets us have water. And now the lot has fallen to the King's daughter and she will be taken to the *stoecheio* tomorrow."

The next day, they brought the King's daughter for the *stoecheio* to devour, and tied her up nearby with a golden chain and went off and left her there alone. When they had all gone, the lad went up to the Princess and found her in tears.

He asked her, "Why are you weeping?"

The Princess told him that the *stoecheio* would come out and devour her, and that was why she wept. So the lad told her he would save her.

When the *stoecheio* came out, the lad gave an order to his dog, and it choked the *stoecheio,* and so the Princess was saved. And when the King heard this, he decided to give the lad his daughter's hand in marriage, and so they were wed.

When he had been there a week, the lad grew restless and wanted to go out hunting. The King did not want him to go, but could not restrain him, so he told him to take servants with him, but he would not and took only his horse and his dog. When he had gone a long way, he grew thirsty and, seeing a hut some way off, went to seek for water. In the hut was yet another old woman, whom he asked to give him a little water to drink, but the old woman told him to let her first strike his dog with her wand and then she would give him water. He told her to strike, but she struck the dog, it was turned into marble; she struck him, too, and turned him into marble, and then she turned his horse into marble as well.

When she turned the lad into marble, the cypress tree withered at home. And the other brother set out to find him. He went past the place where his brother had killed the *stoecheio* and it happened that he put up at the first old woman's house where his brother had put up.

And when the old woman saw him she said, "Forgive me, my son, for not coming to wish you well at your wedding with the King's daughter." The old woman thought he was the other brother, they were so much alike. "Never mind that," he told her. And he straightway set off and went to the King's palace.

When the King saw him, he took him for his son-in-law. "What became of you?" he asked him. "We thought something had happened to you, you were gone so long."

He gave him many excuses why he had been away so long, and the next day went out hunting in his turn, and happened to take the same road as his brother had taken. While some distance off, he saw his brother standing there in marble, with his horse and dog, and recognized him.

He went to the hut and told the told woman to unmarble his brother.

The old woman said to him, "Let me strike the dog with my wand and then I'll unmarble your brother."

The lad said to the dog, "Gobble the old woman up!"

And the old woman said to him, "Tell your dog not to eat me, so that I can unmarble your brother."

"Tell me how to do it," the lad said, "and I'll tell my dog not to gobble you up."

And when she would not, he gave his dog an order and it gobbled her up to the waist.

Then the old woman said to him, "I have two wands, one green, one red. With the green one, I turn things to marble; with the red, I unmarble them."

Then he took the red wand and unmarbled his brother and his dog and horse. He told his dog to gobble up the old woman entirely.

When he had saved his brother, he went back to the Beauty of the Country, and she received him, thinking he was his brother who had beaten her in the fight, and he married her. The other went back to the palace where he had his wife, the Princess he had saved from the *stoecheio*.

They sent word to their parents to come there, too, and they all lived together.

•22• *Anthousa the Fair with Golden Hair*

• ONCE UPON A TIME there was an old woman. The poor soul had been wanting lentil soup for seven years, but could never get it. When she had lentils, she had no onions; when she had onions, she had no oil; when she had oil, she had no water.

So she complained, and said, "Oh dearie me! The poor man wants to wed, but the wedding drums are gone!"

But after this she found all she needed. One day, she took the kettle and went and set it in the stream. The King's son went to water his horse. When the horse saw the kettle, it reared and would not drink. The King's son flew into a rage, gave the kettle a kick, and overturned it.

When the poor old crone saw it, she cursed him, and said, "Oh dearie me! As I have yearned seven years for lentil soup, so may you yearn for Anthousa the fair with golden hair!"

No sooner did the King's son hear this than he began to run round all the villages in turn, searching for Anthousa the fair with golden hair. He searched for three months but could not find her.

After three months he came to a village, and asked,

"Does there chance to live here Anthousa the fair with the golden hair?"

"She does live here," they told him.

"Where is her house? Take me there."

They took him, and when he got there, and looked at the house, it had no stair. How was he to go up?

Nearby he saw a tree and climbed up and looked about him. As he was looking, a *drakaena* came, stood below the house, and called, "Anthousa the fair with golden hair, let down your hair for me to climb."

A lovely girl leaned out and let down her hair, and the *drakaena* climbed up.

After a little her brother came and called, "Anthousa fair with golden hair, let down your hair for me to climb."

Again Anthousa leaned out of the window and let down her hair, and her brother climbed up. They ate and drank, and then her mother and brother climbed down again.

When he saw that they had gone, the King's son came down the tree, went up to the house and called, "Anthousa fair, with your golden hair, let down your hair for me to climb."

When she heard this, she again let down her hair, and the King's son climbed up.

When he had climbed up, he told her he wanted to make her his wife. And she said to him, "And I will take you for my husband. But where am I to hide you now? Let my mother not chance to come and find you here, for she would eat you."

So she wrapped him in a coverlet and put him in the chest. Then she mopped the house so that it should not smell of human.

At nightfall, her mother came and called, "Anthousa fair with golden hair, let down your hair for me to climb."

She let down her hair, and her mother climbed up and began to sniff, saying, "There's a smell of human."

Her daughter told her, "You must have eaten one and the smell still hangs about you."

Next morning, the moment her mother had gone, she got him out of the chest. Then the two talked of running away. But in that house all things could speak. So they would not tell they had

run away, they set to and bound all their mouths, and then they
went.

After they had gone, the old *drakaena* came to the house.
Again and again she called "Anthousa fair, with your golden
hair, let down your hair for me to climb."

But no one answered.

When she saw her daughter did not come out, she climbed the
wall, and called again, "Anthousa fair with golden hair, where
are you?"

All the things had their mouths bound up and could not answer. But they had forgotten to bind the mortar's mouth, and
from the corner where it stood, it answered, "Yesterday the
King's son came; she hid him, and now they have run away together."

When the *drakaena* heard this she became as one mad. She
kept a bear in her stable, and so she went and took it out,
mounted it, and tore after them. She went on and on, a long
way, and finally caught up with them.

The girl had with her her combs and her kerchiefs. When she
saw that the *drakaena* had caught up with them, she threw down
the fine-toothed comb and it turned into a hedge so that the
drakaena could not pass. The bear thrust this way and plunged
that way until, after a thousand tries it made a path and passed
through. On and on it went till it caught up with them again.

When she saw the *drakaena* catching up with them, the girl
threw down the coarse-toothed comb, and it turned into a thicket
of thorns even coarser than the teeth of the comb. For as long as
the bear was entangled in it, they went a long way farther on.
But the bear got through again, and went on and on until it
caught up with them again.

When she saw that the *drakaena* was catching up with them,
she threw down the kerchief and it turned into a sea. The unhappy old *drakaena* wept and pleaded with her daughter to come
back, but she would not hear of it, for she would not leave her
husband.

When the *drakaena* saw that she could not move her daughter,
she turned and said, "You have left your mother, my lass, to follow him, but wait till I tell you what he will do to you. Now, in

the place where you are going, he will leave you in a tree while he goes to fetch his mother to come for you, but his mother will kiss him and he will forget you and wed another. But you must get down from the tree, go where they are making bread for the feast and do what you have to do: take a lump of dough and make two little birds out of it and send them to sit on his window sill and wake him, so that he may think of you."

It all came about as her mother had said. When they drew close to the King's palace, she climbed a tree. She sat and sat and when she saw that no one would come to fetch her, she was in great distress. She turned herself into a gypsy and went to the bakery. She saw them plaiting the dough into loaves and asked, "What is to be done with so much bread?"

They told her, "The King's son is to have a wedding feast, and it is for the feast we are baking."

She walked this way and that till she was able to steal a lump of dough. Then she molded two birds from it, sent them to the King's son's window, and then went back and climbed the tree again.

Now the birds went and sat on the window sill and began to talk, "Do you remember, I wonder," said one to the other, "how for three months you ran about looking for Anthousa the fair with golden hair?"

"I don't remember," said the other.

"Do you remember how you came and climbed a tree and, when my mother went away, you cried: 'Anthousa fair with your golden hair, let down your hair,' and I let down my hair and you came up and I wrapped you in the coverlet."

"I don't remember."

"Do you remember how my mother came and we ate, and as soon as I bade good-bye to her, I brought you out, and we too went away? And when she went to the house and saw I was not there, she mounted a bear and caught up with us?"

"I don't remember."

"Do you remember, I wonder, how I threw down the fine-toothed comb and it turned into a hedge and the bear bit through it and then caught up with us again?"

"I don't remember."

"Do you remember how I threw down the coarse-toothed comb and it turned into a thicket of even coarser thorns, but again she got through and caught up with us. Then I threw down the kerchief and it turned into a sea and she could not cross it?"

"I don't remember."

"Do you remember, I wonder, how you put me in a tree and you went to fetch a carriage for me, but your mother kissed you and you fell asleep and forgot me?"

"Ah, I remember, I remember, I remember!"

The King's son heard all this for he had been awake from the beginning. At first he had not understood what the birds meant, but straightway it all came back to him. So he got up and went to the tree and took Anthousa down, and there was a feast that lasted forty days and forty nights.

I was there too, and the King's wife offered me three golden cups of wine.

•23• *The Shepherd and the Three Diseases*

• ONCE THERE WAS a shepherd who kept his sheep pen outside the village, and grazed his sheep there. He had a little house there, and he would sit in it. One evening, as he was getting ready for bed, he heard a loud knocking on the door.

He asked, "Who is it?"

"Open."

He opened, and saw a woman in black.

He asked her "Who are you, dame? What is it you want?"

She said to him, "I am Pox, Smallpox, and I want you to give me your best lamb, or else I'll take you, and you'll die. Give it to me, and I'll leave you."

Said the shepherd to her, "So far as I remember, and according to what my mother told me, "I've had smallpox, and there's no fear I shall get it again, or if I do, only slightly. So be off with you and let me be, for I have no business with you."

So Pox took up her firebrand and went back to where she had come from.

The shepherd was just settling down for the night—he had even closed his eyes—when he heard another loud knocking at the door.

"Oh, to blazes with it," he said, "who is it this time?" He opened, and saw a woman in black. "What is it you want, dame, at such an hour?" he said to her.

"I am Pestilence and Diphtheria," said she to him, "and I want you to give me your best lamb, or else I'll take you, and you'll die."

He bethought himself, and said to her, "Dame, according to what my mother told me, and as far as I'm aware, I had the pestilence when I was a boy and I may not have it again, so I have no business with you."

So Pestilence took her searing-flail, and left.

The shepherd got onto his mattress, and sleep had not quite taken hold of him, when again he heard—there it was again!— the loud knocking on his door.

"What (in the name of all that's holy) is that?" said he, "I can't get any peace tonight." He opened the door, and saw a woman in black. "What is it you want, dame?" said he.

"I am Plague," said she to him, "and I've come to get you. But give me your best lamb, and I'll not take you."

The shepherd scratched his head: he had never had the plague.

"Come," said he to her, "and I'll give it to you." He took her to the pen, and picked out the best lamb. "Take it," he said to her.

"No," she said to him, "you must bring it to my house yourself."

"And where is your house?"

"Come with me, and you'll see."

The shepherd slung the lamb up on his back, and with Plague before and him behind, they took the road to her house. They went on and on, through deserts and up mountains, but saw never so much as a house for all the hardship. The wretched shepherd was afraid, but he dared not say anything. At last, they saw in the distance a very tall palace with light streaming forth.

"There's my house," said Plague to him.

They went in; the shepherd looked about him, and what should he see, but the whole house full of *kantelas* [oil lamps], hanging from the ceiling and shining as bright as stars. Some were full of oil to the brim, and some only half-full; there were also some just on the flicker, and others on the splutter, ready to go out.

The shepherd ceased wondering at this to ask Plague, "Tell me, what are all those *kantelas?*"

"Those," Plague told him, "are the lives of men. For as long as each man's lamp burns, he will have life. If it goes out, he will die."

"Is my own lamp here among them?"

"Of course it is. Look there!"

The shepherd looked, and saw a lamp full to the brim with oil and shining so bright that it did one's heart good to see it. He saw another beside it with only the water left at the bottom, and it was spluttering, ready to go out.

"Alas," said the shepherd to her, "whose is that?"

"That is your brother's," she told him.

"Can you not take a little from mine, which is brimful, and put it in his and save the poor fellow?"

"Such a thing cannot be done," Plague told him. "The oil is put in once and for all. After that, no more can be either put in or taken out."

"Truly?" said the shepherd. "Neither put in, nor taken out?"

"Truly."

"Then good-bye, for I have no business with you!"

And with the lamb on his shoulder again, he was off at a run the whole way back to the pen, as if the very plague were after him.

The very next day when he went down to the village he heard the passing bell tolling dolefully.

"Good man, who is dead?" he asked.

"Your brother," he was told.

And then he knew that what he had seen was all true.

•24• *The Enchanted Lake*

• Now THE STORY BEGINS—good evening to your worships.

Once upon a time there was a king who had three sons. They grew up and at last were of an age to marry. The old King had three arrows and three bows. He gave one bow and one arrow to each of his sons, and bade them go up to the topmost part of the palace, where each was to shoot his arrow, and wherever it fell, in whatever courtyard, there would he take the daughter of the house to wife.

So they went up to the highest part of the building. The eldest shot his arrow and it fell in the courtyard of a handsome mansion. Here lived a beautiful young girl, whom he married. The second went up and shot his arrow, which fell in a fine house where lived a beautiful young girl, and so he, in his turn, was married. The youngest then remained.

Now, before giving them the arrows, the King had had three new palaces built, and he said, "My sons, you shall marry and live in your palaces with your wives."

The Princes thanked him; the eldest was married, the second was married, and now we come to the third.

The youngest dawdled over the shooting of his arrow; he would shoot it today, he would shoot it tomorrow. In this manner, time went by. The Princes held banquets and invited their father and mother, and there was much rejoicing.

One day, when they were feasting at the eldest brother's house, the King said to the youngest son, "My son, if you wish to have my blessing, shoot your arrow now and get yourself a wife, so that I may see you married, and die happy."

Then the Prince said, "It is far from my desire to go against your wishes, my father. Tomorrow I, too, will shoot my arrow, and wherever it falls, there will I take a wife."

The day dawned, the Prince went up to the topmost part of the palace, shot his arrow, and saw it fly far far away, and fall to earth. The Prince went down to the place where the arrow had fallen, and looked all about him, but saw never a sign of a house of anything there. He went to seek his arrow, and what should he see but a magic lake, and in the middle of it a frog carrying the arrow in her mouth and swimming for her nest.

At once the Prince rushed into the lake and clutched at the frog. He picked her up, still with his arrow in her mouth, and took her home. He put the frog in a room by herself. But how was he to tell his father of this misadventure? He sent away all his servants lest his sisters-in-law should come to hear of it and chaff him about it, and gave himself up to the hunt.

One day, he brought back a deal of game. He hung it up behind the door, and said, "I shall go and confess all to my father, and beg him not to tell my brothers. Yet such was to be my fate."

He went to his father and told him what had befallen. His father was very sad to have brought misfortune on his favorite son, for he loved his youngest child more than the other two. Said he to him, "Ay well, my son, 'twas God's will you should not marry."

While the Prince was with his father, the frog was putting his house in order. And would you believe it, my dears, she stepped out of her skin, and lo! she was a beautiful Princess in silken vestments, very handsome garments they were, too; she rolled up her sleeves, lit the fire, and cooked the game the Prince had brought home from hunting; she laid the table, served the dishes, and then stepped back inside her skin and sat down in her corner.

The Prince returned and entered his house, but what should he see but the room swept, and the food cooked giving off the most tempting smells. "Why, who could have done all this?" said he, and he searched hither and thither, but saw no one. He sat down and ate, not forgetting to set aside for the frog the tastiest portion, which he put on a plate on the table. He then lifted the frog onto the table, and went away.

When he returned, he found the house clean, the dishes washed, and not a soul in sight. "But how can this be?" he said. "Tomorrow I shall go to the hunt, and hang the game I bring back on the door, and hide." The next day he went out hunting, killed a fair number of birds, and hung them up on the door. He changed his clothes, and went down the steps to lock the gate, and then went in by a little door that led into the palace from the garden.

Now when the frog saw the Prince leave, and heard him lock the garden gate, she came out of her skin and was once more a beautiful Princess, so beautiful as to

> *Tell the sun to stay his course,*
> *The star of morn to shine.*

When the Prince saw her, he fell hopelessly in love with her beauty. She went to the window and clapped her hands. The Prince saw a young frog coming plop! plop! up the stairs. As soon as it came up to the Frog Princess, it threw off its skin and set to work, for it had taken the form of a young girl, plucking the fowl, drawing the fire and cooking, with the help of the Princess.

As soon as the work was done, the frog maiden stepped back into her skin and went away. Then the Princess also donned her frog skin and sat down in her corner. So then the Prince left by the small door as quietly as he had come in, and went upstairs. He entered the room where the table stood ready laid, sat down and began to eat. Then he started to walk up and down the room, and at last went up to the frog and fell to stroking it.

"Well, you were to be my fate," he told it, "come what may, I shall henceforth remain a bachelor, for it was you took my arrow in your mouth, and no more shall I seek a wife. But can you not utter at least a word to cheer me, and tell me who it is that comes to cook my food for me?"

The frog looked him straight in the eye, and said nothing.

The tale got about, I don't know how, that his arrow had fallen into a lake and that he now kept a frog in the house.

One day, his sisters-in-law said to him, "Will you not bring us your wife and let us see her?"

"I am not married," the Prince told them, "so how can I bring you my wife?" and, much offended, he got up and went away. When he got home, he found the meal ready, and sat down and ate.

One day, he hid once again and, just as the Frog Princess was going to clap her hands to call the frog maiden, the Prince ran out, seized the frog skin and threw it into the fire. The Frog Princess ran up and down, crying, "I burn! I burn!" and the Prince pulled the skin out of the fire and threw it into a golden basin with water in it. Then he fell at her feet and begged her not to go back into her skin, and to have pity on him.

"Can you not see how sorry is my lot?" he asked her. "Not to be able to go out into the world, and then to be jeered at by my brothers, when you are more beautiful than either of my sisters-in-law?"

"I come of royal stock," she told him, "but we are under a curse and our kingdom now lies below the water. So that we might yet live out our time down there, we have been given the skin of the frog. Thus we can bear with the watery life, everything we have, all our goods and chattels, are in the lake. A wizard has told us that if a man can be found who will love me and not curse the hour he met me, I shall be human again. A frog I have been, and I put you to the test, and now I know you are a good man. I will make you happy; let your sisters-in-law mock all they please."

Then he began to rejoice greatly at his own happiness, whereupon she bade him throw the frogskin into the well and ever after the water would be fresh. This he did, saying, "We will stay together as long as you wish, and say nothing to anyone."

One day, it was the King's feast day. The eldest brother was giving a banquet in his honor to which all were invited. But the youngest brother he mocked at, saying, "Will you not bring us your wife, so we may laugh and chaff and have a merry time together?"

So he went home, downcast.

His wife asked him, "What has made you sad?"

"What, indeed! My brother is holding a banquet because it is my father's feast day and, to be able to laugh at my expense, they have asked me to come with my wife."

"Very well," said she, "if you are of a mind to go, we will, and instead of their laughing at our expense, *we* shall laugh at theirs. Go to the lake where you found me, and call, 'Kye-na-na! Kye-na-na!' Then you will hear, 'Pe-ke-ke! Pe-ke-ke!' You will say, 'Your daughter, Flora, sent me to ask you for the golden wand that stands in the corner, and a silver wand besides, and for one goose egg and two hen's eggs.' As soon as you have them come home."

The harassed Prince did just as she had bidden. He went to the lake, made the call his wife had told him to make, and when he had the two wands and the three eggs, he returned home. Then she asked him when the banquet would be held, and he told her it would be the next day.

The next day, when she tapped once with the golden wand, three slaves sprang out of it; when she tapped twice, a slave girl came out with a chest full of men's and women's garments in cloth of gold, diamonds, and jewelry. She dressed herself in the fine clothes and her husband did likewise, donning the golden sword, the watch, the furs, and the garments in cloth of gold. Then she gave the silver wand to the slaves who went down to the roadway, tapped with the wand, and lo and behold! a beautiful coach, all of gold and drawn by four pure white horses, stood waiting for them in the yard, sparks flying as the horses' hooves pawed the cobble stones. The sisters-in-law kept going to the door and laughing (Ha! Ha! Ha!) and asking when the frog-wife was to arrive.

Just as they were laughing (Ha! Ha! Ha!) anew, what should they see but a beautiful coach, with attendants dressed in gold and pulled by four white horses, come to a halt before their door. They were all agog to see who would alight. Then, as they looked, the attendants got down and handed a beautiful lady out of the coach. They gaped at one another. The Prince got down behind her.

His two brothers ran forward to escort their sister-in-law up into the palace. She went up and kissed her father-in-law's hand. Her father-in-law embraced and kissed her. She then gave the goose egg to her father-in-law. She kissed the hand of one of her brothers-in-law, and gave him one of the two hen's eggs. She kissed the other brother-in-law's hand, and gave him the other egg. So, then, the sisters-in-law began to jeer, "Oh, la! What precious gifts are these! Eggs she offers us!"

Not a word answered she, but only smiled. Then she bade her father-in-law crack his egg, and what should he find inside, but a beautiful crown, all made of diamonds! She took it up and placed it on her father-in-law's head with her own hands. When the two brothers cracked their eggs, they each found inside a watch with a diamond chain.

So then the bride- and groom-to-be said, "Let today also be our wedding day." The feast in their honor was one of much splendor, to the music of instruments and drums, and there was great rejoicing. Their wedding took place that same day, and they lived happily ever after, and may we live even happier.

·25· *Brother and Sister*

• ONCE UPON A TIME there were two poor folk, a brother and his sister. The brother sold wood and the sister stayed at home and looked after the house; she cooked, if there was anything to cook, and did any little job.

One day, when the lad was going to work, a man stopped him, and said, "Will you take this meat home for me?"

"I will," said the lad.

So he took the meat to the house and was given three ten lepton pieces for his trouble. With these, he bought three sardines and took them home to his sister.

"Sister," he said to her, "keep the sardines for us to eat this evening with our bread."

"Very well," said the lass.

After some time, there was a knocking at her door. She opened, and it was three women.

"Ah, my lass," they said to her, "may we sit here and rest awhile, for we have been on the road?"

She took them in, and sat them down. What, now, was she to give them to eat? As she had nothing else but only the three sardines, she got them out, cleaned them, and gave them those, with vinegar and water, for she had not a drop of oil to put on them.

"Forgive me," she said to the women, "but I have nothing else."

"Ah, my lass," said they to her, "we don't know how to thank you."

"Let's change her fortune," said one. "The fortune I give her is, let her comb herself, and fine pearls fall."

"The fortune I give her," said the second, "is, let her wash herself, and the pan fill with fish."

"And the fortune I give her," said the third, "is, let her dry herself, and the towel fill with thirtyleaves and roses."

So the women went away, and the lass was left alone.

"Let me see," said she, "if it were true what they said to me . . . no, never think it, how could it be true?"

But she took up the comb and combed her hair, and lo! the place was full of fine pearls. She went to wash, and at once the basin filled with delicious red mullet, as fat as you please. She went to dry herself—behold! the towel was full of roses. She gathered up the pearls; she gathered up the roses; she set about cleaning the fish, cooking and attending to them. When her brother came home that evening, instead of the sardines, what should he see but those fine fish. The blood rose to his head.

"Sister," he said to the lass, "until now, I have loved you, but, from now on, I shan't be loving you. Where did you get the fish?"

"Brother mine," said the girl to him, "I was good, and I am good. Thus, and thus."

She took him by the hand to show him the roses and the pearls. What joy was his! "So, from today," he said to her, "we are rich!"

The next day they gathered the pearls into a kerchief, and he took them to the capital to sell them. But, at the place where he took them to sell, they would not believe they were his. Where should such a ragamuffin have found pearls? (they said), surely he's stolen them. So they took him to the King to be judged.

"My King," said the lad to him, "I have not stolen the pearls. I have a sister, and whenever she combs herself, fine pearls fall; whenever she washes herself, the basin fills with fish; and, whenever she dries herself, the towel fills with thirtyleaves and roses."

"Truly? Can your sister do what you say?"

"Truly, my King."

"Well, if it is so, bring her here to me. And, if you speak the truth, I'll take her for my wife; otherwise, I'll have your head."

"I'll willingly go, my King, and bring her to you."

The boy went home to fetch his sister, and they got aboard the caïque to go to the King. As they were on the way, the girl was seasick, and a gypsy who happened to be nearby pushed her head down into her apron, so that it would pass. Then the gypsy asked her where they were going, and the lass told her that they were going to the capital, where the king was to take her to be his wife.

When the gypsy heard this she took out a pin, and as the girl bent over her apron she stuck it into her head. The girl became a bird, and flew away.

The gypsy up and got into the lass's clothes and muffled her face well, so that the girl's brother would not see her face and recognize that it was not his sister.

So when they got there, the lad took her to the King. When the King saw her, he was taken aback at her swarthiness and ugliness.

"I've come off the sea, my King, and that is why you see me like this," she told him.

What more could the King say! He called for a bowl to be brought for her to wash in, a comb for her to comb her hair with, and a towel for her to dry herself with. She up and washed herself, but the water was all full of filth and scum; she went to dry herself, and the towel was black with her dirt; she took the comb to comb herself, and—well, what could be worse?—a treasure of nits and fleas fell out.

The King went up in smoke.*

"Seize the liar," he roared," and throw him into prison. As for that flea-ridden sister of his, set her to mind the turkeys!"

The lad called out, telling them that she was not his sister, and that she had been changed, but they paid him no heed. They took him and threw him into prison, and took the evil gypsy and set her to mind the turkeys.

---

* Literally, "The King became a steamship."

The next day, the King went down to his garden to take the
air, for he was sick at heart. Just then, a beautiful little bird came
and sat in a branch above him, and began to chirrup, and said,

"That bird am I, that little bird, that little bird you know of,
"Who combed my hair, and from it fell a store of finest
  pearl,
"Who washed myself, and fine, fresh fish came swimming
  in the basin,
"Who dried myself, and from the towel fell thirtyleaves
  and roses."

The King heard this and it seemed to him very strange. He
called the gardener, and told him, "Set cages around so as to
catch that bird that comes and sings so queerly."
So they set cages the next day, and caught the little bird. The
King took it in his hands, and stroked it. Then, while he was
stroking its head, he somehow stuck his finger with the pin. He
drew it out, and there before him stood the girl, who dumbfounded him with her beauty.
"I am your wife," said she, "and the other is an evil gypsy,
who would have destroyed me."
She combed her hair, and the place was filled with fine pearls;
she washed, and the basin filled with fish; she dried herself, and
roses fell from the towel.
Then the King ordered royal clothes to be brought her, and
she was dressed in them and seated on a golden throne and given
a golden apple to play with. They took her brother from behind
prison bars, but they took the gypsy and cut her to pieces.

· 26 · The Sun and His Wife

• THERE WAS ONCE a man, getting on in years, who was the father
of three daughters, but the unlucky fellow was poor and had to
try and support them by hunting. So he would go out every day,
tracking the hare. One day, he had caught not a one and went
home empty-handed and sighing. His eldest daughter said to
him, "What's the matter, Father, why are you sighing?"

"What should be the matter," he said, "but that I have brought nothing back from hunting, and don't know what we shall eat this evening."

"Ah," said the daughter, "and here was I, thinking you were brooding over marrying me off." The second daughter came up and the same words were said. The youngest, however, more dutiful than the others, said to him, "Don't sit there brooding and sighing, Father; if you never found aught today, you surely will tomorrow."

The next day dawned and the old man again went out hunting. He went hither and thither, but again found nothing; so the poor fellow sat down on a mound and sighed, "Alas and alack!"

That very moment, a very black blackamoor appeared. His name was Alasandalack, and he was the servant of the Sun.

"What is your will with me, old man?" he said to him.

"My will, lad?" said the old man to him. "I never summoned you."

"Indeed you did! Did you not say "Alas and alack"? I'm Alasandalack."

"I can find nothing for my family to eat, poor wretch that I am, and so I sighed."

"And what family have you?"

"Never ask; I have three daughters!"

"Which is the best of the three?"

"The youngest."

"I am the servant of the Sun," Alasandalack told him. "Will you let me take her, for the Sun to wed?"

"I'll ask her, lad. I can't tell you this very moment."

"Very well, then, ask her, and you'll find me here if you say Alasandalack."

The old man went home, and told his youngest daughter, "Such and such happened to me today. So, what do you say, would you be the Sun's wife?"

"I would, Father," she said, "to spare you the burden of having to keep me."

"Well, then, let's go and meet the one I saw yesterday, but don't be frightened, child, when you see what sort of fellow he is."

The girl made ready and they went to the same place, the old man called out, and Alasandalack came and took the girl away through the potholes of the mountain, where the Sun came out, and so to the mansions of the Sun. There the Sun wed with her. The girl was with child. She lived royally in the Sun's mansions, and had only one complaint, but it was a big one. She did not know what her husband was like, for never once had she seen his face. When the Sun was due to return to the palace, his servants gave her a potion to drink, and then she could not see. So she lay beside him without knowing what he was like.

At last, one day, her sisters came to see her. They asked how she was, and she told them, "I am well, never better, but I have one great complaint. I don't know what my husband is like."

"No, truly? How can that be?" they said to her. And she told them it was thus and thus.

"Say no more," they told her. "We'll give you a sponge and, when they give you the potion, put the sponge in it so it won't show."

And so it was! That evening she did not drink the potion, having done as her sisters had bidden her, and she saw the Sun and was struck with wonder. They lay down and the Sun fell into a deep sleep, worn out by his long journey. In the night, she got up and took from inside his head three gold hairs and a padlock with its key. She undid the lock, took a candle and, holding her key in her hand, went about and about inside, amongst wonders without end. There were all manner of things. She walked through workshops where there were tailors sewing and embroidering in gold.

She stopped and asked them, "What is that you are sewing?"

And they answered her, "It is for the Sun's wife and the child she will have."

She went on and on, and then turned back, but as she was going to turn the lock, a drop of wax fell from the candle and scorched the Sun, who at once leapt up crying, "Alasandalack! Alasandalack! The bitch dog has devoured me. Take her," he said to him, "to the wilderness and slay her there, and bring her blood for me to drink."

So Alasandalack led the unhappy girl away; but he took pity

on the poor girl, took her up a mountain and pointed to a forest, saying, "Do you see that forest down there? You must pass through it, saying, 'Long live the Sun.' It is there that his good sister dwells."

So she went down into the forest, saying, "Long live the Sun," and his sister heard her, and said, "Bring her inside. She is my brother's wife." And they brought her in and she stayed there a month or so, and then went on. (Oh, I forgot! Alasandalack had told her to go to such and such a place where his other sister was and say the same.)

So she went on, until the pangs of birth took hold of her. She said, "Long live the Sun, and I am in labor, long live the Sun, and I am in labor."

She within heard her brother's name; she was a *lamia* [flesh-eating-ogress], but when she heard her brother's name she called, "Bring in the woman who is to bear my brother's child. Who is she? Is she his wife?"

Then her belly pained her; the poor woman went in and gave birth to a boy-child with a golden padlock over his heart.

When the Sun's sister saw it, she cried, "That is my brother's child, and this is his wife."

The moment she said it, the Sun came, and there was rejoicing and merrymaking, and all the good things you could ever imagine.

• 27 • *Master Semolina*

• ONCE UPON A TIME there was a king who had a daughter. Many sought her hand in marriage, but she would have none of them. So she took a notion to make herself a husband. She fetched three kilos of almonds, three kilos of sugar, and three of semolina; she ground the almonds and mixed the sugar, almonds and semolina all together, took the mixture in her hands, molded it into a man, and stood him before the patron saint of the house. And then she began her prostrations. Forty days and forty nights she prayed to God, and at the end of forty days God raised the man to his feet. His name was Master Semolina, or Master Semolina Man. He was exceedingly handsome, and his name was known all over the world.

The fame of Master Semolina reached the ears of a distant queen, and she made up her mind to go and take him for her husband. So she built a golden galley with golden oars, and went to the place where Master Semolina lived.

As they arrived, she said to the sailors, "Find the man who stands out handsomest of all, seize him and bring him to the galley."

When the people heard that a golden galley had come, they all went out to see it—among them, Master Semolina. No sooner did the sailors clap eyes on him than they recognized him, straightway seized him, and into the galley with him!

The Princess waited and waited that evening for Master Semolina to come, but in vain! She sought him of this one, she sought him of that one, and she learned that a queen had seized him and gone. What was to be done, what was she to do? She had three pairs of iron shoes made, and set out to look for him.

She came to places and she left them behind her. Finally she drew a long way away from the world and went to the mother of the Moon.

"Good day, foster-mother."

"Well met, young girl. What has brought you, my girl, to this place?"

"Chance brought me here. Would you have seen Master Semolina, Master Semolina Man, anywhere at all?"

"How should I, my girl? It is the first time I have heard the name. Bide here until evening, when my son shall come; he goes all around the world and may have seen him somewhere."

That evening when the Moon came, she said to him, "My son, this maiden wishes to ask you if you have seen Master Semolina, Master Semolina Man, anywhere on your travels?"

"How should I? No, I have not seen him, my girl. It is the first time I have heard the name. Go to the Sun. He may have seen him, for he travels more of the world than I."

That night she slept there, and in the morning they gave her an almond and told her "When you are in need, crack it."

The Princess took the almond and went on her way. She traveled one road after another and had worn out one pair of shoes, when she came to the mother of the Sun.

"Good day, foster-mother."

"Well met, young girl. What has brought you, my girl, to this place?"

"Chance brought me here. Would you have seen Master Semolina, Master Semolina Man?"

"How should I, my girl? No, I have not seen him. But bide here until evening, when my son shall come; he may have seen him, for he travels a great deal of the world."

When the Sun came at evening, the Princess went on her knees to him, and said, "Good Sun, good Master Sun, who travels the world over, would you have seen Master Semolina, Master Semolina Man?"

"How should I? No, I have not seen him. But go to the Stars, who are many. They may have seen someone."

That night she slept there. In the morning they gave her a walnut and told her, "When you are in need, crack it."

Then they showed her the road, and she bade them good-bye and went on her way. She traveled one road after another, and had worn out the second pair of shoes by the time she came to the mother of the Stars.

"Good day, foster mother."

"Well met, young girl. What has brought you, my girl, to this place?"

"Chance brought me here. Would you have seen Master Semolina, Master Semolina Man?"

"How should I, my child? No, I have not seen him. But bide here until evening, when my children come; it may be they have seen someone."

Her children came that evening and she asked them, "Have you seen Master Semolina, Master Semolina Man?"

"No, we have not," said the Stars.

Then up leapt a little one and said, "*I* saw him."

"Where did you see him?"

"In the white lordly mansions, the crane's fledgling, the Queen has him and holds him so well that none may come and take him."

That night she slept there. In the morning they showed her the road, and gave her a hazelnut, saying, "When you are in need, crack it."

She traveled along one road after another and came to the place where Master Semolina was. She went to the palace as a beggar woman, and saw Master Semolina, but said nought.

In the palace there were many geese. She went to the palace servants and said, "Will you let me stay and mind the geese?"

The servants went to the Queen and said, "Lady Queen, there is a beggar woman without who asked to stay and mind the geese. What shall we tell her?"

"Let her do so," said the Queen.

They let her do so. She slept there that night.

In the morning, the moment she got up, she cracked the almond, and out came a gold spinning wheel with a golden spindle bearing spools of gold. When the servants saw it, they ran to the Queen and told her.

When the Queen heard of it, she said to them, "You might go and tell her to give it to me. What use can she have for it herself?"

The servants went and said to her. "Our Lady Queen has asked why you do not give the golden spinning wheel and the spindle to her. What use can you have for it yourself?"

"I will give it you, but for one night you must give me Master Semolina."

The servants went and told the Queen.

"To be sure I'll give him to her," said the Queen. "What harm could come to him?"

So that night, when they had eaten, the Queen gave Master Semolina a potion, and the potion had sleep in it. As soon as he had drunk it, he fell asleep; then the servants picked him up and carried him to the beggar woman, and took the golden spinning wheel with the spindle.

When the servants had gone, the Princess began to speak to Master Semolina, "Why do you not waken? Am I not she who made you? Who mixed the almonds, the sugar, and the semolina, and made the dough? Who wore out three pairs of iron shoes to come and find you, and yet you have not a word to say to me? Have you no pity, light of my life?"

These words the Princess spoke all that night, but never did

Master Semolina Man as much as stir! In the morning the servants went and picked up Master Semolina, the Queen gave him another potion, and he awoke. No sooner had the servants left the Princess than she cracked the walnut and out of it came a golden mother hen with golden chicks. When the servants saw the golden mother hen with her golden chicks, they ran to the Queen to tell her about it.

"Make haste," said the Queen, "and tell her to give it to me. What use can she have for it herself? And if she should ask for Master Semolina Man, I will give him to her. What harm can come to him? And what harm came to him, indeed, that night I gave him to her?"

So the servants went to her and said, "Why do you not give us the golden mother hen with the golden chicks? What use can you have for them yourself?"

"If you will give me Master Semolina for another night."

"We will," said the servants.

The Queen once more had Master Semolina drink a potion to make him sleep, and as soon as he had fallen asleep the servants picked him up and carried him to the beggar woman, took the golden mother hen with the golden chicks and went. When they had gone, the Princess again began to say the things she had said on the first night, but Master Semolina did not so much as stir! In the morning the servants came again, and picked up Master Semolina and went away.

Then the beggar woman cracked the hazelnut, and out at once came a golden clove tree with golden cloves upon it. When the servants saw the golden clove tree with the golden cloves upon it, they ran and told the Queen, and she said, "Make haste and tell her to give it to me, what use can she have for it herself? And if she asks for Master Semolina again, I'll give him to her."

So the servants went and told her.

But next to where the beggar woman dwelt, there dwelt a tailor, and he sewed at night and so heard everything the beggar woman had been saying.

He sought out Master Semolina and said to him, "Begging your pardon, sire, but I should like to ask you something."

"Ask me," said Master Semolina.

"Where do you sleep at night?"

"What a question! At home, of course, where else?"

"Master Semolina, I have not slept a wink for two nights because of that beggar woman who minds the hens. She sits up all night saying, 'Master Semolina, why do you not waken? Did not I wear out three pairs of iron shoes on the way here to find you, and even so you will not speak to me?'"

Master Semolina now saw what had happened, but he said nothing. He went and saddled his horse, strapping onto it a saddlebag full of gold florins.

That night the Queen again gave him the potion, but he only made as if to drink it and fall asleep. Then at once the servants picked him up and carried him to the beggar woman, taking away with them the golden clove tree with the golden cloves upon it.

As soon as the servants had gone and the Princess again took up her complaint, Master Semolina Man leapt to his feet and embraced her and on the instant they had mounted the horse and were on their way.

The next morning the servants went to fetch Master Semolina Man, but not a trace could they find of him! They ran wailing to the Queen and told her. Then she, too, began to weep and wail, but to no avail!

So then she said, "I'll make a husband myself," and on the instant set her servants to grind a quantity of almonds, which she mixed together with sugar and semolina and so molded a man and began her prostrations. But instead of prayers, she uttered curses, and after forty days the man turned rotten and they threw it away.

The Princess and Master Semolina Man went to their kingdom and lived so well they could live no better. I was that way myself and went all over the kingdom.

.28. The Crab

• ONCE UPON A TIME there was a king and queen who had for neighbors a priest and his wife. And the King was so fond of the

Priest that he often said to him, "We must marry our children, one to the other," and the Queen said the same to the Priest's wife.

Such was their wish and so did it come about. The Queen was with child and bore a daughter such that the sun tore his raiment and ran wild at her beauty; the priest's wife was with child and bore—a crab. The Princess grew up among gold and silk, and got prettier every day; the Priest's crab grew up in the basket where they kept him, and got bigger and bigger. By the time the Princess was eighteen years old, the King had forgotten the promise he had given to the priest and wanted to marry his daughter to a prince.

So then, one day, the crab called to his mother, "Mother, you must go and tell the Queen to keep her promise and give me the Princess."

So the Priest's wife arose and went and said to her, "O Queen, our children are now grown and we must marry them. My crab bade me tell you not to forget the bargain we made before the children were born."

To escape from this bargain, the King, who was present and had heard, told the Priest's wife, "If your son will wager that he can take away, in one night, the mountain that stands before my palace and keeps out the sun, then I will give him my daughter."

"So be it, my King," said the Priest's wife, and went and told the crab.

When the crab heard what had been said, he became as one dead and neither ate nor spoke all night. And, that very night, a multitude of *drakoe* came together and dug up the mountain and leveled it. So, when the King awoke next morning, he found the palace full of sunshine, and he said, "I am late in waking, and the sun is now high in the sky."

Then, when he got up, he looked and behold! the mountain that faced the palace had disappeared and a great plain stretched before him. The King was in great distress, but what to be done? Since the bargain was thus, he had to marry the Princess to the crab. So preparations were made for the wedding, and the King sent a carriage and a golden basket to the bridegroom's house. The crab was placed inside the golden basket; then the

Priest's wife got into the carriage and took the basket, with the crab in it, on her lap, and they went to the palace. Not to make a long tale out of it, the wedding took place, and the Queen wept bitterly from grief that her daughter, the Princess, so beautiful as she was, should marry a crab instead of a prince.

That night, when the bride was alone with the crab, there stepped out of the crab's shell such a fine young man as surpassed all the princes in the world for good looks, and he told her not to grieve, and that if she could keep their secret for three weeks, she would save him, but if she should disclose it, she would lose him. And thus he was a crab by day and at night became a handsome man. And the Princess was full of joy at her good fortune, while her mother grieved till she dripped and guttered like a candle.

When Saturday came, the young woman said to her husband, "What are we to do now, for tomorrow is Sunday, and we must go to church?"

Then said her husband to her, "Get up early tomorrow and go with your mother, and I will come after, but take heed—a still tongue or you will lose me."

So on the morrow, she went to church with her mother, and later her husband went also. Her mother saw him and began to weep and wail.

"There's the groom for *you!* He must surely be a Prince who has come to woo you, and now he will hear that you are wed and go away."

Her daughter sat mute; she was sorry for her mother's grief, but did not speak. This again befell on the second Sunday and the third. But, on the third Sunday, the Queen wept so much that her daughter feared her mother would die, so she told her the secret. When she went back to her palace, she found neither crab nor anything at all.

Who then wept and beat her breast and pined away? The good Princess of our tale. She went and, weeping, told her father what had befallen her and besought him to give her a saddlebag full of florins and three pairs of iron shoes for to go and seek her husband. The King could do nothing but give them to her. She put on men's clothes and set forth.

For two years she went from country to country and from place to place, always asking for her husband, but none could tell her aught. At the end of those two years, the second pair of shoes began to wear out. So she found a place where three roads met, and there she had an inn built; any traveler who passed that way she took inside and tended him. She would take no money from him, only asked him to tell her what he had seen and heard on his travels, and after that he would go on his way. The third year was just drawing to its close when two beggars came that way. The one was lame, the other blind.

When she had taken them into the inn and given them food and drink, she asked them to tell her what they had seen and heard on the road.

The lame one answered, "On the way as we came, we grew hungry and sat down beside a stream to eat. I had three rusks; I took them from my bag and went down to the stream to dip them in the water and soften them. But in the stream there ran a current and it carried my rusks away downstream, and I began to run on my lame leg to catch up with them. I ran as hard as I could, but the water ran ever faster than I, until I came to a hollow wherein the water flowed. Here I saw some steps descending, and so I hobbled down, too, and there I found a great door. Through the door I saw a palace. In I went and there I saw an oven with many loaves of hot bread in it. I stretched out my hand to take a loaf when, quick as lightning, up got the baker's shovel and rapped me over the knuckles and said, 'Wait till the lords have eaten first; then you may take one.'

"Farther on, I saw a caldron full of food a-cooking. I stretched out my hand for the ladle to taste a little, and quick as lightning the ladle got up and rapped me over the the knuckles and said, 'Wait till the lords have eaten first; then you may have your share.' I saw three doves go into a room and drop into a crystal basin, and when they had bathed they turned into three fine young men as bright as angels, and sat down at the table to eat. The dishes took themselves to the table. Then one of them picked up his wine glass and said, 'To the health of the fair one who did not keep the secret—weep, ye doors, weep, ye windows!' And all at once he began to cry, and with him, the doors and windows. The second young man did the same. Then the third man said, 'To the health of the most fair lady who did not keep her promise for one more day and lost me—weep, ye doors, weep, ye windows!'

"And thereupon he began to cry more than all the others crying with him. Afterward, they once again became doves and flew away. Then I, too, took a plate and filled it with food; I took two loaves as well, and left the castle and went to find the blind one, who was bewailing my absence. We sat down together and ate the food and the loaves and then we came on here to find a place for the night."

Then the Princess said to the lame one, "Can you find that place again and take me there?"

"That I can," said the lame one.

The next day, the Princess set out with the lame one. They entered the castle. As the Princess went past the oven, the oven said to her, "Welcome, my lady!"

As she went past the caldron, the same, "Welcome, my lady!"

When the beating of the doves' wings could be heard, the door said to her, "Hide behind me, my lady."

She hid, and soon after the three doves came and dived into the crystal basin and became three most handsome young men. The Princess at once recognized her husband, the youngest of the young men, but she held back and did not speak. Then they began to eat.

When the time came for them to drink the toast, the first said, "To the health of the most fair lady who did not keep the secret. Weep, ye doors, weep, ye windows," and at once they all began to weep. The same with the second. When her husband's turn came, he said the same, but instead of crying this time, the doors laughed, and the windows laughed.

"I bade you weep!"

But they would do nothing but laugh.

Then he got up and went to break them, but whom should he see but his wife!

"Ah, that is why they would not weep, but laughed, because you are come."

But she ran, quick as lightning, and snatched up the wings, threw them on the fire, and burnt them.

Then her husband said to her, "You have saved me," and joyfully they all departed and went home to the palace.

Great was the joy of the King and Queen. They had a second wedding: forty days and nights the feasting lasted, with eating and drinking and merrymaking.

Neither was I there, nor need you believe it.

·29· *The Sleeping Prince*

• Now THE STORY BEGINS—good evening to your worships.

There was once a king that had a most beautiful daughter. He loved her very much, for when she was very small, her mother had died, and so he had no one in the world but that little girl.

An order came to him to go to war, and he was at his wit's end to know how his daughter would fare without him. The daughter came in and saw that her father was sad.

She said to him, "What has made you sad, Papa?"

"What, indeed, my child, but that I have been ordered to war, and am sorry to leave you here alone."

"Go well, my Father, and return well. I shall sit with my nurse and wait for you. But come soon, for I have no one else to care for at home." The father left for the war, she put a gold kerchief on the frame to embroider and give to him when he came back from the war.

One day, as she was at her embroidery, a golden eagle came by her window, and said, " 'Broider away, 'broider away, a dead man you'll have for a husband one day."

The Princess said nothing, but stared at the eagle. The next day it again came by, and told her the same.

Then said the Princess to her nurse, "While I was sitting at my embroidery, an eagle came by and told me, ' 'Broider away 'broider away, a dead man you'll have for a husband one day.' "

"When it tells you so again," her nurse said to her, "you say, 'Take me to see him.' "

The eagle again came by and told her the same. Then said she to the eagle, "Take me to see him."

The eagle lowered its wing, and said to her, "Climb upon my wing, and I'll take you to see him." She climbed upon the eagle's wing and it took her away. When the eagle had gone a fair distance, there was a wide-lipped well and the eagle went in and left her in the courtyard, and flew away.

In the well stood a beautiful palace. The dogs slept in the courtyard. She walked on and saw horses, asleep, too; she went up to the palace, and saw the servants asleep, too. She walked into a room all of gold, and saw a handsome Prince who slept as one dead. Beyond the bed was a table, and on the table a paper, and the paper said, "Whatever maiden enters here and pities the Prince for his youth, must stay and watch over him three months, three weeks, three hours, and three half-hours, and never sleep, for when he sneezes she must say to him, 'Bless you, my King, may you live for ever; I am she who has watched over you three months, three weeks, three hours, and three half-hours!' Then will the Prince wake, and whoever has had patience enough to do this, her will he have for his wife, and with the Prince all those in his palace who have slept, will awaken."

The Princess saw what she had come to. Said she, "What else can I do but stay here now and watch over him till he sneezes, and then say, 'Bless you, my King, may you live for ever; I am she who has watched over you three months, three weeks, three hours, and three half-hours.'"

That evening when it grew dark, all the house was lit with lights, but there was never a sign of who had lighted them. She saw a table before her with divers dishes: she ate, but never saw who it was that brought them. And so the time went on. She tried not to sleep, so she might say to him, "Bless you, my King, may you live for ever!"

Three months went by, three weeks, and three days. One day, as she sat, she heard a voice, "Serving maids for hire!"

So she called, "Wait! Wait! I'll have a serving maid. Let them all bend over the well so that I may see their faces and choose one for company." She saw one that pleased her, and said, "Let the maid down."

They let her down, and on the same rope the princess tied a cloth with the hiring price in it, and they took it and went. She dressed the maid in pretty clothes and told her she had taken her for company. Then—the poor Princess here was sleepy—she said to her, "I'll sleep now, with my head on your lap, and in half an hour do you wake me, for if the Prince sneezes, I must say to him, 'Bless you, my King, may you live for ever, I am she who has watched over you three months, three weeks, three days, three hours, and three half-hours.'"

The serving maid said to her, "Sleep, my lady, with your head here on my lap, and in half an hour I will wake you."

No sooner had the Princess fallen asleep than the Prince sneezed.

Then said the serving maid to him, "Bless you, my King, may you live for ever . . ."

Then at once the King woke up and embraced her, and said, "You will be Queen, and the richest queen in the world."

Then he ran and fetched water and sprinkled it over all his attendants, his beasts, his dogs, his all. Then he turned back to his wife, and saw a lass asleep on the ground.

He said, "But who is this?"

"Indeed, my King, yesterday some serving maids came by, and I hired one, and they let her down through the well. I shall now wake her."

"No, let the poor thing sleep, and then send her to mind the geese."

When the Princess awoke, she looked about her, and saw not a sign either of the Prince or anything at all.

Said she, "What has happened to the Prince? Where is he?"

"Indeed, the Prince sneezed, he awoke and saw the two of us here, and said he wanted me, and for you to go and mind the geese."

To this the Princess said nothing, but rose and went down to mind the geese.

When he had gone round the palace, the King also wanted to go to war.

So he said to his wife, "What would you have me bring you from my journey?"

"Bring me a crown of diamonds," said she.

Then the King also went down to the lass who minded the geese, and said to her, "What would you have me bring you?"

"Bring me, Lord King, the millstone of patience, the hangman's rope, and the butcher's knife. If you do not bring me what I have asked you for, my King, your ship will neither go forward nor go back."

The King left her and went and finished his business. He bought the Queen's diamond crown and he boarded his ship and set sail for his homeland. Although the sail had been hoisted, the ship would go neither forward nor back. At this all were astounded; they hauled the anchors this way and that, and could not tell what the matter was.

Said one of the men on the ship, an old man, to the Prince, "My King, live for ever! Would you have been asked to make a purchase you did not remember to make?"

"Why—that's true!" said the King. "A lass I have to mind the geese told me to bring her the millstone of patience, the hangman's rope, and the butcher's knife."

"I'll go, my King, and get them for you," said the old man. "But you must look out for that lass, for she has a great sorrow, and you must attend and see what she will do."

The old man bought the things and gave them to the King, and at once the ship moved forward as if on wings. So the King came to his palace, gave the diamond crown to his wife, and then he went down and gave the other things to the lass.

That evening, the king went down and stood outside the room where the lass slept, and heard her say, "I was a princess, the only daughter, my father went to the war and I had set myself to embroider him a golden kerchief, when an eagle came by my window, and said, ' 'Broider away, 'broider away, a dead man you'll have for a husband one day!' I said to him, 'Take me to see him.' The eagle took me on its wing and brought me, lowered me into the well, and led me to the palace. I watched over him, without sleeping, for three months and three weeks, and then the serving maids came by overhead and I hired a maid for company. When it was time for the King to wake and sneeze, the serving maid said to him (for I was sleeping), 'Bless you, my King, may you live for ever . . .' Now, as I have no one to whom to tell my sorrow, I brought you to see what you would tell me. From the Princess that I was, to come to minding geese! Butcher's knife, what say you I should do?"

"Knife yourself!"

"Hangman's rope, what say you I should do?"

"Hang yourself!"

"Millstone of patience, what say you I should do?"

"Have patience!"

"What patience can I have? Hangman's rope, what say you I should do?"

"Hang yourself!"

The King was watching what was going on inside through the keyhole. When he saw that she had mounted to tie the rope and hang herself, the King gave the door a kick and rushed inside and embraced her, saying, "It was you who saved me! And you did not tell me, but let me send you to the geese? You are a Queen, you are my wife, and I'll go straightway and hang the other one with the rope you would have used to hang yourself with."

Then she said, "I do not want our marriage to begin with killing, only set her free to go where she will, for she did me great harm and I do not wish to set eyes on her again. Let us go to my Father, at our palace, to kiss his hand and have our wedding."

They went to the palace—her father had returned, five or six days before, from the war—and the King told him he wanted him to be his father. And with pipes, lutes and drums, great rejoicing took place, the marriage rites were held, and they lived right well—may we live better.

· 30 · *The Turtle and the Chickpea*

· ONCE UPON A TIME there was a fisherman, a widower who had no children at all.

He went one day to fish and caught nothing, but there was a turtle caught up in his nets; so he said, "Such is my luck; so I'll take it home," and he took it and kept it in his house.

But where his house had once been full of rubbish, the day after he took home the turtle, he found the house cleaned and shining like crystal, and the poor fisherman wondered who could have done it. One day he took some fish home, and at midday he went to light a bit of a fire to cook the fish and he saw that the fish were no longer on the spit.

"That cat has never taken the fish till now! How can she have taken them?" But in a corner of the room he saw steamed fish in the kettle, fried fish on one plate and baked on another. He saw that the house had again been cleaned and swept, and he was amazed.

"Who can have done it, I wonder?"

So the next day he kept watch and he saw come out of the turtle's shell a maiden whose beauty had no match in the world.

When she came out, he seized her and said, "Is it you, then, who keeps my house, unbeknown to me?"

And he broke the turtle shell, and the maiden stayed. He crowned her in holy matrimony and made her his wife.

The King of that place was unmarried; so he gave all the girls a veil to embroider, and whoever embroidered the best would be his wife. He also gave one to the fisherman's wife, for he thought she was his daughter. And without knowing why she was to embroider it, she sat down and embroidered on it the sea with fish and with ships. Other girls also embroidered, as the King had ordered that these girls were to go on the same day and each show her veil. So each took her veil, and the fisherman's wife went, too.

When the King saw her, he was astounded at her beauty. He looked, too, at the veil she had embroidered, and it was the best of all. He said that he would wed with her, but she answered that she was married to a fisherman.

"But why did you embroider the veil?" asked the King.

"Because I did not know why you had ordered the veils to be embroidered. I embroidered it for your pleasure."

"Bid your husband come here," the King said to her.

"As you will, Lord King," she said, and went home and told her husband, "The King has bidden you go to him."

The poor fisherman went and said to the King, "What is your will, Lord King?"

"The wife that you have is not for you. So either you provide a meal of fish to feed all my army till they have their fill or I shall take your wife away from you."

"It is well, Lord King," answered the fisherman, and went home and told his wife, "Alas, wife, that veil has brought us misfortune. The King has ordered me to feed all his army with fish for one day, or he will take you for himself; he says you are not the wife for me."

"Let the King sleep on it," said his wife. "And you, husband, go to the place where you fished me up and call to my mother to give you the little fish kettle."

So the fisherman went to the sea, and called, "Lady mother of the sea, come, for I have need of thee."

A woman came out from the midst of the sea, and said to him, "Welcome, son-in-law, and greetings. What is your wish?"

"Your daughter sent me to you for the little fish kettle."

"It is well, son-in-law," she said, and went down and brought him a fish kettle big enough for only one plate of food.

She gave it to her son-in-law, and he went and said to his wife, "Why, cook in this, and it won't be enough for me, let alone the King's army."

"Never you fear, husband, this kettle can suffice for ten times the King's army; only go and invite the King and his army to come tomorrow to our table."

So the fisherman got up and went to the King and said to him, "Tomorrow, Lord King, be so good as to come, and the meal will be ready."

So the next day the King summoned his army and they went and sat down in a wide place. He brought three servants to bear the dishes.

The king's servants went forward, and the fisherman said to them: "Ask the King what dish he would like first?"

They went and asked the king and he ordered them to bring him fish soup to begin with. The fisherman's wife put the ladle in the fish kettle and brought out all the bread they needed. Then, again from the kettle, she took out as many bowls of soup as there were men in the King's army.

When the soup had been eaten, the King ordered steamed fish. The fisherman's wife again put in the ladle and brought out steamed fish. Then the King ordered, in turn, fish with onions, fried fish, baked fish, and fish done in all kinds of ways. And all these dishes came out of the fish kettle, until the King's army had had their fill and got up and went about their business, and the fisherman saved his wife.

When several days had gone by, the King again summoned the fisherman, and said to him, "That woman is not the wife for you. Either you feed all my army with grapes tomorrow, or I shall take your wife away from you." (It was the month of January.)

"It is well, Lord King," said the fisherman, and he went complaining home, and said to his wife, "The King has set his eye on you, wife, and is doing all he can to take you away from me. Now he's ordered me to feed all his army with grapes. Where can we find grapes at this time of year?"

"Never you fear, husband, I shall never be the King's wife, but I shall make a King of you. Go now to my mother, and ask her for a pannikin of grapes."

The fisherman went to the sea, and called, "Lady mother of the sea, come, for I have need of thee."

The Sea came forth, and said to him, "Greetings, son-in-law, greetings, indeed. What is your wish?"

"Your daughter sent me to you for a pannikin of grapes."

"At once, son-in-law," said the Sea, and went and brought him a pannikin of grapes.

It had in it barely an *oka* of grapes, and he took it to his wife and said, "These grapes are hardly enough for me."

"Never you fear, this is a wonder-working pannikin, so go to the King and tell him to come with his army and eat his fill of grapes."

The fisherman went and said to the King, "The grapes are ready; so be so good as to come with your army."

The next day, the King summoned his army and they went and sat down in the same wide place, and the King's servant went to the fisherman's house and bore the grapes back in platefuls; the fisherman's wife took them out of the pannikin and it never emptied itself until the army had eaten its fill and the King took them away with him.

The fisherman went home, and said to his wife, "I saved you again today, wife. But we shall see what else our King (may he live for ever) will think up."

"Never you fear, husband, I'm here, never fear."

After several days had gone by, the king summoned the fisherman, and said "That woman is not suited to you: she is the wife for me. So now I want you to bring me a man two hands' span tall, with a beard three hands' span long."

"As you will, Lord King (may you live for ever)," he replied, and went.

He went to his wife, and said, "Now we're up against it, wife. The King wants us to bring him a man two hands' span tall, with a beard three hands' span long."

"Never you fear husband. That, too, will be done. I have a brother of that like. Go to my mother and ask her to send back with you my brother, Chickpea, so that he may rock our child in the cradle."

The fisherman went to the sea, and called, "Lady mother of the sea, come, for I have need of thee."

The Sea came forth, and he said to her, "Your daughter sent me for you to send her Chickpea, so he may rock our child in the cradle."

"It is well, son-in-law," said the Sea, and called, "Chickpea, go to your sister and rock her child."

"It is well, I'm coming; just let me feed the chickens."

When he had fed his chickens, he mounted a cockerel and came out of the midst of the sea. The fisherman saw that he was two hands' span in height and had a beard three hands' span long that fell to the ground.

The fisherman went on ahead and after him Chickpea on the cockerel, and they went to the house.

"What is your will with me, sister?"

"Go to the King for him to see you, then put his eyes out, and make your brother-in-law king."

"It is well, sister," answered Chickpea.

The fisherman went in first, and after him Chickpea, before the King.

"What is your will, Lord King?" asked Chickpea.

"I called you so I might see you," said the King.

"And now have you seen me?" he asked him.

"I have," said the King.

Then Chickpea said, "Leap, cockerel, and put out the King's eyes."

The cockerel leapt and put out the King's eyes, and from the pain of the pecking, the King died.

Then said Chickpea to the King's Council of Twelve, "Will you make my brother-in-law King, or shall I set my cockerel on you?"

"We'll make him King," said the Council.

And they put the fisherman on the King's throne and brought his wife to be Queen, and they are reigning to this day; they have Chickpea on his cockerel as their knight, and he rides up and down in the palace.

• 31 • *The Seven Ravens*

• ONCE UPON A TIME there was a father who had seven sons and no girl-child. Every day he prayed to God to send him a daughter, to be a comfort to him in his old age. God heard his prayer and sent him a daughter, but she was a very weak little creature. In order to gain strength and keep well, she had to be dipped in spring water. Therefore the father sent his sons to bring him a pitcher of water, but on the way they broke the pitcher and were afraid to return.

The father waited, and the mother, too, waited and waited, but they did not come. Thereupon the father grew angry and said, "My curse upon them! May they turn into seven black ravens!" Hardly had he spoken when the seven black ravens flew over the house.

At once, the father regretted the curse he had laid upon them, but in vain, for it is written, "Where is he who would give as much as a fig for a thousand and one acts of repentance?" He could not take back his curse. So they were left with only the girl-child. But she, so little as she was, did not know that she had brothers, until, one day, when she had grown, she heard a neighbor say, "She is well-grown now, but what is to become of her, a pretty wench, with all her brothers gone?"

Hearing this, she went at once and asked her mother, "Mother, did I have brothers that were lost?" Her mother saw that the truth could no longer be hidden from her and she told her all that had befallen. One morning, they found the girl was gone. She had set out to find her brothers.

"I cannot live in comfort, and my brothers in misery," said the girl-child.

She took with her a ring that belonged to her mother and on she went until she came to the end of the world. There she found the Sun, but she could not stay, for he was too hot, so she went on to the Moon. But no sooner had she entered than the Moon said, "I smell the smell of human flesh."

The lass got up at once, left that place, too, and went to the Stars. The Stars received her graciously, and asked what she was seeking.

"I seek my brothers," said she, "whom I lost in such-and-such wise."

Of all the Stars the Dawn Star took most pity on her and gave her the leg of a bat, saying, "Take this little bone and keep it by you, for otherwise you may not open the door of the tower where your brothers are."

The girl took the bat leg and wrapped it in her kerchief and went on her way. On and on she went till at last she reached the tower and found it locked. She took out the bat leg and knocked with it on the door, and it opened at once. A tiny little man appeared before her.

"What are you seeking, my lass?" said he to her.

"I seek my brothers," said she to him, "the seven ravens."

"The seven ravens are not here, but come in if you will, and sit down and wait for them."

After a while the little man began laying the table and put out seven plates and seven glasses of wine. The girl went up and tasted a morsel of the food on each plate and drank a mouthful of wine from each glass. And in the youngest brother's glass she left the ring she wore. The seven ravens came at midday and sat down to eat. The first one went to taste his food and said, "Someone has tasted the food on my plate."

"And on mine," said the second.

"And mine," said the third, and the fourth, and the fifth, and the sixth, and the seventh.

They went next to drink their wine, and the youngest one found his mother's ring in his glass.

"Why, our sister is here!"

"If it is our sister, we are saved."

So then she came forth and they at once took on human form, and they took their sister with them and returned all together to their father's house. Everyone was exceeding joyful and they all lived happily ever after, and may we live even more so.

· 32 · *Poppies*

· THERE WAS ONCE an old woman who had a daughter she would send to gather fresh grass. One day in May, when the fields were full of flowers and all the trees spreading their leaves, the daughter went into the field, but instead of gathering grass she began to pick poppies! She had a needle and she sewed them on her dress. As she was sitting there, my dears, bedecking herself from top to toe with poppies, the three Fates came by and laughed to see her; even the youngest of them laughed, who had never laughed before.

So the three Fates said to the girl, "Because you have made our sister laugh, we shall each give you a wish."

"May the flowers you are wearing turn to brilliants and diamonds," said the first.

The second said, "May you become the fairest in the land, and when you speak, may roses, roses, fall from your mouth."

The third and youngest said, "You who made me laugh, now the King will come by, this very hour, and make you his wife; no sooner will he see you than he will fall madly in love with you."

And such was her fate. And so it ended, my dears, with the King coming by that very hour, and no sooner had he set eyes on her than he stood and stared in amazement at her beauty, and he said, "Are you human or spirit?"

She answered, "Human."

Then he said, "Come here to me," and he took her up and put her on his horse and brought her to his mother.

When she saw her, his mother said, "Why, my son! What is this? Such a being is surely a spirit!"

"No, mother," he said, "it is a woman, never fear."

Not to make too long a tale of it, he ended by making her his wife. They lived happily together.

One day, as she sat in her chamber, combing her hair, she began to laugh.

The King asked her, "Why do you laugh?"

"Well, my dear," she said, "I'm laughing because your beard puts me in mind of our palace brush."

"Indeed!" said the King, at once, "is that how you look on me?" He summoned his twelve councillors and bade them reach a decision. And they advised him to have her killed.

So then the Fates who had been watching over her, saw what a plight she was in.

"Just see," they said, "what the silly girl has brought on herself!" and they built themselves three frigates, turned themselves into three handsome young men, and made their way to where she was. Then they began to fire off their cannons.

"Three royal ships, three royal ships have come!" and the people ran out to see the ships.

The King put on his uniform to go and receive the strangers.

The strangers said to him, "We hear you have our long-lost sister with you."

"We have," said the King, and he was much afraid. So he took the young men to the palace. Baked meats were served, and when they had sat down and eaten, they said, "We wish to see our sister."

So they went to the Queen's chamber, and said to her, "Foolish girl, whatever possessed you to tell him that? Isn't it enough that we made you a Queen, but you must think up such an insult to the King? He has made up his mind to have you killed. But as we are the Fates and watch over you (for did you not make our sister laugh?), take this little brush that is all brilliants and diamonds, and hang it behind the door. If the King should come in and ask what it is, you answer, 'My Lord King, this is what I meant, for such is the one we have in the palace.' Let it be seen that you are as rich as this, and next time, be careful. Because you made our sister laugh, unhappy girl, we'll do you this favor, as the King was just about to have your head cut off."

Then they bade her good-bye, the King bade them good-bye, and they went aboard their frigates and sailed away. So the King returned to the palace, and went into the Queen's room. Just as he was closing the door, he saw something golden—the beautiful little brush—behind the door, shining fit to dazzle him.

He said, "What is this thing?"

"It's what I meant was like your beard."

When he heard this, he said, "Ah, the poor woman! I was wrong to wish her killed. It was not her intention to mock me, but to honor me, and I took it otherwise." And he loved his wife all over again, they lived happily ever after, and may we live happier.

Neither was I there, nor need you believe it.

·33· *The King's Godson and the Baldchin*

• ONCE UPON A TIME there was a King who had to leave on a long journey. He boarded the caïque—in those days there were no steamships, only sailboats—the anchor was weighed and the ship set sail. As it was on the way, the caïque went adrift and set the King down in—let's say—Cyprus. Where they set him down there was no town nor even a village; so the King and his servant found themselves all alone at night and in winter weather in this deserted place. They strained their eyes in this direction and that, and saw a light shining far away.

"Well," said the King to his servant, "all we can do is take that road until we come to that light and whatever's waiting for us there." They went, and found a shepherd in his hut.

"Good evening, shepherd."

"Good evening. Pray walk in."

No need to ask if he made much of them. Well, of course, a great man is easy to pick out. The shepherd got up and killed a lamb, roasted it, and they sat down to eat. It so happened that, that very night, the shepherd's wife gave birth to a boy.

Then the King said to the shepherd, "I am King So-On-and-So-Forth of Such-and-such, and I should like to christen the child who was born tonight and then leave."

"As you will, O King (may you live for ever)," said the shepherd. The King stayed three days and christened the child.

On the day he was about to leave, he took off his ring and gave it and a letter to the shepherd and told him to send his god-child, when he had reached legal age, to seek his godfather. And in the letter it said that if he met a lame man, a blind man, or a baldchin on the way, he was not to take them with him.

When the boy reached sixteen years of age, his father told him, "My son, take this ring and this letter, and go and seek your god-father, the King."

The boy took the ring and the letter and set out to find his godfather. As he was on the way, he met a lame man.

"Where are you going, my son," the lame one asked him.

"I'm going," he said, "to seek my godfather, the King."

"Won't you take me with you, my lad who has all the virtues? Perhaps the King would take me into his employ."

"Very well, uncle." he said to him, "come along." And he took him with him. As they went on their way, the lame man would halt and every so often sit down to rest.

"I'll tell you what, uncle," said the lad, "I'll go on ahead and you come after." He had not gone far before he met a blind man.

"My son who has all the virtues, where are you going?"

"I'm going to my godfather, the King."

"Ah, my son, to whom God has granted the gift of sight, will you not take me with you?"

"Very well, uncle," he said to him, "come along."

The lad had a good heart and could not find it in him to say no. But as they went along the way, the blind man, too, grew tired. "Well, now, uncle," he said to him, "I'll go on ahead and you come after."

The lad went on ahead. Farther along, he met a baldchin.
"Where are you going, good fellow?" the baldchin said to him.
"My godfather, the King of Such-and-Such, left me this ring
and letter and I'm going to seek him."

"I'll tell you what," said the baldchin to him, "take me with
you and tell him I'm your kinsman, perhaps he'll have work for
me."

"Very well," said the lad, "come along."

They went on and on until they came to a plain with not a
drop of water anywhere. Farther on, they came to a well. The
well was deep and they were thirsty.

Then said the baldchin to the lad, "I'd go down myself, but
you are nimbler. I'll tie you with the rope and you go down.
Don't be afraid."

The baldchin tied the lad and lowered him into the well. He
sent up water and the baldchin drank.

"Hi!" called the lad, "now pull on the rope and get me out."

"Get you out?" said the baldchin. "After all I went through to
get you in, now I'm to get you out?"

The lad wept and pleaded, but he would do nothing.

"However," said the baldchin, "if you'll give me the King's
ring and his letter and say that I am his godson and you my servant, I'll save your life."

What could the lad do? To save his life, he had to agree.

"No," said the baldchin, "you must first swear to me you'll
never tell."

Then the lad swore, "May I die and then live ere I breathe
word of this."

Then the baldchin pulled on the rope and got the lad out.
They again set forth and reached the palace. Rat-tat! on the door.

The servant came and said, "Who is it?"

"I am the King's godson," said the baldchin. "Here's a letter
from him and his ring."

"Oh, if you're the King's godson, come inside."

The King's joy, when they told him, knew no bounds. But
when they went before him and he saw them, the baldchin like
Satan and the lad like an angel, he was amazed. But what was

he to do? He kept the baldchin at the palace and sent the lad out as (let's say) a cowherd. In time the King's old servingwoman grew fond of the lad.

One day, when the lad was in the palace he noticed a swallow's nest. When the male flew up, the she-swallow scolded him for idling on the way and not bringing the little ones their food at the right time. The lad understood what she was saying, and laughed.

"You see, Lord King?" said the baldchin. "He's laughing at me for being a baldchin."

"Why do you do that?" said the King to him.

"No, Lord King," said the lad, "I'm laughing because the she-swallow scolded her mate for tarrying with the food for their young."

"Aha!" said the baldchin, "so he understands the language of animals and birds! Then send him, Lord King, to bring back Pipiree's Bird from darkest India."

"Look you," said the King to the lad, "either you go and fetch it or off goes your head."

"I'll go," said the lad.

The king's old serving woman saw that the lad was downcast and asked him what the matter was. He told her the story.

"And now he's sending me to bring back Pipiree's Bird from darkest India," he said.

"Ah," said the serving woman, "you're being sent to your death. Such a many have gone, none has brought it back and all have been killed. But," said she to him, "there is a mare that flies when you mount her. As you draw near to India you will see great fires. When you see them, halt and stay there for three days, for every three days the fires go out at morn, and when they go out, strike the mare with your cane and go and seize the bird. It is on a golden tree, and the moment you catch it, make haste to return." And so it was. The lad did as the old woman had told him and, the morning the fires went out, he seized the bird. Cannons fired and fired after him, but he was hit by none. And he brought back Pipiree's Bird.

When he saw him, the baldchin was thunderstruck, for he had not thought he would come back alive. After many days had passed, the baldchin said to the King, "Godfather, let's send the lad to fetch us Golden-Hair."

"O dear heaven," said the King, "do not ask such a thing of the lad, for many have been there and none has returned; she has built towers out of heads and fortresses of bodies."

"No," said the baldchin, "the lad is able and can bring her."

Then the King called the lad, and said, "You shall go and bring Golden-Hair."

Again the old woman found the lad deep in gloom. "What is the matter, my lad?" she said. "What has made you sad?"

He told her his story and then said, "I am sent to bring back Golden-Hair."

"Indeed, my child," said the old woman, "what has been asked of you is very hard. But hear what you must do. Tell the King to give you forty skin bags of honey, forty skin bags of millet and a saddlebag full of sovereigns, and, wherever you go, do good and God will see you succeed." Then she showed him the way.

Then the lad went to the King and said to him, "Give me forty skin bags of honey, forty skin bags of millet, and a saddlebag full of sovereigns, and I will go and bring back Golden-Hair."

"Very well," said he, "take them."

The lad took them, fetched his horse, and set off. Toward evening he reached a large well.

"Here," said his horse to him, "leave me a little to graze while you sleep." So he slept.

"Get up," said his horse to him, "and save souls."

He got to his feet, and what should he see? A snake striving to eat an eagle's young that were in the nest. He climbed the tree and killed the snake with his sword. Then the eagle flew up.

"Is it you," it said to him, "who comes every year and eats my young?" And it swooped down on him to peck his eyes out.

Then the young birds cried out, "No, Mother, it is he that saved us: see the snake that would have eaten us! It was he who killed it."

"Tell me," said the eagle to him, "What would you have me give you for the good you have done me?"

"I," said he to the eagle, "am a man and you're a bird, so what could I hope to gain?"

"Take this feather," said the eagle to him, "and whenever you need me, singe it a little and I'll come."

He took the feather and put it in his pocket.

On and on they went, lost their way, and entered a wood. There the lad saw a crowd of ants.

"Dismount," said his horse to him, "and lead me aside so we don't trample any ants."

He dismounted and led his horse aside, but as he was leaving the forest the King of the ants called to him, "Hello! Which way did you come? You didn't trample my army?"

"No," the lad answered.

Then it called to its army and asked them.

"We are all safe and sound!"

"Are you hungry?" the lad asked the ant.

"Faint with hunger," it told him. "We came into this forest, but found nothing."

He threw them the forty skin bags of millet, whereupon the ants fell on them like creatures possessed and filled their bellies.

"Well, now," said the King of the ants, "for the good you have done us, what can we do for you?"

"What, indeed," he said. "What can an ant do?"

"Take," it said to him, "this wing, and when you need me, singe it a little and I'll come."

"I will," he said, and he put it away with the other.

From there they then went down to the sea and rode along the seashore. On they went till they saw a great fish that had been thrown out into shallow water. The poor creature was twisting this way and that, but it could not get into deeper water. It was at the edge of the shore and near to dying. He went and picked it up—in gentle fashion—and threw it toward the open sea. Once in the deeper water it came to itself.

"Well, now," it said to him, "for the good you have done me, what can I do for you?"

"What, indeed," he said. "I am a man, you are a fish. What can you do for me?"

"Take this bone," it said to him, "and whenever you need me, singe it a little and I'll come." He took the bone as well and put it away with the other things.

Then on they went until they came to a stream. In the stream he saw a swarm of bees that the current was carrying away. So he put down his sword like a bridge and the bees climbed onto it. When they had come out, he threw them the forty skinbags of honey he had with him. When they had eaten the honey, they came once more to their senses and revived.

"Well, now?" said the Queen Bee to him, "for the good you have done us, what would you have us give you?"

"I," said he to them, "am a man and you are bees. What could you do for me?"

"Take this stinger, and when you need me, singe it a little and I'll come."

He took this, too, and laid it away with the rest. They went on a little and saw an old woman.

"Is it here, Mother, that Golden-Hair lives?" the lad asked her.

"It is here, my child, but do not ask more. (Only a lad, too— the pity of it!)"

He did not falter, but went straight to the King, her father.

"Greetings," said the King. "How is it you've come?"

"I've come," he said to him, "for your daughter."

"Very good," said the King to him, "for it happens that I have her to give away. But first I have something to say to you. If you can do it, you shall have her."

"Say on, Lord King, and I'll see what it is."

"This ring of my daughter's I shall throw into the middle of the sea, and if you can find it in three days, you can have her." Then he went down to the sea on his horse and sat down to think.

"What," said the horse to him, "is making you so thoughtful?"

He told it what the King had said.

"But we," said the horse to him, "have the bone that was given us by the fish we saved. Just singe it a little and we'll see what it has to say."

He singed the fishbone. In a short time up came the fish. "What is your wish?" it said to him.

"Now is the time," said the lad, "for you to save me. The King has thrown his daughter's ring into the depths of the sea and says I must find it in three days. If I don't, he'll have my head."

"Never fear," said the fish. "In three days I shall have found it. You sit down here at the edge of the sea and smoke your cigarette, and don't worry."

And straightway the King of the fish summoned all the fish and said, "Quick, go and find the ring."

They sought it here, they sought it there, but no ring. At last, an old fish said, "Yesterday I swallowed just such a little thing."

"Quick," said the King, "get out of the water and dry it out of you."

The fish got out onto dry land and dried it out of itself.

"There you are," it said to him, "take the ring."

He took it straight to the King, Golden-Hair's father.

"That's all very well," the King told him, "but I have something else to tell you. If you can do that, too, I'll give you my daughter."

"Tell me," said he, "and I'll see."

"I shall mix together one kilo each of all the seeds that are sown on the land, and if you can sort them out in one night, I'll give you my daughter."

Now what was he to do? He fell into deep gloom.

But again his horse said to him, "We have a wing, taken from the ants. Just singe it a little."

He singed the wing and along came the ant.

"What is your wish?" it said to him.

"What, indeed! The King has mixed together a kilo each of all the seeds that are sown on the earth and he's given me one night to sort them out, otherwise he says he'll have my head."

"Oh, don't worry about that," said the ant to him. "I'll call out my army at once and they'll sort them out in three hours."

So the ants came up and sorted them out in two hours. Later, when the King went to look in the store, he saw them all sorted out, here the wheat, there the oats, here the corn, there the millet.

"Well, now," the King said to him, "so you've done that, too. One more thing will I have you do. If you can bring me the water of life, I'll give you my daughter."

Then the lad singed the eagle's feather, and along came the eagle.

"What is your wish?" it said to him.

The lad told him what the King had commanded.

"Ah, never fear," the eagle said. "You must make a saucer of gold and go to the mountain that opens and shuts by itself, and I'll come there, too."

He made the saucer of gold and took it to the mountain. Then the eagle took it on its wing and flew into the mountain, dipped the saucer into the water of life, and flew out and gave it to the lad. The next day the boy took the saucer of water to the King.

"All well and good," said the King to him, "but let us see if this is the water of life." He summoned a *gelati* and a blackamoor. "Slay the blackamoor," said the King to the *gelati*.

The *gelati* struck at the blackamoor and slew him. Then he set up his head, poured the water of life on it, and the blackamoor came back to life.

"Very well," said the King to him. "Now I shall give you my daughter, but I am going to dress forty maidens in red and among them will be my daughter. They shall all turn their heads away, but if you can pick her out and lead her away, she's yours."

Then the lad went home and sat down to think. Then he remembered the bee's stinger, singed it a little, and up came the bee. "What is your wish?" it said to him.

"Such and such the King told me, and I don't know what to do. I'm afraid all my trouble will be for nothing, for, instead of Golden-Hair, I might pick out some gypsy."

"Never fear," said the bee to him, "because I shall go and as she changes her clothes, I shall put a mark on her and then when they stand in a row, I'll go and perch on her so that you'll know which is she."

The bee went and got into the palace and flew about as Golden-Hair was dressing. She drove it off, but it still flew about her.

"Alas, my dear Mother," she turned and said to her mother, "even the bees are sorry for us. The time has come for us to part."

Then in came the forty maidens and stood in a row. He saw the bee fly up and sit on the Princess, the foremost of them all.

"Well, now choose," the King said to him. He pretended he did not know which to choose. He looked here, he looked there.

"I'll take this one," he said, "and be my luck as it may." And he took the first. The King's heart missed a beat when he saw him choose her.

"Well, well," he said to them, "it was your luck, my brave lad, to choose my daughter."

He took her and brought her straight to the baldchin. When the baldchin saw Golden-Hair, he took her to the King and said, "Now that Golden-Hair is here, let the lad climb the apple tree and pick the red apples at the top."

"No, dear heaven," said the King, "those apples have never been picked by anyone. Wait till they fall off by themselves. Don't you see how high they are?"

"No, Godfather," said the baldchin, "the lad is able and can do it."

Once the King had gone, the baldchin set the lad to climb the tree. Just as he was going to pick the apple on the very top, the branch broke, and down went the lad holding the apple. And as the lad lay there lifeless, the baldchin dug a pit and threw him in it. Then he took the apple to Golden-Hair.

When she saw it she said, "But who are you?"

"I, said he, "am the master of the lad who brought you here. I am your husband."

When she heard this, she screamed. "Get out of here," she said, "and quickly!"

Her screams brought the King running.

"What made you scream?" he asked her.

"Take this baldchin out of here," she said to him, "for I can't abide the sight of him, and fetch me my husband who brought me here."

"Where is the lad?" the King asked the baldchin.

"He fell off a tree and was killed," he told him, "and I have him buried in a pit."

"Quick," Golden-Hair told him, "take him out and let me see him. Let no part of him be lost."

The baldchin sent for the dead lad to be brought.

When Golden-Hair saw him, she took some of the water of life from the saucer of gold, and sprinkled it over him, and at once the lad came back to life.

"Aha!" he said to him, "now, Baldchin, my oath is ended. I died and came back to life. Now I can tell everything."

He sat down and told the whole story from the beginning. Then the King ordered the baldchin to be tied to the horse's tail and they put the lash to the horse and it broke the baldchin to pieces. He married the lad to Golden-Hair, ordered joy and lilac blossoms, and then he put him on the throne.

·34· *The Navel of the Earth*

· THERE WAS ONCE an old king who had three sons and three daughters. When the moment came for him to die, he called for his sons and daughters. "Pay heed, my children, to what I shall ask you to do. Give your sisters to whoever asks for them first, be he lame, blind, or however he may be, give, if you wish to have my blessing."

"Very well," said his children, and the King gave up the ghost.

After a shortish-longish while, a lame man presented himself to the eldest Prince and asked for his eldest sister in marriage. When the Prince heard this, he grew angry and said to him, "Ah, churl face who seeks my sister! February cripple, pockmarked thing! Get out of my sight, and quickly, or I'll tear your other rib out!"

So the unhappy lame man got up with a flea in his ear and went to the second Prince, but here, too, he got the rough edge of his tongue. Then he went on to the youngest Prince's palace.

When the Prince heard that he was seeking his eldest sister in marriage, he said, "Splendid! I'll give her to you, why not? It was my father's command, and I can but obey."

So he gave her to him and he married her and took her away.

Hardly had a shortish-longish while gone by when a one-eyed man presented himself to the eldest Prince and sought his second sister in marriage.

"Ugh! away with you, one-eyed rascal, coming here for the King's daughter," he said to him. "Get out of my sight, and quickly, or I'll have your other eye, one-eyed villain."

He, too, fled from the eldest and went to the second, but he also turned him away. Then he went to the youngest, and this one gave her to him. After some time, along came a beggar in rags and went to the eldest Prince and asked for his youngest sister in marriage.

When the Prince saw him and learned that he was after his sister, he was like a demon in his rage, and said, "Ugh, you raggletaggle! Look what we've come to now! A lousy beggar, no less! Get out of my sight, you scum, coming here after the King's daughter!"

The poor man fled to the second brother, but he all but had him flogged. Then he went to the youngest and he gave her to him with all his heart. So he took her away with him.

After some time had passed, the young Prince decided to go and win the Beauty of the World. So he closed up his palace and rode off on his horse to win her. Now many princes had wanted to win the Beauty of the World, but they could not, so she slew them and took their heads and built a tower with them. But she still needed one head more to finish off the tower. It might be our own prince's head.

So when he came to that country, he went before the King her father, and told him he had come to win his daughter.

"Very good," said the King, "and I shall give her to you. I shall shut you up in an underground room for forty days, and in that time you will think out what the features are of the navel of the earth. At the end of forty days, I shall let you out to tell me what you have thought. If you haven't found it, my daughter shall have your head to put on her tower, for she is building a tower of human heads and needs one more to complete it—it might well be yours."

"It might well," said the Prince.

So they put him in the underground room and brought him food and water.

One day, when he had thought and cudgeled his brains to find what the features were of the navel of the earth, he became dizzy with thinking, and got up to take a stroll. As he was strolling, he noticed a small window. He went up and opened it and saw another world. He climbed through the window, came upon a staircase, and went down forty steps. Then he found a path and took it to escape from his prison. He went on walking until noon, when he found a tower, and outside the castle, near the door, a spring and a tree. He drank water at the spring and lay down in the shade of the tree to rest.

As he was lying there and thinking, a Moorish woman came down from the castle to fetch water, saw the Prince, and said, "Welcome, pretty lad."

"Well may I find you," said the Prince.

"And how is it you are here in these parts where not even bird on the wing will come?"

"Indeed, my fate drove me this way and here I am."

When the Moorish woman had filled her pitcher, she went back to the castle and told her mistress that a handsome youth was below at the spring, resting himself.

"Run and bid him come up!" said her mistress.

The Moorish woman went and invited the Prince to the tower. No sooner did the mistress clap eyes on him than she rushed up to him and embraced and kissed him on both cheeks, for she was the Prince's eldest sister. The lame man, the blind man, and the beggar, who had married the princesses, were brothers and all were *drakoe*. Then the Prince's sister asked him how he came to be in that place. The Prince told her that he had come to win the Beauty of the World and had been shut up in an underground room to think out what the features were of the navel of the earth, and had found a little window which led him out to that place.

"You should not have gone and been caught in such a place," his sister said to him, "but fate has helped you and brought you here. It may be that the *drakos* or his brothers know what those features are." Then she hid him lest the *drakos* should come in angry and eat him.

A little while later, in came the *drakos* and said, "Phew, the castle smells of human."

"It is nothing," said the Princess, "you have come in from outside, that's all."

When the *drakos* had eaten to his heart's content, the Princess said to him "Well, now, supposing one day a brother of mine should come here, what would you do to him?"

"If the eldest or the second should come, I should tear them to pieces."

"And if the youngest should come?"

"Ah, the youngest," said the *drakos,* "made me his slave by his good manners; if he should come, I would rise from my place for him to sit and I'd build him a castle of his own to live in."

"Well, he has come," said the Princess.

"What, has he?" said the *drakos.* "And, if he has come, why have you not brought him to me?"

"I was afraid you might do something to him," said the Princess.

"What should I do to him? Come, bring him to me."

The Princess went and brought him. When the *drakos* saw him he got up at once and kissed him on both cheeks and sat him down in his place and then asked him how it was he had come to those parts. And the Prince told him what had befallen him.

"And now I have come to you," he said to him, "to tell me, if you know, what the features are of the navel of the earth, for I am all but out of my mind with thinking about it."

Then the *drakos* said to him, "I do not know what the features are of the navel of the earth, but stay here as long as you like, and then go to my brother who married your second sister. He might know."

After staying there a number of days, he was put on the road and went on to his second sister. When she saw him, she was amazed that he should be in those parts. He told her, too, what had happened to him, and she told him in her turn. And after the *drakos* had come and had eaten and was in a good mood, she led up to the matter, asking him what he would do if any of her brothers should come. He too said that if her elder brothers should come, he would tear them to pieces; but if the youngest were to come, he would treat him like a king. After all this, she brought him to the *drakos,* who, in his turn, embraced and kissed him on both cheeks and asked him what need he had to be in those parts. The Prince told him, too, of his trouble. And he, in his turn, sent him to their other brother, who had married the Prince's youngest sister.

So he went there, to cut the story short—for the children are sleepy and the tale is a long one—and when his sister saw him, she embraced and kissed him, then hid him so that the *drakos* would not eat him. And when the *drakos* had eaten his fill of his favorite victuals, the Princess led up to the matter and then brought him out. When the *drakos* saw him, he jumped for joy. And when he had embraced him, he sat him down in his own place.

"Tell me, now," he said to him, "what trouble has brought you to these parts where never a human treads?"

When the Prince had told him his troubles, the *drakos* said to him, "I don't know what the features are of the navel of the earth, but I shall now find out. Follow me."

He followed him up to the highest part of the castle and the *drakos* whistled a whistle such that the mountains rattled with the noise and he saw the wild beasts break out from inside the mountains and from off the trees. The plain filled with all sorts and conditions of animals, wild and tame, that called, "What is your will, Master?"

And he said to them, "Which of you has ever been to the navel of the earth and can tell us what its features are?"

But none had chanced to go and none answered him.

The *drakos* scolded them and sent them away. Then he whistled again another kind of whistle, and all the winged creatures of the air, big and small, flocked together, even the flies and gnats. He asked them the same, but none could give him an answer. As they stood there in thought, they saw an eagle coming from afar and shining like the sun. As it drew closer, they saw that it was loaded, at the throat and on the wings, feet, and body, with diamonds, gold, silver, and pearls.

The *drakos* said to it, "Why have you tarried?"

And the eagle answered, "I was sick with the mange, O Master. And I remembered hearing from my old grandfather that whoever gets the mange should go to the navel of the earth where three springs flow, bathe himself in that water and be cured. As I was in sore need, I took the road and went. There are three springs there: one runs with gold, one with silver, one with diamonds, and at each spring stands a tree that bears pearls.

So I went and stood under the spout of each spring in turn and bathed and was cured of the mange. Then I loaded myself with gold, silver, and diamonds, and I sat on the tree and loaded myself with pearls. Just then I heard the whistle and took the road, and as I was heavily laden and old, I was a long time coming; so please forgive me. Now come and unload me."

When he had unloaded it, the *drakos* asked, "What else is there at the navel of the earth?"

"There are many trees that bear all kinds of ornaments," said the eagle.

Then the *drakos* gave the word, and all the winged creatures flew away. The ornaments that he had taken from the eagle he tied in a cloth and gave to the Prince, saying, "Now with your own ears you have heard what the features are of the navel of the earth. Take these ornaments and show them to the King as proof."

After staying a good many days at the castle with his sister and brother-in-law, he bade them farewell and left. He called at the other castles and bade his sisters and brothers-in-law farewell, then took the road and again found the little window, got back into his prison, and called to be taken out and brought before the King.

And the King asked him, "Well, how have you fared? Have you thought what the features are of the navel of the earth?"

"I have, Lord King, but let the Princess come too and hear what they are."

The King gave the order for the Princess to come before him. When the Prince saw her, he was dazzled by her beauty.

And she, too, asked him, "Have you discovered what the features are of the navel of the earth?"

"I have, Princess," he said. "At the navel of the earth flow three springs; at each spring stands a tree that bears pearls, and one spring runs gold, the next spring runs silver, and the third diamonds. Hold out your apron and I'll give you the proof of it."

The Princess held out her apron, and the Prince emptied into it the ornaments that the eagle had brought. When the Princess saw them, her eyes lit up.

He said to her, "The gold, silver, and diamonds are from the springs, and the pearls are from the tree."

Then the Princess said to her father, "For how many years, my Father, have I sought for him and he for me! It is a pity that we took the lives of so many young men wrongly. So it is he I shall have for my husband."

The King gave his consent and married them and ordered the wedding feast and revels to go on for forty days.

·35· *Cinderello*

• THERE WAS ONCE a woman who had only one child. The lad never went outside the house, but sat at the hearth in the cinders. His mother called him Cinderello.

One day his mother said to him, "Do go out, for a little, my child. What ails you that you never go outside?"

"Give me a ten lepton piece, and I will," said Cinderello.

His mother gave him a ten lepton piece; he took it and went out. When he reached the road, he saw some lads about to kill a little dog.

He said to them, "Here, lads, give the little dog to me, and I'll give you a ten lepton piece."

He gave them the money, took the little dog, and went home.

Another day his mother again said to him, "Do go out for a little, my child."

Said Cinderello, "Give me a ten lepton piece, and I will."

His mother gave him a ten lepton piece, Cinderello took it, and went outside. As he was walking along the road, he again came across some lads who were about to kill a little cat.

Said he, "Give that little cat to me, and I will give you this ten lepton piece."

He gave them the money, and took the cat. He took the cat home and again sat down at the hearth.

Another day his mother again said to him, "Do go out for a little, my child."

Said Cinderello, "Give me a ten lepton piece, and I will."

His mother gave him a ten lepton piece, and Cinderello went out. As he was walking, he again came across some lads who were about to kill a little snake.

Said he, "Give that little snake to me, and I'll give you this ten lepton piece."

He gave the money, took the little snake, and brought it home.

When he had raised all three animals and they were grown, the little snake said to him one day, "I want you to take me back to my country."

Cinderello got up, set the snake down before him, and, with him following behind, they set off.

As they were on the way, the snake turned and said to him, "My father is the King of the snakes. Now when we get there, all the snakes will fall upon you, but never you fear, for I shall call out and they will leave you. And when we get to my father's house, he will try to give you many things because you saved my life. Don't you take anything, but ask for the ring that lies under his tongue."

When they got there, the little snake gave a whistle, and snakes began to come up until the place was full of snakes. Among them was a snake as big as up to there. This was their King. When the snakes saw Cinderello, they swarmed over him and would have eaten him. The little snake called out, and they left him.

Then the little snake went up to his father, and said, "It was this lad, Father, who saved me from death. By now I should have been forgotten. That is why I have brought him here today, for you to give him whatever he may ask of you."

The big snake took him home with him, and said, "What would you have of me for saving my child?"

Said Cinderello, "I would have nothing," said he, "but the ring you have under your tongue."

Then the King of the snakes said, "You ask a great deal, but for my son's sake I will give it to you."

Cinderello took the ring and went. On the road he grew hungry.

"The snake," said he, "offered me so much and so much and I

would have nothing but this ring, and now I'm dying of hunger."

He was angry and threw down the ring, but suddenly a blackamoor leapt out of it, and said, "What is your command, Master?"

"What shall I command?" said he. "Food to eat!"

Quickly the blackamoor laid a table with food and wine and whatever your heart desired.

When Cinderello had eaten his fill, the blackamoor cleared it away, and went back into the ring. The lad took up the ring, came back to his village, and lived with it right well.

One day, Cinderello said to his mother, "Mother, go to the King, and bid him give me his daughter in marriage."

His mother said to him, "What is our station, dear boy, that the King should give us his daughter?"

And he said to her, "Do as I tell you, and go."

Off went the poor woman to the King.

When she entered, she said to the King, "My son wants your daughter for his wife."

Then the King said to her, "If, in such-and-such a square, your son can feed my army till they can eat no more, I will have him as my son-in-law. I will give him forty days. If he cannot do this in forty days, I will have his head."

His mother went back and told him. The days went by, and Cinderello kept to himself. When thirty-nine days had passed, the King sent word that the days were all but at an end and that he should not pretend to forget it. The lad sent back word to say he was aware of it and that he need have no fear. When the fortieth day came, he took the ring and went to the square where the army was to be fed.

He struck the ring once, out came the blackamoor, and said, "What is your command, Master?"

"I want you," he said, "to fill this square with food."

The blackamoor up and filled the square with food, the soldiers went and ate their fill, and still there was food left over.

Then the King again said to Cinderello's mother, "When," said he, "your son has built, also in forty days, a road stretching from your door to mine, all of pieces of gold, I'll have him for my son-in-law."

When the forty days had passed, the lad struck the ring on the ground and ordered the blackamoor quickly to make a road, from his door up to the palace, all of pieces of gold, before the King got up. The blackamoor up and did it before you could count to three.

The King got up and opened his window to look out, and what should he see! He was wonderstruck at the sight of the road.

Again he called the lad's mother, and said to her, "Just one more thing must your son do, and then I'll have him for my son-in-law. I want him," he said, "to build a castle better than my own palace. I'll give him another forty days; if he cannot, I'll have his head."

To cut a long story short, when the forty had passed, the lad again struck the ring on the ground, the blackamoor came out and made a castle better than the King's. The King opened his window that morning, and saw it. It was all made of gold.

The Cinderello's mother went to the King, and said, "My son has done all that you ordered him to do."

Then the King told her to make ready for the wedding, and the old woman went and told her son what the King had said to her. And when all was ready, the King married his daughter to Cinderello in the new palace, and set a blackamoor to watch over them. So as not to lose the ring, Cinderello always kept it under his tongue. But the blackamoor who guarded them was cunning and one day said to the Princess that she should ask her husband where he drew such a strength. Cinderello told her about the ring, and she told the blackamoor.

"Will you not take it from him for me to see a little?" the blackamoor asked her.

So she went while her husband was asleep and somehow took the ring out of his mouth and gave it to the blackamoor.

Once he had it in his hands, he struck it once on the ground, the blackamoor came out, and said, "What is your command, Master?"

"Take away," said he, "that man who lies asleep there, with his mattress, and put him down in the road, without waking him; then pull down this castle and build it in the depths of the sea with me and this woman in it."

The blackamoor of the ring destroyed the castle, threw poor Cinderello out into the street, and then built the castle in the depths of the sea and put in it the blackamoor and Cinderello's wife. Next morning, Cinderello woke up to find himself sleeping in the road, with never a sign of wife or ring. He got up in despair, went to the King, and told him of the harm that had come to him. Then the unlucky lad went home.

The cat went and rubbed itself up against him, and mewed, and said, "What's amiss, Master?"

"What should be amiss, Puss," said he to her, "but that harm has come to me. At night as I slept, the blackamoor took my ring and my wife away and has gone."

"Quiet yourself, Master," said the cat to him, "I'll bring it back to you. Fetch me the dog for me to ride and I'll go and get the ring."

So he fetched the dog, and the cat mounted him and passed through the sea. She went on till she found the castle and walked up on the ceiling. That evening the mice were having a wedding. The cat swooped down and seized the bride.

So the mice began to squeak, and plead, "Give us back the bride, and take whichever one of us you fancy."

"I shan't give her back to you; but if you go and fetch me the ring the blackamoor has in his mouth, then I'll give her back to you."

"Don't harm the bride, I'll go and get it for you," said one of the mice.

So the mouse went and dipped his tail in the honey, then he stirred it round in the pepper, and then went and put it up the blackamoor's nose as he lay asleep. The blackamoor sneezed, out came the ring, and the mouse seized it and took it to the cat. Then the cat let the bride go free and the mice went on with the wedding. The cat took the ring, came down from the ceiling, mounted the dog, who leapt into the sea, and they went back to their master.

When they were almost out of the sea, the dog said to the cat, "Let me see the ring, too."

The cat did not want to give it to him, but the dog threatened to throw her into the sea. So the cat was afraid and was about to give it him, and what should happen but the ring slipped away from them, and fell into the sea.

"What have you done?" said the cat to the dog. "How can I go to our master without the ring?"

When they got out, Cinderello asked them what they had done. Then the cat said that they had found the ring but the dog made them lose it in the sea. The dog said never a word. Again Cinderello sighed. As she sat, the cat saw the fishermen hauling in their nets, farther along the shore. Cats like fish, you know, so she went up to the fishermen and cried, "Miaow, miaow!" The fishermen took pity on her and threw her a deal of fish. As she was eating them, what should she find in the belly of one but the ring! She picked it up with such joy, and took it to Cinderello.

He took it and went to the King, and said to him, "Do you wish me," said he, "to bring you back the blackamoor and your daughter?"

"Of course, if you can do it," said the King, "don't stand there doing nothing."

Then Cinderello struck the ring on the ground, and the blackamoor came out and said to him, "What is your command, Master?"

"Take the castle," said he, "that stands in the sea, and bring it just as it is and put it where it was before."

So the blackamoor of the ring went and took the castle and set it up outside the King's palace, where it had stood before. The King went upstairs with a sword and slew the blackamoor, and gave his daughter back to Cinderello. He kept the little cat and the dog at the palace, and they lived right well.

· 36 · The Mill

· ONCE THERE WERE two brothers, one a gentleman and the other poor. The gentleman used the poor brother as a shepherd. On the Saturday before Easter the gentleman picked out the lambs to be killed for Easter Day. When they were ready to be sold, his brother asked him to let him kill a lamb to eat with his children and his wife at Easter, which was the next day.

His brother, who was a miser, picked a quarrel with him. "What, you ingrate, aren't you content that I give you work and feed you bread, but you must ask for lamb as well?"

The poor man did not open his mouth, but when they had sold the lambs and only one was left unsold, he said to his brother, "May I have this lamb?"

"Take it," said he, "and go to the Devil's dam!"

So bitterly was the poor man offended by these words that he decided he would neither go home nor anywhere else, but would travel up hill and down dale, until he found the Devil's dam. He ran like a man possessed. He went on and on until it grew dark. Finally he sat down to rest.

As he was sitting there thinking, he saw a light. He got up again, and went toward it. When he drew close to the light, what should he see but a great table with the Temptations—all the demons gathered together—sitting around it in a circle, drinking and eating.

When they saw him, one called, "Greetings, uncle."

Another, "Greetings, uncle! How is it you've come here to see us? We've been here so many years now and no one has visited us yet. What happened that brought you here?"

All the demons asked him the same.

The man said, "I have come for no reason other than that my brother gave me this lamb and told me to go to the Devil's dam, and I took the lamb and came to find you."

They bade him eat, but he refused.

They asked him, "What would you like us to give you in return for the gift you've brought us?"

"Whatever you have in your hearts," said he, "give me."

They gave him a mill for grinding coffee, and told him that if he turned the mill it would bring forth whatever he wanted— piastres, pieces of gold, food, any kind of thing—but bade him not give it to any man, whatever he might be offered. The man took it and returned home on the Saturday night before Easter.

Easter Day dawned. His children were weeping for they had no bread to eat nor any clothes to wear; they bewailed their fate. When their father came, he took out the mill, turned it a little, and brought from it loaves of bread, cooked dishes, gold pieces, clothes, whatever your heart desired. They got up in the morning, changed clothes, and went to church, full of the joys of living.

Now his brother saw his brother's wife and children changed, and dressed in fine clothes. "There's something going on here," he said to himself.

He asked here, he asked there, he questioned the children again and again, and at last he learned that his brother had a mill which brought forth these things. He went to his brother himself and asked him, but the brother denied it at first.

"Come, tell me," he said, "it was your children who told me about it."

The other had, willy-nilly, to admit it. Now his brother fell to pleading with him to give him the mill and he would give him a treasure of piastres and make over to him all his possessions. The other agreed, but first went home, turned the mill and filled a chest with pieces of gold, then went and gave the mill to his brother. His brother was not content, now that he had the mill, to stay in the village, but took it with him to Constantinople to show to everyone. As he was crossing over in the boat, the demand went round for salt. He up and turned the mill to bring out salt, but the mill would not stop. It turned by itself, and poured and poured out salt, till the boat was so full that it sank, and all were drowned!

The renounced ones took back their mill, but the poor man now had much gold and lived a golden life.

• 37 • *Myrsina, or Myrtle*

• ONCE UPON A TIME there were three sisters who were orphans. Neither father had they nor mother.

One day they thought they would find out who was the best of the three. So, just as the sun was about to rise, they went onto a sun porch and stood, the three of them, in a row and said to the sun, "Sun on the sun porch, who is the best of us all?"

And the sun said, "One's as good as the other, but the third and youngest is better still."

When the two elder sisters heard this, they bit their lips and went home with bitterness in their hearts. The next day, they both put on their best clothes, decked themselves out in their finery, but the unhappy youngest, whose name was Myrsina, was obliged to wear her worst and dirtiest, and again they went to consult the sun.

And when he came out on the porch, they said again, "Sun on the sun porch, who is the best of us all?'

And the sun again said, "One's as good as the other, but the third and youngest is better still."

When Myrsina's sisters heard this they burned with shame and went home, much humbled. On the third day they again consulted him, and the sun again told them the same. Then the two were more than ever consumed with envy and plotted together to get rid of the unhappy Myrsina. "Our mother has been so many years dead and very soon we must go and rebury her; but we must make all ready this evening, for our mother is buried far away on the mountain and we ought to leave very early." And the luckless Myrsina believed it, and next day she took some soul bread and *kollyva* and they set off to rebury their mother. They walked and walked and came to a wood and halted under a beech tree.

Then the eldest said, "Here, this is our mother's monument. Bring the pickax for me to dig."

"Oh dear," said the other. "Look what we've gone and done, forgetful ninnies that we are! How are we to dig? We've brought neither fork nor pick. Now what are we to do?"

Then the eldest one said, "One of us shall go and get the pickax."

"I'm afraid," said the second.

"And if I," said Myrsina, "as much as see a bird fly suddenly from a tree, I shall be stiff with fright."

"Listen," said the eldest, "you stay here, Myrsina, and we'll go and get the pick, because none of us can go alone. You sit down and look after the *kollyva* till we come."

"Very well, but come quickly, for I'm afraid to be alone."

"Oh, we're back already!" they said, and went gleefully off.

Poor Myrsina sat and waited and waited till the sun went down. Then, when she saw night was falling and she was all alone on the mountain, she began to cry. She cried so much that even the trees took pity on her.

A beech tree told her, "Don't cry, dear lass, only let that breadring you are holding roll, and wherever it stops there shall you bide, without a fear in the world."

Then Myrsina set the bread rolling and ran after it. Following it one way and the other, and without seeing where she was going, Myrsina ran into a pit. There she saw a house before her and went inside. Now in this house there lived twelve brothers, the Months, who spent all day going about the world and came home only late at night. When Myrsina came, there was no one at home. Then Myrsina rolled up her sleeves, took up a broom and cleaned all the house, and then sat down and cooked a delicious meal. Then she set the table, ate a little, and hid herself in the loft. Then the Months came home. They came in, and what should they see but all the house swept, the table set, and everything ready! What had been happening?

So then they said, "Who is it that has done this for us? Let him not be afraid, but come out, and if it's a lad, we'll make him our brother, and if a lass, our sister."

But no one answered. So they all ate and wondered some more and then went to bed. In the morning they were soon up and away. Then Myrsina came down from the loft, and again cleaned the house and sat down and made a pie, but what a pie! The kind of pie you lick your lips over when you eat it. Then, when evening came, she set the table and put out all the dishes. Then she cut herself a little piece of pie, ate it, and again went and hid in the loft. In a little while the Months came home, and when they saw everything was ready, they hardly knew what to say.

And they said, "But who is it that has done this for us? Let

him not be afraid, but come out . . ." And they said this and so
many other things, but in vain! Myrsina would not come out.
Then they sat down and ate and then went to bed.

Then the youngest said, "I shan't come with you tomorrow,
but stay here and hide, and find out who it is that comes and
does all this for us."

And so, when God sent a new day, they all got up and went,
and only the youngest stayed behind and hid behind the door.
Then down came Myrsina to do what she had done before.

But just as she was coming down, the youngest Month seized
her by the skirt, and said, "And so it's you, lady, who has done
all these things for us and won't tell us but keeps hidden! Don't
be afraid. You'll be like our own sister to us: something we
asked for in heaven and found on earth."

Then Myrsina took courage and told him how her sisters had
left her, and how she came to be in the house. And she set to and
did all the work she had done before. She cleaned all the house,
cooked, and made everything ready, like a true housewife. Late
that evening, when the Months came home and saw Myrsina,
they were very glad. They hardly knew what to do for gladness.
Then they sat down and ate and went to bed, like good little
brothers.

They got up early, and said to Myrsina, "Little sister, do as you
have done for us, and this evening you will see what brothers we
can be to you."

Then they went off. Myrsina did all the housework as she had
before, and as it was growing dark, she went outside the house
and waited for her brothers.

She had not been waiting long when the Months came home,
and said, with gladness, "Well met, little sister!"

"Welcome home, brothers!"

"How did your day go?"

"Well. And yours?"

"Never mind us. If your day goes well, then so does ours."

"Come away in, now, and rest your limbs. You are tired, and
the meal is ready."

"That's true, Myrsina, you're right. Let's eat, for we are very
hungry this evening."

Then they came in and sat down at table. And when they had eaten, you should have been there to see! One gave Myrsina earrings of gold, the next a garment of cloth of gold embroidered with the heavens and stars. Another two brought her dresses embroidered with the earth and crops, and the sea and fishes; another—but to hear it all, you'd think you were in a fairy tale. And so Myrsina lived with the Months as happily as could be.

When her sisters learnt that Myrsina was alive and well, they were eaten up with envy and made plans to poison her. And straightway they baked a pie with poison in it, and went to find Myrsina. It was just as the Months had gone.

Rat-tat! they knocked on the door.

"Who is it?" Myrsina answered from inside.

"Why, Myrsina, have you forgotten us so soon? Open the door. It is your sisters that have worn themselves out searching for you on the mountain."

"My sisters dear!" said Myrsina, and at once opened the door and embraced them and began to weep.

Then they said, "But what did you suppose, Myrsina? We went home as fast as we could go, found the pickax, and came back for you. We looked everywhere, but no Myrsina! So then we said, When Myrsina was left alone, she was afraid and someone must have passed by and she would have gone with him to some village . . . and the long and short of it is, Myrsina love, we heard later you were here, and here we are to visit you. But we can see you are well, little sister!"

"Oh yes, I'm well, I couldn't be better."

"So we see, but take care not to leave here, as they're so fond of you. We'll be going now."

"Why won't you stay?"

"No, we're in a hurry, another time. Stay well, Myrsina."

"Go well."

"We'll often come and see you. Ah, there! you see? We nearly forgot—here, take this pie—it's one of those we baked for our mother's soul. Now you eat it for our mother's soul."

And Myrsina took it. And when they went, she cut a piece for the dog they had there. And straightway the poor thing fell dead.

Then Myrsina knew that the pie had been poisoned and that her sisters had tried to poison her, so she did not eat it. She threw it in the oven and burnt it.

After many months had passed, Myrsina's sisters heard that Myrsina had not been poisoned. And they procured a poisoned ring and came again to where Myrsina was. They knocked on the door, but Myrsina would not open.

Whereupon they said, "Open the door, Myrsina, we have something to tell you. Look, we have brought you our mother's ring, for when she died you were only little and knew nothing about it. And when our mother was on her deathbed, she said, 'Lest you have my curse, give this ring to Myrsina, when she grows up.' And we don't want to go to hell, so, as you're grown up now, take your ring."

Then Myrsina opened the window and took the ring. And no sooner had she put it on than she fell to the ground like one dead. That evening, when the Months came home and saw Myrsina lifeless, they raised such lamentation as made the countryside ring. And after three days they took her up and dressed her in gold, laid her in a golden casket, and kept her in the house.

A good while after, a prince chanced to pass that way. And when he saw the chest, it pleased him so much that he asked the lads to let him have it. At first they would not give it to him, but after much persuasion they let him have it. But they warned him never to open it. And the Prince took the chest and brought it to his palace. And one day he fell very ill and nearly died.

Then he turned and said to his mother "Mother, I shall die and never know what is in that chest. Bring it for me to open. But all you others must leave the room."

And when they had all gone outside, he opened the chest, and what did he see? Myrsina, all dressed in gold and so beautiful that even though lifeless she looked like an angel. Then the Prince was struck with wonder. And when he came to himself and saw the ring Myrsina wore, he said, "Let me see if there is anything written in the ring that will tell me what this unhappy girl's name is."

And no sooner had he taken it off her finger than Myrsina woke on the instant and leapt out of the chest.

She began to ask, "Where am I? Who brought me here? Why, this isn't my home. Where are you, brothers mine?"

"I'm your brother now," said the Prince, "and you're in the King's palace."

And then he told her all that had happened: how he had bought the chest with her in it from the Months, and how she had lain lifeless inside until he had taken off the ring and brought her back to life.

Then Myrsina remembered her sisters, and said, "Alas! Your Grace, be sure you throw that ring into the sea, for it is poisoned and bewitched. It was brought to me by my sisters and the moment I put it on my finger, I was poisoned and fell into the state I was in when you found me."

Then the Prince bade Myrsina tell him all her story. And when he had heard it, he swore bitterly, and said, "Though those sisters of yours be at the ends of the world, I'll find them and punish them, for . . ."

"Please, your Grace, do nothing," said Myrsina. "Let them be, do nothing to them. Let them have their punishment from God."

Then the Prince was appeased. And when his illness was over, he lost no time in marrying Myrsina, and they lived happily together.

When her sisters heard that Myrsina was alive and had married the Prince, they could not contain their envy. And they came to the palace to poison her.

They entered and asked a manservant, "Where is Queen Myrsina? We are her sisters and have come to visit her."

"Wait there," said the manservant, "and I will inquire, for without the King's permission no one may see Myrsina."

Then he entered and said to the Prince, "Sire, there are two young women outside who say they are Queen Myrsina's sisters and wish to see her. Shall I let them in?"

Then the Prince said to one of his gentlemen-in-waiting, "Quickly, seize those women and get rid of them as best you know how. For they have come here to poison Queen Myrsina."

Then they seized the two sisters and what they did with them I don't know. I only know that they were never seen or heard of again.

But Myrsina and the Prince lived and thrived, and Myrsina's name was on everyone's lips for her beauty and good works.

I have been to the palace and seen Myrsina. And when I took my leave, they gave me a string of gold coins to take home with me. But as I was going by Melachro's house, her dog came out and ran after me. To save myself I had to throw down the coins and the dog picked them up and ran off. But should you get up very early in the morning, at sunrise, take a sop of bread and throw it to Melachro's dog, and she will give you the gold coins.

· 38 · *Maroula*

· Now THE STORY BEGINS—good evening to your worships.

Once upon a time there was a woman who had no children and every day she asked God to give her a child. One morning, as she stood at her window, she turned to the Sun, and said, "Good Master Sun, Master Sun, give me a child and when it is twelve years old, you can come and take it."

The Sun heard her plea and gave her a pretty little girl, as pretty as the morning star. She called her Maroula and she was full of joy that she had a child. The more Maroula grew, the prettier she became, and soon she was twelve years old. One day, as she was going to the spring for water, the Sun saw her and turned himself into a brave young lad and went up to her and said, "Ask your mother when she'll give me what she promised."

"But who are you?" Maroula asked the lad.

And he answered, "You tell your mother what I said, and she'll know who I am."

"Very well, I'll tell her," said Maroula, and picked up her pitcher and went home, and said to her mother, "Mother, when I was at the spring, I saw a lad, but what a lad! He was so handsome, he shone like the Sun. And his face! And he told me to ask you when you will give him what you promised him? I asked him who he was, and he told me you'd know who."

And her mother sighed, and said, "I know the lad, my lass. But tell him, when he finds you again, that you forgot to tell me."

The next day, when the lass again went to get water, the Sun came down, and asked her, "Did you tell your mother what I said?"

"I forgot to tell her," she told him.

Then the sun gave her a golden apple, and said to her, "Take this apple and put it in your headdress. This evening, when your mother undresses you before bed, the apple will fall out and you'll remember to tell her."

Maroula went straight home, and said to her mother, "The lad who told me to ask you when you would give him what you promised, found me again and gave me this apple, telling me to put it in my headdress so that when you undress me this evening, it will fall out and I'll remember to tell you."

"When he finds it, he may take it," said her mother, and made up her mind not to send her little girl any more for water.

For a long while she did not send Maroula for water and then she grew bolder and sent her. But, when the Sun saw her, he turned into a young lad again and came down and asked Maroula what her mother had said to her about the promise she had made.

"Ah," said Maroula, "she said, when you find it, you may take it."

Then the Sun took Maroula by the hand and took her far away to his palace, which had a beautiful garden before it. The Sun was away all the day and left Maroula in the garden to play, and in the evening he came round to his palace again. But poor Maroula, however much she was given in the Sun's palace, thought of her mother and sat all day in the garden and wept, and said:

> As my mother's heart withers and colder grows,
> So will the Sun's lettuces fade in their rows:
>   Fell yourself, tree, fell yourself.

And she would put up her hands and tear her cheeks. And the lettuces faded and the trees fell with Maroula's tears.

In the evening the Sun would come and see Maroula with swollen eyes and scratched cheeks.

"Who did this to you, Maroula, my dear?"

"The neighbor's cockerel came and fought with ours and I went to part them and they scratched me."

The next day, Maroula sat in the garden and wept again and tore at her cheeks, and said:

> As my mother's heart withers and colder grows,
> So will the Sun's lettuces fade in their rows:
> Fell yourself, tree, fell yourself.

The sun came that evening and again saw her with her cheeks torn.

"Who has done this to you again, Maroula, my dear?"

"The neighbor's cat came over to ours and they fought and I went to part them and they scratched me."

Maroula went again the next day to the garden, and when she sat down, she remembered her mother and again made her cheeks run with blood, and wept, and said:

> As my mother's heart withers and colder grows,
> So will the Sun's lettuces fade in their rows:
> Fell yourself, tree, fell yourself.

So all the lettuces withered and all the trees fell and the garden was strewn with logs and tree stumps.

The Sun came that evening and saw Maroula, all bloodstained.

"Who has done this to you again, Maroula, my dear?"

"I got caught in a rosebush," said Maroula to him, "and it tore me with its thorns."

But when he got out the next day, the Sun said to himself, "What if I went to see what Maroula does in the garden?" So he turned back and what should he see but Maroula, weeping and clawing at her cheeks.

He drew close to her, and said, "Why are you crying, Maroula, my dear? Can it be you are unhappy here?"

"No," said she, "I'm not unhappy."

"Then why are you weeping? Can it be you want to go back to your mother?"

"Yes, I want to go back to my mother," said Maroula.

"Well, since you want to go to your mother," said the Sun to her, "I will send you home."

So he took her by the hand to the edge of the garden, and there he began to call, "Little lions, little lions!"

Up came the lions.

"What is your will, Lord?" they said to him.

"Will you take Maroula to her mother?"

"We will."

"And on the road, what will you eat if you hunger, and what drink, if you thirst?"

"We'll eat her flesh and drink her blood."

"Run away, and quickly, too," said the Sun to them. "You will not do for me."

Then he called, "Little foxes, little foxes!"

Up came the foxes.

"What is your will, Lord?" they said to him.

"Will you take Maroula to her mother?"

"We will."

"And, on the road, what will you eat if you hunger, and what drink, if you thirst?"

"We'll eat her flesh and drink her blood."

"Get away from here, and quickly," said the Sun to them.

Then, once more, he called, "Little deer, little deer!"

Up came the deer.

"Will you take Maroula to her mother?"

"We will."

"And, on the road, what will you eat if you hunger, and what drink, if you thirst?"

"Fresh, fresh grass, and clear, clear water."

"Go with my blessing," said the Sun to them, and he lifted Maroula up and sat her on the antlers of one of the deer, adorned her with gold coins, and sent her home to her mother. On and on went the deer, and it grew hungry.

It came across a cypress tree, and said to it, "Bend, cypress, and I'll set Maroula down."

The cypress bent over and the deer set Maroula down upon it.

"Now I'll just go and graze a little," said the deer to her, "and then I'll come for you. But don't call out, unless you chance to need me, so that I can eat."

"Very well," said Maroula, "go."

Under the cypress tree there was a well, and nearby lived a *drakaena* who had three daughters, and she had sent one of her daughters to bring water from the well. So when she bent over to lower the bucket into the well, she saw Maroula's face reflected in the water and thought it was her own. So she threw down her bucket and danced back home.

"Did you bring the water?" her mother asked.

"Would you send a girl the likes of me for water?"

Her mother bided her time and sent the second daughter to the well, but as soon as she saw Maroula's face in the water, she, too, took it to be her own. So she, too, threw the bucket away and went running home to her mother.

"Would you send a girl the likes of me for water?"

Then she sent the third daughter to the well, but the same thing happened. Then the mother herself up and went to the well. She bent and looked into the water and saw Maroula's face. She looked up, saw the girl, and burst out laughing.

"Oh, my dear young woman," the *drakaena* said to her, "it was you that my daughters saw in the water and that turned their heads, and it was for you I left kneading my dough. Come down and I'll eat you."

"Make your bread first," said Maroula to her, "and then come back and eat me."

The *drakaena* ran home and kneaded her dough in a hurry and then ran back to Maroula.

"I've kneaded the dough," she told her, "so now come down and I'll eat you."

"Make your bread first," said Maroula, "and then come."

So she ran and made her bread and came running back.

"I've made it," she said," now come down and I'll eat you."

"Run and heat the oven first and then come and eat me."

The *drakaena* went and heated the oven and came back.

"I heated it," she told her. "Come down and I'll eat you."

"First put your bread in, before the oven goes cold," Maroula bade her, "then come and eat me."

The *drakaena* went off to put the bread in the oven, and then Maroula called out, "Little deer, little deer!"

The deer heard and came running.

"Quick," Maroula told it, "the *drakaena* wants to eat me."

Then the little deer said, "Bend, cypress tree, and I'll take Maroula."

The tree bent and the deer took Maroula and began to run. On the way, they met a mouse, and the deer said, "Mouse, if the *drakaena* meets you and asks if you've seen us, tell her some story and keep her from following us."

After a while, the *drakaena* came along, and said to it, "Here, mouse, have you seen a girl on a deer?"

The mouse said, "I did find a tress of hair."

The *drakaena* said, "That's not what I asked you. Have you seen a girl on a deer?"

"Just wool-gathering!" said the mouse.

"That's not what I asked you. Have you seen a girl on a deer?"

"Just yarn-spinning!" said the mouse.

"That's not what I asked you. Have you seen a girl on a deer?"

"Just cloth-cutting!" said the mouse.

"That's not what I asked you. Have you seen a girl on a deer?"

"I have," said the mouse. "Hurry, and you'll catch her."

As the deer ran and drew closer to her mother's house, the dog sensed that it was Maroula and began to bark, "Bow-wow! It's Maroula coming! Maroula's coming!"

And her mother said, "Sh! Naughty dog! Would you have me die of grief?"

Then the cat on the rooftop sensed it was she, and mewed, "Miaow, miaow! Here's Maroula coming!"

And her mother said, "Shoo! Naughty cat! Would you have me die of grief?"

Then the cockerel sensed her coming, "Cock-a-doodle-doo! Cock-a-doodle-doo! Here's Maroula coming!"

And her mother said, "Hush, naughty bird! Would you have me die of grief?"

Just as the deer came to the house, the *drakaena* caught them up, and, as the deer was going in at the door, the *drakaena* was able to catch it by the tail.

"Ouch, my tail, my tail!" cried the deer.

As it came inside the house, Maroula's mother got up to welcome it, "Welcome, welcome, and, as you have brought me my Maroula, I'll put on your tail for you," and she got a little wool and put on its tail.

And she lived happily ever after with her little girl, and may we live even happier.

Part III
Tales of Kindness Rewarded and Evil Punished

The Twelve Months

· ONCE UPON A TIME there was a widow woman who had five children, but she was so poor she hadn't so much as a brass farthing. She could find no work to do except once a week, when a gentlewoman of the neighborhood had her in to bake her bread. But for her trouble she did not give her even the corner of a loaf to take for her children to eat, but the poor woman went home with the dough on her hands and there she washed them in clean water and this water she boiled and made gruel and this the children ate. And with this gruel they were satisfied the whole week till their mother went again to make bread at the gentlewoman's house and returned, with hands unwashed, to make them gruel again.

The gentlewoman's children, for all the food they had, so much and so rich, and for all the fresh bread they fed on, were like dried mackerel. But the poor woman's children were filled out and chubby, like plump red mullet. Even the gentlewoman was amazed and spoke about it to her friends.

Her friends said, "The poor woman's children are filled out and chubby because she takes away your children's luck on her hands and gives it to her own children. That is why they get fat and yours grow thinner and dwindle away."

The gentlewoman believed this and when the day came again for making bread, she did not let the poor woman leave with her hands unwashed, but made her wash them clean, so that the luck should stay in her house. And the poor woman came home with tears in her eyes. When her children saw her and saw that she had no dough on her hands, they began to cry. On the one hand, the children wept, and on the other, the mother.

At last, like a grown woman, she steeled herself and calmed her tears, and said to her children, "Dry your eyes, my children, and weep no more, and I'll find a piece of bread for you to eat."

And she went from door to door and barely found someone to give her a stale corner of bread. She dipped it well in water and shared it among her children, and when they had eaten, she put them to bed and they fell asleep. And at midnight she left the house without looking back lest she see her children dying of hunger.

As she walked through the wilderness in the night, she saw a light shining on a high place, and went up toward it. And when she drew close to it, she saw it was a tent, and from the center hung a great candelabra with twelve candles, and underneath it hung a round thing like a ball. She went into the tent and saw twelve young men who were talking over what to do about a certain matter. The tent was round and to the right of the entrance sat three young men with their collars open, and in their hands they carried tender grass and tree blossoms. Next to these young men sat another three, with their sleeves rolled up, and coatless, carrying in their hands dry ears of wheat. Next to these sat another three young men, each with a bunch of grapes in his hand. Next to these sat another three young men, each huddled over himself and wearing a long fur from the neck to the knee.

When the young men saw the woman, they said, "Greetings, good Aunt, be seated."

And after greeting them, the woman sat down. And when she was seated, they asked her how it was she had come to that place. And the poor widow told them of her plight and her troubles. Seeing that the poor woman was hungry, one of those who wore furs got up and laid the table for her to eat, and she saw that he was lame. When the woman had eaten her fill, the young men began to ask her all kinds of things about the country, and the woman answered as well as she could.

At last the three young men that had their collars open said to her, "Now, good Aunt, how do you get on with the months of the year? How do you like March, April, and May?"

"I like them well, my lads," answered the widow, "and indeed, when these months come, the mountains and fields grow green, the earth is gay with all kinds of flowers, and from them comes scent, so that a body feels revived. All the birds begin to sing. The husbandmen see that their fields are green and rejoice in their hearts and make their granaries ready. So we have no complaints against March, April, and May, otherwise God would send fire to burn us for our ingratitude."

Then the next three young men that had their sleeves rolled up and ears of wheat in their hands, asked, "Well, and what have you to say to June, July, and August?"

"Nor can we complain over those three months, because, with the warmth they bring, they ripen the crops and all the fruits. Then the husbandmen reap what they have sown and the gardeners gather their fruit. And indeed the poor are made happy by these months, for they do not need many and costly clothes."

Then the next three young men that carried grapes, "How do you get on with the months of September, October, and November?"

"In those months," answered the woman, "folk gather grapes and make them into wine. And they are good besides in that they tell us that winter is coming, and folk set about getting in wood, coals, and heavy clothing, so as to keep warm."

Then the three young men in furs asked her, "Now, how do you get on with December, January, and February?"

"Ah, those are the months that care for us greatly," said the poor woman, "and we love them very much. And will you ask for why? Here's why! Because folk are by nature insatiable and would like to work the whole year round, so as to earn much, but those winter months come and cause us to draw into a corner and rest ourselves after the summer's labors. Folk love these months because, with their rains and snows, they cause all the seeds and grasses to grow. So, my lads, all the months are good and worthy and each one does his work, may God preserve them. It is us folk who are not good."

Then eleven of the young men made a sign to the first of those who carried grapes, and he went out and very shortly came back with a stoppered jar in his arms and he gave it to the woman, saying, "Come now, Auntie, and take this jar home with you to raise your children on."

Joyfully the woman took the jar on her shoulder, and said to the young men, "May your years be many, my lads."

"May the hour be good to you, good Aunt," they answered, and she went.

Just as dawn was breaking, she came back home and found her children still asleep. She spread out a cloth and emptied the jar onto it. When she saw that it was full of gold pieces she all

but went out of her mind for joy. When it was well and truly
light, she went to the baker's and bought five or six loaves and
an *oka* of cheese and woke her children, washed and tidied them,
set them to say their prayers, and then gave them bread and
cheese, and the little dears ate until they were truly full. Then
she bought a kilo of wheat and took it to the mill and had it
ground, made it into dough, and took the loaves to the bakery to
bake. And just as she was returning from the bakery, with the
board laden with bread on her shoulder, and was almost home,
the gentlewoman saw her and suspected that something had happened to her and ran up to her, to learn where she had got the
flour to make bread with. The poor woman innocently told her
all.

The gentlewoman was envious and made up her mind that
she, too, would go to see the young men. So, that night, when
her husband and children were asleep, she slipped out of the
house and took the road and went on till she found the tent
where the twelve months were and greeted them.

And they said to her, "Greetings, mistress, how is it you have
consented to visit us?"

"I am poor," she answered, "and I have come to you for help."

"Very good," said the young men, "and how are things where
you come from?"

"They might be worse," she answered.

"Well, how do you get on with the months?" they asked next.

"How, indeed," she answered. "Each one is a sore trial. Just as
we are getting used to the heat of August, straightway September, October, and November come along and chill us so that this
one gets a cough and that one catches a cold. Then the winter
months, December, January, and February, come in and freeze
us, the roads fill with snow, and we cannot go out, and as for
that lame-john of a February . . . !" (Poor February was listening.) "And then those accursed months March, April, and May!
They don't consider themselves to be summer months, and all
they want is to act like winter ones, so they make the winter last
nine months. And we can never go out on the first of May and
drink coffee with milk in it and sit on the new grass. Then come
the months June, July, and August—they're the ones that are

mad to stifle us with sweat by the heat they bring. Indeed, on the fifteenth of August, we are all in a fit of coughing and the bitter winds spoil our linen on the clothesline. What more can I say, lads? Our life with the months (may curses befall them) is a dog's life."

The young man said nothing but made a sign to him who sat in the middle of those bearing grapes.

And he got up and brought in a stoppered jar and gave it to the woman, and said, "Take this jar, and when you get home, lock yourself up in a room alone and empty it out. See that you do not open it on the way."

"I won't," said the woman.

She went and joyfully came home just before dawn. Then she locked herself in a room all alone and spread out a cloth and unstoppered the jar and emptied it out. And what came out of it? Nothing but snakes. They coiled themselves about her and devoured her alive; she left her children motherless, for it is wrong for one to accuse another. But the poor woman, with her true heart and her sweet tongue, went up in the world and became a great lady, and her children flourished. There! That's what they call a happy ending!

.40. *The Two Neighbors*

• Good evening, and the story begins.

Once upon a time, there were two neighbors, who could find no work in their village. So they agreed to go and work in foreign parts, and they went. The one would cheerfully work for any wage, however small, while the other, even if he was offered a good wage, say fifty drachmas, would not go to work. He worked one day in seven, and then he would sit and eat and drink, and so time went by. The first worked every day; sometimes he earned a great deal, sometimes only a little. He was able to save and put aside three thousand drachmas.

After two years had passed, they met, and the first said to the other, "I'll tell you what, neighbor. Let's go back to our homes. We have been long enough in foreign parts. I miss my wife and children, and long to see them again."

"Let us go, then," said the other, "but how should a man return? I haven't the tenth part of a drachma to my name."

"I," said the first, "have put aside a sum from my wages. If you wish, I can lend you a thousand. When we return home, you can find work and pay me back."

To cut a long story short, they agreed. The first lent the other a thousand, and they set off for home.

But, once the idler had the thousand in his pocket, a demon began whispering to him to keep it and not pay it back.

So he said to the good man, "Have you ever been told that God demands acts of evil?" (They were talking as they went along the road home.)

"What I have always been told," said the first, "is that God demands acts of goodness, not evil."

"It is as I told you," said the second.

"But what I have always heard," said the good man, "is, 'Do good, and it will be done to you.'"

"I'll lay you a wager," said the other. "Let's accost three men on our road, and ask them. If they say that God demands acts of evil, you lose your thousand; if they say, acts of goodness, I lose the wager, that is, I hand you back your thousand."

The first man agreed to this. "So be it," said he.

So they walked on and on, and came across a shepherd seated on a rock, with his flock grazing about him. It was a demon in disguise!

They went up to him, and said, "Tell me, old man, if you can: Does God demand acts of goodness or acts of evil?"

"Not acts of goodness, my sons," said he. "One of you might stand here, talking to me, while the other goes and steals a sheep. That is all in all, these days."

"You see?" said the second man.

They walked on and on, and on their way down, they met a priest, with a sack full of offerings over his shoulder, again the demon in disguise.

They asked him, "Tell us, Father, if you can. Does God demand acts of goodness or acts of evil?"

"Not acts of goodness, my sons," said he. "One of you might stand here, talking to me, and the other snatch the sack off my shoulder. That is how things are, these days."

"You hear?" said the idler.

They went on their way and saw in a forest a boy cutting wood, a fine little fellow, and asked him the same thing.

"Today, all that counts is, grab, run away, eat, drink, that is what God demands today, and that's the right of it,"

The good man lost the thousand, willy-nilly.

"What matter," he said, "if I lose the thousand! It can't be helped, since that is the right of it."

"Now," said the other, "that is over and done with. Come and eat now, for surely both of us are hungry."

They sat themselves down. But no sooner was the food laid out before them than the demon again began whispering to him to seize the other two thousand the good man had in his pocket. All of a sudden he leapt upon him, blinded him with a stick, took his money, and threw him over a nearby precipice. The first man groaned with the pain as he lay there under the precipice.

"Glory be to God!" said he. "What a sad pass I'm in. I have only myself to blame. Why did I want to take him with me? Couldn't I have returned alone? What need had I to lend him money?"

After a long time groping about, right and left, under the precipice, he at last found a wild pear tree, and sat down, in ruin and despair, at its roots. At nightfall, he climbed up the wild pear tree so that wild beasts should not devour him. After a while, he heard voices and other sounds—it was a whole regiment of demons. It was in this place that the excommunicates met and made their plans.

Then said their thrice-accursed leader to one of the demons, "And what have you been doing today?"

"Today," said he, "I went to the Princess, who sat embroidering at the frame. I harassed her here, I tormented her there until

I blinded her with the needles. The palace was all in a turmoil today."

"Well done!" said the leader. "If they did but know it, there's a pit near the pear tree here, and they have only to wash the Princess's eyes in some of the water from it for her to see again on the instant."

The injured man up the pear tree heard all.

Then the leader asked another demon, "And what have you been doing today?"

"What else, my Lord, but the work I have been doing these forty years! Do you mind what it is? I go to a place where the monks are building a monastery, and pull it down. I shall never let them finish the job."

"If the monks did but know it," said he, "they have only to slay a *Karaggliozi*-faced lamb—white, with black around the eyes —at every corner, before they begin to build, and you could never pull it down," the leader said.

"What have you been doing?" he asked another.

"Today," said he, "there were two men walking along the road together, and I set one of them to blind the other, take his money, and throw him over the precipice."

"If he, too, did but know it," said the leader, "he has only to wash his face in the pit that has water in it, to have his sight again."

The man up the pear tree heard all this.

When the blessed dawn came, and the demons went away, he came down from the pear tree, and by groping his way about at last found the pit with the water in it, washed his face in it, and so his sight came back. Then he went to a vegetable garden, cut himself a marrow, and filled it with water from the pit. Then, after trying for some time, he at last climbed up the precipice and got back on the road again. He made his way to the place where the monks were building the monastery. The instant they saw him, the monks brought him food and did all they could for him.

And he in his turn asked them, "How goes the world with you, holy folk?"

"Never ask, good Christian," said the monks. "We have been

working these forty years to build a monastery. As much as we build by day is pulled down again to the very foundations during the night, and what is to be done about it we cannot tell."

"Bring me," said he, "four *Karaggliozi*-faced lambs, and I will do what I will do, and the monastery will never again be pulled down."

The next day the monks brought him the lambs. He slew one at each of the four corners of the monastery and then bade them build it up. The monks built up the monastery and, truly, it was never pulled down again.

"What reward are we to give you for the great good you have done us?"

"I want nothing," he said, "but a suit of clothes and a knapsack."

He took up the clothes, the knapsack, and the marrow full of the miracle-working water, and set out for the place where the hapless Princess lived.

He entered the city and at last stood outside the palace, among a noisy throng of people.

So he began to cry, "Miracle doctor! Miracle doctor!"

The people began to jeer, the children ran after him, and all the folk laughed fit to burst. The King heard the laughter, and was very angry. He sent his henchman to see what was amiss and why the folk were laughing, when, inside the palace, there was only weeping. So the henchman went out and they told him what the matter was, and when he had passed it on to the King, the King ordered him to be brought up.

They brought him up into the palace, and when he saw the Princess, he said, "King, I will cure the Princess, but the doctors must first leave the room."

When this was done, he took a small piece of cloth and bathed her injured eyes with the water, and the Princess had her sight back on the instant.

The King all but went mad with joy, and said, "What shall I give you?"

"I want nothing, sire."

"Then take her for your wife; it was you who cured her. What would have become of her without her sight?"

"I am married," said he, "and have children, and I am from such-and-such a place (Mytilene, let us say)."

"Then," said the King, "I appoint you governor of that place to keep order there in my name."

He gave him two bags of gold and dressed him in full dress uniform.

So he went back home covered in glory. When he got there, he issued a proclamation that all the people should assemble in the church, for the governor wished to speak to them, and all the people came—it was a royal order, was it not?

He was dressed in such a way that no one knew him. When the assembly dispersed, he opened wide the doors of the church and placed a sack on one side and another on the other, and put a handful of gold pieces in each.

As the man who blinded him came out, he said, "Wait here, I want you."

He also stopped the man's wife, and when all had departed, he said to her, "I will give you two or three handfuls of gold because your husband has made me so rich. It was he who gave me all this treasure."

"When?" said the bad man. "I do not know you."

"But *I* know *you!* I'm the one you blinded and threw over the precipice. There I found a wild pear tree and groped about until I found all the treasure you see here."

The other stood there, gaping.

The next day, he went and sought out a friend of his and said, "Let us go to this place, and, when we get there, you blind me and throw me over the precipice. I'll give you three gold pieces, if you agree to do it."

"I agree," said the other.

So they went to the place where the bad man had harmed the other, the good man. The friend blinded the bad man and threw him over the precipice, and left him.

He groped his way about, and at last came upon the wild pear tree, and climbed up, expecting to find treasure there.

At nightfall, the demons came, their leader mad with rage. He summoned the two demons, the one who had hurt the Princess and the other who had pulled down the monastery, and said,

"Who told *you* to go and tell the monks to slay lambs to complete the monastery, and who told *you* to take the Princess water from the pit to wash her eyes with and get her sight back?"

And thereupon, my dears, he began to beat, belabor, and kick them until they howled for mercy. Under his blows, the demons fell flat on their backs and they saw him sitting up there in the wild pear tree.

"It wasn't us told them," they said, "there's the one who did it," and they pointed up to the bad man as he sat there in the pear tree. Then all the demons fell upon him, pulled him down from the tree, and tore him to pieces.

And that was the end of him, and never may worse befall.

•41• *Truth and Falsehood*

• ONCE, Truth and Falsehood met at a crossroads, and after they had greeted each other, Falsehood asked Truth how the world went with him. "How goes it with me?" said Truth. "Each year worse than the last." "I can see the plight you are in," said Falsehood, glancing at Truth's ragged clothes, "why, even your breath stinks." "Not a bite has passed my lips these three days," said Truth. "Wherever I go, I get troubles, not only for myself, but for the few who love me still. It's no way to live, this." "You have only yourself to blame," said Falsehood to him. "Come with me. You'll see better days, dress in fine clothes like mine, and eat plenty, only you must not gainsay anything I say."

Truth consented, just that once, to go and eat with Falsehood because he was so hungry he could hardly keep upright. They set out together and came to a great city, went into the best hotel, which was full of people, and sat and ate of the best. When many hours had gone by, and most of the people had gone, Falsehood rapped with his fist on the table, and the hotelkeeper himself came up to see to their wants, for Falsehood looked like a great nobleman. He asked what they desired.

"How much longer am I to wait for the change from the sovereign I gave the boy who sets the table?" said Falsehood. The host called the boy, who said that he had had no sovereign. Then

Falsehood grew angry and began to shout, saying he would never have believed that such a hotel would rob the people who went in there to eat, but he would bear it in mind another time, and he threw a sovereign at the hotelkeeper. "There," he said, "bring me the change."

Fearing that his hotel would get a bad name, the hotelkeeper would not take the sovereign, but gave change from the reputed sovereign of the argument, and boxed the ears of the boy who could not remember taking the coin. The boy began to cry, and protest that he had not had the sovereign, but as no one believed him, he sighed deeply and said, "Alas, where are you, unhappy Truth? Are you no more?"

"No, I'm here," said Truth, through clenched teeth, "but I had not eaten for three days, and now I may not speak. You must find the right of it by yourself, my tongue is tied."

When they got outside, Falsehood burst out laughing and said to Truth, "You see how I contrive things?"

"Better I should die of hunger," said Truth, "than do the things you do." So they parted forever.

·42· *The Old Man and the Three Brothers*

• ONCE THERE WERE three brothers who set out for foreign parts to look for work. As they were on the road they came to a deserted place and sat down near a spring to eat and rest themselves. As they were eating, they saw an old man coming toward them with his little stick.

"Good day, my brave lads," he greeted them.

"Long life to you, Gran'fer," they answered him, and the youngest cut him a piece of bread, and said, "Sit yourself down, Gran'fer, and eat a bite of bread."

The old man took the bread and sat down. In that deserted place there was a flock of crows.

The old man said to the eldest brother, "What would you like to be yours, my lad, here in the world where you are now?"

"I should like," he answered, "for all those crows to be sheep and for the sheep to be mine."

"Very well," said the old man. "But if a poor man came and asked you for a cup of milk, would you give it to him, if you had so many sheep?"

"That I would," said the lad, "and whatever he wished for, milk, cheese, whey, or whatever."

Rap! The old man beat with his staff on the ground and the crows became sheep. The whole place was white with sheep. The lad got up, gathered in the sheep, and stayed on there. The second two continued on their way with the old man. On they went till they came to a forest.

Then the old man asked the second brother, "What would you wish to have, my lad, here in the world where you are now?"

"I should like, Gran'fer, for all these holm oaks to be olive trees and for them all to be mine," said the lad.

"Very well," said the old man to him, "as you'll have so much oil, would you give some of it to a poor man?"

"That I would," he answered him.

Rap! The old man beat with his staff on the ground and the holm oaks became olive trees on the instant. And the lad stayed in that place and set up a chandlery, filled barrels with oil, and loaded them on ships.

The youngest brother was left alone with the old man, and they went on their way together. When they came to a crossroads, they sat down at the spring that was there, to rest.

The old man said to the lad, "But aren't you going to ask for anything?"

"I, Gran'fer, should like for this spring to run honey."

"And would you give honey to the poor, if they asked you for some?"

"I would."

The old man beat with his staff on the ground, and honey at once began to run forth from the spring. The lad stayed on at the crossroads, selling honey and doling it out to the wandering poor. The old man went off on his own business.

After some time had gone by, the lad left a paid hand at the spring, to dole out the honey, and he set off to visit his brothers, for he had missed them. On the way, he looked for olive trees but saw a forest of holm oak. He went farther on looking for sheep, but saw only crows, and never an oil merchant or a sheep farmer.

And as he stood and wondered, he saw the old man coming along once more, and the old man said to him, "You see? Your brothers did not do as they said they would. They did not give the poor of the good things I bestowed on them. That is why I took back the sheep and the olives. But you were as good as your word; therefore, receive my blessing."

And even before his words were ended, the old man disappeared.

•*43*• *The Cardplayer in Paradise*

• ONCE Christ went into a cardplayer's house and told his wife that He would come that evening to dinner. The cardplayer made ready and brought in fish for three persons—himself, his wife, and his guest. But that evening, Christ came with his twelve Disciples.

The man and his wife up and said they doubted they could feed so many, but Christ blessed the food, they all ate, and there was food left over. When Christ was leaving, He revealed Himself and asked the cardplayer what He could do for him in return.

He thought, and said, "Let me always win at cards, for it is my work, and when I die, take me into Paradise."

"It is well," said Christ, and disappeared.

All his life, the cardplayer beat everyone at cards. The time came for him to die, and before he went to the next world, he told his wife to put the playing cards inside his coffin. He died, and was saved.

The road to Paradise first ran through Hell. When he arrived outside Hell, the Devil called him inside. The cardplayer agreed to play cards with him, and if he lost, to go to Hell, but if he won, to take away one of the damned with him. They began to play, and at the end the cardplayer found himself the winner of twelve of the damned. At last, they set off for Paradise. The card-player found Saint Peter's gate and bade him call Christ. Christ came and was told that there were thirteen people there at the gate. "I told you," Christ said, "I would take only you into Paradise, and you have brought twelve more."

"I beg Your pardon," the cardplayer said, "but You said You would come to my house on Your own, yet You brought me twelve more to feed."

What could Christ do, but let in the twelve?

·44· *The Devil Who Wore Out Forty Pairs of Tsarouchia*

• ONCE, a thief was going along his way, when he met the Devil, and the Devil asked him, "Where are you off to?"

"I'm looking for work, I'm a poor man."

"Shall we go along together?" the Devil asked him. "I'll make you rich. Tell me what work you do."

"I steal," he told him.

"Ah, that's the best kind of work! I'm the Devil and I'll help you so that no one shall catch you at it."

The thief went on stealing for forty years, and in the forty-first year he was caught. They put him in prison and sentenced him to hang. They took him out onto the gallows to hang him, and put the noose around his neck.

Then the Devil turned up, arched his back for the thief to stand on, and told him, "Never fear, friend, I'm here. Just look beside you, friend. What do you see?"

"I see an ass loaded with old *tsarouchia* [Peasant's studded clogs]".

"I couldn't carry those *tsarouchia*. I've waited forty years, chasing after you to bring you to this moment when you would hang."

And he ducked out from under him, and the thief hanged.

•45• *The Child Who Was*
Poor and Good

• ONCE UPON A TIME there was a poor woman who had four girl-children. To raise them, the unhappy creature went out to work. A harder worker you could not have wished to find, but even so, her daily wage all went on food. She was barely able to earn enough to purchase their daily bread. She had to let them go about unclad and unshod, for there was not a mite left over to buy them clothes. If ever some good Christian dame were to give her some old, worn garment, she would make it over for the eldest, and then would cut it down to fit the second and the third. For the fourth and littlest girl nothing remained. Winter and summer she went about in only a ragged little shirt, barefoot and barechested.

One year, the winter was severe with rain, cold, and snow! The unhappy fourth child shivered and could not get warm. At last, she said to her mother: "Mother, I must leave this place and go and find another mother who can make me a little garment now and then. I shall die if I stay here longer. I cannot go on with only this little shirt to wear."

So the child left her home and walked and walked. On the road she found a little bird under a tree. The bird was young and featherless, and it had fallen from the nest. Little squawks came from its beak for it had not the strength to fly back up the tree and would die down on the ground. The child was sorry for it. She took it in her little hands and warmed it between her palms. She looked about her, and when she saw a man coming along the road, she asked him to put the bird back in the nest. And so it was she who saved it.

The child again went along her way and passed amid some branches. She saw a spider spinning its web, up and down, back and forth, the web growing and growing the while, you might have thought there was some great haste about it.

The child halted, and said, "I will not break the web, but go round the other way, so as not to grieve the spider."

The spider said, "Thank you, my good child. What would you have me do for you in return for your kindness to me? Where are you going, all unclad and barefoot?"

"I am going to find some cloth and take it to my mother to make me a little garment, for I am cold."

"Go, then," said the spider to the child, "and on your return, come this way again and tell me what I can give you in my fashion."

So the child went on, and farther away she came across a bramble. As she tried to go past it, her little shirt caught on its thorns and was torn to shreds, so that she was mother-naked. The poor child fell to crying—it would have broken your heart to see and hear her.

Her sobs were heard by a lamb that was grazing in the meadow a little way off.

The lamb said to the child, "What ails you, child? Why do you weep? Have you had a whipping?"

"Oh," wailed the child. "I was going to find a little garment to keep me warm, and as I was going past the bramble it tore my little shirt to shreds and left me mother-naked."

So the lamb asked the bramble, "Wherefore did you this harm? What is to become of the child now?"

"Give her some of your wool and I will card it. Let her give it to her mother to make her something to wear, for wool will keep her warm," said the bramble.

The lamb began to walk all round and around the bramble, the wool came off on the thorns, and the child plucked it off already carded. When she had gathered a fair quantity, she said, "Thank you, little lamb! Now I will run back to my mother, so she can set about spinning the yarn, weaving it, cutting the cloth, and sewing it, so that I can wear it when I go to Communion at Christmas."

She was running on her way, full of joy, when it crossed her mind that her mother would not have time, going out to her work every day as she did, to do all this by Christmas, and she at once grew sad. When she reached the foot of the tree where the bird's nest was, what do you think! There, before her, was the bird's mother.

"You dear child!" said the bird's mother. "How can I thank you? How can I repay your goodness in saving my little one's life? What is that you have in your arms?"

The child told her that it was the wool the lamb had given her, and that she was hurrying to take it to her mother to spin, weave, cut, and sew to make her a little garment to wear at Christmas when she would go to Communion.

"Let me spin it for you," said the bird.

She took it in her beak, and flew up very high, so as to pull it into a long thread. And by the time she flew down again (if you could only have seen!), she had spun the thread and rolled it into a ball. The child took it and went on her way. When she got to the spider's web, the spider was waiting for her.

"Well, how did you fare? Did you find anything at all?"

When the spider saw the balls of thread in the child's arms, it took the thread and began to weave it, quick as lightning, and as fine as any weaver.

The child took the cloth to her mother, who cut it into a little dress, sewed it, put it on the child, and made her pretty. She went to the church, and all the folk kissed and hugged her for being so fine and warmly clad.

Part IV
Tales of Fate

Chance and the Poor Man

• THERE WAS ONCE a good man, but he had never any gain from his labors. So he decided to go in search of Chance and ask her to help him. He set out and on the way he came across a lake that he must cross, but could not, for there was no ferry. While he stood there at a loss, a big fish came up and asked him where he was going. The man told it his story, and said that he was going in search of Chance, but could not get across the lake.

Then said the fish, "I will take you, but ask Chance about a pain I have in my back."

"Very well," said the man, and he sat on the fish's back and crossed the lake. Once across the lake, he followed the road and came to a kingdom ruled by a young and very handsome King, but, as often as he fought, he could never win. Here, the guards arrested him as a foreigner and brought him to the King, who asked him where he was going. The man told him his story.

"Go your ways," said the King, "but, I pray you, ask Chance for me why it is I never win my wars."

"I will," said the man, and took his departure. On his way, he met a farmer plowman who sowed but had never reaped. The farmer asked the man where he was going and the man told him his story.

"I pray you," said the farmer, "when you find Chance, ask her why, though I sow, I never reap."

"Very well," said the man, and went on his way.

After he had been on the road some time, he reached the place where Chance lived and went to her and asked her to help him. Chance received him fairly, and told him to go back home, and she would send him three occasions when he might help himself to become rich.

"Thank you very much," said the man, "but I will also ask you to help a farmer who sows but never reaps what he sows." Chance told him that under the surface of the field there was a great treasure, and that was why the seeds that were sown never bore fruit. As for the King, she said that he was a woman and, because of the natural cowardice of women, never won. As to the fish, she said that it had a thorn in its back that was hurting it. Having thanked Chance, the man took his departure. When he came to the farmer, he told him what Chance had said. The farmer begged him to stay and help him take the treasure out of the earth and they would share it. But the man did not wish it and went on his way.

Then he came to the King, who received him and asked him what answer Chance had given him. He bent down to the King's ear and told him what Chance had said about him. Then the supposed King proposed that the man become her husband so that *he* would be King. But the man, not wishing to have so many cares, declined to become King and went on his way.

After this, he came to the lake, where he found the fish, and by blowing gently on its back, he got out the thorn. To show its gratitude, the fish told him that under the lake was an ancient city that had sunk, and in it there were precious things which the fish would bring out for the man to take. But even then the man did not wish it and went off home to wait in bed for Chance to carry out her promise and send him riches.

•47• *The Ill-fated Princess*

• ONCE UPON A TIME there was a Queen who had three daughters she could not settle with husbands. The Queen thought it a sore burden that other girls should marry, while these, who were Princesses, were all but growing old, unwed. One day a beggarwoman came to the palace asking for alms. Seeing the Queen so distressed, she asked what the matter was, and she told her about her sorrow.

Then the beggarwoman said to her, "Mark well what I tell you. Tonight, when your daughters are asleep, you must watch and see how each of them sleeps, and come and tell me."

This the Queen did. That night she watched and saw that her eldest daughter slept with her hands on her head, the second had her hands on her bosom, while the third had them folded in her lap. When the beggarwoman came the following day, the Queen told her what she had seen.

Then the beggarwoman said to her, "Attend to me, my Lady Queen. It's she who had her hands folded in her lap that is the ill-fated one, and it is her evil Fate that hinders the Fates of the others."

When the beggarwoman had gone, the Queen sat deep in thought. "Listen to me, Mother," her youngest daughter said to her, "do not be sad. I heard it all and now I know that it is I who hinder my two sisters from being wed. Have all my dowry rendered into gold pieces and sewn into the hem of my dress, and let me go."

The Queen said no, and asked her, "Where would you go, my child?" But she paid no heed. She dressed herself in nun's clothing and, after bidding her mother farewell, set forth. As she was leaving by the palace gate, two bridegrooms rode up for her sisters.

So the unhappy girl went on and on, until at evening she came to a certain village. Here she knocked on the door of a cloth dealer's house and asked him to let her spend the night there. He told her to go up to the best chamber, but she refused and said she would stay downstairs.

That night her Fate came and began to rip up the cloths that were stored downstairs, tearing them into shreds and wreaking chaos all around, for all the girl begged her not to. But would the Fate pay any heed to her? She made her cower by saying she would tear her to pieces as well. At daybreak, the dealer went down to see how the nun had spent the night. When he saw all the damage—his wares destroyed, and the house turned upside down—he said to the girl: "Alas, lady nun! What harm is this you've done me? You have ruined me. What's to become of me now?"

"Bide awhile, bide awhile," answered she, and opened the hem of her skirt, and took out some gold pieces, and said, "Are these enough for you?"

"They are, they are."

And so she bade him good-bye, and again went on her way. On and on she went, until it again grew dark and she knocked on a glass merchant's door. The same happened there. She asked to spend the night downstairs, and again her Fate went in the night and left nothing standing. The next day, the glass merchant went to ask how the nun had spent the night, and saw the chaos that had been wrought. He cried out in protest, but when she had filled his hands with gold, he was appeased and let her go. The unfortunate girl again followed her road, until she came to the royal palace of that country. There she asked to see the Queen and besought her to give her work.

The Queen, who was a keen-witted woman, saw that it was a noblewoman hiding behind the nun's veil, and asked her if she knew how to embroider in pearls. She answered that she was very well able to work in pearls, and so the Queen kept her beside her. But when the ill-fated girl sat down to embroider, the pictures came down from the wall, snatched the pearls from her, tormented her and would not let her be for as much as a moment. The Queen saw all this and was sorry for her.

Often, when the servants came to complain that the dishes had been broken in the night and that it was she who had done it, the Queen replied, "Be still, be still, for she is a Princess and a noblewoman, but she is under an evil Fate, poor thing."

So one day the Queen said to her, "Listen to me, my child. You cannot go on living in this fashion, with your Fate pursuing you, unless you find a way to change your Fate."

"But what must I do?" the girl asked her. "What must I do to change my Fate?"

"Listen well to me. You see that high mountain that seems so far away? On it, all the Fates in the world live together. There they have their palaces, and that is the road you must take. Go up to the very top of the mountain, seek out your Fate, give her the piece of bread that I shall give you, and say to her, 'Fate who decreed my fate, change my fate.' Do not leave, whatever she may do to you, until you have seen her take the bread in her hands."

And that is what the Princess did. She took the bread and went up the pathway until she came to the top of the mountain. She knocked at the garden gate, and a very handsome young woman dressed in fine clothes opened the gate and came out.

"But *you* are not mine," she said, and went inside again.

After a while, another came out, just as beautiful and fine.

"I don't know *you*, my good girl," she said, and went away.

Another came, and yet another, and many came out, but none knew her to be her own, until one, disheveled and ragged, torn and filthy, came to the door.

"What are you looking for here, you foolish girl?" she said to the Princess. "Split you, hang you, begone! I'll have your heart out!"

The ill-fated girl handed her the bread, and said, "Fate, who decreed my fate, change my fate."

"Begone! Go and tell your mother you must be born again, put to the breast, and lulled to sleep. Then come here, and I'll change your fate."

The other Fates said to her, "Change her fate, for you have given her an evil one. Is she, a Princess, to be tormented in this fashion? Give her another fate, give her another."

"I will not, so let her be gone!"

At that moment, she took the bread and hurled it at the girl's head, and it rolled right down. The girl picked it up, and took it to her again, and said, "Take it, good Fate, and change my fate."

But she spurned her, and threw stones at her.

At last, with the pleading of the one Fate and the other, the girl's persistence in giving her the bread, the evil Fate was obliged to say, "Give it to me," and snatched it.

The girl stood trembling before her, afraid she was about to throw it at her again, but the Fate held on to it, and said, "Attend to what I say! Take this ball of thread," (and she threw her a ball of silk thread), "and take good heed! You must neither sell it nor give it away, but when it is sought of you, you must demand its weight in gold. Go now about your business."

The girl took the ball of thread, and went back to the Queen. Now she was no more troubled.

In the neighboring land, the King was ready to wed, and the bride's dress still lacked a quantity of silk that must match. The people at the palace had been seeking far and wide for something to match. They had heard that in the neighboring kingdom there was a young woman who had a ball of silk thread. So they went and asked her to bring the thread with her to the bride's palace, so they might see if it matched the dress. When they got there, they put the ball of thread against the dress, and saw that it was one and the same. Then they asked how much she would take for it, and she replied that she would sell it only by weight. They brought up the scales and placed a quantity of gold pieces on the other side, but the scales never moved. They went on putting in pieces of gold, but in vain.

Then the Prince himself got on the scale, and then the silk was balanced, so the Prince said, "Since your silk weighs as much as I, then, for us to have the silk, you must have me."

And so it came about. The Prince married the Princess, and there was great joy; they lived well, and may we live even better.

·48· *The Sackmaker*

• ONCE THERE WAS a sackmaker who sang as he wove his net, and this is what he sang:

> I stopped it up myself.

Day and night he sang this song. One day the King came by and heard him sing:

> I stopped it up myself.

Again and again. He came by again at night and still the sackmaker was singing the same song:

> I stopped it up myself.

The King went into the workshop. When the sackmaker saw him, he put down his work and got up and took off his fez and crossed his hands on his breast. And the King said to him, "I have something to ask you, craftsman, but you must answer me truly."

"Let me know what it is, Lord King, and I'll answer you truly," replied the sackmaker.

"Day and night I come by your workshop and I hear you al-

ways singing the same song, 'I stopped it up myself.' Tell me
how you came to like this song, and why you sing that and no
other."

"Alas, Lord King, what am I to answer you? I sing my own
poverty. I am very poor and I begged and prayed God to show
me what my fate was that I was not able to go forward in life,
but remained so poor. So that night (the night I said my prayer
to God), when I fell asleep, I dreamed that I was in a place
where there were a thousand springs. Some ran like rivers, and
some ran like brooks, some ran so that the pipe could not hold
the water, and some ran little, some ran much, some had one
pipe and some two, some three, and some even more, and some
only dripped, plop, plop, plop. And I asked a man, 'What are
these springs?' And he told me that they were the fates of every
man. 'Since it be so,' I said to him, 'which is my own fate?' He
showed it to me, and I saw that it only dripped. I thought the
pipe must be stopped up and so I stuck a little piece of wood in
it to unstop it. But I stopped it up even worse, for it did not even
drip after that. 'Ah,' said I, 'I stopped it up myself.' And with
that yearning I woke up and made a song of the words and
I sing it night and day and bewail my ill fate."

The King went away without saying anything. The next evening, he sent round a pie in a piedish by a servant, who said to
the sackmaker, "The King sends you greetings and this meat
pie."

The servant gave it to him and went away.

The sackmaker held the pie in his hands, and said to himself,
"And if we ate this pie tonight, what good would it do us?
There are five of us, it will not be enough. I'll take it to the
cookshop and ask the man there to give me two or three loaves
of stale bread and any cooked food he has left over, and that will
last us one or two days; what good will this pie do us?"

He did as he had said. He took the pie to the cookshop, and
said to the man there, "Here, I'll give you this pie and you give
me one or two loaves of stale bread and some cooked food for
me and my children to eat."

The man at the cookshop took the pie and gave him two or
three stale loaves and some cooked food that was left over, and

he took it home and he and his children had enough to eat for two or three days. Before he went home, the man at the cookshop cut a piece of the pie to taste it, and found its filling was all gold pieces! When he saw them, he was amazed—what sort of pie was this! He took out the gold pieces and tied them in a napkin and went joyfully home.

The next day, the King again came by and heard the sack-maker still singing the same song:

I stopped it up myself

That evening he sent him a goose stuffed with gold pieces. Again the sackmaker took it to the cookshop. The man there said so many flattering things when he saw it.

And the sackmaker said to him, "Now here's this goose; if we eat it tonight, what good will it do us? Tomorrow we won't have bread to eat. Here, take it and give me some loaves of stale bread and a deal of cooked food for me to feed my children with."

The man at the cookshop took up as many stale loaves and pieces of bread as he had left and filled a sack with them, ladled out a dish of cooked food left over from earlier, and gave them to a hireling of his to carry to the sackmaker's house. As soon as the sackmaker had gone, the man at the cookshop opened the goose. It was full of gold pieces and he was beside himself with glee. Early next morning, the King again came by the sackmak-er's workshop and again heard him singing the same song. The King wondered why he was still singing it and went in, and said to him, "How has the world been faring with you, craftsman?"

"How indeed, Lord King. I work at my craft to earn my bread," replied the sackmaker.

"How did you like the pie and the goose? Were they good?" the King then asked.

The other said to him, "Alas, my King, what can a pie and a goose avail five hungry mouths for one or two meals? If I eat goose today, I shan't even have bread to eat tomorrow. So I took both to the cookshop and exchanged them for cooked food and bread and we have been living off the like all these days."

When the King heard this, he said to himself, "It's certainly true you stopped your own luck."

The King went away back to the palace. On his way home, the sackmaker would pass over a bridge. So the King filled a bag with gold and gave it to two of his men, and said to them, "Go and keep watch on the sackmaker, but see you don't go too close. When he shuts up his shop to go home, you go on before and put this bag right in the middle of the bridge so that the sackmaker is sure to see it and pick it up. But be very sure no one else comes along and takes it."

When it was growing dark, the King's men took the gold and went to watch for the sackmaker. When he had put up the shutters of the shop, barred them and had come out to lock the door before leaving, the King's men went on before, left the bag of gold in the road over the bridge, and then they hid under the arches.

But when the sackmaker drew close to the bridge, he said aloud, "So many years have I been crossing this bridge with my eyes open, for once let me cross it with my eyes shut and see if I get across. If I fall off the bridge and am killed, at least let there be an end to a life so full of hard luck." (The King's men heard this.) The sackmaker then closed his eyes, crossed the bridge and never saw the bag of gold.

When he had gone some distance farther on, the King's men came out, picked up the gold and went to the King. When he saw the bag, the King asked them, "Why have you brought back the bag with the gold in it?"

"Were we to have gone away and left it on the bridge? When the sackmaker was nearly on top of the bag, he said, 'So many years have I been crossing this bridge with my eyes open, let me cross it for once with my eyes closed,' and he closed his eyes and crossed over and never saw the bag. He even came close to tripping over it."

"Oh, the Devil take him, the dolt! It's surely true he stopped up his spring of fate himself." And, early the next day, he called him, and said, "Look you, my good man, you have no sense at all. The pie and goose you treated very sensibly when you exchanged them, for you did not know what there was inside them. I had filled them with pieces of gold to make a rich man of you. But why, you silly fellow, did you close your eyes yesterday to cross the bridge with your eyes shut, so you never saw the bag of gold that I had had placed there and never picked it up and got to be rich?"

"I'm not to blame, Lord King, my fate willed me to do so."

Then the King sent one of his men to bring the man from the cookshop, to whom he said, "Why, liar and trickster, did you wrong this man? When you saw that the pie was full of gold and the goose as well, why did you not give him half the gold at least, instead of piling dry bread and the dregs of your cookpot on him? Go, posthaste, and bring him the gold pieces just as you found them, because I sent them to him myself."

He went and brought them and the King gave them to the sackmaker, and said to him, "You yourself stopped up your spring of fate. I wanted to unstop it for you in secret, but I couldn't for your own stupidity. Now take this gold and go and live in comfort and stop singing that song."

The poor sackmaker took the gold and became a merchant.

Part V
Jokes, Anecdotes, and
Religious Tales

The Riddle

• THERE WAS ONCE a king who had a daughter he wished to marry off. So as to get her a good husband, he thought he would devise a puzzle. He took two eggs, one from a white hen, and one from a black, and said, "Whoever can tell which is the white hen's egg and which the black hen's, will marry the Princess, but if he cannot, his head must come off."

Everyone got word of this. Princes from all the countries of the world tried, but none could solve the puzzle, and so he had their heads cut off.

Then a shepherd boy heard of the King's puzzle, and said to his mother, "Mother, I'll go, too, and try to tell the black hen's egg from the white hen's."

"Oh dear, my son, why should *you* go? So many clever princes have gone there and met their death. You are a peasant's son and only graze your sheep each day; are *you* to solve the puzzle?"

"I will go like them, Mother, and try my luck."

The poor mother saw very plainly that there was nothing to do but to set to work and bake him a pie and put enough rat poison in it to kill an ox. She put it in his woolen *tagari* [shoulderbag] and said, "Take your little dog, Pretty-pie, with you, and when you are hungry, eat this pie. First throw a piece to Pretty-pie, and then eat of it yourself."

So our shepherd boy set out for the great city. As he was on the way, he felt hungry, so he sat down by the side of the road and brought out the pie. He first cut off a piece and threw it to Pretty-pie, but, no sooner had she eaten it, than she at once stretched out her legs and died. Then he threw away the pie and sat there, staring at his dog that he had loved so much. Just as he was about to go on his way, he saw three ravens fly down and fall upon the body of the dog. But no sooner had they eaten of the dog, than they were poisoned and fell dead.

The boy took heed of all this, and went on his way. He walked on and on, the pangs of hunger growing fiercer as he went. He had nothing else in his *tagari*. He became so weak he could barely stand on his feet. While he was wondering what to do, he caught sight of a ruin—a deserted church. He went up to it, and saw different things lying about—paper, broken *kantelas,* and icons. But he saw nothing that he could eat. He looked around the other side, and saw a cow that had died with young. "What am I to do now?" he said. "I am so hungry."

He took a piece of glass from the broken windows of the church, opened the cow's belly with it, and took out the calf. He began to cut it up, but how was he to eat it raw? He gathered up the leaves of the psalters to build a fire with them and roast the calf. And now, how was he to light it, for he had no match to strike? He struck one stone against another, beat out a spark, lit the paper with it, and cooked the meat. Of course, the meat could not roast well over a fire of paper, so it was both roasted and unroasted when he ate it.

When he had eaten and somewhat stilled the pangs of hunger, he said, "Now that I'm thirsty, what's to be done? Where shall I find water to drink?"

He searched all around, but not a drop of water could he find. He happened to raise his eyes, and saw a *kantela* that held water topped with oil. He took it down, poured off the oil, and drank the water from the lamp. When he had eaten and drunk as best he could, he set out afresh for the city.

When he came to the King's palace, the soldiers saw him, and called, "What is it you want here?"

"I want," said he, "to solve the King's puzzle."

"Get away with you, dolt! Solve the King's puzzle, indeed!"

But he persisted, "What can it matter to you? I will solve it."

The King heard the noise outside, and ordered them to let him come in. When he saw the boy, the King shook his head and laughed.

"So many have come," he said, "and now you, too, poor boy, have come to solve the puzzle. Bring the two eggs."

The eggs were brought.

"Will you tell us, now, which is the white hen's egg, and which the black hen's?"

"I'll tell you, my Lord King, which is the white hen's egg, and which the black hen's, but first I'll ask you a riddle of my own, and, if your Highness can answer it, then I will answer yours."

The King laughed again, he thought it so comical.

"Have you such a riddle as I shall not be able to answer?"

"Be that as it may," said he, "if you solve it, well and good. If you do not, then I will not solve yours."

"Let's hear it, then," said the King.

So the shepherd boy said:

> The sweet pie finished off the Pretty-pie;
> Poor Pretty-pie, dead,
> Three black fellows fed;
> I have eaten what's born and what's still in the bellykin,
> Roasted on alphabet letters;
> I have drunk water that's neither of earth nor yet of the
>   welkin.

"Beshrew me!" said the King. "Who told you such a riddle?"

"No one told it me," said he. "I thought it out in my own brain."

The King then called his counselors, but not one could solve the riddle. And because he saw that the boy was so clever, the King decided to give him his daughter in marriage, only he begged him to explain the riddle, that he might know what it meant.

"I was a poor shepherd boy," he answered, "and my mother did not want me to come here. But when she saw that my mind was made up, she made me a pie and I gave a piece first to my little dog. No sooner had the dog eaten it, than she died, and the ravens that ate of my dog died, too. Then I became very hungry. I could barely stand for hunger. I set out to see what there was to eat. I found a church, and near it, a dead cow. I took the calf out of her belly, and ate it. But, so as to eat it, I cooked it over a fire of psalter leaves. And the water I drank was neither of the earth nor of the welkin, but the water of a *kantela* hanging in the church."

And so it was that the shepherd boy wed the King's daughter and there was great joy and revelry at the marriage feast. His old mother came and stayed at the palace and ate chicken, while before in her village she had eaten only bread and onion.

·50· *What Is the Fastest Thing in the World?*

• ONCE THERE WERE two brothers who ran a farm together. One of the two was clever, the other was a dullard.

One day the clever one said to the dullard, "Brother, I want to divide the farm between us."

"Divide away," said the unfortunate dullard.

So on a certain day the clever one divided the farm and chose his part. The field was not all good—half was first-rate land and the other was barren. The clever one chose and took the good half and left the useless half, the barren land, to the dullard.

The unhappy dullard had also wanted the good half, and as there was nothing else he could do about it, he went to see the King. The King at once sent a soldier for the other brother, so they might come to a compromise, but not they! Both wanted the good half. So then he bade them divide the field in another way, so that each should get some of the good and some of the bad, but, again, not they! Both wanted the good half. When he saw them so determined, the King had the idea of setting them a riddle and whichever of the two could solve it, would take the good land. So he said to them, "So you may quarrel no more, I'll set you a riddle and whoever can solve it, will take the good land."

Both said yes. Oh, the clever one was in great spirits! He said to himself, "My brother is a dullard. I shall solve the riddle."

So the King said to them, "I want you to tell me what is the fastest thing in the world. I'll give you eight days to think about it."

Off they went to their homes. The clever one began to think. Said he, "It'll be this; it'll be that; it'll be the other." Anything in the world could be it.

The poor dullard was not up to thinking anything. So he worried and sighed all day and all night.

He had a daughter that had no match in the world for beauty, and she asked him, "What is it, Father, that makes you sigh?"

So he told her the story, how the King had set them a riddle to solve, and whoever solved it would take the good land.

"And what is this riddle, Father?"

"He wants us to tell him the fastest thing in the world."

"Do not distress yourself, Father," she said, to him, "and, the day you have to go, I'll tell you how to answer and win."

The man breathed again. The days passed, and the time came for them to go to the King. Then he went and asked his daughter, and she told him, "You will say, Father, that the fastest thing in the world is the mind."

So they went to the palace, the King put his question. The clever one said that the fastest thing in the world is the bird.

"Wrong," said the King to him.

"The horse, then."

"Wrong," said the King again. "Now you," he said to the other.

"O King, live for ever," said the dullard, "the fastest thing in the world is the mind, for while we are here, the mind may be in America."

"Right," said the King," you have found the answer to that one; I'll set you another. You shall tell me what is the heaviest thing in the world."

The clever one said to himself, "I'll find the answer to that one, at least." So he again went home and began to think.

The poor dullard was sure of himself. "I've my daughter who will tell me," he said to himself. So he told her that he must know what was the heaviest thing in the world.

So his daughter said that on the day they were to go she would tell him. The poor girl was afraid for him. "He might," she thought, "say it out loud, for my uncle to hear and tell the King and win."

The eight days that the King had allowed them had again passed and he went and asked her. She said to him, "Go and tell him that the heaviest thing in the world is fire. And if he asks you why, tell him it is because no one can lift it."

They set out for the palace, the King put his question. First, the clever one said that the heaviest thing in the world was emery stone.

"Wrong," said the King to him.

"Iron."

"Wrong again."

Then said the other, "The heaviest thing in the world is fire."

"And why?" the King asked him.

"Because we cannot lift it."

"That's right," said the King. "But I shall set you another, and when the eight days are up, you shall come again and then your case will be over. You shall tell me what thing we need most in the world."

So they again went off home. The clever one again fell to thinking. He said to himself: "What is it? What is it not? It's money!"

The other one told his daughter about it. "I'll tell you, Father," said she.

So when the time again came he went and asked her, and she told him, "You will say that the thing we need most in the world is ground, and when he asks you why, you will say that if there were no ground, what should we stand on?"

They again went to the palace. The other said that the thing we need most in the world is money.

"Wrong," said the King.

"Bread."

"Wrong."

Then the poor dullard said the thing we need most in the world is ground.

"Right," said the King. "Now the good land is yours."

So then there was nothing the other could say about it.

Before they left, the King took the winner into another room of the palace, and said to him, "I want you to tell me who has been giving you the answers you've brought here."

"Alone I did it," he told him.

"You're not telling the truth," said the King. "I want you to tell me who gave them to you. Now you have nothing more to fear. The farm is yours."

So the man sat down and told him he had a daughter and that she had given him the answers.

"Bring her to the palace tomorrow," he said to him, "for me to see."

The poor old man called his daughter and they went to the palace. The moment the King saw her he was amazed at her beauty. At once he made her the proposal to become his wife.

"I never heard the like," said the maiden. "Your Grace a King, and I a poor girl!" said she. "Never!"

"What can that matter to you, as I want you for my wife? One thing only I ask of you. We shall have a paper drawn up, which you will sign to say you will never meddle in my affairs; if you ever do, you shall choose whatever you wish to be yours in my palace, and go away."

So they agreed, the paper was drawn up, and the maiden signed it. The wedding took place and they lived happily together. The girl did not meddle in the King's affairs and the King was pleased.

One day when a few years had gone by, the Queen was sitting at the window and she saw a man coming along with his loaded donkey. Suddenly, his donkey fell down dead in its tracks. The peasant ran hither and thither to fetch help. Just then, another came by with his donkey and saw that the dead donkey had a new packsaddle. So he took off his donkey's old packsaddle and took the new one. The two peasants began to quarrel—the one said that the new packsaddle was his, the other said it was his.

The Queen had seen the wrongful deed from her window above, and called, "Let the peasant with the dead donkey take the new packsaddle that was his." And so it was done, since the Queen had given the order.

The king heard how the Queen had delivered judgment over the packsaddle and went to the palace in anger and at once said to the Queen, "Make ready to leave, as you did not keep to our agreement."

But the clever Queen said to him, "I will leave at once, only let us eat together this evening."

"Very well," he said to her. But when they were eating, the Queen put a sleeping draught in the wine and no sooner did he drink than he fell asleep. At once she ordered the royal carriage to be brought. When it had been brought, she ordered them to pick up the King as he slept and put him inside, and off they went to her father's house.

When her father saw her, he was afraid and asked her, "What's amiss, my child?" But she told him that the King was sleeping and he must be quiet. Then they picked up the King and put him in the bed. Next morning, when the King awoke, he looked all about him, for he did not know where he was. He clapped his hands and at once the Queen appeared and said to him, "What is your will, Majesty?"

"I want to know where I am."

"You are in my father's house."

"And who gave you permission to bring me here?"

Then she showed him the paper they had drawn up to say that she might choose for her own whatever she wanted from the palace, and then she said to him, "I wanted neither your riches nor your possessions, but you only I wanted and you I took."

Then the King laughed, and said to her, "Well done! You are cleverer than I am, and from now on I give you the right to judge all my affairs."

So they got up and went back to their palace

and lived and expired
and children and grandchildren sired.

· 51 · *Princess Plumpkins* (*Pachoulenia*)

• ONCE UPON A TIME there were two kings whose lands neighbored upon each other. Now one of them had three male children and the other three girls. The King with the sons took pleasure in teasing the other King about this, and so it was that when they came across each other on their way to the Kings' club, he would say, "Good morning, Lord King, with your three fillies!" The other unhappy man hardly knew what to answer. He grew melancholy and would not eat or anything.

One day, when this had gone on for a long while, his youngest daughter, Plumpkins, who was very sharp-witted, asked him what the matter was.

"It's nothing, my dear," he answered.

"How can it be nothing, Father? Either you tell me or I do

away with myself!" What, then, could the King do but tell her?
She burst into laughter. "What!" she said, "is that what's mak-
ing you sad? If he says it again, you say to him, 'Good morning,
Lord King, with your three colts!' "

The other two daughters, who had heard this exchange, began
to mock, "And is that why you are sad? We thought he had sent
you an emissary to ask for our hands in marriage, and you were
sad at parting with us!"

So the King did as Plumpkins had bidden him. The other
King (the one with the sons) was angry, "So!" he said, "so!" and
racked his brains for some difficult riddle to puzzle the other.

A few days later, he said to the other King, "I want you to
bring me a kilo of grain, already ground, that must both be flour
and not be flour. Either you do what I demand or I take your
best piece of land." The unhappy King "put on mourning." * He
told Plumpkins what had happened. "But is that all that troubles
you, Father dear? Whatever he says to you, come straight and
tell it to me, and never fret."

And immediately Plumpkins gave an order to a hundred car-
penters to cut planks and scrape them down to sawdust and to
put the sawdust in bags. Then they took them to the other King.
When he saw so many full bags just as he had demanded, he
was flabbergasted.

"Hold hard," said he, "won't I set him a riddle to puzzle
him!" And, indeed, as they were on their way that evening to
the club where the Kings go, he said to Plumpkins's father,
"Now, Lord King, I want you to bring me a can of milk, that
must both be milk and not be milk, or else I take your best piece
of land!"

"It is well," said the King, all in a tremble, "I will look to it."
And he at once went home and told Plumpkins.

"Never fret, Father dear, put your trust in me. Order a great
number of horses to be put to work, and bring a bottle and fill it
with the froth from their lips and take it to him for milk." And
so he did. He took a milk can full of this froth to the other. And
no sooner did the King (the one with the sons) clap eyes on it
than he became as wild as a hornet.

* Became sad, melancholy.

"But who is it that helps you to come out the winner?" he said to the other.

"It is my daughter, Lord King, Plumpkins is her name."

"*She!*" said he, "a woman, to vie with *me?* Bring her to dine with us tomorrow."

And, indeed, at midday on the next day, Plumpkins dressed herself and combed her hair and went there with her father. But, once at table, she let no food pass her lips.

At this the King asked, "Why do you not eat?"

And to this she replied, "Your Majesty, the dishes you have here are not to my liking. I am accustomed to eggs done on the spit. Please order the cook to do me two."

So the King gave the order to the cook, but how was the unhappy man to set about roasting eggs on the spit! It could not be done. So the King, in some distress, had to tell her that such a thing could not be done.

"Very well, your Majesty," said Plumpkins. "Whatever you asked of us was done, yet you cannot bring me two eggs done on the spit. Think no more about it. I can very well have nothing at all to eat."

Whereupon the King desired to find some means of pleasing her. "Tell me, my Lady," he said, "what gift I may make you."

Then Plumpkins said:

> A lettuce, made of thirty more, of thirty lettuce made,
> And on the lettuce let there be gold lettuces arrayed.

At this the King was altogether dismayed. "But how am I to gratify your wish, if what you ask is impossible?"

"Then, your Majesty," said Plumpkins, "I have beaten you."

"No, indeed!" said the King. "I must have one more try. You take my youngest son, who is the worthiest young man in the kingdom, and try to cross the great river. Whichever of the two crosses first to the other side and brings me back the Parrot of Happiness will be the winner. If my son is the one that brings the bird to me, I shall have your head cut off. If you should bring it, I will make my son your bridegroom."

To this Plumpkins most readily agreed. The next morning she

went to her father's stable and ordered the best horse to be saddled. Then she dressed herself like a horseman and at the hour
of midday rode down to the river. There she found the other
King's son, trying to empty the river with a teaspoon in order to
get over to the other side. When she saw this, she laughed until
she could laugh no more. Then she gave her horse a stroke with
the crop and leapt into the river. In a very short while she was
across. But now the hardest part was to come. The Parrot of
Happiness was guarded by a fierce dragon, while the Prince who
owned the bird watched all night long lest it be stolen, for when
the parrot opened its beak, gold fell from its mouth. Plumpkins
gave the dragon a potion to make it sleep; then she went to the
Prince and told him (it seems) that she desired to see the Parrot.
The Prince consented with pleasure. But while they were both
shut up in the room, Plumpkins dealt him a blow and knocked
him down. Then she seized the bird and made off. She left a
paper stuck on the door, saying, "I was a woman, and tricked
you!" Then she mounted her horse and crossed the river. The
Prince was still standing there, trying to empty away the water
with a spoon, so Plumpkins ran with the Parrot to find his father
at the palace. The instant the Parrot saw the King, it shot out a
shaft of flame from its mouth that went straight at the King and
burned him to ashes. And so Plumpkins married his son.

·52· *The Vinegrower, the Priest, the Frankish Priest, and the Chotzas*

• A CERTAIN VINEGROWER went to his vineyard and there found a
chotzas, a Frankish priest, and a priest of our own Church picking the grapes.

The vinegrower thought he would teach them a lesson, one by
one. First of all, he caught the chotzas.

"Just tell me this, you filthy chotzas," said he to him, "who
told *you* to pick the grapes? Never mind *them,* at least they're
Christians." And there and then, he beat the chotzas black and
blue.

When the other two priests heard the vinegrower say, "Never mind them, at least they're Christians," they said to themselves, "That's good, we've got away with it."

When he had finished with the chotzas, he went up to the Frankish priest, and began: "Here, you churl of a Frankish priest, who gave you permission to come to my vineyard? The other's our own priest, so, damn it, that doesn't count." (Now our own priest was very glad to hear this.)

Pata-kioutou! there and then, he settled the Frankish priest's hash for him, too. "As for you, Father," he said to our own priest, "what am I to do with you? Is this what you used to teach us every time, in the Church?" He let *him* have it, too, and in this way carried out his duty with discretion.

·53· *Eggs*

• IN THOSE DAYS there was a captain who had a sailing ship. Once, he came into port and went to a tavern to eat. He went inside, and asked the tavern keeper, "Have you anything cooked for me to eat?"

"I have not, my poor friend. All the dishes I had have been eaten. I might have two or three fried eggs; will they do you? Shall I bring them?"

The captain said yes and sat down to eat. As he was about to eat, a sailor came along and told him they were weighing anchor, as a wind had come up. So the captain left the food and ran straight back to his ship. He went aboard, and they weighed anchor, but could not steady the ship. God and Saint Nicholas helped, and saved the ship from the storm.

It was five or six years before he entered that port again. Once there, the captain went to pay for the eggs as he had had it in mind to do. He had remembered that he still owed for them.

The tavern keeper gave him an astronomical bill, saying, "Those eggs, if I had sat the hen on them, would have hatched into four birds, two cocks and two hens."

He took him to court, since, egg for egg, bird for bird, the tavern keeper would take his ship and still leave the bill unpaid.

The captain roamed about in a daze—to lose his ship for four eggs! He went to another tavern where all the old men gathered; there was a criminal lawyer there. He saw that the captain was upset, he found out what his case was, and went and sat beside him.

"Captain, order me up a cup of wine, and worry no more. I'll get you your boat back tomorrow."

The captain gave the order and the cup of wine at once was brought for the lawyer. He drained the cup and wrote out a brief, which he took to the court. The brief named him as lawyer.

The next day dawned. It struck nine, ten, eleven o'clock; it was nearly noon. All those who were bringing suit had assembled, and still our lawyer had not come. At about a quarter of twelve, there he was, coming to the fore! He sang as he came.

The judge said, "Oh, well done, dear man! You've kept us waiting here so long, we're all dying of hunger!"

"Oh, let me be, brother. I bought five *okades* of faba beans yesterday, and sent them home to my wife. She took it into her head to cook them all at once. We ate them all day yesterday, and again this morning, and still had a lot left over. I took the rest out to plant them, and that is why I wasn't here on time."

The tavern keeper spoke up, and asked him, "However can a man plant cooked beans?"

So the lawyer answered him, and said, "However can chicks hatch from cooked eggs?"

The lawyer lost no time in winding up his case and delivering verdict: "Captain, you had four eggs, four piastres, and two for the bread, six piastres. Pay him, and let him go about his business!"

The judge agreed with him and the captain won back his ship. As a reward, the captain paid the tavern keeper to give the lawyer drink for as long as there was wine in the barrel.

·54· *The King and the Basket Weaver*

(*Or, How with One Zwanziger a Man May Pay Off an Old Debt, Lend Money at Interest, and Feed Eight Mouths.*)

• THERE WAS ONCE a king who every evening would go about in disguise, observing how the people did in his kingdom. One evening as he went about, he heard a lyre being played on the other side of a door, and a merry noise of singing and dancing. He opened the door and went in. "A very good evening to you," said he to the folk. "Welcome," they answered, "sit you down." They gave him a tidbit to eat and the *bourikia* to drink wine from. He was somewhat revolted at this, but he could do nothing but eat the tidbit, drink wine from the *bourikia,* and wish them well. Then he set himself to asking the man who played the lyre what work he did, how life treated him, whether he earned much, and suchlike.

"Good sir," the other said to him, "I am a weaver of baskets and, God be praised, I jog along as best I can. I make one Zwanziger a day, and with this I contrive to pay off an old debt, lend money at interest, and feed eight mouths."

The King was bewildered at this, for he could not get it clear in his head how this basket weaver could, on only one Zwanziger a day—or fifty lepta, if you will, for such was the value of the Zwanziger in those days—contrive to do so much. So he said to him, "Tell me," said he, "how you contrive to do it. Is your debt a large one," he said, "and do you truly lend money at an interest?"

Then the basket weaver smiled, for he saw that the King had understood nothing of all this, and he took him by the arm and led him to another room in the house and there showed him an old man and an old woman sleeping on a bed. "Behold!" he said, "the old debt that I repay. That is my father and mother who bore me and raised me, and now I pay off that old debt, or, if you will, I repay in their old age what they did for me in their youth."

Then he ushered him back into the room they had been in at first and showed him four children making merry, and said, "Behold! there is the money I lend at interest. Those," he said, "are my children, and in feeding them now, I lend at interest, for when I grow old they will repay what I did for them by looking after me. I feed," he went on, "eight mouths: two, if you will, my wife's and my own; four, my children's, make six; and two, my father's and mother's, make eight."

Then the King, in his turn, took the other by the arm and led him into a corner, and with no one by to see, unbuttoned his coat and showed him the royal crown hanging at his breast. The poor basket weaver was dumbfounded at the sight and knew not what to say to his having had the King himself in his house. But the King bade him take courage, and said, "Never fear, for I shall do you no harm. Only you must not tell any man what you have told me if you do not see my face; otherwise, if you tell and do not see my face, be sure that I will have your head."

"I hear and obey, Lord King, may you live for ever!" replied the poor basket weaver, much afraid. The King then bade farewell to all, and took his leave.

The next day, he summoned his Council of Twelve, and said to them, "If you are worthy men, tell how a man, with the one Zwanziger a day that he earns, can pay off an old debt, lend money at an interest, and feed eight mouths."

He gave them the space of three days, and the one among them who should find the answer he would make his Grand Vizier. So then they put on their thinking caps and thought and thought, but could not find the answer, till at last they put their heads together and agreed that the King could not have thought this out alone, but had heard it in the place where he had been the night before. So they ran about and went here and there, asking at this, that, and the other house, "Would a certain man have come here last evening, with such and such a look about him (so to speak)?" but nothing did they discover, until at last, after turning and turning about, hither and yon, would you believe it! they came to the basket weaver's house.

"Would a man have come here last evening," they asked the basket weaver, "with such-and-such an air (so to speak)?"

"Yes," said the basket weaver, "and it was the King (may he live for ever!) who condescended to come into my poor house and keep us company a while."

At this they all drew a long breath. "Would you," said they, "have told him thus and thus?"

"Yes," said he, "I did."

"Will you not tell us, too," said they, "what it was?"

Said he, "I may not, for he commanded me to tell it to no one."

"Tell us," said they, "and take ten pounds (let us say) for your trouble."

"I will take nothing," said he. "Whatever you say, and whatever you give me, I can never tell you."

"We beg and pray you," said they to him, "and take twenty pounds—thirty—take fifty—a hundred—two hundred—three hundred—five hundred—here, take a thousand!"

When the basket weaver saw the thousand pounds, he said to himself, "Good man, if I take these thousand pounds, my children could live right royally. And, as for my head, well and good! As long as my children can have a happy life, let me lose my head." So he up and took the thousand pounds, and told them all.

Then they ran to the King and gave him the answer. The King knew that they could not have found it without help and that the basket weaver must have told them. So the King's order was given for the basket weaver to be brought before him.

"Did I not tell you," said the King, "to say nothing to anyone, unless you saw my face? Now you will get your deserts and your head will come off." And thereupon the block was made ready for the beheading.

"Lord King, may you live for ever," said the basket weaver then, "you commanded me to say nothing unless I saw your face. Yet I did not see it but once, nor only twice, but a thousand times did I see it," and he laid out in a row the thousand pounds he had been given. "Behold!" said he, "is that not your face? And that? And that? Behold your face a thousand times over, not once alone." (For, of course, he had been given a thousand pounds and had seen a thousand faces of the King engraved upon them.)

And then the King marveled at the basket weaver's cleverness and said to him, "You are the one most fit to be my counselor and Grand Vizier." And he dismissed his Council of Twelve, made the basket weaver his Grand Vizier, and our good basket weaver was Grand Vizier to the end of his days. He lived a happy life, and may we live happier.

·55· Otto's Astronomer, Watchmaker, and Doctor

• WHEN OTTO CAME to Greece, he sent to Europe for an astronomer, a watchmaker and a doctor to come and teach the Greeks. They got off the boat at Patras, got on a horse, and set out for Athens. Night fell while they were on the road, and they stayed at a mill. The miller cooked them a *bougatsa* and a chicken and brought them good wine. They sat down and ate. For his part, the miller took the *bobota* off the fire, set it down piping hot and began to eat. The doctor stared hard at him.

When he saw the way the miller was eating, he said to the others, in their own language: "You see him? He'll burst tonight with the food he's had. We'll tell him to make our beds outside, and let his own people come at sunup and find him."

So they told him to put their beds outside. Said he, "My lords, do not sleep outside, for it will rain hard in the night." The astronomer went outside, looked at the sky, and said, "He doesn't know what he's talking about. Let him put our beds outside."

But that night there was a heavy rainstorm; so they knocked on the miller's door, and he let them in. After a short while, they called to him to get up and help them make ready to leave. "Go to sleep," said he to them, "it's not time yet. It's two o'clock." But they insisted. He lit the lamp, and they looked at their watches and saw the miller was right.

The watchmaker asked him, "How comes it you can tell the time?"

"Well, now, my donkey will just have brayed," said he.

The astronomer asked, "How comes it you knew it was going to rain?"

"This afternoon my pigs were rolling and squabbling," said he to him.

"And how did you contrive to eat all that *bobota?*" asked the doctor.

"I put my head under the tap, drank water, and got it down that way."

Then the foreigners turned aside and said among themselves, "What business have we here with the Greeks, whose pigs are astronomers, whose donkeys are watchmakers, and whose taps are doctors?" And they went back the way they had come.

·56· *The Priest's Son and the Sickles*

• ONCE A PRIEST fell ill and sent his son out with the farmhands to reap. That night, when the son came home, the priest asked him, "Well, my son, have you reaped a fair yield?"

"Oh, Father, if you knew the trick I played them," the son told him with pride. "I hid the sickles, and they've been all day looking for them!"

·57· *The Baldchin and the Drakos*

• ONCE THERE WAS a shepherd who had a great many sheep and goats, and would have made a lot of cheese, but when he tried to get on with the cheese making, a *drakos* would come and eat it all up.

One day it happened that a tipsy baldchin came upon him in the pasture. So they sat down and ate together, and each told the other his troubles. When the baldchin heard that a *drakos* came and ate the cheese, he said to the shepherd, "What would you give me for killing the *drakos?*"

The shepherd answered, "As I stand to lose my income, and earn nothing by all this, I'll give you half my sheep, but know that tomorrow is his day for coming here."

"Be easy on that score," said the baldchin, "think nothing of that."

The next day, when they woke, the shepherd said to him, "Hello! Are you ready? Here he comes, this minute!"

The baldchin had forgotten all about it. So when the shepherd told him, "Thus and thus, you gave your word you would kill the *drakos,*" he beat his brains, thinking what to do, for he had given his word and did not want to go back on it, but he was afraid to fight the *drakos.*

He beat and beat his brains a long while, and then he said to the shepherd, "Go and bring about twenty-five flower cheeses, and cast them here and there, in the pasture and on the path."

The shepherd did as the baldchin had told him, and sat down to wait. In a little while, there came a sound like thunder, a big noise. Said the shepherd to the baldchin, "Look out, he's coming! That big noise was his footfall."

When he drew near, the baldchin stood before him, and shouted with all his might, "Watch out, get away, or I'll squeeze you to pulp, as I do these stones."

He picked up a flower cheese off the ground, squeezed it between his hands, and ate it.

When the *drakos* saw him squeeze the stones and eat them, he was afraid. He took up a stone and tried it, but to no avail.

"Let's see you squeeze another," he said to the baldchin.

"Here you are, then," said the baldchin, and he picked up another cheese, and squashed it to a pulp.

"Heaven forbid," said the *drakos,* "don't eat me, and I'll take you to my palace, where I and my forty brothers will make you our master."

"Come here, then," said the baldchin, "bend down and pick me up." The *drakos* lifted him onto his shoulder, and they were at the palace in no time.

No sooner had they arrived than the other brothers got wind of the baldchin, and called, "Why, there's a smell of human flesh. Bring it for us to eat."

"For Heaven's sake!" said the *drakos* to them, "don't let him hear you, or he'll squash us all to pulp. Don't be misled by his size, he can eat stones. Thus-and-thus happened to me in the pasture I went to." And he told them what the baldchin had done in the pasture.

That evening they sat down to eat at table. The baldchin saw that they did not take the meat off the bones or anything, but crunched it all up together and swallowed it down. He ate his meat, and the bones he secretly slipped down his neck so that they fell into the bosom of his shirt. The time came for them to drink wine. He saw that they had gourds for glasses.

"If I were to drink only half of that," he said to himself, "I should be blind drunk." So he said to the *drakoe*, "For your own good, give me only a small glassful, because I get mean when I'm drunk, and if I drank a few of those gourds, I wouldn't leave a house standing, nor a man, for that matter."

"Oh, Heaven forbid, master, drink as you please."

The next day, at dawn, they went out to play ball. The *drakoe* had a ball that weighed forty *cantaria* and were wont to go into the open country to play to see who could throw it farthest. One picked it up and threw it a mile, another threw it two miles: all had a turn, and some threw farther and some threw not so far.

When it came to the baldchin's turn, the *drakoe* said to him, "Come on, baldchin." Although he could not move it, the baldchin bent down, and placed his hands on the ball, and all at once raised a shout:

> 'Ware, Constantinople, and Smyrna, beware.
> The baldchin will now shoot his bolt through the air.

When the *drakoe* heard Constantinople and Smyrna, they cried, "Don't, for Heaven's sake, we've got sisters in Smyrna and Constantinople, don't kill them. Enough, enough!"

The next day, they needed to fetch in water. So the baldchin said, "Bring the barrel and the rope, and I'll go and fetch it."

"No, no, master," they said. "There's no need, we'll fetch it."

"No," said the baldchin, "I want to go, for I'm tired of sitting and doing nothing."

So they brought him the barrel and the rope, but the rope alone was too heavy for him to lift!

So he said to a *drakos,* "Pick them up and take them to the spring and fill them, for I will not deign to lift them myself."

One of the *drakoe* picked them up and took them to the spring and left them. Then the baldchin went and after a thousand tries wound the rope round and round in the spring, and then sat down to wait, for there was nothing else he could do! He knew they would come looking for him.

That evening, when he heard the footfall of the *drakos* who had come to see what had happened to the master, he began to sing out, " 'Way, haul away, we'll haul away, Joe!" and made as if he were pulling on the rope.

"For Heaven's sake, master!" said the *drakos,* "you'll spoil the spring, and we shan't have any water. What was it you wanted to do?"

"Well," said the baldchin, "I mean to take out the spring, and put it near the palace, so that we don't have to come here every day with that silly little barrel that I wouldn't deign to lift with my little finger."

"No, no, master, let me lift it."

"Come and lift it, then, and lift me up on it."

The *drakos* picked up the barrel and the rope, and lifted up the baldchin, too, and they went back to the palace.

Next day, they went out to cut wood. The baldchin got them to carry the rope and the axe for him. They left him in a forest, and then spread out, one going this way, the other that. He again set to work and tied trees a-many with the thick rope, and sat down.

When he saw them at a distance coming to look for him (for he had tarried), he began to cry out, "Haul, haul away!"

"God forbid, master, you'll ruin the forest."

"No, indeed, I'll stay and load 'em on my shoulders, one by one, till I've a load like yours," said he.

"There's no need, master, leave 'em be, we'll bring them along." So he tricked them yet again, and they hoisted the wood and put him atop, and so went back to the palace.

Many days went by in this way, until he grew weary of it and was afraid, to boot, lest they find him out; so he said to them, "Let one of you lift me up and take me to my house and, when it suits me, I'll come back in a while and look you up."

"Very well, master," said they to him, for they, too, wished to be rid of him.

So one of them lifted him onto his shoulder, and off they went. When they drew near to the village, he was afraid lest anyone should see him and call out and the *drakos* might know him for what he was and eat him; so he said to the *drakos*, "Put me down now, and come along behind me in secret, so that I can show you my house."

When they came to the house, he put the grindstone down on the floor and turned it, whirr! whirr!, and said to the *drakos*, "Watch out, I'm going to eat you. See here, I'm sharpening my teeth," and he turned the grindstone very fast, "and don't any of you go and worry the shepherd any more, or I'll eat you all up!"

The *drakos* ran off, looking behind him for fear he was being followed. From then on, no *drakos* bothered the shepherd. The baldchin got half the sheep as the shepherd had promised him, and he lived well, and may we live better than he.

· 58 · *Eli*

· ONCE UPON A TIME there was a fellow called Eli who had taken his wheat to be ground at the mill. He got up on his mule and went off to fetch it. After fetching it, he stopped and unloaded his mule and left it to graze while he lay down to sleep. Another came along with his ass laden with maize. When he saw Eli asleep, he took his wheat, loaded it onto the mule, and left him the ass with the maize. He took off Eli's straw hat and put his own cap on his head, he took off Eli's shoes and put his own clogs on his feet, and he took his mule and the wheat, and went.

A while later, Eli awoke. He looked around for his mule, and saw the ass. He opened the sacks, and found maize. He put his hand on his head, and felt the cap. He looked for shoes, and found clogs on his feet.

"Here!" said he, "I'm not Eli! I had a mule, wheat, a straw hat, shoes!"

He went to his wife, and called to her, "Eli's wife, Eli's wife! Where's Eli?"

"He went to the mill."

"And what beast did he have with him?"

"He had a mule."

"What crops did he have?"

"Wheat."

His wife knew him by his voice, for it was night when he called to her.

"Come along, husband, what goes on there? Why don't you come up into the house?"

"Oh no, I'm not Eli—I never wore clogs, or had an ass."

But his wife came down, opened the door to him, and they lived well; may we live even better.

·59· *Loading the Ass*

• THERE WAS A MAN came down to Chora to buy. He bought almost sixty *okades* of merchandise, loaded his ass with it, and mounted. On the way, he bought twenty-five *okades* of wheat, had it put in a sack and hoisted it onto his own shoulder as he mounted the ass. But the ass would not budge.

When the village people saw this, they said to him, "How can you put such a load on that animal and then sit on him?"

He said to them, "Are you so blind you can't see I'm carrying twenty-five *okades* on my own shoulder?"

·60· *The Miser of Castro*

• A MISER, an inhabitant of Castro,* once gave a piece of cloth to an artisan to make him a cap. He asked him, "How much will it

* Formerly the capital town of Chios.

be? The artisan told him, "Ten piastres." Said the miser of Castro, "No, that is too dear. I'll give you ten piastres for making me two." Said the artisan, "I will." Then the miser said, "Will you make me four?" Said the artisan, "I will." "Will you make me five, six. . . . ten? For the same price as two?" The artisan agreed to make him ten caps from the same cloth for the same price as two.

The next day, the artisan brought him ten little caps, as small as small. "What!" said the miser of Castro, "those would fit an infant. How do you expect me to wear them?" The artisan replied, "How did you tell me to make them, good sir? Did you not tell me to cut ten out of the same cloth?" "Yes, but did I tell you to cut them so small? Oh, let me at him!" So, thereupon, they came to blows, and all the little caps got torn into tiny shreds.

.61. *The Cowardly Chiots*

• THERE WAS A GREAT BATTLE, and of three thousand, only three remained. The first hid in a tree, the second on a *doma* [rooftop], and the third behind a wall. Regiment upon regiment of Bashi-Bazooks came by, but none saw them hiding.

One Bashi-Bazook at the rear knocked his pipe out on the tree. The man in the tree took the pipe for a sword and thought he was going to cut the tree down, so he cried out to him, from up the tree, "Hold hard, my lord! I'm coming down." He came down and the Bashi-Bazook slew him. When he saw that his blood was black, he said, "How black the Giaour's blood is!"

The second, hidden on the roof, called out, "He would eat olives, my lord, though I told him not to." "Ah, so there you are, come down," said the Bashi-Bazook. When he came down, he slew him as well.

The third, who was behind the wall, said, "I'm better off for saying nothing," and the Bashi-Bazook slew him, too.

.62 . *The Chatterbox*

• ONCE UPON A TIME there lived an old man and an old woman. They were both good people, but the old woman was a great chatterer, none more so. She was also somewhat silly. Whatever her husband said to her, whatever went on in her house, she went at once and told the neighbors, and so the whole village heard.

Once, the old man went to the forest to cut wood. While he was cutting a log, the ground he was standing on gave way all of a sudden, and his legs went in deep. The old man was taken by surprise and struggled to get out of the pit. All at once, he felt some hard thing under his feet. He dug, and what should he find but a tub full of gold pieces!

"What luck!" he said, "but what am I to do with it, for my old woman will hear of it, and, as soon as she does, everyone will know."

He sat down at the root of a tree and began to think. He thought and thought and found what to do.

He got up and put the tub of gold pieces back in its place, covered it very carefully and went back to the village. He bought a hare and a big fish and returned to the forest. He hung the fish on a tree, and then went to the river where he had cast his nets, shut the hare up in the fish pot and put the fish pot in the nets among the reeds.

When he had done all this, he went back to his house and said to his wife, in a low voice, "Wife, a great piece of luck today!"

"What, husband? What happened? Tell me, so I can be glad, too!"

"Yes, but don't you go and tell it all over the village."

"I swear to you, I'll tell nobody. By the saint who sees us from the icon, I won't tell."

"As you've sworn, I'll tell you. In such-and-such a manner, wife," he said, very low, in her ear, "I've found a tub full of gold pieces."

"And why did you not bring it home?"

"I thought it was better for us to go and fetch it together."

The old woman made haste to get herself ready, tied on her kerchief, and followed her husband into the forest.

On the way, the old man said to his old woman, "You know what I heard, wife? I heard it said that in our time, the fish grow in the forests and the beasts of the wild lands live in water."

"Whatever nonsense is that, poor soul? Don't tell me you believe it."

"Don't *you?* Then come and see for yourself if it's true."

He took her to the tree where he had hung the fish.

"That's queer!" said the old woman. "How could the fish have grown up there?"

The old man made as if he could not believe his eyes.

"Well, how long are you going to stand there?" the old woman said to him. "Get up and cut off the fish and we'll have a fine soup this evening."

The old man climbed the tree and cut down the fish. Then they went on their way again and came to the river.

"I can see something hopping about in my fish pot," said the old man, and ran toward the patch of reeds. "Quick, come and see! A hare's in the fish pot!"

"So it was true what they told you. Take the hare out, we'll have it *stiphadho,*" said the old woman.

The old man got out the hare and they went on to the treasure. He unearthed the barrel and they took it home in secret. From that time on, the old man and woman were rich and began to live the pleasant life.

When some time had gone by, the old woman, who couldn't keep a secret, began to invite her neighbors to her house and spend a lot on evening entertaining. The old man was worried and scolded her.

"You've no call to scold," she told him. "I have as much right as you to the barrel and the gold."

At this, the old man lost patience. He knew that if they went on spending as his wife was spending, in a very short while they would be as poor as they were before, so he hid the barrel of gold. His wife got angry and went to the judge to complain.

"Sir Judge," she said, "my husband hasn't been the same since he found a barrel full of gold pieces. He no longer wants to go to work or get drunk. I want to take the gold pieces from him, so *you* give them into my keeping."

The judge told the clerk to call the old man and he also bade the village elders come to the hearing.

"Treasure? Green horses!" * the old man said to him.

"Don't pretend you don't know! Your wife came and complained to the judge that ever since you found the barrel of gold pieces, you've changed, you're a different man."

So there was nothing the old man could do but follow the clerk and appear in court. The elders were all gathered there.

"Begging your pardon, your worships. What treasure is this you want me to see about? My wife must have dreamed it. She'll have told you a lot of nonsense, as is her wont."

"Don't give me that, husband! I remember it all and I'll tell it as it happened. We went to the forest and we saw a fish hanging on the tree."

"Fish on the tree!" said the judge.

"Yes, Sir Judge. Then we went on to the river and we found a hare in the fish pot."

The village elders laughed fit to burst.

"Go away, my good woman," said the judge to her, "and let's have no more of your nonsense."

So the old man kept the treasure and no one ever believed his wife again.

.63. *Ninety-nine Hens and a Rooster*

• ONCE THERE WAS A COUPLE who had ninety-nine hens and a rooster. One evening they were talking, and the man said, "Wife, let's sell a few hens and get a little money."

Next day, a peddler called and the wife got all the hens and the rooster and gave them to him.

The peddler said to her, "I forgot to bring my money with me,

---

* An idiom like the American "Horsefeathers!"

so I'll leave you the cock as a pledge." She agreed. Then said the peddler, "Won't you let me have your donkey to carry the hens? How am I to get so many home?" "Take her, too," she said to him.

Then he asked her for her bitch dog to watch over the hens on the way. "Take her, too," she said to him.

At last he asked her for the gun that was hanging on the wall to protect himself from an enemy, should one appear on the way. "Take that, too," she said to him. And so she handed over them all.

When her husband came home that evening and they were sitting and talking, she told him she had handed over all the hens.

"I told you," said the husband, "to hand over a few hens."

"What matter? I let him have them all, and I let him have the donkey, too, to carry them, and the dog to watch over them, and your gun."

He was angry at this, but said nothing.

Next morning, he set off for a village, aiming, in his turn, to cheat some woman. On the way as he went, he came to a well and there found a girl drawing water.

"Where are you from?" asked the girl.

"From the Other World," he answered.

"Would you have seen my mistress's Takis?"

"Yes," said he. "We were together there. He is well, but he lacks money, shoes and clothes for his back."

The girl ran and told her mistress. When her mistress heard that there was a man from the Other World who had brought a message from her son, she took the man into her house, attended to his wants, and gave him money for Takis as well as clothes, shoes, and other things.

As soon as he had gone, the woman's husband, who was an officer, came home, and she told him that she had sent her son in the Other World clothes, shoes, and some money. He saw that a trickster had duped his wife, and made haste to mount his horse and chase after the thief. He caught him up near a mill. The thief saw that the officer was after him and he went into the mill and told the miller to hide, for they were after him. The miller ran and climbed a plane tree and hid in it. Inside the mill, the thief had covered himself in flour.

When he got to the mill, the officer dismounted and called the miller to hold his horse and at once ran to catch the one who was up in the plane tree. To get up the tree, he took off his boots and began to climb the plane tree. Then the thief put on the boots, mounted the horse, and away!

When he found out what had been done to him, the officer returned home, and said to his wife, "You, wife, gave money, clothes, and boots for Takis, but I gave my boots and horse; so our Takis can go on horseback."

.64. *The Sievemaker and the Ass*

• The sievemaker had a hen and told his wife to sit it on some eggs and hatch out chicks, and when these, too, grew to be hens, to sit them on eggs and hatch out more hens, and sell them to get money to buy a young ass.

"Ah," said his wife, "let me put our child to ride on it, so that I don't have to carry the weight of him on the back of my neck."

"No," said the sievemaker to her, "you will not put the child on the ass and hinder its growth."

"I will so."

"You will not."

"I will so."

"You will not."

The sievemaker got angry, seized his wife, and beat her black and blue.

.65. *Three* Pecheis *of Paradise*

• Once there was an emir who had a terrible sore. He called all the doctors, but not one could cure him, and each one gave him up for lost.

Then, one of his men said to him, "Lord, there is a doctor I know of, one Hobrius. Should we not summon him and see what he can do?"

"Fie upon you!" replied the emir. "Am I to employ a Jew? Have you ever witnessed any good come out of Jewry? That vile race!"

But at last he consented to see Hobrius, and when Hobrius had examined the sore, he said, "I will cure you, my Lord, I stake my life on it."

"By the Lord Allah, good Jew," answered the emir, "If you can cure me, I will give you something your race has never yet delighted in."

The doctor undertook the cure, gave the emir herbs to take, and brought him back to health.

"Well done, friend Jew!" said the emir. "By Allah, it's a pity you are not a Turk, a man such as you!"

"Alas, my Lord," replied the doctor, "what's to be done, when each man follows his own faith!"

"So be it, my friend," said the emir to him, "I will pray to the Prophet in your behalf, and give you a paper that you must guard well, for it will bring you to salvation."

So the emir went inside, and when he came out again, he gave the doctor a paper covered with Turkish writing. Hobrius, who in truth was expecting Turkish pounds, took the paper, shaking his head, and put it in his pocket, made a low bow, and left. Once outside, he betook himself to a tax collector, who was a friend of his, and showed him the emir's paper. The unhappy Jew had supposed it to be an order on the bank to give him money. When the tax collector read it, his eyes started open and he gasped and stared long at Hobrius.

"Good friend," he said, "how did you come, good friend, by this?"

"Thus and thus," Hobrius replied. "Emir Hamet gave it to me for curing his sore."

"God save you, friend Jew," said the Turk to him, "you are a lucky man, good friend!"

Hobrius jumped for joy at this, thinking he was going to get a potful of piastres. "But what is it?" he said to the tax collector, "what is written there, good sir?"

"Do you know what this is, friend? It's a title deed that gives you the right to three *pecheis* of Paradise, where no Jew has ever been."

The unhappy Hobrius all but went out of his mind, not knowing whether to laugh or cry, but he restrained himself before the Turk and said, "God grant that it be as you say, good sir, and may Adonay take years from me and give days to our Lord and master."

The Turk still held the paper and read it over and over, and, at last, after much thought, he said to him, "A favor would I ask of you, friend Jew," he said. "What will you do with all of three *pecheis*? Will you not give one *pechys* to me, for which I will pay you fifty pounds, if you will."

By this time, Hobrius was again in possession of himself and he now put on a special air. "What's that you say, good sir?" he said to the other. "Am I to sell one *pechys* of Paradise for fifty pounds? Who would sell it so cheap? It's not in my interest, good sir, begging your pardon."

"Come, come, good friend," said the Turk to him, "I'll give you a hundred pounds; if I had more, I'd give it, but I have not."

"Well, then," said Hobrius, "as a great favor to you, good sir, I'll stint myself of so much in the world-to-come."

The Turk counted out the hundred pounds. Hobrius took them and wrote on the back of the emir's paper that one *pechys* had been sold to such-and-such a man and would be handed over to him in the next world. Thus Hobrius was made glad, the Turk was made glad, and, at his devotions on Friday, he showed a friend of his a paper, signed by Hobrius, to the effect that he had sold him one *pechys* of room.

His friend then lost no time in running to seek out Hobrius. "I have a favor to ask of you," he said. "Sell me one *pechys* as well, for which I'll pay you two hundred pounds." "I cannot do so, good sir," said Hobrius, "how can I make one *pechys* of room in Paradise over to you?"

"I beg you, friend, I beseech you, and three hundred pounds I'll give you." And so Hobrius contrived to sell another *pechys*.

It came to the ears of other Turks, pashas, and beys who had carried out many crimes, and they came running to Hobrius to sell them the other *pechys*. Hobrius again put on a special air. "Where am *I* to go?" he said. "Would you put me out of Paradise? It is not just."

"Three hundred pounds!" said one. "Four hundred pounds!" said the other. "Five hundred pounds!" said one pasha, who was guilty of the greatest number of crimes.

"Well, then," said Hobrius, "for your sake, my Lord, I will go to hell for the rest of time, as a favor to you." And he sold the last *pechys*.

When the Grand Emir heard of it, he cried on him from the castle top. "The curse of Allah upon you, Jew!" he said to him. "What have you done, you dog? Would you sell the three *pecheis* of room I gave you? Ptui! May Allah's curse fall on you, Jew of Satan!"

"What would you have me do, my Lord?" Hobrius asked him. "I asked myself, what would there be for me in Paradise? Will there be another Hobrius like me, there? Only your lordship will be there and you would treat me like a dog, 'Ptui! here, Ptui! there, you Jew!' What sort of life would that have been for me?"

.66. *The Honest Wife*

• ONCE UPON A TIME there was a married couple. The wife was sitting at the window when a man came by on the road and said to her, "Noukou." She had no notion what he meant. He came by the next day and she was at the window. Again, he said to her, "Noukou."

That night, when her husband came home, she said to him, "If you but knew, husband mine! A man came by today and said, 'Noukou.'" "And what did you say to him?" "Nothing." "You foolish wench, you should answer, 'Naka,' and if he says, 'When?', you should say, 'Tonight'."

The man came by next day and said to her, "Noukou," and she answered, "Naka." "When?" "Tonight."

He came that evening. "Be seated," she said. "My husband is away from home. He is going abroad. I have cooked a meal."

They sat down and ate. Rat-a-tat! on the door. "Oh!" said she. "It's my husband! Where shall I hide you? I'll put you in a sack and hide you under the bed."

The door opened and in came her husband. "Good evening to you." "God be with you. Have you not gone?" "No. There were no ships. I go tomorrow. Have you anything to eat?" "Oh, husband. I fetched home a piece of meat." They made a good meal. "Your health, husband!" "Your health, wife!" They drank well.

When they had eaten, "Listen, wife," said he, "I have a mind tonight to beat the flax you have under the bed." "Never bother your head, poor soul, about that now. I'll beat it tomorrow." "I'll beat it now and rid you of the burden." He picked up the threshing stick, pulled out the sack with her sweetheart inside, and dealt it (and him) many a blow and all but beat him to pulp. Then the husband got him out of the sack and took him home, and he had to stay in bed I don't know how long.

And, one day, when he had gotten back his health and strength, he passed by his sweetheart's house. She was at the window and said to him, "Noukou."

> Bid me neither Nouk' nor Nak';
> You'll ne'er again put me in the sack!

.67. *What Am I to Say?*

• A BUTCHER ONCE GAVE a poor man some tripe. The poor man went down to the sea to wash it, and as he brought it out of the water and was holding it up, a sailing ship went by. When the captain saw the poor man holding up the tripe, he thought he was waving with his handkerchief to be picked up. On putting his boat in to shore and finding out the truth of the matter, he laid hold of the poor man and dealt him a goodly blow, saying, "The next time, when you meet a ship or anyone else, say:

> Good luck attend your stern and may winds belly out your
>   sail:
> May you ne'er see bird on the wing to follow in its trail."

The poor man took good account of this after the blow he had received, and as he went on his way, he met a hunter; he never hesitated, but greeted him and said:

Good luck attend your stern and may winds belly out your
    sail:
May you ne'er see bird on the wing to follow in its trail.

On hearing this, the hunter laid hold of him and dealt him a blow in his turn, saying, "You hound, what words are these?" "But what would you have me say?" asked the poor man. Said the hunter, "Do you say:

May you case five and ten each day,
One hundred every week."

As he went along his way, the poor man came to a village. He went into a cottage and saw that a wake was being held. He greeted them and said, "May you case five and ten each day, one hundred every week." On hearing his words, the villagers laid hold of him and dealt him more buffets and told him to say, "Let this be the one and only: may no one among you ever come to such harm."

He went on to another village, where a wedding was taking place. He went to the wedding, greeted the folk, and said, "Let this be the one and only; may no one among you ever come to such harm." They, too, laid hold of him and buffeted him in their turn and told him to say, "May such joy ever be yours: may the power and zest you put into making this feast be yours when you come to eat it."

Further along the way, he met a man relieving himself, greeted him, and expressed the wish that such joy might ever be his and that the power and zest he had put into making the feast be his when he ate it. The other arose, seized him and dealt him a resounding blow.

"Here's a go!" said the poor man. "You all give me such blows that I can't tell what to be saying." "Here's what you say," the other told him, " 'Phew! Those turds! How they stink!' "

He went on and came to a village where the priest was saying mass in the church. He went inside, whereupon the priest went up and sprinkled him with incense. "Phew! Those turds! How they stink!" said he to the priest. The priest seized him and the villagers all but split him up the middle with blows. Then he took to his heels and went back to his village and so escaped more buffetings.

•68• *Almondseed and Almondella*

• ONE DAY A POOR MAN was passing by the weaver's in his neighborhood, and saw a black hen tied to the weaver's shop by a red string. When he went home he heard his neighbor calling that her black hen had been stolen and for pity's sake to find it. So he called to her, and said, "If you give me two piastres, I'll show you where it is."

She accepted, and he took a book and made as if he were reading in it, and then said, "I've found it! It's in such-and-such a workshop, so run and get it." She ran and got it and gave him two piastres.

Then his own wife said to him, "Seems it's paying work, so why not be a seer?" So he decided to be a seer, and say what seers say.

As he was sitting at the crossroads one day, the King's servants came by and they asked him what child the Queen would bear, girl or boy. So, not knowing what to say, he made as if he were reading in his book and began saying, over and over, "Boy, girl, boy, girl . . ." So they got tired of listening to this, and went.

It came about that when the Queen gave birth, she bore a boy and a girl, twins. Then the servants remembered the seer, and told the King what he had said to them.

At this time, the King had been robbed of his coffer, and when he heard this about the seer, he had him brought to the palace in triumph, with the army and bands of musicians along. The poor seer trembled with fear, but what was he to have done? How was he to know who had stolen the coffer?

One day went by, then two, then three, and he just sat there.

One evening, he asked for a dish of almonds to be brought him, and shelled and ate them. Now, the thieves were three. One was outside the door and trying to see if the seer would guess right. When he had taken a fair quantity of almonds, the seer felt sleepy, and said, "The first has come" (first sleep, he meant).

When he heard this, the one outside was afraid. So he went, and said to the others, "Listen, fellows, the seer has found us out. I went and stood outside his room; he heard, and said, 'The first has come'." They would not believe him, so the second went and stood behind the door.

The seer woke, and shelled more almonds and ate them. He grew tired again, and said, "The second has come." The second thief heard him, and went and told the others. "He's found out about me now," he said to them. "I went and listened, too, and he said, 'The second has come'." The third went to see.

The wizard again awoke and shelled more almonds, and ate. He grew tired again, and said, "The wobbly woman's son has come" (the third sleep, he meant).

So he went, and told the others, "That devil of a seer knows about us."

So then they all went, beat on the door, and cried out to the seer, "We know you're a good wizard and know about us all three, only don't give us away to the King, and we'll show you where we put the coffer." They went, and showed him.

Many days went by. The King asked him, "Well, seer, what have you found out?"

"I've found out something," he said to him. "Send me a servant to do the digging."

He sent him a servant, and they went and dug in the garden, brought up the coffer intact and full of gold pieces. The King was overjoyed, and showered him with gifts and more gifts. And, when they had eaten at midday, the King took the seer out into the garden. As they were walking there, the King picked an almond from an almond tree, and said to him, "If you're really a seer, let's see what you'll say to this. What have I here, in my hand?"

The poor seer, whose name was Almondseed, and whose wife's name was Almondella, was terrified, and said, "Well done, Almondseed, that Almondella allowed to fall into the King's hands."

The King thought he meant the almond that he held in his hand and the almond tree it had come from, and he was very glad and gave him a deal of gold, and he went home and lived well, and even better.

·69· *The Village of Lies*

• ONCE THERE WAS A FATHER who had three sons. When he felt that death was near, he bade them beware of losing themselves in the village of lies. On their father's death, the sons set out to find work in another place. As they went on their way, they were benighted in a village of lies. There a priest found them and asked them to stay with him, and they did.

That night, when they had eaten, the priest told them, "This village is a village of lies, and we are in the habit of taking it in turns to tell a lie."

First, the priest told one, "There once was a big rock and the people of all the villages had tried to roll it away and could not, but when I came, I moved it all by myself."

Then said the eldest and the second son, "We keep a flock of fifty thousand goats."

Then the youngest said, "My father had forty beehives and I would go every morning to count both the hives and the bees. Once it fell out that one bee was missing. I went up a mountain, it seemed low to me; I went down again, it seemed to me high. I went on as far as the seashore, and there I saw a man who had our bee yoked to a cow and was ploughing a field. I unraveled a thread from my cap and caught the bee in it from where I stood and brought it back to the other bees. As I was going on my way, I got word that my godfather was to be christened and I was to go to the Almighty for some oil. And I went and found a marrow plant that had been forty years a-growing. I climbed from leaf to leaf until I came to the Almighty, got the oil, and came down again from leaf to leaf. While I was coming down, I grew weary and fell asleep, and a donkey that had been dead forty years got up and ate the marrow stalk right up to where I was sleeping. I awoke and saw the marrow stalk was eaten and wondered how to get down. I searched in my pocket and found a length of twine. I unwound it once, but it was not enough; I unwound it twice, and it stretched all the way and I came down. As I went on my way, I grew thirsty. I found a well, cut off my head, threw it in so as to fill it with water, and went on. But, on the road as I went, I forgot I had no head; so I went back to the well, where I found a fox eating it. I threw a stone into it, and the fox left the head as well as a letter saying that the priest should take his family and go and the three brothers remain in his stead."

·70· *The Man With the Pie*

• A ROGUE ONCE ASKED two others to go to his house. He baked a pie and said, "We'll eat the pie when we've seen which of us has had the best dream. Sleep now."

They slept. He with the sharpest wits got up in the night and ate the pie. Then, when the others got up, the first one said, "I saw myself going up and up. There, I found Paradise. What a crowd of people there are, there! They live well."

The second said, "I got a ladder and went down and down. There, I found Hell. The torments of the damned! Don't ask me to describe them!"

"And I," said he with the sharpest wits, "I saw the one go up and the other go down; so I got up and ate the pie."

Part VI
Legends

The Swallow

· ONCE A YOUNG MAN LOVED a maid who cared for him not at all. So what did he do to win her? He changed his clothes and sold apples in the streets.

He came and stood below his beloved's walls, crying, "Apples! Fine apples!" Not knowing it was he, she asked, "How much are your apples?" "I will sell them all, mistress, for a measure of millet." "Very well, we will buy them from you," answered the maid.

So he entered, was given the measure of millet, and handed over the apples. But as he went to empty the millet he upset it on purpose all over the floor, and so he sat down and gathered it into his coat, grain by grain. The maiden perceived the young man's foolishness and laughed. She told him that there was no need to pick up all the millet in that way, for they would give him another measure. But he would not have it and said there was no help for it, he must gather them up in that way. And he gathered until nightfall. Then he asked them to let him stay the night in the house so he might finish his work. They suspected nothing and so did not refuse him, but only deplored his wrong-headedness.

When they all retired for the night the young man took good heed of where his beloved would sleep, and at midnight went into her chamber, laid hold of her, and fled, with no one any the wiser, not even the maid herself, she slept so deeply. Only when it was again day did she perceive that she was not in her father's house but in an unknown place with the young man who loved her but whom she did not love. At once she saw the trap he had laid for her and made up her mind never to speak a word. He tried a thousand and one tricks to induce her to let fall a word, but to no avail—she remained as though dumb.

Thus a long time went by, and when the young man saw that he would not have his way, he decided to marry another, one who would at least speak. The maid was at the place where the marriage crowning was to take place, standing senseless with grief, so that she was not even aware of the burning candle she

was holding, and it all but burned her fingers. When the bride
saw this, she could not contain herself, and pulled off her wedding raiment, crying to the other maid:

> Alas! Unlucky girl, who play'st the silent ox's role,
> Why art thou not, too, blind as is the mole?

The maid, who until then had been mute, was wroth at this
and turned and said to the bride, "While I have borne suffering
for three years and never uttered a word, could you not suffer for
one moment in silence?"

When the young man heard his beloved speak, he flung himself upon her to take her in his arms, and caught hold of her
braided hair, but she became a swallow and the tresses were left
in his hands. Only two locks remained to her, and these make up
the forked tail of the swallow.

•72• *Phlandro*

• IN THE OLD GREEK TIMES there was a maiden of noble birth
called Phlandro. The name Phlandro means "She who loves her
husband," and as she was named, so did she come to be. She
loved her husband with all her heart and soul, so much, indeed,
that she gave up all her worldly goods and turned to stone for
love of him.

It so befell that a young merchant captain, handsome and
hardy, fell in love with Phlandro and courted her, and they were
betrothed. After the betrothal he had a new ship built, and when
the boat was done, their wedding took place. After the wedding
the ship was launched and he embarked and set sail.

Then Phlandro began to wait and watch on the shore. Her
heart was full sore at her husband's departure, and nigh to breaking. She stood and watched the ship as it sailed away, weeping
bitterly so that her tears mingled with the waves and they grew
bitter and evil and ran rough and wild until they whipped themselves up into a storm. On their way they fell upon the ship and
drowned Phlandro's husband, so that he never returned. But

Phlandro came again and again to the quiet seashore to watch and wait.

So the months passed till they grew to a year, then two, then three, with never sight nor sound of the ship. And Phlandro wept and cursed the sea, and her tears dried up for she had no more to shed. And she besought God to turn her to stone, and her prayer was granted. God turned her into a barren rock in human shape as would be worn by a thousand years of the waves' beating. And the human shape of the rock may still be seen. The sea wave beats and howls upon it, and its voice, the wailing voice, is one with the wailing of the sea.

Many years later, Dame Chadzighianni, a Christian noblewoman, who had had two ships built for her sons, made an offering to the Holy Virgin and built a shrine for the safety of her sons as they fared over the sea. And this shrine brought a blessing and calm to the wild sea wave that until then had been the curse of all that coast.

·73· *The Searing Breath of the Katevatos*

• THE KATEVATOS IS a fierce old man with white hair; in winter he wrestles with the other spirits on the peaks of Liakoura. When the elements struggle thus, Liakoura trembles, groans, sighs, and covers herself with snow, for she cannot endure the spirits' raging. And later, when the Katevatos has overcome them all, he goes to his crystal palace and rests. His breath is the terrible blast that petrifies both man and beast. March is the worst month for him.

It would be about a hundred years ago now that a monk named Gherotheo from the Monastery of Blessed Luke felt the desire to see the Katevatos' palace, as well as the elements' wrestling match and the terrible searing wind. He took with him bread and firewood and whatever else he needed, and went up to Liakoura one November, and there he shut himself up in a cave on the highest peak, which is called Lykeri. Here he lived up to the middle of March and he saw all he had been wishful to see. But although he still had sufficient bread and firewood for his

needs, so much did he fear the howling of the elements as they
vied with one another, so much did he fear the shock of their
blows and their stamping, the thunder and lightning of the heavens, and the groaning of Parnassus, that there was no strength
left in him. And the searing March blasts blew and withered him
up and sucked his blood, until he saw Death standing clear before him. So then he rose and wrote on the wall of the cave:

> I saw the elements wrestling, saw their halls,
> But nought I feared like the frightful Marchtide squalls.

And the smoke from the unlucky Gherotheo's fire may still be
seen on the wall of the cave.

·74· *The Lake Spirits of Peristera and Xerovouni*

• MOUNT PERISTERA HAS many peaks and on the highest of these
there is a small but bottomless lake; it isn't much more than four
hundred meters long, but it has water a-plenty. There is another
lake on Mount Xerovouni. Here all the creatures drink the
water, but the large beasts and the goats never go up to drink,
for they know full well it is bewitched. And truly, in each of
these there dwells a spirit.

Once—not over fifty years ago— the spirits came out to hold a
contest. They agreed that each was to take whatever the other
sent him. The spirit of Xerovouni hurled snowballs at the other,
and he swallowed them down. But then the spirit of Peristera
began to throw balls made of lamb's innards that he had first
sprinkled with salt. He obtained the ingredients for these from a
shepherd whom he had obliged to give him the entrails from his
sheep. The spirit opened up each sheep, took out the innards, and
then sewed it up, and the sheep was none the worse for it. But
after he had swallowed every one of many such balls, the spirit
of Xerovouni couldn't take any more and burst.

At once, then, the spirit of Peristera ran up and opened the other's breast, took out the heart and put it on a spit, setting the shepherd (who had been there all this time, looking on) to turn the spit until the roast was done. But he could not turn it, because not only was it big and heavy in the ordinary way of things, but all the heavier for being bewitched. So he ordered him to rub the heart three times with his finger and then lick it. The first time he licked his finger he felt strength enter his body, the second and third times he became as wild as a beast. And he too went into the lake and dwelt there, for now he was bewitched.

From that time forward, nothing was heard of the shepherd, none knew what had become of him. He appeared to one friend alone, and him he swore on the Holy Writ to secrecy; the friend was a dairyman, or cheesemaker as we call them. Only to him did he appear, and bade him bring him the skim (the top of the milk, I mean, that they use for making butter), and told him that if ever he wanted to see him, he should come to the lake, climb up on a white rock, play on the pipes, and he would appear. Only he made him swear to say nothing to anyone. So it often happened that the friend would come and pipe and the possessed one would appear.

After some time had gone by, the shepherd's mother, who had never given up hope that her son was alive, began to suspect. So she pleaded with him, weeping tears, till he took pity on her, and said, "Up, then, and come with me, and you shall see Ghiannis." So he brought her to the rock where their meeting place was and hid her behind him.

No sooner did he begin to play the pipes than the possessed one sprang up, and no sooner that, than the old woman fell on him and embraced him, calling out, "My son! my son!" and I don't know what all. In a rage, the possessed one turned upon the other and shouted, "Cheese curdler is your calling, cheese curdler ever be, and night and day you'll curdle cheese, and never profit see!" And they never saw him again.

Some time passed and there was a fair in a village called Tyrnavo, which stands below Nizopolis, some two hours' journey from the lake. The possessed one appeared in the fairground and seized the fairest daughter of the village, whom he had known some time before he was bewitched. He took her down with him into the lake and bewitched her too. The village folk stood as if turned to stone at her being spirited away like that before their eyes.

The maiden, indeed, had two fine brothers, fearless and brave they were. They lost no time in getting after the spirit. But when they reached the lake, the spirit leapt in with the maiden and the waters closed over them. The youths then decided to dig into the slope of the mountain and make a gully, about two men's stature in depth, and the water began running into it. Just then the earth began to tremble, and there came down an enormous rock, big as this room, and dammed the gully. (Both gully and rock may be seen to this day.) The brothers went away in despair.

Many years ago now, in 1876, an old man, by name Kazako (I don't recall his Christian name), told me that a little while before, in '73, he'd happened to go to the lake very early one morning before the sheep went to drink, and saw, so he said, the spirit's wife sitting beside the lake and combing her hair. When she saw him, she at once sprang into the lake, forgetting to take her things. So the old one went up and found her comb, looking glass, and a tress of hair, pretty as you please, all golden. The old one picked them up. But that night the spirit came to the pen where he was sleeping alongside the sheep, dealt him a blow, and said, "Take the things back where you found them." And he did.

·75· *New Airs*

• WHEN KING ALEXANDER HAD BEEN to the wars and conquered all the kingdoms of the world, and all the inhabited world trembled at his name, he summoned three wise men, and asked them, "Tell me, O ye who know the writings of destiny, what must I do to live for many years more and enjoy this world that I have made all my own?"

"O King live for ever, your strength is manifold," answered the wise men. "But what destiny has written may not be unwritten. There is one thing alone that can allow you to enjoy your kingdoms and your glory so well that you will wish to be immortal and live for ever, like the eternal hills. But it is hard, oh, hard indeed!"

"I do not ask if it is hard, but only what it may be," said Alexander.

"Ah, then, sire, let it be as you command: it is the water of life. Whoever drinks of it need never fear death. But he who goes to seek it must pass between two mountains that beat unceasingly one against the other. Not even a bird on the wing may pass. How many nobles and princes of renown have lost their lives in this terrible trap! And once you pass between the mountains there is a *drakos* who guards the water of life with unsleeping eye. Slay the *drakos* and the water is yours!"

Then, on the instant, Alexander ordered that his winged horse, Bucephalus, be brought to him—the animal who, though wingless, could yet fly like a bird. He mounted, put the spur to his black steed, and was on his way. With a touch of the whip he pressed ever onward. He slew the *drakos* and took the glass vessel that held the water of life. But once the misguided one had returned to the palace he failed to take good care of the water. His sister looked it over and, without a thought as to what it might be, poured it all away. It chanced to fall upon a wild onion plant and that is why the wild onion will never wither away.

Some hours later, Alexander went to drink of the water of life, but what had become of it? He asked his sister, who told him that as she had had no idea of what it was, she had poured it away. The King nearly went mad with grief and frenzy, and he laid a curse upon her that she should become fish from the waist down and suffer torture until the world should come to stand in the middle of the ocean.

The gods heard him, and ever since, those who sail the sea in ships may see her twisting and turning in the waves. Even so, she does not hate Alexander, and whenever she sees a ship, will ask, "Does Alexander live?" And if the master of the ship is at a loss what to answer and should say, "He is dead," the maiden in her great grief will stir up the sea with her hands and her unbound fair hair, and the ship will sink. Those who know better will answer, "He lives and reigns," and then the long-suffering maid will be of good cheer and happily sing sweet songs. From her the sailors learn new airs and bring them home from sea.

•76• *The Nereids' Cave*

• A LITTLE BELOW Nether Astrakoi is the Nereids' Cave; from this cave there flows, clear and cold, an abundance of water. Nereids dwell there, and when they take their bath the waters rush out in a turmoil. And every eight or ten years there is a little drought, and then oranges and orange leaves come forth with the water.

There was a peasant from the village of Sgourokephali who excelled at playing the lyre, and the Nereids took him to the cave and entertained him. He fell in love with one of the Nereids, and to find the cure for this ailment went to an old crone living in his village and confessed his passion to her. Her advice to him was, one moment before cockcrow, to seize his beloved by the hair and hold her tight; though she change into different beasts he was not to weaken but to hold her fast till cockcrow.

So the young man went to the place where he was wont to go; the Nereids took him to their cave, and he began as before to play the lyre and they to dance. But as cockcrow drew close, he rushed up and seized his beloved by the hair. She at once turned into a dog, then a snake, then a camel, and even into fire, but the young man did not weaken and held her fast until he heard the cock crow, and the other Nereids vanished. Then his beloved became young and lovely as before, and followed him to his village. They lived together for a year, at the end of which she bore him a son, but never did she speak a word.

This strange and unbearable dumbness of hers brought him again to visit the same old crone and tell her of his sorrow. And this time she advised him to heat the oven well, take the child in his arms, and say to the Nereid, "Since you will not speak to me, I will take your child and burn it," and make as if to throw the child into the oven. He did as the old crone had bidden him. No sooner did the Nereid hear from him than she cried, "Unhand my child, you dog!" Thereupon she seized the child and vanished from his sight.

But the other Nereids would not again admit her to their cave, because she had borne a human child. And so she was obliged to live in a spring they call Loutsa, near the Nereids' Cave. And there she may be seen two or three times a year, holding her child in her arms. And the other Nereids can be heard singing and dancing in the Nereids' Cave, but no longer to the strains of the lyre.

·77· *Kaemene Island*

· MANY YEARS AGO now, close on one hundred and fifty, Gaffer Laemos' boat was crossing to Rhodes. While they were on the open sea a squall blew up, and being in danger of their lives, they had to put in to the shore of an unknown little island. They dropped anchor and landed. A few hours had passed and it was getting light when they suddenly saw three mules coming down laden from the mountain. Each one had a heavy load—there were three great paniers. As they came to the shore they turned about, still laden, and went back the way they had come, and a while later they returned laden and did the same. This they repeated many times.

On seeing this strange sight, the mules coming and going always laden, with no sign of anyone driving or loading them, the sailors stared at one another in amazement. Indeed, one of them went up to one of the mules and struck it with a stick he was holding. At this it turned and said, in a human voice, "Do not strike me, cousin!" He was much taken aback on hearing this and stood and stared at it. Then it said to him, "It may seem strange to you that I should call you cousin. Know, then, that I was not born a mule but that I am a man and now do penance. I am Matais the priest, your cousin, who spoke flattering speeches to many, and swore many a false oath. And these other two are from the same place as we are" (and he gave their names) "and do penance alike. This place is called Kaemene and is near Santorini. Go to our hometown, do some good action, and pray for us, so that our souls may find a little rest."

Notes
to the Tales

PART I

Introduction

A fair number of animal tales have been passed on to us from antiquity under the name of Aesop; not, I suspect, because he created all the so-called Aesopic fables, for which we have the splendid critical editions of August Hausrath and Ben E. Perry, but because of the practice among the ancient Greeks of having an inventor ready at hand to account for every phenomenon and every custom. Thus, Aesop was presented as being the author of all the droll anecdotes. The "joy in relating" the old Aesopic fables, hypothesized by Otto Keller and Hausrath, is not evident from the concise versions of the preserved collections. Because of their brevity and their moral content, the Aesop tales were used in the schools of rhetoric for centuries as models for students in correct writing. They thus became linguistic essays whose main virtue was their concise form. But the oral tradition, wherein the word flows clear and unforced, like water from a natural spring, preserves the relationship to the original forms more closely than does literary tradition. Of course it is impossible for us to know how long these tales survived in oral tradition before Demetrius Phalerius first collected them in 316 B.C.

It is true that not all ancient tales survive nowadays in the oral tradition of the Greek people. However, those modern tales which correspond to ancient ones are more complete than their predecessors; see, for example, no. 18, "Crab and Snake" and no. 19, "Shepherd and Snake" in this selection. They show a more logical connection of the details, and they do not depend mainly on the formulation of a moral, as do the old classical tales. Therefore, modern tales help us to restore the narrative aspects of the ancient tales. Also, there are cases where only hints of the existence of an ancient tale are found, and these hints are often preserved in one or two lines, or even in a proverb; in such a case, the modern tales are able to fill in the gaps of the ancient tradition. Thus see no. 8, "Hedgehog and Fox."

The Middle Ages drew exhaustively upon this treasury of classical myths, but in so doing wrought modifications: the moral element was suppressed and the element of anecdote reinforced. From the myths came wonder tales and droll animal stories, featuring commonly animals such as the bear, fox, and wolf. As von der Leyen observes (*Märchen,* p. 251) the ancient myths reached Europe through Byzantium. The animal tales were especially well liked in the north and thence traveled toward the south and east.

That animal tales continue to thrive among the Greek people, particularly in Pontus and Cyprus, is shown by the rich harvest gathered some years ago, when the Folklore Archives of the Academy of Athens circulated an appeal to schools for the recording of animal tales by the pupils. The collection of this excellent material has now reached 3500 tales.

· *1* · The Fox and the Wolf Go a-Fishing

Type 2B, *Basket Tied to Wolf's Tail.* Athens Folklore Seminar MS 816. Transcribed by Aspasia Lalaouni in Konistrae, Euboea, in 1961. The tale was told by her mother, who had it from her illiterate grandmother, who died in 1932 at the age of one hundred and five.

Wishing to keep for itself the lamb it has stolen in company with the wolf, the fox invites the wolf to go fishing and hangs a basket around its neck (or tail), which eventually pulls it down under the water. Usually this tale is combined with Type 123A, *Fox Buys Colt and Leaves It at Home.* The fox has in its possession a lamb of which it is very fond. The wolf changes its voice, breaks into the fox's hut and eats the lamb. Using for bait the fish it has hung up in its lair, the fox lures the wolf to go fishing in the sea. It hangs a pot on the wolf's tail, so that it may catch a lot of fish, and the wolf is pulled under. A Magara Propontis variant is in Megas, *Begegnung,* no. 10.

This tale is widely told in the rest of Europe, but usually the wolf's demise is brought about by the attachment to its tail (Type 2, *The Tail-Fisher*). The bear (wolf) is persuaded to fish with his tail through a hole in the ice. His tail freezes fast, and when he is attacked and tries to escape, he loses his tail. For numerous versions see Bolte and Polívka, 2: 111; von der Leyen, *Märchen,* p. 108; Liungman, *Volksmärchen,* p. 4; Polites, *Laographia,* 5 (1915): 459–68; Ranke, *Folktales of Germany,* no. 1; and Seki, *Folktales of Japan,* no. 1. As Kaarle Krohn observes (*"Bär (Wolf) und Fuchs,"* *Journal de la Société finno-ougrienne,* 6 [1889]: 26), the animal that has a short tail is not the wolf but the bear. It is therefore likely that the story has an etiological beginning and comes from northern countries, perhaps Scandinavia, whence it would have passed into Germany and France, and there have been told with the wolf in place of the bear. In southern countries, however, such as Greece

NOTES TO THE TALES

and Spain, where the waters of the lakes do not freeze in winter, the attachment to the wolf's tail made no sense. Another manner of fishing therefore had to be implied in order to lead to the drowning of the wolf.

There are in the Athens Folklore Archives and Athens Folklore Seminar seventy-three variants of this tale, nine of which have been published.

· 2 · The Nun Vixen

Type 20D*, *Cock and Other Animals Journey to Rome to Become Pope.* Compare Type 61, *Fox as Confessor.* Recorded in Negades, Epirus, in 1848. It was first printed in translation in Hahn, *Märchen* (2nd ed.), p. 101, no. 90; and later in the original in Pio, *Contes,* p. 54. It was reprinted by Megas, *Paramythia,* 1st Ser., p. 3, no. 1. See version in Megas, *Griechische Volksmärchen* p. 19, no. 10.

In the variant from Adrianopolis, Thrace (Athens Folklore Archives, MS 394, p. 36), the birds come out of the vixen's belly alive (Motif F913). On the disguising of the wolf, fox and cat as monks, in order to delude their victims, see Polites, *Paroemiae,* 3 (1903): 572 ff. and *Laographia,* 2 (1901): 693 ff. Also see Bolte and Polívka, 2: 207 ff. Similarly, the fox is pictured in monk's disguise, with a rooster in front of him, in an illustration to *Reynke de Vos,* a copy of which is in the Staatsbibliothek in Wolfenbütel (Lübeck, 1498, p. 18; new edition by A. Leitzman, Halle, 1960). These data are courtesy of Dr. Inez Diller. Compare also the fables of Aesop (Halm, nos. 16, 87; Hausrath, no. 7; Perry, no. 7), in which a cat disguises itself as a doctor and monk. There are eight published variants and many unpublished ones in the Athens Folklore Archives and Athens Folklore Seminar.

· 3 · Lion, Wolf, and Fox

Type 50, *The Sick Lion.* The fox pretends to seek a remedy for the lion; advises him to skin the wolf. This tale was recorded in Cromne, Pontus, and printed in Ἀστὴρ τοῦ Πόντου (*Star of Pontus*), 1 (1885): 103, no. 5. It was later reprinted in Ἀρχεῖον τοῦ Πόντου (Pontine Archives) 16 (1951): 85, no. 5, and by Megas, *Paramythia,* 2d Ser., no. 1. There is a version from Pontus in Megas, *Begegnung,* no. 2. The story is found in Aesop as "Lion, Wolf and Fox" (Halm, no. 255; Hausrath, no. 269; and Perry, no. 258). Also see Moser-Rath, *Predigtmärlein*, no. 135.

·4· Fox and Stork

Type 60, *Fox and Crane Invite Each Other*. Athens Folklore Archives MS. 25, p. 241. Recorded by S. Anagnostou in Lesbos, 1901. Published by Megas, *Paramythia*, 1st Ser., p. 17, no. 2, and translated in Kreschmer, *Märchen*, no. 23. For variations see Aesop, Halm, no. 34, "Fox and Stork;" Polites, *Paroemiae*, 1: 268; and Moser-Rath, *Predigtmärlein*, no. 88. There are sixty-two variants in the Athens Folklore Archives and Athens Folklore Seminar, four of which are published.

·5· Rooster, Fox, and Dog

A version of Type 62, *Peace among the Animals*. It is included in the Greek catalogue under the supplementary number *62 A *The Fox and the Cock*. Athens Folklore Seminar MS 579, recorded in 1955 at Trikala, Thessaly, by Maria Katrona.

This version is very similar to the Aesop fable "Dog, Rooster, and Fox" (Halm, no. 255; Hausrath, no. 268; Perry, no. 252), in which the fox is advised to wake the doorkeeper (dog) that sleeps in the hollow tree and to tell him to open the door. See the text in Megas, *Begegnung*, no. 3, and Megas's note in *Laographia*, 21 (1962): 483 ff. The more than one hundred unpublished variants in the Athens Folklore Archives and Athens Folklore Seminar come from various parts of Greece.

·6· Ten Years the She-Fox, Eleven the Wee Fox

This tale is not found in the Aarne-Thompson Type Index, but is included as no. 69, *The She-Fox Aged Ten, the Young Fox Eleven*, in the Greek catalogue. The present version was collected in Argos.

For other texts see Nearchos Klerides, "Historíes ton Zoön tis Kyprou," *Kypriakae Spoudae*, 13 (1949–50); Megas, *Paramythia*, 2d Ser., no. 4; and *Laographia*, 4 (1912–14): 299, where the tale illustrates the proverb "The vixen one hundred years wise, the fox cub one hundred and one." This is said about children who surpass their parents in either good or bad qualities. See also Polites, *Paroemiae*, 1 (1901): 432, 455, 464.

In a variant from Cyprus (Klerides, "Histories," p. 47, no. 2, "The Sparrow's Command"), the sparrow commands his children to fly away if they should see a man bending down, for he would be about to throw a stone. His young ones reply, "And what if he has the stone in his pocket?" "Well done, my child, your schooling is over; off you go, and live on your own!"

Similar versions from Macedonia and the Aegean are found in Miliopoulos and Vonderlage, *Mazedonische Bauerstuben*, p. 35, "Goodman Kostas the Blackbird" (collected in Salonica in 1952), and Carnoy and Nicolaïdès, *Traditions*, p. 186, "Le Moineau et ses enfants." Examples from the Middle Ages and modern times are recorded in Bolte and Polívka, 2: 239 ff., as notes to Grimm 157. Twenty variants are known of the first type (the fox) and four of the second (the sparrow or other wily bird).

·7· The Fox in the Pit

This tale is not included in the Aarne-Thompson Type Index, but is recorded as number *34C, *The Fox Falls into the Pit,* in the Greek catalogue.

See Nearchos Klerides, "Histories ton Zoön tis Kyprou," *Kypriakae Spoudae,* 13 (1949–50): 18, no. 2; and Megas, *Paramythia,* 2d Ser., p. 18, no. 5. The fox accuses God of not having given him wings so as to catch birds, but as he is looking up at the birds in the trees, he accidentally falls into a pit. Gratified that there was no water in the pit—otherwise he would have been drowned—he accuses himself of not having been content with what God has given him. Compare the tale of the astrologer who falls into a well while gazing at the stars (Aesop, Halm, no. 72; Hausrath, no. 40; Perry, no. 40).

·8· Hedgehog and Fox

Type 105*, *The Hedgehog's Only Trick.* The hedgehog inveigles himself into the fox's lair, and by raising his prickles, forces the fox out of the hole. Collected by C. Coryllos in Patras. Printed in *Laographia,* 1 (1909): 322, no. 4. Note by Polites, *Paroemiae,* 1: 328; reprinted by Megas in *Laographia,* 18 (1960): 488.

A variant of this fable also collected in Patras is published in *Laographia,* 2 (1910): 692, as "The Hedgehog and the Snake." The hedgehog, who has not troubled to make his own burrow for the winter, asks the snake to let him copy the design of his nest. As soon as the hedgehog gets inside, he uses his prickles to keep the snake out. Eviction is also the theme of two stories of the hare kept out of its burrow by the hedgehog, both collected in 1938, the one by a high school student in Xeropegadon, Naupactos (Athens Folklore Archives MS 1205 [140: 35], p. 3 published in *Laographia,* 18 [1960]: 486, no. 2), and the other in Asemochorion (Athens Folklore Archives MS 1264 [140: 94], p. 3). Variants appear in Hahn, *Märchen* (2d ed.), p. 103, no. 91, and Argenti and Rose, 1: 588, no. 41. There are nineteen unpublished variants. Another Greek variant of the story from southern Italy is published in Morasi, *Studi,* p. 76. See also Legrand, *Recueil de contes,* p. 181, "Le Chèvre et le renard," in which the fox and the wolf are afraid of the horns of the goat that has gotten itself inside the fox's lair. The hedgehog forces it out.

This fable of the hedgehog and fox is obviously of ancient origin. The poet Archilochus (Diehl, *Supplementum,* p. 103) refers to it in the verse:

πόλλ, οἶδ ᾿ἀλώπηξ, ἀλλ ᾿ἐχῖνος ἐν μέγα.

(The fox is very wily, but the hedgehog goes one better.) When the fox draws near, as Ion says in the fifth century, the hedgehog curls up into a ball of spikes so that the fox may not touch it, let alone bite it. In this modern Greek fable, the ancient tradition is afforded a most adequate succession, and yet another fable is added to the Aesopic collection. See Megas, "Some Oral Greek Parallels to Aesop's Fables," *Humaniora,* p. 206; and *Laographia,* 18 (1960): 486 ff. Compare also von der Leyen, *Märchen,* p. 254, no. 111.

·9· *Wolf, Fox, and Ass*

Type 122J, *Ass Begs Wolf to Pull Thorn out of Foot before Eating Him.* Motifs J1608, "Ass's Charter in his Hoof"; K551.18, "Respite from Death Granted until Wolf Reads Horse's Passport." Athens Folklore Archives MSS 189, 258. Collected by M. Philintas in Kyzikos, Asia Minor, in 1894. Published in Megas, *Paramythia,* 1st Ser., p. 14, no. 3, and translated in Megas, *Griechische Volksmärchen,* no. 3.

This fable is set forth in the Mediterranean epic, *The Hagiography of the Illustrious Ass (Synaxarion tou Timemenou Ghadarou),* and is found in Wagner, *Carmina Graeca Medii Aevi,* pp. 112, 124 where it illustrates the proverb, "He ate the lettuce leaf without vinegar." (For a study of this proverb by Polites see *Laographia,* 7 [1918]: 646.) The proverb expresses the chief meaning of the fable: the weak are condemned for the slightest of shortcomings, while the strong and cunning are forgiven the most serious sins. When the two partners, wolf and fox, take the ass off on a sea voyage, they hear his confession and condemn him; however, the ass uses the same guile in order to save himself: he asks the wolf to read the document written by his father and concealed in his hind hoof, or else to remove a nail from his hoof before eating him, and then, with one good kick, breaks the wolf's teeth, or sends him flying into the sea.

The first subtype for this tale is found in the Aesopic fable about the ass who pretends to be limping in order to save himself from the wolf's jaws (Aesop: Chambry, no. 282; Halm, no. 334b; Hausrath, no. 198; Perry, no. 187). According to Polites (*Laographika Symmeikta,* 1: 193), "most of the poems about Reynard are on the model of this fable, referring, some to a mare, some to a colt." There is an extensive bibliography on this in Bolte and Polívka, 1: 77. See also Wesselski, *Märchen,* p. 250, and Wossidlo and Henssen, *Mecklenburger Erzäheln,* p. 207, no. 16. Moreover, a Caucasian fable found in Dirr, *Märchen,* no. 39, and a Turkish variant from Kastamones (Eberhard and Boratav, Anlage C. no. 4, p. 414) have the same plot as the modern Greek version.

Variants of this fable are in *Laographia,* 17 (1957–58): 141 f., 177. These involve another type of the ass and wolf (or fox) fable which is told widely in Greece and may be also compared with the medieval tale "De Lupo et Asino" (Steinhöwel, *Aesop,* p. 203; and Grimm, *Reinhart Fuchs,* p. 424). The fox goes into the field and steals the straps that harness the oxen to the yoke. The ass undertakes to get them back; he goes into the field and lies down as if dead. Foxes bring the yoke harness and fasten one end to the ass and the other around their necks in order to drag the ass to their lair. Suddenly the ass leaps up and pulls the foxes into the village (*Laographia,* 21 [1963–64]: 119, 466. Compare Kretschmer, *Märchen,* no. 21, and Bolte and Polívka, 3: 74–75). The ruse whereby the ass pulls the foxes into the village is in Type 47C, but appears as a piece of cunning on the part of the fox at the wolf's expense: the fox ties one end of a rope to the horns of a cow they both intend to eat and the other to the wolf. The cow pulls the wolf home, where he is skinned (Motif K1022.2). In the parallel Greek tales this ruse is attributed to the ass at the fox's expense.

For two United States Negro texts of a seemingly dead mule (colt) coming to life when a buzzard tries to eat him, see Richard M. Dorson, *American Negro Folktales*, nos. 8, 28.

· *10* · Man, Snake, and Fox

Type 155, *The Ungrateful Serpent Returned to Captivity*, plus Type 154, "*Bear-food*," and Motif K235, "Creditor killed or driven away." The fox agrees to help the man in return for his geese. The man goes for the geese, but instead brings dogs in his bag. The dogs chase the fox to his hole. Eberhard-Boratav Type 48. Athens Folklore Archives MS 25, p. 210; collected in 1901 by S. Anagnostou in Lesbos. Published in Megas, *Paramythia*, 1st Ser., p. 19, no. 5. Alternative version in Megas, *Begegnung*, no. 18, and Megas *Griechische Volksmärchen*, no. 5.

Compare Grimm, *Märchen*, no. 99 "Der Geist im Glas"; Bolte and Polívka, 2: 420; von der Leyen, *Märchen*, no. 167, p. 325; Moser-Rath, *Predigmärlein*, no. 30, p. 126; and Polites, *Laographia*, 2 (1910): 161 ff., in which variants are recorded. Also consult Dawkins, *Modern Greek in Asia Minor*, pp. 334, 439; *Laographia*, 9 (1926): 254; Pontine Archives, 14: 37; *Thrakika*, 17: 108 (translated in Dawkins, *More Greek Folktales*, p. 9, no. 3); Rossi and Caracausi, *Testi Neogreci*, p. 127, no. 20 and p. 396, no. 2; Morosi, *Studi*, p. 75; Legrand, *Recueil de contes*, p. 187. Also see Giese, *Märchen*, no. 54, and the Aesop fable "Countryman and Snake" (Halm, no. 97; Hausrath, no. 62). For comparative versions see Eberhard, *Folktales of China*, no. 67, and Noy, *Folktales of Israel*, no. 57, both published in the present series.

· *11* · Cat, Lion, and Man

Type 157, *Learning to Fear Men*. Instead of the fox, the cat undertakes to convince the lion of the frightfulness of man. They see a woodcutter who tricks the lion by catching its paws in a cleft tree (Motif K1111). Recorded by P. Papachristodoulou in Saranta Ecclesias, Thrace. Printed in *Laographia*, 1 (1915): 395; reprinted in *Thrakika*, 1 (1928): 216; Megas, *Paramythia*, 2d Ser., no. 2; and Loukatos, *Laographika Keimena*, p. 28, no. 8. A version is found in Ranke, *Folktales of Germany*, no. 7; as well as in Perdika, *Skyros*, vol. 2, p. 122; and Thumb, *Handbuch*, p. 294.

Compare Type 151, *Man Teaches Bears to Play the Fiddle*, and see Bolte and Polívka, notes to Grimm No. 72. Compare also the Aesopic fable "Archer and Lion" (Halm, no. 403; Hausrath, no. 281). There are six published and twenty-two unpublished Greek variants. Sixteen American Negro texts of Type 157 are given in Richard M. Dorson, "King Beast of the Forest Meets Man," *Southern Folklore Quarterly,* 17 (1954): 118–28, although the American oikotype does not have to K1111 motif.

· 12 · The Old Woodcutter and the Lion

Type 159B, *Enmity of Lion and Man.* Fable culminates in a proverb. Published by Kyriazis, *Cypriot Proverbs,* p. 259 and republished by Megas, *Paramythia,* 2d Ser., no. 3, and in *Griechische Volksmärchen,* no. 13. See Polites, *Paroemiae,* 4 (1904): 34–36; compare Krumbacher, *Moskaner Sammlung,* p. 115. There are eight published variants in *Laographia,* 4 (1912): 467; 5 (1915): 393; 19 (1961): 232, and twelve unpublished variants in the Athens Folklore Archives and Athens Folklore Seminar.

· 13 · Why the Dog Chases the Hare

Type 200C*, *Hare and Hunting Dog Conduct a Store (Inn) Together.* An etiological fable in which the dog lends his shoes to the hare so that he might quickly run and fetch water for the king (lion). He takes them, but never returns.

Told by Polychrones Travakoullas in the Carpathian idiom and published by Michael G. Michaelides-Nouaros, "Symmeikta Karpathou" ("Carpathian Miscellanea"), *Laographia,* 10 (1932): 254. Variant in Megas, *Begegnung,* no. 4. There are three published and 24 unpublished versions, in which the reason for the hostility between the hare and the dog varies. See also Polites, *Paradoseis,* 1 (1904), no. 1009.

· 14 · Ox and Ass

Type 207A, *Ass Induces Overworked Bullock to Feign Sickness.* Athens Folklore Seminar MS 1162 C, p. 127. Recorded by Maria Lioudaki in Merambelou, Crete in 1938, and published in Lioudaki, *Stou Pappou ta Gonata* ("At Grandpa's knee"), p. 16. Reprinted in Megas, *Paramythia,* 2d Ser., no. 6, and in *Griechische Volksmärchen,* no. 15. Compare the Aesopic fable "Goat and Ass" (Halm, no. 18). In a Chiote variant in Argenti and Rose, 1: 557, no. 40, the fable occurs as an episode of Type 670, *The Animal Languages*. There are five published and twenty-nine unpublished variants.

·*15*· Ass and Camel

Type 214A, *Camel and Ass Together Captured because of Ass's Singing* (Motif J2137.6) and Motif J2133.1, "Camel with Ass on his Back Dances." Collected by T. Kostakis in Vatika on the Isthmus of Kyzikos, Asia Minor, and published in *Laographia*, 17 (1957–58): 111.

The fable is made up of two episodes based on the two motifs above. The second, the camel's revenge, depends upon the first, the ass's singing, because of which the camel, being the slower of the two, tastes the gardener's switch. A version from the Caucasus is in Dirr, *Märchen*, no. 35; an Arabic text is noted by Chauvin, *Bibliographie*, 3: 49, no. 1. The Greek variants of this fable are given by Megas in *Laographia*, 17 (1957–58): 145.

·*16*· The Mouse and His Daughter

Type 2031C, *The Man Seeks the Greatest Being as a Husband for His Daughter*. Catalogued by Megas as Type *217A, *The Mouse and her Daughter*. Motif L392, "Mouse stronger than wall, wind, mountain." Athens Folklore Archives MS 205, p. 25. Collected by M. Philintas in Kyzikos in 1893, it was published in Megas, *Paramythia*, 1st Ser., p. 30, no. 8, and in *Griechische Volksmärchen*, no. 8.

This fable is found in the *Directorium Humane Vite* of Johannes de Capua (p. 238), and corresponds to Indian texts in Hertel, *Indische Märchen* (pp. 57–59) and to the Turkish fable from *Humajun-name* in Giese, *Märchen*, no. 56. See also Megas's article in *Laographia*, 19 (1960–61): 630 ff. For additional versions consult Pino-Saavedra, *Folktales of Chile*, no. 50; and Seki, *Folktales of Japan*, no. 13.

·*17*· Owl and Partridge

Type 247, *Each Likes His Own Children Best*. Published in Nearchos Klerides, "Historíes ton Zoön tes Kyprou," *Kypriakae Spoudae*, 13

(1949–50): no. 40; Megas, *Paramythia*, 2d Ser., p. 26, no. 9; and Megas, *Griechische Volksmärchen*, no. 16. See Polites's notes in *Laographia*, 5 (1915): 621. The older construction is that of the Aesopic fable of the fertility race (Crusius, *Babrii fabulae Aesopeae*, no. 56). For other versions see Georgeakis and Pineau, *Le Folklore*, p. 98; Loukatos, *Laographika Keimena*, p. 47 no. 4; and Chadzioannou, *Kypriakoe Mythoe* (*Cypriot Tales*), no. 36. There are five published and twelve unpublished variants.

·18· Crab and Snake

Type 279*, *Snake Trying to Surround Crab Refuses to Straighten Itself Out*. Athens Folklore Archives MS 672, p. 41. Recorded in 1914 by Father P. Stamboulas in Megara, and published by Megas, *Paramythia*, 1st. Ser., p. 24. Reprinted in *Humaniora*, p. 196. and *Laographia*, 18 (1960): 471.

This is the Aesopic fable of the snake and the crab (Chambry, no. 291; Halm, no. 346; Hausrath, no. 211; Perry, no. 196), but the modern Greek tale is fuller in the telling. According to the ancient version, the crab advises the snake to improve its manners, and as the snake disregards his advice, the crab lies in waiting until the snake is asleep, then seizes it by the neck with its claws and kills it. Seeing the snake now lying straight out like a rod in its hole, the crab says, "You should have been straight like this before: if you had been straight, you would not have suffered this punishment."

Wienert gives us the meaning of the tale as follows: "Die Schlange kann trotz allen Ermahnungen des Krebses von ihren krummen Wegen nicht lassen." Similarly, Thompson's Motif-Index contains the reference, J1053, "Snake disregards warnings to improve his manners, is eaten by crab." But the truth of the moral which underlies the last words of the crab is seemingly otherwise: one should be straight and sincere in manner, for crookedness will be punished. Moreover, this is the meaning implied in the best version: those who approach their friends with evil intent come to grief themselves. However, in the narrative of the tale, no "crookedness" is evident on the part of the snake against the crab. Thus, the crab kills his friend the snake in indignation at the snake's failure to conform with his advice on moral behavior.

But the story is different in the modern Greek version. Here, the killing of the snake is justified as being most logical and natural:

after the crab does the snake the honors of his nest, the two friends lie down to sleep. Then the snake, pretending that it is the habit of snakes to sleep coiled up, twines itself around the crab and begins squeezing the breath out of its body. So the crab's deed in killing the snake inside its nest is fully justified as self-defense against the cunning intentions of its friend the snake.

The antiquity of this tale is borne out by the reference made to it in verses attributed to the poet Alcaeus (ca. 6000 B.C.):

'Ο καρκίνος ὧδ' ἔφα
χαλᾷ τὸν ὄφιν λαβών.
εὐθὺν χρὴ τὸν ἑταῖρον ἔμμεν
καὶ μὴ σκολιὰ φρονεῖν.

(So spoke the crab, having seized the snake in its claw: A friend should be straight, and not think with design.)

·*19*· Shepherd and Snake

Type 285D, *Serpent* (*Bird*) *Refuses Reconciliation.* Athens Folklore Archives MS 230, p. 132. From the collection of Father Symeon Manasseides, of Chatzigyrion, Eastern Thrace, 1884. Published in Megas, *Paramythia,* 1st Ser., p. 27; and in Megas, *Griechische Volksmärchen,* no. 7.

In the published text, the tale has an idyllic quality: the shepherd's child walks among the sheep, stroking them and playing with them. The child does not see a snake gliding through the grass and treads on its tail. In its pain, the snake turns and bites the child, who dies of the poison. However, in four of the variants of the fable (from Pontus, Lesbos, and two from Thrace), the mishap is not fortuitous: the shepherd's eldest son plots against the snake's life so as to become master of all its treasure. Although he cuts off only the tip of the snake's tail, the snake kills him with its bite.

Exactly the same configuration is to be found in the five variants of the ancient fable in Koraes, *Mython* (1810 ed., no. 141, p. 338), which was included in the critical editions of Chambry (no. 81) and Hausrath (no. 51, ii), whereas in the remaining variants (Chambry, no. 81; Halm, no. 96b; Hausrath, no. 51, i and iii) the countryman misses the snake and strikes a stone instead. In the Koraes variant, he fails to strike the snake's head and kill it, but succeeds in cutting off the end of its tail. In his later reconciliation with the snake, he brings "flour and honey" to its nest—offerings usually made to propitiate the spirits. Thus, the snake's response to the countryman's invitation refers here not to the cleft stone, but to its severed tail, as in the modern Greek fable. But this variant too leaves the plot of the Aesopic fable open to conjecture, for it is not evident what determines the friendship between the countryman and the snake, which, even after his child's death, the countryman seeks to renew by bringing gifts, nor why the ostensibly friendly snake should cause the child's death.

The obscurities in the texts of the written tradition can be explained by the oral versions which have been preserved on the lips of the Greeks of Thrace, Lesbos, Pontus, and the Peloponnese. In the modern Greek variants (Megas, *Humaniora*, pp. 200–202; *Laographia*, 18 [1960]: 478–81) the connection of events is reasonable. The friendship of the man and the snake is based on the animal's gratitude for the offer of milk. The killing of the countryman's son does not take place at the beginning of the tale and without reason, as in the ancient texts, but rather occurs as an act of revenge by the snake against the greedy, ungrateful son, who attempted to kill the snake during his father's absence in order to acquire its treasure. Thus the countryman's endeavor to be friends with the snake after his return is explained, not by his fear lest the snake kill him also but by his wish for the reward that the snake was likely to give him. So he offers the same food that the snake has preferred from the beginning—milk.

The fable of the shepherd and snake corresponds, as we know, to the story in the *Panchatantra;* yet, for chronological reasons, Bolte and Polívka agree with Crusius and with Marx that it does not have its origin in India but is an invention of the Greeks. Concerning its original form, see Polites, *Paradoseis,* 2: 1096 ff., and Megas, *Humaniora,* pp. 198–205. See also *Laographia,* 18 (1960): 476–86, for variants. In the oral tradition, the fable constitutes a well-reasoned and self-contained tale; it is widely told, as appears from its many variants recorded in Bolte and Polívka, 2: 462 ff.

PARTS II, III, and IV

Introduction

In each of these tales the hero is given great tasks to perform: he is sent to confront danger in faraway places, and his quest is not essentially the treasure, kingdom, and wife that he ends by acquiring, but the end is the adventure itself (Max Lüthi). Thus the basic element is the spirit of enterprise that comes out in the action. The principal action is not determined by the ends to which the tale leads but by the manner in which the hero passes through the world of marvels and uses his fantastic powers, in the face of struggle and hardship, to attain his final victory. The difficult road that leads to the eventual reward is the theme of the action.

On the hero's way to success, the supernatural world plays a part either benevolent or hostile. This is the same supernatural world that operates in the realms of myth and popular legend. In the popular saga, the narration of an event, however unlikely it may be, is believed by the people to be true. But whereas in the tale the action is dynamic and ends in success, in the legend the action is passive; its aim is the event, the actual experience, and it very often ends in tragedy. This seems truly to be one of the intrinsic differences between these two kinds of popular narrative, one of which portrays heroic action, the other actual, but disarranged, human experience of the world, real and perceived (Kurt Ranke).

Yet another difference emerges, involving the nature and origin of figures of the mythical world. In the legends of the Greek people there survive, under the same or only slightly changed names, the demoniac figures of Greek myth: the Fates (*Moerae*) and Chance (*Tyche*), the Nereids (*Neraides*), and Gorgonas, the Witch (*Ghello*) and the flesh-eating Ogress (*Lamia*), Ogres (*Drakoe*) and Ogresses (*Drakaenas*), the Spirits (*Stoecheia*) and Charos. As mentioned in the Introduction, we find, apart from these survivals from the Greek past, *Stoecheia* also imported from the East: the Blackamoor (*Arapis*), probably the *Omorphe tou Kosmou* or Beauty of the World (*Giousel Dougnia*), and many more.

In order that the tale-making ability of the imagination of the Greek people may be appreciated in all its amplitude, a few examples of these figures have been appended to the selection of Greek legends.

·20· *The Monk*

Type 551, *The Sons on a Quest for a Wonderful Remedy for their Father,* combined with elements of Type 304, *The Hunter.* For an analysis see Type 550, *Search for the Golden Bird:* Ib; II; IIIc, d; IVa, c; Vb (Motif L161 "Lowly hero marries princess"). Athens

Folklore Archives MS 311, p. 106. Collected in 1873 by C. N. Chatzopoulos in Saranda Ecclesiae, Thrace; published in *Thracian Archives*, 4 (1937–38): 177–87, and reprinted in Megas, *Paramythia*, 2d Ser., no. 30, and in Megas, *Griechische Volksmärchen*, no. 53.

The special elements of this version are as follows. The remedy for the king's loss of sight is soil from a distant kingdom where the people sleep six months of the year and are awake for the other six months (Motif F771.4.4). The youngest of the king's three sons takes the road from which no traveler returns. He dupes the ogres who think him their lost youngest brother, whose stature has diminished through slaving for his captors. He kills the beast, the ogres' grandsire, which ate its children as soon as they were born (Chronos theme). He arrives at the distant kingdom and finds everyone asleep. He sees a sleeping princess in the castle, and without waking her takes various tokens (as in Type 304, IIIa, Motifs H81.1, "Hero lies by sleeping girl and leaves identifying token with her," and H81.1.1, "Hero takes token from sleeping princess"). He kisses the sleeping princess, roses fall, and with these he saves himself from the ogres as they pursue him on his return journey: with one of the roses he dries up the mud over the road and escapes; with the other, he restores the mud and prevents the ogres from following. The princess comes to his country seeking her betrothed, as in Type 304 (Motif H81, "Clandestine lover recognized by token").

Compare Grimm, *Märchen*, no. 111, Bolte and Polívka, 2: 503; and von der Leyen, *Märchen*, no. 13. For Greek variants which have been translated see Hahn, *Märchen* (1st ed.), p. 286, no. 52; Legrand, *Recueil de contes*, no. 145, "Le Dracophage"; Mitsotakis, *Volksmärchen*, p. 152, no. 18; Argenti and Rose, 1: 476, no. 1; Dawkins, *Modern Greek in Asia Minor*, nos. 355, 379. Also see Hahn, *Märchen* (1st ed.), p. 90, no. 6 (2d ed.), p. 319, no. 6; Pio, *Contes*, no. 9; Schmidt, *Griechische Märchen* p. 113, no. 18; Kretschmer, *Märchen*, no. 41; and Rossi and Caracausi, *Testi Neogreci*, p. 475.

· 21 · The Twin Brothers

Type 303, *The Twins or Blood Brothers* with elements of Type 300, *The Dragon Slayer*. Analysis: Ia, II (cypresses as life tokens that, at the birth of the twins, are planted and grow out of the fish's head [Motif E761.3 "Life token: tree (flower) fades."]); III (The first brother goes in search of the Beauty-of-the-World [*Omorphe tou Kosmou*]; he carries out the tasks set by the king, father of the princess, with the princess's help; on winning the wrestling match with the blackamoor—the Beauty herself changed into a blackamoor by a magic potion—he goes off and saves a princess from an ogre and marries her [Motif R111.1.3, "Rescue of princess (maiden) from dragon"]; transformation by a witch follows); IIIa, d; IVa; Va. Collected in 1848, in Negades, Epirus, and first published by Hahn, *Märchen* (1st ed.), p. 166, no. 22, then, in the original, by Pio, *Contes* p. 60; reprinted Megas, *Paramythia,* 2d Ser., no. 18 and translated in Megas, *Griechische Volksmärchen,* no. 41.

The contest with the Beauty-of-the-World (*Omorphe tou Kosmou*), also demoniac in nature, is found in a Thracian variant collected in 1894 (Athens Folklore Archives MS. 223, p. 67, no. 6), published in Megas, *Begegnung,* no. 9: "The Fisherman's Son and his *Gorgona*" (Type 303: Ia; II [As Life-Tokens, the Cypresses], III [as in Type 300], c, d; IVa, b, c; Va [Motif B512, "Medicine shown by animal"]).

I wish to note only the variants of this tale that appear in foreign tongues: Hahn, *Märchen* (2d ed.), p. 214; Schmidt, *Griechische Märchen,* p. 118, no. 23; Legrand, *Recueil de contes,* p. 161; Mitsotakis, *Volksmärchen,* p. 140; Georgeakis and Pineau, *Le Folk-lore,* p. 103, no. 13; Dawkins, *More Greek Folktales,* no. 38; Dawkins, *Modern Greek in Asia Minor,* p. 489; Rossi and Caracausi, *Testi Neogreci,* p. 152, no. 26. In the *Folktales of the World* series, see Christiansen, *Folktales of Norway,* no. 72; Ranke, *Folktales of Germany,* no. 29; Seki, *Folktales of Japan,* no. 15; and Pino-Saavedra, *Folktales of Chile,* no. 5. For other variants, see Megas, *Paramythia,* 2d Ser., p. 222, note to tale no. 18.

The tale of the twin brothers is widely told, as is plain from the many variants in Bolte and Polívka, 1: 528 ff. Compare Grimm, *Märchen,* nos. 60, 85; and von der Leyen, *Märchen,* nos. 7, 8. It was extensively studied by Kurt Ranke in *Die zwei Brüder,* but the question of its origin has given rise to some controversy. Some have associated it, because of many common elements, with the ancient Egyptian tale of the two brothers, recorded c. 1200 B.C. and first made known in Europe in 1859. Liungman (*Volksmärchen,* pp. 50 ff.) sets it in the Byzantine era (A.D. 300–1500) and surmises that it passed from Constantinople, after the fall of that city, to Italy and thence to Western Europe. According to Ranke it is not very old, and is in no way related to the Egyptian *Batamärchen* but probably originated in France in the fourteenth century.

· 22 · *Anthousa the Fair with Golden Hair*

Type 310, *The Maiden in the Tower,* plus Type 313, *The Girl as Helper in the Hero's Flight.* Athens Folklore Archives MS 149, p. 58. Collected by A. Christides in Iena, Eastern Thrace in 1890; published, Megas, *Paramythia,* 1st Ser., p. 88, no. 9; translated Megas, *Griechische Volksmärchen* no. 29.

On this beautiful tale, see Bolte and Polívka 1: 97 ff., 2: 517, notes CDH[1] and von der Leyen, *Märchen,* no. 32; Grimm, *Märchen,* no. 12, "Rapunzel." Recent studies of this tale are those of Max Lüthi, *Fabula,* 3 (1959–60): 95 ff., "Die Herkunft des Grimmschen Rapunzelmärchens," and Michael Meracles, *Laographia,* 21 (1963–64): 416 ff. Lüthi demonstrates that the source of the German Rapunzel is the French Persinette of "Mademoiselle de la France," while Meracles, working on the basis of twenty-two Greek variants, two Serbo-Croatian, and one Corsican, concludes that the girl shut up in the tower is originally not the adopted but the true daughter of the ogress (or witch) and that the birthplace of this tale is in southeastern Europe.

The theme of the hero, a brave lad under the curse of an old woman, is used in a Slavic tale (Bolte and Polívka 1: 50). For the other elements of this tale, see Bolte and Polívka 2: 526 ff., 140 ff., Politis, *Laographia* 2 (1910): 147 ff., and Dawkins, *More Greek Folktales,* no. 49. A variant from Rhodes is in *Laographia,* 21 (1963–64): 120 ff., 467. For other versions see Seki, *Folktales of Japan,* nos. 23, 24; Christiansen, *Folktales of Norway,* no. 78; and Dégh, *Folktales of Hungary,* nos. 3, 8.

· 23 · *The Shepherd and the Three Diseases*

Type 332A*, *Visit in the House of the Dead.* Athens Folklore Archives MS 1159E, p. 83. Narrated by a seventy-five-year-old woman of Koroni, Messenia; collected, 1938, by Georgia Tarsouli; published *Laographia,* 17 (1957–58): 145; reprinted Megas, *Paramythia,* 2d Ser., p. 203, no. 42; translated in Megas, *Griechische Volksmärchen,* no. 68.

Of the same type as *Godfather Death* (Type 332), the version we have here is nevertheless in the tone of the droll tale. The common man not infrequently jokes about the bitter things of life and so pokes fun at unrelenting Charos; Charos, indeed, appears in certain

Greek variants of the tale published in *Laographia*, 4 (1912–14): 73; 15 (1953–54): 418, no. 39; and 17 (1957–58), 146; also found as "The Thrush" in Miliopoulos and Vonderlage, *Mazedonische Bauerstuben*, p. 49.

The cave with the lighted candles is also found in tales of the common type in Grimm, *Märchen*, p. 44. In those it is Death who leads the godfather to the cave, shows him his own life-candle, but snuffs it out, punishing him for having been a cheat (Bolte and Polívka 1: 381, note D²; Motif E765.1.3). There is nothing of the droll in this form of the tale, as in the variants from Lesbos in Carnoy and Nicolaïdès, *Traditions*, p. 144, and Garnett, *Women of Turkey*, 1: 185. See notes by Megas in *Laographia*, 17 (1959): 145–48, as well as von der Leyen, *Märchen*, p. 130; Moser-Rath, *Predigtmärlein*, no. 21; and Grimm, *Märchen*, no. 44.

·24· *The Enchanted Lake*

Type 402, *The Mouse (Cat, Frog, etc.) as Bride*. Told by Marianna Kambouriglou of Athens; printed in "Athenaika Paramythia," *Deltíon Historikes Ethnologikes Hetaerias*, 1 (1893): 330, no. 11; reprinted in Megas, *Paramythia*, 2d Ser., p. 89, no. 21; and translated in Megas, *Griechische Volksmärchen*, no. 44.

The theme of the three princes finding wives by the shooting of arrows is a usual introduction in tales of this type from Greece, Slavic countries, Turkey, Finland, and also from Arabia and India (Bolte and Polívka, 2: 38; Eberhard and Boratav Types 86, I, 1 and 87, I, 1; Cosquin, *Contes*, pp. 282, 292, 303). The youngest prince's arrow falls in a lake; retrieving it, he finds a frog and brings it home. The frog helps him on his father's quests; he obtains the best gifts and the most beautiful bride and wins the kingdom. In Western European variants the hero follows in the direction shown by the feather that the king blows into the air (Grimm, *Märchen*, no. 63, "Die Drei Federn"; von der Leyen, *Märchen*, no. 62).

The main theme here is the spouse with the animal exterior. At the basis of the construction of this tale is the magical nature of the wife concealed in an animal skin until the young man to whose lot she has fallen through the shooting of the arrow throws the skin into the fire and obliges her to remain ever afterward at his side. Megas endeavored to show in *Hessische Blätter für Volkskunde*, 49–50 (1958): 147, that the time and place of the destruction of the skin are significant in the formulation of the tale. For the union of mortal man with a woman of supernatural nature, see Bolte and Polívka 2: 269–71. A version of this popular tale is found in Pino-Saavedra, *Folktales of Chile,* no. 14.

·25· Brother and Sister

Type 403A, *The Wishes.* Analysis: IIc; IIIb; IVb, d; Va, b; VI, with the following special features. Instead of the Savior and Peter, the three Fates bestow on the poor but hospitable girl marvelous gifts (Motif D1454.1.2), e.g., that pearls should fall from her hair when she combs it. While attempting to sell the pearls in town, her brother is arrested as a thief and taken to the king; when he hears of the sister's gifts, the king asks for her hand in marriage; as the girl is on her way to marry the king, a gypsy-witch changes her into a bird with a pin and takes her place; the bird sings strange songs and is caught; when the pin is drawn out, the spell is broken.

Athens Folklore Archives MS 1467, p. 8. Collected by Georgia Tarsouli in Koroni, Messenia, 1921; published in Megas, *Paramythia,* 2d Ser., no. 15.

This tale is widely told in Greece. A beautiful Cretan variant has appeared in Megas, *Begegnung,* no. 6, "The Two Sisters and Christ." Translated variants are found in Hahn, *Märchen* (1st ed.), p. 193, no. 28; Kretschmer, *Märchen,* no. 62 (Epirus); Schmidt, *Griechische Märchen,* no. 13 (Zante); Dawkins, *More Greek Folktales,* no. 11 (Thrace). A version also appears in Seki, *Folktales of Japan,* no. 29.

·26· The Sun and His Wife

Type 425L, *Padlock on the Enchanted Husband.* Athens Folklore Archives MS 36, p. 279, no. 7, collected by D. N. Sarrhos in Epirus, 1888–1892. The Epirot storyteller did not recall the end of the tale and it has been completed from a variant told on the island of Naxos (Athens Folklore Archives MS 1545, pp. 354–68). See Swahn, *Cupid and Psyche,* p. 34, subtype L. Analysis: I 16; II 8 Helios (sun) = Husband, *Ach-chach* (Alasandalack) = Servant; III 3, 4; IV 1a. (The heroine obtains a candle and sees her husband; she wakes him by dropping wax on his body); VI, 1, 2a.

Variants include one unpublished text in Athens Folklore Archives, MS 355, p. 15, collected by I. Drakos in Moschonesia, an islet near Chios; Hahn, *Märchen* (2d ed.), p. 80, no. 73 (Crete);

Roussel, *Contes,* p. 91, no. 44. There are five unpublished variants from Naxos, Paros, Crete, the Dardanelles, and Philadelphia (New Sehir) in Asia Minor. Swahn correctly divides his material for the tale type *Amor et Psyche* into subtypes in accordance with the episodes leading to the reunion of the husband and wife. Of these, the most important is subtype A, having many elements in common with the tale of Apuleius. See Megas, *Begegnung,* no. 17, and Megas, *Griechische Volksmärchen,* no. 47.

There are 379 variants of this tale known to me (as against the 35 known to Swahn), from all regions of Greece. Also see Bolte and Polívka, 2: 229; von der Leyen, *Märchen,* 68; Grimm, *Märchen,* no. 88; Liungman, *Volkmärchen,* pp. 91–98.

·27· *Mr· Semolina*

Type 425A, *The Husband is a Vivified Image. Long, Wearisome Search. Three Nights to Sleep with Husband.* Given in Swahn, *Cupid and Psyche,* as Type 425B. Athens Folklore Archives MS 22, pp. 28–34; collected 1914, by D. Ioannou in Haghia Anna, Euboea; published in Megas, *Paramythia,* 2d Ser., p. 115, no. 25; translated by Megas, *Griechische Volksmärchen,* no. 48.

The principal motif of the subtype is the recovery in three nights (Bolte and Polívka, 3: 406; von der Leyen, *Märchen,* no. 71; Grimm, *Märchen,* no. 193, "Der Trommler"). According to Swahn, this is an "innovation" under subtype A, which principally belongs to France, whence it spread to almost all of Europe and Asia Minor, more particularly to Ireland, Denmark, and Norway. It is represented in Greece by 28 texts out of 379 known. A version of Type 425 is in Noy, *Folktales of Israel,* no. 58.

·28· *The Crab*

Type 425D, *Vanished Husband Learned of by Keeping Inn (Bath-House).* See analysis by Swahn, Type 425D. Athens Folklore Seminar MS published in Megas, *Paramythia,* 2d Ser. no. 26; translated in Megas, *Griechische Volksmärchen,* no. 50; variant in Megas, *Begegnung,* no. 20, from Thrace.

Principal theme: the free hostelry (Motif H11.1.1: "Recognition at inn [hospital, etc.] where all must tell their life histories"), which is also found in the Greek novel, *Libestros et Rhodamné,* and most probably came to the West from the East by the same route taken by the returning Crusaders. Also see Bolte and Polívka, 2: 255[1] and 503; von der Leyen, *Märchen,* no. 13; Grimm, *Märchen,* no. 111, "Der gelernte Jäger").

·29· The Sleeping Prince

Type 425G, *False Bride Takes Heroine's Place as She Tries to Stay Awake. Substitute Bride. Recognition When True Bride Tells Story to Objects.* See Swahn, Type 425G. Variants are in Dawkins, *Modern Greek Folktales,* 175, no. 32, "The Prince in a Swoon"; Dawkins, *More Greek Folktales,* no. 5; Hahn, *Märchen* (1st ed.), p. 121, no. 12, and Geldart, *Folk-lore,* p. 62. Greek text published in Pio, *Contes,* p. 49; *Laographia,* 21 (1963): 130 and 469, no. 3; Carnoy and Nicolaïdès, *Traditions,* pp. 127–43, no. 7; *Folk-Lore,* 12 (1901,) 320, no. 24. The story of the sleeping prince and of the substitute bride is also found in Type 894, *The Ghoulish Schoolmaster and the Stone of Pity.*

·30· The Turtle and the Chickpea

Type 465A, *The Quest for the Unknown.* Collected by S. Manassides in Aenos in 1885. For the material of this type of tale, see comments on tale no. 27 above, as well as Megas's articles in *Hessische Blätter für Volkskunde,* 49–50 (1958): 135, "Der um sein schönes Weib Beneidete;" and *Laographia,* 17 (1957–58): 149–69, 177 ff. Published in Megas, *Paramythia,* 1st ser., p. 46, and in Megas, *Griechische Volksmärchen,* no. 24.

·31· The Seven Ravens

Type 451, *The Maiden Who Seeks Her Brothers.* Analysis: Ia, c; IIa, IIIa. (The spell is broken with the girl's departure for the tower, which she opens with the bat's claw.) Athens Folklore Archives MS 1462, p. 104; collected by Maria Lioudaki, 1938, in Chersonesos, near Herakleion, Crete; published in Megas, *Paramythia,* 2d Ser., p. 51, no. 17; translated in Megas, *Griechische Volksmärchen,* no. 40.

Nearest to this text is the variant from Lesbos, published in Megas, *Paramythia,* 2d Ser., p. 45, no. 16, "The Twelve Brothers Turned into Birds" (Ia, b; IIb; IIIb; IVa, b [dumb girl accused of witchcraft because she goes out at night to gather plants of which she makes shirts for her brothers], Va). The tale goes on to recount sufferings in storylike manner and the punishment of the witch-stepmother. Other variants: from Zante, "The Nine Wild Swans and Fair Helen," *Laographia,* 11 (1934): 452, no. 12; from Patmos, "The Nine Eagles," *Laographia,* 16 (1956): 170, no. 24; from Carpathos, "The Twelve Brothers," Michaelides-Nouaros, *Laographika Symmeikta* ("Folklore Miscellany"), p. 328, no. 9; from Astron Kynosoura in the Peloponnese, an anecdote in Athens Folklore Archives (collected by Polites, Athens Folklore Archives, unpublished collections, 102, pp. 1–4).

The variants come from islands at one time under Italian and "Frankish" rule (after 1204 A.D.); so possibly the tale originated in Italy. See von der Leyen, *Märchen,* no. 44, Grimm, *Märchen,* nos. 9, 25; Bolte and Polívka, 1: 69, 227. Compare also Liungman, *Volksmärchen,* no. 105 and Ranke, *Folktales of Germany,* no. 32.

· 32 · *Poppies*

Type 514*, *The Unlaughing Fate.* Athens Folklore Archives MS 1387, 401, no. 51; collected by Adamantios Adamantiou in Tinos, Cyclades; published in Megas, *Paramythia,* 2d Ser., p. 131, no. 28, and translated in Megas, *Griechische Volksmärchen,* no. 51.

The theme of this tale is the unsmiling Fate, made to laugh by a poor girl, who is given beauty and is destined to become a queen.

In this text from Tinos no reason is given why the queen laughs, and the episode is created in which the king's beard is likened to the privy brush. The reason referred to in other variants is her mother's obstinacy. Even when her daughter becomes queen, the mother pursues her with the same insistent questions: what became of the food she had begged, which her daughter gave to the poor old man or the three old women, and so on. This trait is recalled by her daughter the queen, who laughs. Obviously the episode gives rise to an extension of the tale, which resembles the Turkish form in Eberhard and Boratav, Type 164. The episode of the king's beard is found in two other Turkish tales (Eberhard and Boratav Type 34, IV, 4, and Type 132, IV, 4).

The tale may be grouped with further stories of the "Unsmiling (or Unlaughing) Fate" as *514D. See Megas, *Festschrift für Friedrich von der Leyen,* p. 61, "Die Moiren als Funktioneller Faktor im Neugriechischen Märchen."

·33· The King's Godson and the Baldchin

Type 531, *Ferdinand the True and Ferdinand the False,* plus Type 554, *The Grateful Animals.* Collected by K. Chadzioannou in Cyprus, published in *Kypriaka Chronika* ("Cypriot Chronicles"), 9, (1933): 293; translated by Megas, *Griechische Volksmärchen,* no. 27. This story has been dealt with by Megas in his monograph *Der Bartlose in Neugriechischen Märchen,* in which he showed the lacunae in the tradition of the German *Kinder- und Hausmärchen,* no. 126 and went on to analyze the type on the basis of forty Greek texts. To the variants noted there may be added: Dawkins, *Forty-five Stories from the Dodecanese,* p. 56, no. 3; Dawkins, *Modern Greek Folktales,* p. 182, no. 34; Dawkins, *More Greek Folktales,* p. 59, no. 10; Pontine Archives 18: 286, no. 2; *Makedonicon Hemerologion,* 1: 312. Also see Grimm, *Märchen,* no. 126; von der Leyen, *Märchen,* no. 46; and Liungman, *Volksmärchen,* p. 149.

·34· The Navel of the Earth

Type 552, *The Girls Who Married Animals.* Athens Folklore Archives MS 186, p. 19: collected, 1883, by Symeon Manasseides in Aenos; published in Megas, *Paramythia,* 1st Ser., p. 103, no. 11; reprinted, *Jahresgabe* (1957), 7 ff., 21 ff.; translated in Megas, *Griechische Volksmärchen,* no. 31.

This tale differs from the widely known type at several points. The dying king commands his three sons to marry his three daughters to the first who should happen to ask for their hands in marriage. A lame man, a cross-eyed man, and a beggar present themselves (ogres, kings of the wild beasts and birds). The youngest gives away his sisters and then sets out to win *Omorphe tou Kosmou* (Beauty of the World). The test question is, what are the features of the navel of the earth? He learns the answer from the eagle who arrives last at the gathering of the birds (compare the fable of Melampus, *Apollodorus* 1, nos. 9, 11).

Compare Grimm, *Märchen,* no. 197; von der Leyen, *Märchen,* no. 178; and Bolte and Polívka, 3: 425, in which the Greek variants are recorded. To these may be added: Kretschmer, *Märchen,* no. 26; Dawkins, *Modern Greek in Asia Minor,* pp. 272 ff., 379 ff., and Dawkins, *Modern Greek Folktales,* p. 121, no. 23.

The young man is helped in finding the unknown place by his

supernatural brothers-in-law (Ilines, Bilines, Alamalakousses in Hahn, *Märchen*, no. 25; Pio, *Contes*, no. 40; and Tsun Matzun in Kretschmer, *Märchen*, no. 26), which replaces the "navel of the earth" in the Thracian variant. It is probable that we have here popularized traces of the ancient representation of the navel of the earth, similar to those preserved in the Thracian tradition of the navel of the sea (Polites, *Paradoseis*, no. 554). Also see *Laographia*, 3 (1912): 700; W. H. Roscher, *Omphalos*, p. 9, note 13, and his study *Der Omphalosgedanke bei verschiedenen Völkern*, p. 2. For an Indian representation of the navel of the earth, calling to mind the eagles of Zeus, of which gold likenesses stood near the navel of the earth at Delphi and on top of pillars before the altar of Lycean Zeus, see Roscher, *Omphalos*, pp. 55 ff., 126, plates VI, 1, VIII, 3. See also Roscher, *Neue Omphalosstudien*, p. 20, and his article "Kleine Beiträge zur Religionwissschaft und Volkskunde," part 1, "Omphalos," *Laographia*, 7 (1923): 207–14.

· 35 · Cinderello

Type 560 *The Magic Ring*, Ib, II; IIIa, b, c; IVa, c. The final episode in which the cat and dog return is worthy of note, as it corresponds to practically all the Greek variants and to four out of twelve of the Turkish variants (Eberhard and Boratav Type 58, III, 5): the dog asks the cat, while swimming, to give him the magic object, threatening to throw her into the depths of the sea if she refuses. The ring (or stone) falls into the sea and a fish swallows it; the fish is caught in the fishermen's nets; they throw it to the cat and the ring is found (compare Type 736A [Motif N211.1], *The Ring of Polycrates*).

Collected in 1905 by Paul Kretschmer in Lesbos, and published by him in *Der heutige lesbische Dialekt*, p. 524, no. 21, and in *Märchen*, no. 11; reprinted in Dawkins, *Modern Greek Folktales*, no. 9 and in Megas, *Griechische Volksmärchen*, no. 26.

Widely told in Greece, there are seventy-two variants of which twenty-two are printed; see *Laographia*, 10 (1962): 428. Translated texts are published in Hahn, *Märchen*, 2d ed., p. 109, no. 9, p. 202 (Epirus, Euboea); Geldart, *Folk-Lore*, p. 42; Boulanger, *Contes*, p. 155 (Corfu); Paton, *Folk-lore*, 10 (1909): 201 (Lesbos); Carnoy and Nicolaïdès, *Traditions*, p. 57 (Lesbos); Argenti and Rose, 1: 464, no. 14 (Chios); Dawkins, *Forty-Five Stories from the Dodecanese*, p. 75, no. 4 (Astypoloea); Dawkins, *Modern Greek in Asia Minor*, pp.

457, 329, 507 (Cappadocia); Miliopoulos and Vonderlage, *Mazedonische Bauerstuben*, p. 25. Versions of this tale are found also in Pino-Saavedra, *Folktales of Chile*, no. 24, and Eberhard, *Folktales of China*, no. 62.

· 36 · The Mill

Type 565, *The Magic Mill*, Ib, c; IIc. Athens Folklore Archives MS 25, p. 34; collected in 1901 by S. Anagnostou in Lesbos. Published in Megas, *Paramythia*, 1st Ser., p. 72, no. 6, and translated in Megas, *Neugriechesche Märchen*, no. 21.

See Bolte and Polívka, 2: 438; von der Leyen, *Märchen*, no. 23; Grimm, *Märchen*, no. 103; Liungman, *Volksmärchen*, pp. 167 ff.; Kretschmer, *Märchen*, p. 337, no. 50. Versions are also found in Eberhard, *Folktales of China*, no. 49 and Seki, *Folktales of Japan*, no. 39. Greek variants are in Kretschmer, *Märchen*, p. 216, no. 50 (Arcadia); *Zographios Agon*, 2 (1896): 21, no. 2 (Lesbos), and p. 70 (Crete); Koutras, *Ninety Mourabades*, pp. 22 ff., no. 31 (Daies, Doumelia); and Miliopoulos and Vonderlage, *Mazedonische Bauerstuben*, pp. 47 ff. Anecdote variants from Aetolia, Pelion, and Lesbia are in the Athens Folklore Archives.

· 37 · Myrsina

Type 709, *Snow White*. Athens Folklore Archives MS 188, p. 82; collected in 1888, by I. Proios in Macedonia; published in Megas, *Paramythia*, 1st Ser., p. 53, no. 4, and translated in Megas, *Griechische Volksmärchen*, no. 19.

One of the most beautiful tales in the whole collection, the present text reveals certain points of difference from the common type: cruel sisters instead of a murderous stepmother; the questioning of the sun instead of a magic mirror; abandonment in the woods, instead of attempted murder; and the Twelve Months in place of dwarfs.

On the questioning of the sun, see Polites, *Laographika Symmeikta* ("Folklore miscellany"), 2: 137 ff. Also see Bolte and Polívka, 1: 453; von der Leyen, *Märchen*, no. 37; Grimm, *Märchen*, no. 53; Liungman, *Volksmärchen*, p. 108. This tale is widely told in Greece; at least sixty-six variants are known. Translations are available in Legrand, *Recueil de contes*, p. 133 (Chios); Boulanger, *Contes*, pp. 61, 87, 133 (Corfu); Schmidt, *Griechische Märchen*, p. 110, no. 17 (Zante); Dawkins, *Modern Greek in Asia Minor*, p.

441, no. 1 (Cappadocia); Rossi and Caracausi, *Testi Neogreci,* p. 208, no. 34. Also see Dawkins, *Modern Greek Folktales,* p. 113, no. 20. A foreign variant is found in Pino-Saavedra, *Folktales of Chile,* no. 28.

·38· *Maroula*

Type 898* *Daughter to be Given to Sun when Twelve.* Collected by I. Zographakes in Crete; published in *Parnassos,* 8 (1884): 712; and translated in Megas, *Griechische Volksmärchen,* no. 17.

This charming Greek tale illustrates the undying love between mother and child. The childless mother asks the Sun for a girl-child and promises to give her to him when she is twelve years old. This is done. The Sun learns of the girl's longing to return to her mother and gets helpful animals (hares or deer) to take her back. She avoids the efforts of a *lamia* to overpower her and succeeds in returning home. It is classified by Stith Thompson among the novelle, and rightly, since it is the offering of the child to the Sun that brings about her birth; but the Sun does not appear as an evil spirit (as in similar cases, e.g., Types 810–814), but sympathizes with the daughter in her longing for her mother.

There are twenty-five Greek variants, and translations can be found in Hahn, *Märchen* (1st ed.), p. 245, no. 41, p. 396; Schmidt, *Griechische Märchen,* p. 104; Megas, *Begegnung.* no. 5.

·39· *The Twelve Months*

Type 480, *The Spinning-Women by the Spring. The Kind and Unkind Girls.* Introduced by Type 750F*, *The Old Man's Blessing.* A poor woman gives children water in which she has washed her hands after making bread for her rich sister; as to the other elements, cf. Type 480; IIg; Ve (In the abode of the Twelve Months); VId; VIId; VIIId. For the Twelve Months, see Bolte and Polívka, I, 107. A detailed study of this type is Warren E. Roberts, *The Tale of the Kind and Unkind Girls.*

Athens Folklore Archives MS 110, p. 196; collected in 1882 by Symeon Manasseides in Aenos (Eastern Thrace); published in Megas, *Paramythia,* 1st Ser., p. 63, no. 5; reprinted in *Von Prinzen, Trollenn, und Herrn Fro,* p. 39; translated in Megas, *Griechische Volksmärchen,* no. 20.

This is one of the most beautiful tales passed on to us in the last two decades of the nineteenth century by Father Symeon Manasseides from Aenos and other villages of Eastern Thrace. It is similar in its descriptiveness and its moral effect on children to the Grimms' tale "Frau Holle," no. 24, to which it has been related (see Bolte and Polívka, 1: 207; von der Leyen, *Märchen*, p. 54). Variants in translation are found in Kretschmer, *Märchen*, p. 338, no. 52; Dawkins, *Modern Greek in Asia Minor*, p. 254, no. 2; p. 347, no. 4; p. 399; Dawkins, "The Twelve Months," *Laographia*, 7 (1923): 285; Dawkins, *Modern Greek Folktales*, p. 452, no. 76; Megas, *Begegnung*, no. 7; Briggs and Tongue, *Folktales of England*, no. 2; and Dorson, *Buying the Wind*, pp. 206-9 (from Kentucky). There are twenty-two published and forty unpublished variants in the Athens Folklore Archives and Athens Folklore Seminar.

· *40* · *The Two Neighbors*

Type 613, *The Two Travelers (Truth and Falsehood)*, Ia, b, d; IIa; IIIa, b; IV. Recorded by Eumorphia Sava in the village of Polychnitos, Lesbos, 1957; published in Megas, *Paramythia*, 2d Ser., no. 31, and translated in Megas, *Griechische Volksmärchen*, no. 54. There are twenty-four known variants, of which twelve are printed. The wager in the majority of these is: Which wins, truth or falsehood? or, Which comes out on top: good or evil?

I refer only to the published variants in translation: Hahn, *Märchen* (1st ed.), p. 209, no. 30 (Epirus); Kretschmer, *Märchen*, no. 64; Pio, *Contes*, p. 227 (Syra); Mitsotakis, *Volksmärchen*, p. 135, no. 16; Garnett, *Women of Turkey*, 2: 286; Dawkins, *Modern Greek in Asia Minor*, pp. 389, 483 (Cappadocia); Dawkins, *Forty-Five Stories from the Dodecanese*, no. 32 (Kos); Miliopoulos and Vonderlage, *Mazedonische Bauerstuben*, p. 41 (West Macedonia); Klaar, *Klephtenkrieg*, pp. 159-62 (Epirus).

According to Bolte and Polívka, 2: 480, this widely told tale has its probable beginning in the Orient. At all events, in 1930 a tale written on papyrus of the twelfth or thirteenth century B.C. was discovered by Allen H. Gardiner, who gave it the title, "The Blending of Truth." Truth and Falsehood are brothers who quarrel over which of them governs the world. See text and notes in Emma Brunner-Traut, *Altägyptische Märchen*, pp. 44, 240. Compare von der Leyen, *Märchen*, no. 92; Grimm, *Märchen*, no. 107; Massignon, *Folktales of France*, no. 45.

·41· *Truth and Falsehood*

In the Greek list, this tale is given the supplementary *613D, *Truth and Falsehood*. This text, from Argos in the Peloponnese, was published in *Laographia*, 4 (1912–14): 297, no. 1. There are two unpublished variants from Eleia and Carpathos. Whereas in the preceding tale Truth wins, in this one Falsehood's hold over the world is admitted. The tone, at the close, is that of the droll.

·42· *The Old Man and the Three Brothers*

Type 750D, *Three Brothers Each Granted a Wish by Angel Visitor*. Collected in Naxos by Dialechti Zeugoli in 1924; published in Megas, *Griechische Volksmärchen*, no. 61.

Widely told in Greece as a religious tale, the content in this form is as follows. An old wayfarer (Christ) grants the wishes of three brothers. The first wishes for the rooks to turn into sheep; the second, for the water of the spring to turn into wine or oil; the third, that he might marry a wife who thinks the same as he does. When they get rich, the two elder brothers use the old beggar shamefully; their life again becomes what it was before. The youngest takes the beggar into his house to spend the night and he and his wife decide to slay their child so as to be able to treat the beggar's sores with the child's blood (or with its ashes, after burning it in the oven). The child is found alive and well the next morning in the oven; Christ (the old wayfarer) has brought it back to life.

The last episode is a variant of the second episode in Type 750B, in which the poor peasant kills his only cow for the sake of a stranger (Christ), but next morning he finds the cow alive in the stable (Motif Q141, "Reward: man's cows magically multiply"), as in the Greek tale of Saint Philip and foreign tales of other saints. The sacrifice of a child constitutes one of the basic elements in the tale of Faithful John, who is brought back to life with the blood of his master's child (Type 516C, Bolte and Polívka I, 46D, Motifs E113, "Resuscitation by blood; and S268, "Child sacrificed to provide blood for cure of friend.") According to E. O. Winsted, whose study on this theme appeared in *Folk-Lore* 57 (1946): 139, "The Self-sacrificing Child," the idea of blood sacrifice came from India and spread to western Europe. Also see Dawkins, *Modern Greek Folktales*, pp. 227, 415. The tale as a whole seems to have spread particularly in eastern Europe, as Kretschmer observes (*Märchen*, p. 337, no. 51); Kretschmer also records Bulgarian, Serbo-Croatian, Hungarian, and other variants. Armenian, Albanian, and Berber variants have been recorded by W. R. Halliday, in Dawkins, *Modern Greek in Asia Minor*, p. 253 and by Dawkins, *Modern Greek Folktales*, p. 415. For the text of Greek variants (thirty-one in number), see *Laographia*, 17 (1957-1958): 130-31. An additional thirty-six are unpublished. I note here only those translated: Kretschmer, *Märchen*, no. 51; Klaar, *Klephtenkrieg*, 43-51; Dawkins, *Modern Greek in Asia Minor*, p. 523; Dawkins, *Modern Greek Folktales*, no. 70; Miliopoulos and Vonderlage, *Mazedonische Bauerstuben*, pp. 95-97.

·43· The Card Player in Paradise

Type 750H*, *The Notary Enters Heaven*. Collected from a fifty-one year old woman, M. Nicolaidou of Argyroupolis, Pontus, by P. Nicolaides, undergraduate in Chaldia, Pontus; published in *Laographia*, 17 (1957-58): 626 ff.

Sixteen Greek variants are known from various parts of the Greek-speaking region from Pontus to Calabria and Cyprus. Of these eight have been published, having the following content: Christ and Apostles are shown hospitality by a card player: he is granted a wish (Q145 "Miraculously long life as reward." Q142 "Magic treasure as reward for humility"), and asks that he may always win at cards (N221 "Man granted power of winning at cards") and be received in Paradise. He lives and dies peacefully; on his way to Heaven, he enters into Hell and plays cards with Satan. By winning twelve times, he is able to take twelve souls out of Hell with him (E756 "Contest over souls"). To Christ, who tells him He was expecting him alone, he answers that he also expected Him to come alone to dinner, but that He came with twelve more. Thus, they all enter Paradise. According to another variant from Pontus, Saint Peter lets the card player and the twelve redeemed souls into Paradise, but takes away his deck of cards and sends them back to Hell. Pontine Archives, 15 (1950): 116-18, no. 4. Also see variants in *Laographia*, 11, (1934-37): 506 (Zante); Klaar, *Klephtenkrieg*, pp. 82-85; *Mélanges offerts à Merlier*, 2: 379-95 (Cephallonia); Rossi and Caracausi, *Testi Neogreci, pp.* 303-6 (Calabria); von der Leyen, *Märchen*, no. 17; Grimm, *Märchen*, no. 82.

·44· The Devil Who Wore Out Forty Pairs of Tsarouchia

Motif M212.2 "Devil at gallows repudiates his bargain with robber." Collected by Th. Kostakis in Tsakonas, Asia Minor; published in *Laographia*, 17 (1957–58): 108, no. 6; reprinted in Megas, *Paramythia*, 2d Ser., p. 199, no. 40; translated in Megas, *Griechische Volksmärchen*, no. 60.

The tale has as its subject the degradation of man in coming to an agreement with the devil. Variants known to us number four: from the Peloponnese (*Laographia* 6 [1917–18]: 650); from Cephallonia (Polites, *Paroemiae*, 4, [1904]: 378, where the word *diabolos* [devil] occurs forty-three times); and two anecdotes, one from Chalkis and one from Thebes, both in the Athens Folklore Archives. But the tale is told more widely than appears from the *Paroemiae*, in which the tale has been condensed (see *Laographia*, 18 [1959]: 138). The theme of the footwear that the devil wears out in the pursuance of his aim is reproduced exactly in a medieval tale (Wesselski, *Märchen des Mittelalters*, p. 244, no. 54: "Die Schuhe des Teufels") as well as in many variants (Bolte and Polívka, 2: 178).

Apparently this tale is widespread among the people and in literature. It is included in the Motif-Index but not in the Type Index, and is classified in the Greek catalogue of tales under the supplementary number, *821C, *Devil Promises Help*. Connected to this tale is the story of deceiving the devil by the feigned hanging of the man with whom the agreement has been made, found in Estonia (Aarne, *Estnische Märchen und Sagen*) and in the international catalogue (Type 1190*, *The Man Thought Hanged* [K215]). See the two Greek variants in *Laographia*, 17 (1957–58): 139.

·45· The Child Who Was Poor and Good

Cumulative tale: The Poor Child's Clothes: bird—spider—thornbush—lamb. Collected by Niki Perdika in Skyros and published in *Skyros*, 2: 225, no. 22; translated in Megas, *Griechische Volksmärchen*, no. 38.

·46· Chance and the Poor Man

Type 460B, *The Journey in Search of Fortune*. Athens Folklore Archives MS 846, pp. 4–7; collected in 1888 by C. Stamoulis in

Drakeia, near Volos, Thessaly; published by Megas in *Laographia,* 15 (1953): 6–7.

Tales of this type are based on the theme of the journey to find Chance, who controls the affairs of men. The requests put by various beings to the hero of the tale along the way further constitute a basic element of the story, in establishing the means whereby Chance is able to come to the aid of the poor man. The Greek tales of a journey to meet Chance set out the plot independently and not as an extension of the well-known tale of the rich man and his son-in-law (Type 930), the form in variants from western Europe. These variants have retained elements of the original substance of the tale, as Aarne concludes at the close of his study *Der Reiche Mann und Sein Schwiegersohn* (p. 180). In the supposed original form, the poor man tells Chance (or God) what he wants, and Chance (or God) answers benevolently each time, "You will have your chance on your return." Thus also in the Thessalian tale, "Chance received him favorably and told him to return home and she would send him three occasions (i.e., opportunities), which he might turn to account and so become rich." But whereas in the Indian and Annamite variants, which apparently agree with the *Ur*-form, the hero of the tale does indeed take advantage on his return journey of the opportunities that present themselves and arrives home a rich man, in the Greek tale he does not understand Chance's words and misses his chances. Thus, the outcome of the story has the idea that misfortune originates in failure to take advantage of opportunity.

Megas has made an extensive study of the Greek and other variants of this tale in *Laographia,* 15 (1953): 6–19; Dawkins also studied them in *Forty-Five Stories from the Dodecanese,* pp. 358–68, no. 35 and in *More Greek Folktales,* no. 12. According to Dawkins, in the tales of chance we may see, in simple fashion and without moralizing, the Greek attitude to the problems of human life that relate to Man's fate, chance, and moral values (*Folk-lore,* 61 [1951]: 422).

·47· *The Ill-fated Princess*

Type 938A, *Misfortunes in Youth.* Classified by Megas among the Tales of Fate, no. *735E; Eberhard-Boratav Type 136. Athens Folklore Seminar MS 15, p. 36; collected by a student, K. Athanassatos, in Cephallonia, 1959; published in Megas, *Paramythia,* 2d Ser., p. 172, no. 33, and translated by Megas in *Griechische Volksmärchen,*

p. 244, no. 55. See Megas' contribution to *Laographia*, 15 (1953): 20–36. Compare also Lo Nigro, *Racconti populare siciliani*, no. *735.

·48· The Sack-Maker

Type 947A, *Bad Luck Cannot Be Arrested*. Eberhard-Boratav, Type 131. Athens Folklore Archives MS 186, p. 227; collected in Aenos by S. Manasseides, in 1883; published by Megas, *Paramythia*, 1st Ser., p. 120, no. 13, and translated in Megas, *Griechische Volksmärchen*, no. 37.

For comments on the tale of the poor villager who is unlucky in everything, see Polites, *Laographia*, 1 (1909): 668, and *Laographia Symmeikta* 2: 47 ff. For variants see Kretschmer, *Der heutige lesbische Dialekt*, p. 536; Dawkins, *Modern Greek Folktales*, 460, no. 79A; a monthly supplement of the daily newspaper, *Athens* (1909), p. 1650, collected in Thessaly; unpublished variants from Eurytania, Epirus, Thrace and Euboea.

PART V

Introduction

There are two other forms of narrative used by the people that stand out clearly among the tales they tell: jokes (or droll tales) and anecdotes, and religious tales.

The Droll Tale has no leanings toward the marvelous and the other world: its sphere of reference is that of the real world. The foolish and comic things of this world are recounted in the spirit of exaggeration. The Droll Tale has no particular style; its only aim is to make its audience laugh, for this kind of narrative springs from the dry and facetious humor of the people, from man's fundamental need of laughter to raise him above the cares and trials of his daily life.

The Droll Tale draws its action from the various possibilities that present themselves in the life of social man and in human character. In respect of man's occupations there is typification: for example, the miller, who habitually figures in tales of lying, typifies the swindler who is outclassed by the youth in the lying contest. Sometimes the heroes of the tales are brought to Heaven or Hell, but here the situation is set forth in the manner of parody and with

an entirely human tendency to blaspheme; they may also be brought
into some comical sort of collision either with Saint Peter or else
with the Devil and his dam. The Religious Tale, on the other hand,
follows the opposite direction; it does not take us aloft but brings
the divine down to earth. The sojourn of the gods on earth is, of
course, an extremely ancient and widely broadcast theme and, since
this descent necessarily leads to contact with man, the Religious
Tale often goes hand-in-hand with the Droll Tale. For example,
the Cephallonian's deck of cards, which is blessed by Christ in
return for the hospitality he offers Him when He comes with the
Apostles to Cephallonia (no. 43), the devil who wears out forty
pairs of *tsarouchia* (no. 44), and many others, are subjects that link
the Religious Tale with the Droll.

Like the ordinary tale, the Religious Tale may contain miracles
and magic, within the sphere of religious belief. Again like the
ordinary tale, the Religious Tale tends to assemble events both rare
and perilous, and the hero of the Religious Tale is stronger than
the temptations and tribulations to which he is exposed (see Kurt
Ranke, "Betrachtungen zum Wesen und zur Funktion des Märchen," *Studium Generale. Jahrg.* 1958, Heft II, pp. 647–64).

·49· The Riddle

Type 851, *The Princess Who Cannot Solve the Riddle.* Athens Folklore Seminar MS 111, p. 4; collected by undergraduate Maria Valasi
in Nauplion, 1959; published in Megas, *Paramythia,* 2d Ser., p. 182,
no. 36.

Polites extensively treats this type in *Laographia,* 2 (1910): 581.
See variants in *Laographia,* 21 (1963): 488. The chief difference
between the variants lies in the formation of the riddle, which, in
foreign texts (Bolte and Polívka, 1: 188; von der Leyen, *Märchen,*
p. 167) also refers to the adventures of the youth: the poisoned
ravens (as in our tale), and the riddle of the murdered lover
(Motif H805), to which Megas gives the supplementary number
*851B. There are sixteen recorded variants. The riddle is set by the
daughter or the adulterous wife of the king, the one with a view
to betrothal, the other threatening capital punishment. See Megas,
notes in *Laographia,* 21 (1963): 489; Dawkins, *Forty-Five Stories
from the Dodecanese,* no. 22, p. 252; Dawkins, *Modern Greek Folktales,* no. 67, p. 404; Legrand, *Recueil de Contes,* p. 29.

One form of this tale type is to be found in the story of *Turandot*

(Type 851A), of which we have two Greek variants (from Athens and Crete). See the notes in Kretschmer, *Märchen,* p. 329.

·*50*· *What is the Fastest Thing in the World?*

Type 875, *The Clever Peasant Girl,* Ib, III, IV, V. Bolte and Polívka 2: 349. Athens Folklore Archives MS 1545, p. 332; collected in Naxos by Dialekti Zeugoli, in 1930; published in Megas, *Griechische Volksmärchen,* no. 36.

See von der Leyen, *Märchen,* no. 76, p. 194; Dawkins, *Modern Greek Folktales,* no. 45, pp. 399–402, and *Forty-Five Stories from the Dodecanese,* nos. 20, 21. Variants are found in Argenti and Rose, 1: 436, no. 4; and Kretschmer, *Märchen,* no. 24; and there are texts in the Athens Folklore Archives. Tales of this type deal exclusively with instances of wit, particularly in the Slavic variants: e.g. "What is the sweetest thing—sleep. What is the fastest—the eye (or, thought)," and so on. This type of question and answer was already extant among the ancient Greeks and was furthermore introduced by them into philosophy. Cf. von der Leyen, *Märchen,* p. 194; Pino-Saavedra, *Folktales of Chile,* no. 36; Ranke, *Folktales of Germany,* no. 47; and Noy, *Folktales of Israel,* no. 61.

·*51*· *Princess Plumpkins* (*Pachoulenia*)

Type 884, *The Forsaken Fiancée: Service as Menial.* Recorded in Zante by M. Minotes from the narrative of Mimika Drongites, an illiterate villager of Volimes, forty years of age; published in *Laographia,* 11 (1934–37): 459, no. 15. This tale constitutes a version of Type 884, presenting considerable originality, for which reason it has been entered in the Greek catalogue under no. *884D, *Girl Dressed as Man Mocks the Prince,* contents as follows:

Two kings are brothers, one having three (seven, or nine) sons, the other three (seven, or nine) daughters. The first jeers at the second for having only girls. The youngest daughter undertakes to prove that girls are worth more than boys and sets out, earlier than her uncle's son, to bring the Water of Life, or some other precious commodity, from foreign parts. In male attire, she rides her horse across the river, while her cousin struggles to empty the river with a walnut shell (or spoon), before he will cross it. Arriving in the foreign country, she enters the service of the prince, who has in his possession the object of her quest. He suspects that she is not a man and, following her mother's advice, puts her to the test first in the garden to see if she will pick the flowers; second in the store to see if she will first look at women's clothing; third in sleep to see if the flowers put in her bed will be fresh next morning; and fourth in the bath. In the last test she tricks the prince into falling into the water himself; she then seizes the Water of Life (or the Parrot of Happiness) and departs, leaving the mocking words, "I came with my honor and leave with my honor." On her return to her country, she finds her cousin at the riverside, still holding the walnut shell. The prince she has tricked finds out where she lives and sells her two turtle doves, given him by his mother who is a witch. They bring her, asleep on their wings, to his house and he marries her.

In *Laographia*, 10 (1962): 438–45, Megas dealt with tales that have as their theme a girl who joins the army as a man in the place of her aging father or her brother (Type 514, *The Shift of Sex*, and Type 884, *The Forsaken Fiancée*). There he referred (pp. 443–45) to seven variants of the Plumpkins tale, among which are a text from Thera (1885) in Dawkins, *Modern Greek Folktales*, no. 47b (note, p. 312); from Chios, in Argenti and Rose, 1: 584, no. 56; three anecdotes from Naxos and also a Cretan anecdote. Five more anecdotes may be added to these from Lamia, Epirus, Cephallonia and Crete.

The Turkish tale in Eberhard-Boratav, Type 374, and the Sicilian in Gonzenbach, *Sicilianische Märchen*, 1: 114, no. 17, are similar. The Epirot tale of "The Princess Who Went to War" (Hahn, *Märchen*, 1st ed., p. 114, no. 10, and Pio, *Contes*, 57, no. 19) also present some originality; it has been given the number *884C. Tale No. 69, "The Swallow," in this volume is also a version of this type.

· 52 · *The Vinegrower, the Priest, the Frankish Priest, and the Chotzas*

Type 910F, *The Quarreling Sons and the Bundle of Twigs*. From Cyprus; published in Chadzioannou, *Kypriakoe Mythoe* ("Cypriot tales"), p. 34, no. 3. This tale bears some resemblance to the Aesopic fable "Three Bulls and a Lion" (Aesop: Halm, no. 394). While the three bulls are grazing together, the lion dares not attack them, but after he has cunningly contrived to separate them, he eats them singly, one by one. The fable (Halm, no. 103) demonstrates that there is strength in unity. See also Hausrath, no. 53, Perry, no. 53, "The Children of the Farmer."

·53· *Eggs*

Type 821B, *Chickens from Boiled Eggs*. Athens Folklore Seminar MS 1270; collected, 1960, by undergraduate Anna Papamichael, in Syme, Dodecanese; published in Megas, *Paramythia*, 2d Ser., p. 196, no. 39; translated in Megas, *Griechische Volksmärchen*, no. 59. In this version, however, the lawyer is not the Devil, and the tale more probably belongs to Type 920A, *The Daughter of the King and the Son of the Peasant*, part 2, "The Suit over Eggs" (Motif J1191.2, "Suit for chickens produced from boiled eggs"). See Bolte and Polívka, 2: 368, (note 1), and von der Leyen, *Persische Märchen*, no. 17. There are nine Greek variants: Kretschmer, *Märchen*, no. 35 (Crete); five in manuscript from the Peloponnese, one from Aetolia, one from Cyprus, and one from Crete.

·54· *The King and the Basket Weaver*

Type 921A, *The Four Coins,* combined with Type 922B, *The King's Face on the Coin*. Riddle-tale collected by S. Stathis in Cythera, 1909; published in *Laographia*, 2 (1910): 363. There are seventeen variants with the same plot from different parts of Greece, of which one, from Chios in Asia Minor (1957), has been translated into German in *Begegnung*, no. 23. See also Dégh, *Folktales of Hungary*, no. 17.

·55· *Otto's Astronomer, Watchmaker, and Doctor*

Type 921C*, *Astronomer and Doctor at Farmer's House*. From Arkadia; published in *Laographia*, 6 (1917): 246. Variants in the Athens Folklore Archives are from Epirus, Lemnos, and Crete.

·56· *The Priest's Son and the Sickles*

Published by Chadzioannou, *Kypriakoe Mythoe* ("Cypriot tales"), p. 44, no. 13. A numskull story.

·57· *The Baldchin and the Drakos*

Types 1060 *Squeezing the (Supposed) Stone;* Type 1063B, *Throwing Contest: Trickster Will Throw Stone;* Type 1049, *The Heavy*

Axe. Bolte and Polívka, 1: 149 (B1), 3: 333 (a, b); and von der Leyen, *Märchen,* no. 25.

Athens Folklore Archives MS 174, p. 127; recorded in Telo, the Dodecannese, by Kammas, 1895, and published in Megas, *Paramythia,* 1st Ser., p. 127, no. 1. Translated by Megas in *Griechische Volksmärchen,* no. 65. Variants are found in Hahn, *Märchen* (1st ed.), no. 18; from Tinos in Pio, *Contes,* p. 203 and Hahn, *Märchen* (2d ed.), p. 211; from Epirus in Pio, *Contes,* p. 34 and Hahn, *Märchen* (1st ed.), p. 173; from Syra in Pio, *Contes,* p. 224 and Kretschmer, *Märchen,* no. 33; from Cappadocia in Dawkins, *Modern Greek in Asia Minor,* p. 551; from Epirus in Høeg, *Les Saracatsans,* 2: 45–49, no. 9; and in Rossi and Caracausi, *Testi Neogreci,* pp. 167–73. There are many unpublished variants from the Peloponnese, Aetolia, Euboea, and Smyrna. An American version from the southern Appalachians, North Carolina, is in Dorson, *Buying the Wind,* pp. 168–72, "Jack the Giant Killer."

· *58* · *Eli*

Type 1284, *Person Does Not Know Himself.* Bolte and Polívka, 1: 335 (c), pp. 340–41. Athens Folklore Archives MS 34, pp. 3, 4, collection by N. G. Polites from Cerpini, Kalavryta, Peloponnese. Published by Megas in *Paramythia,* 1st Ser., p. 137, no. 3; translated in Megas, *Griechische Volksmärchen,* no. 66. See also von der Leyen, *Märchen,* no. 147, and Grimm, *Märchen,* no. 34, "Die kluge Else." Variants are in *Laographia,* 4 (1912–14): 491, no. 60, and 13 (1951): 118. See Noy, *Folktales of Israel,* nos. 69, 70.

· *59* · *Loading the Ass*

Type 1242A, *Carrying Part of the Load.* A rider takes the mealsack (or the plow) on his shoulders to relieve the ass of his burden (Motif J1874.1). Published in *Laographia,* 10 (1929): 473, no. 12. There are four variants from the Peloponnese, Doris, and Macedonia. The present text was collected in Chios. The inhabitants of the island of Chios are famous for their droll and witty humor. Droll tales from Chios have been published by Vios in *Laographia,* 4 (1912–14) and 6 (1917–18). The two following tales were also drawn from Vios's collection.

·60· *The Miser of Castro*

Type *1272A, *The Stingy Man's Caps,* in the Greek catalogue. Published in *Laographia,* 4 (1912–13): 479. The miser orders the tailor to make him ten caps instead of one from the same piece of cloth. This anecdote from Chios, the sole example of its kind, is much to the detriment of the inhabitants of Castro, formerly the capital of Chios.

·61· *The Cowardly Chiots*

Type *1298, *The Foolish Fugitives,* in the Greek catalogue. Published in *Laographia,* 4 (1912–13): 480, no. 10.

This Chiot story, lampooning the inhabitants of the village of Vrontado, refers to the time of the Massacre of Chios (1822). Although it appears to belong to recent times, it draws its model from the Philogelo of Gerocleus, which runs as follows: There are two cowardly pedants: one hides in the well, the other in the thicket, so that when the soldiers lower a helmet into the well to draw up water, the one hiding in the well thinks that a soldier is coming down and, through his pleading not to be pressed into service, gets himself taken. When the soldiers tell him that if he had kept quiet, they would have passed him by, the one in the thicket says, "Well, pass *me* by, then, for I kept quiet." This modern Greek tale, like several others that draw their models from antiquity, is obviously an ancient heritage of the Greek people.

·62· *The Chatterbox*

Type 1381, *The Talkative Wife and the Discovered Treasure.*
Transcribed in 1957, from the narrative of a female refugee from Eastern Thrace by undergraduate Domna Sakellari. Athens Folklore Seminar MS 1449, p. 1; published by Megas, *Paramythia,* 2d Ser., no. 44 and translated in Megas, *Griechische Volksmärchen,* no. 70.

See the notes of Moser-Rath, *Predigtmärlein,* no. 118. Of the Greek variants there are seven unpublished, and six published, of which two are translated: one from Crete, in Kretschmer, *Märchen,* no. 30, and the other from Chios, in Pernot, *Études néolelléniques,* 1: 161, and reprinted in Thumb, *Handbuch Neugriechischer Volks-*

sprache, p. 286. An excellent version of this well-known tale is found in Dégh, *Folktales of Hungary,* No. 13.

·63· Ninety-nine Hens and a Rooster

Type 1385, *The Foolish Wife's Pawn,* combined with Type 1540, *The Student from Paradise.* Analysis in Bolte and Polívka, 2: 440 (a, b, c, d). See von der Leyen, *Märchen,* p. 142 and Grimm, *Märchen,* p. 104, "Die klugen Leute."

Athens Folklore Archives MS 264; collected by undergraduate Georgia Jonko in Perichora, Ioannina, 1957; published in Megas, *Paramythia,* 2d Ser., no. 45; translated by Anna Spitzbarth in "Neunundneunzig Hühner und ein Hahn," *Volkshochschule,* 32 (1963), Zürich, Heft 10, p. 314, and Megas, *Griechische Volksmärchen,* no. 71. Greek variants are found in Schmidt, *Griechische Märchen,* p. 125, no. 25 and in the Athens Folklore Archives. A version collected from Pennsylvania Germans entitled "The Great Need" is printed in Dorson, *Buying the Wind,* pp. 132–33.

·64· The Sieve-Maker and the Ass

Type 1430A, *Foolish Plans for the Unborn Child. Air-Castles for the Unborn Colt.* Anecdote from Cyprus, published by Chadzionnou, *Kypriakoe Mythoe* ("Cypriot tales"), p. 56, no. 28. The woman looks forward to putting her child on the ass's back (or the child looks forward to riding it). The husband beats the wife (child), because she would hinder the ass's growth.

There are two variants from western Greece (Akarnania and Arta). For foreign variants, see Bolte and Polívka, 3: 275–76; von der Leyen, *Märchen,* no. 151; and Grimm, *Märchen,* no. 168.

·65· Three Pecheis of Paradise

No. *1540C in the Greek catalogue. This Droll Tale was transcribed in Ioannina, in 1894, from an elderly man's narrative; published in *Laographia,* 1 (1909): 333. In lieu of a fee the Turkish governor gives the Jewish doctor who has cured him a paper awarding him three *pecheis* of space in Paradise. The Jew sells them to three Turks; his excuse is that a Jew would have a hard time of it, insulted and ill-used, among the Mussulmans in Paradise.

There are no other recorded variants.

·66· The Honest Wife

Type 1730, *The Entrapped Suitors*. Recorded in Zante, 1932, told by Maria Karamalike of Lykoudi, aged 70, who was unable to read or write; published in *Laographia*, 11 (1934–37): 508, no. 39. Of the thirty-eight Greek variants fifteen are published. For translations see *Folk-Lore*, 11 (1900): no. 8 (Smyrna); Argenti and Rose, 1: 568, no. 47 (Chios); Hallgarten, *Rhodos,* pp. 28–30, 127–32, 132–34, 219–21 (Rhodes); Nicolaïdès, *Contes licencieux,* p. 174.

·67· What Am I to Say?

Type 1696, *What Should I have Said (Done)?* This droll tale from Patras was published in *Laographia*, 3 (1911): 668.
Variants of this very familiar tale are told by Greeks and other peoples. There are four published and twenty-nine unpublished texts. See *Laographia*, 3 (1911): 499–500; 10 (1929–32): 420; 16 (1956–57): 408; Hahn, *Märchen* (2d ed.), p. 154, no. 111; Hallgarten, *Rhodos,* pp. 148–51. A text brought to Illinois from Ireland is in Dorson, *Buying the Wind,* pp. 343–44. For an historic-geographic study of this tale, "Was hätte ich sagen sollen?" see Martti Haavio, *Kettenmärchen* (Helsinki, 1929).

·68· Almondseed and Almondella

Type 1641, *Doctor Know-All*. Analysis: I, II, III (Bolte and Polívka, 2: 402a, b, c). Athens Folklore Archives MS 53, collected by Panaghiotides in Babourochoria (western Epirus), 1902; published by Megas, *Paramythia,* 1st Ser., p. 134, no. 2.
In *Laographia*, 17 (1957–1958): 124–29, 175, there are recorded thirty-one Greek variants, which are closely compared with Turkish and European parallels. Certain elements of the Greek variants are not found in any of the foreign parallels and may be considered peculiar to the Greek Droll Tale. In addition, there are twenty Greek anecdotes providing further variants. That this Droll Tale is generally of eastern and particularly Indian origin, having already been recorded in India in the first or second century A.D., is shown in Bolte and Polívka, 2: 411.
For variants in this series see Eberhard, *Folktales of China,* no. 11, and Ranke, *Folktales of Germany,* no. 54. Dorson, *Buying the*

Wind, pp. 253–56, prints a Louisiana French version, titled "Roclore."

·69· *The Village of Lies*

Types 1920, *Contest in Lying;* 1920D*, *Climbing to Heaven;* 1960D, *The Great Vegetable;* 1960G, *The Great Tree.* Collected by G. Roussias in Xerochori, Euboea, and printed in *Laographia,* 3 (1911–12): 498.

The participants in a lying contest are usually a miller and a young man or boy. The miller is represented here as typifying slyness and mendacity, and he is usually a baldchin. The youth presents a steady tissue of episodes, which are not found in the contest of lying in the Aarne-Thompson Type Index. The usual content of these tales in Greece is as follows:

The miller (or priest), usually a baldchin, and the youth wager a pie against the fee for grinding the youth's flour (or the price of the grinding against a mule) for the one who will tell the biggest lie. By putting in too much water, the miller puts all the flour into the pie. The miller tells of a large squash (or watermelon), an axe, or a camel-driver with twelve camels, that falls through a slit into the squash (Type 1960D). The youth tells a story about the bee that was lost (Motif X1861), found yoked together with an ox; a walnut tree grows out of the wound at the back of the bee's neck, and a field sown with grain grows on the top of the walnut tree that is reaped with the sickle that was stuck in a wild boar's buttocks; a paper that falls from the boar's wound says:

> Alpha, beta, gamma, eta;
> This the youth who wins the *pitsa!*

A variant tells of the youth's going up to heaven by the stem of the squash, to invite the godfather to his father's christening (Type 1962, *My Father's Baptism*), and his coming down by a thread (which, single, does not suffice, but, double, is more than he needs) and the further wonderful adventures of the liar, like the loss of his head and the foxes' seizing it. This form is in a Byzantine verse-tale, probably twelfth century, printed in *Laographia,* 1 (1909): 567 et seq. and in Type 852, *The Lies.* Here the initial premise varies considerably. Instead of a youth and a miller, there are three brothers who, in spite of their father's order, go to an inn owned by a baldchin or spend the night at the house of a priest-liar and take turns in the contest in lying. The two elder brothers lose their mules or become the slaves of the innkeeper (or priest), but the third and youngest beats him and wins the inn (or the priest's house), as in our tale.

See the transcription of Greek variants (forty-eight in number) in *Laographia,* 17 (1957–58): 132–37, in contrast with the Turkish (Eberhard-Boratav Type 358) and European (Bolte and Polívka, 2: 506–16) parallels. See also Polites, *Laographia,* 2: 197. For translated Greek variants see Georgeakis and Pineau, *Le folk–lore,* p. 140; Dawkins, *Modern Greek in Asia Minor,* p. 535 (Cappadocia); Hahn, *Märchen* (1st ed.), p. 242, no. 39 (Epirus) and p. 313, no. 59 (Euboea); Høeg, *Les Saracatsans,* 2, no. 11 (Epirus). There are also many anecdotes in the Athens Folklore Archives and Athens Folklore Seminar.

Other versions appear in Briggs and Tongue, *Folktales of England,* no. 90, and Noy, *Folktales of Israel,* nos. 24, 44.

·70· *The Man With the Pie*

Type 1626, *Dream Bread.* Collected by D. Loukopoulos in Aetolia and printed in *Laographia,* 12 (1938–48): 597, no. 3. Eight Greek variants are printed in *Laographia,* 17 (1957–58): 137–76. An American version from Maine is in Dorson, *Buying the Wind,* p. 91, "Three Irishmen Have a Dream Contest."

·71· *The Swallow*

The legend of the transformation of the swallow was collected by Vlassios Scordelis in Stenimakos (northern Thrace), published in *Pandora,* 11 (1861): 452–53, and reprinted in Polites, *Paradoseis,* no. 343.

The principle of this legend is reasonable, since the swallow's tail is indeed scissorlike in form, but its composition of fairy tale–like episodes is roughly done. In particular it contains elements of tales of the maiden who goes to war as a man (Types 514 and 884), the plot of which is as follows.

Theodora becomes a soldier in the place of her father or brother and endures tests, usually three, to see if she is a man or a woman. She often has her little dog, an embodiment of her father's blessing, as a companion. She speaks with mocking words. The king's son, who is the object of this mockery, comes to her home selling spindles, recognizes her from her broken (or gold) tooth, and abducts her by magical means while she sleeps. She wakes to hear the prince's roosters. Because of her suffering, she is struck dumb, and the prince abandons her to marry another. At the wedding, the bride cannot be quiet, "Mute girl, your hand is burning!" The mute girl finally speaks and the prince marries his first love.

This narrative appears in *Laographia*, 20 (1962): 440–42, where Megas recorded the Greek variants (sixteen in number). See especially Hahn, *Märchen* (1st ed.), p. 114, no. 10; Pio, *Contes*, p. 57, no. 19 (Epirus); Dawkins, *Modern Greek Folktales*, no. 47a (Thrace); Hahn, *Märchen* (2d ed.), p. 124, no. 101 (Poros, Peloponnese); *Laographia*, 20 (1962): 385, 438–40, no. 11. For Bulgarian and Romanian texts, see Polites, *Paradoseis*, pp. 938–40, no. 343. A related story in this volume is no. 51, "Princess Plumpkins."

·72· *Phlandro*

Collected by A. Papadiamantis in Sciathos and published in *Techne* (1899), p. 132; reprinted in Polites, *Parodoseis*, no. 277.

The theme of this legend was provided by the shape of a rock on the island of Sciathos, in which the ready imagination of the people discerned a human form. An ancient model is found in the myth of Niobe. This etiological legend gives an explanation of why the sea is rough.

·73· *The Searing Breath of the Katevatos*

Collected by G. Kremos in Arachova, Parnassus, and published in *Nea Hellas*, no. 35 (October 26, 1874); reprinted in Polites, *Paradoseis*, no. 264, and in Schmidt, *Griechische Märchen*, p. 144, no. 13.

The *Katevatos* (from the ancient Greek *Kataibatis*) is a wild wind that blows down from Parnassus, to which a personality has been ascribed by the local inhabitants much in the same way as such winds were made persons by the ancients, who thought of them as Titans or giants. The people imagine that the tempest is the wrestling of the winds. They interpret wind changes as the victory of whichever wind is blowing.

·74· *The Lake Spirits of Peristera and Xerovouni*

Told by Dinos Sarantis, head drover of Perivoli ton Grevenon (West Macedonia); collected by Polites in 1898 and published in *Paradoseis*, no. 501, pp. 270–81.

"This most beautiful legend," says Polites, "teaches us that new legends are made every day and wedded with mythical elements, remnants of ancient mythology that have been treasured by the Greek people. The imaginary world of mythical creatures is so closely united with the real, that its limits are hard to define, and a man who has up to now lived in close cohabitation with his fellow men may quite conceivably overstep the boundaries and change into a supernatural being. The young shepherd, whose help is sought by the spirit, himself becomes a spirit and, seizing the maiden he loves, bestows on her the same unearthly spirituality as his own (*Paradoseis*, p. 1123).

It is thought that each lake, just as each mountain, has its own spirit who often wrestles with the spirit of the neighboring lake. The lakes are also thought to be related by nature to the spirits that personify the winds, the battle between which, as in the preceding legend, is represented by a storm. That spirit wins which takes on a man as its ally. This idea seems to be an echo of the ancient myth of the Battle of the Gods and Giants, in which the gods win with the mortal Heracles as their ally (see Polites, *Paradoseis*, p. 1122, no. 497).

According to our legend, by tasting the spirit's heart the shepherd of Mount Peristera is endowed with tremendous strength and, upon throwing himself into the lake, becomes a spirit of great might. The belief that a man may become a hero by partaking of a food which bestows divine strength underlies many ancient myths, according to Polites (*Paradoseis*, pp. 1129 ff.). An example is the myth of Glaucus, the fisherman: it was he who ate the imperishable grass, or, in one variant of the myth, drank of the immortal spring, and became a god. Later he threw himself into the sea and became a sea divinity. This myth emanates from a very old and widely held superstition that the attributes of any body, before it becomes food, are passed on to whoever partakes of it, for it is imagined that in the tasting, the spirit that has dwelt in the food is also absorbed. Thus Achilles was fed on the entrails of the lion and the wild boar and the marrow of the bear, and in this way acquired their strength and vigor (Polites, *Paradoseis*, p. 1133, and see p. 1052 for Greek superstitions regarding spirits in general).

·75· *New Airs*

Collected by I. Kondylakis in Crete and published in *Hebdomas* (1887), no. 27, p. 5; reprinted in Polites, *Paradoseis*, no. 552.

This story belongs to the Modern Greek tales of the *gorgonas*, or spirits of the sea, and connects the *gorgona* with Alexander the Great as his sister. The *gorgonas* are the sea divinities of antiquity perpetuated by the Greek people, who imagine them, as the ancient Greeks imagined the Tritons, as having a fish's tail instead of legs. This tradition was dealt with by Polites in a special study (*Parnassos*, 2 [1878]: 259–75, in *Laographia*, 3 [1911]: 172–80, and in *Paradoseis*, pp. 1165 ff.). According to Polites, a fusion is observable in the legends of the *gorgonas* with the ancient myths of the Medusa and of the Syrens, as well as that of Scylla. As with the ancient Syrens, whose prime characteristic was their singing, so the *gorgona* of modern Greek legend is presented as playing the lyre and singing sweet songs whereby the sailors learn new airs.

The immortal water corresponds to ambrosia, and the two mountains that beat unceasingly one against the other are the Planctae Petrae, the rocks near Scylla and Charybdis, through which, according to the Homeric epics (Odyssey 62), not even a bird might pass. Beyond the Planctae were the streams of Oceanus and the ambrosial lilies whence the doves brought ambrosia to Zeus, but each time a dove would be crushed between the rocks as they shut together. In some variants, the mountains, as they closed, cut off the tail of Bucephalus, famed among the people as Alexander's horse.

·76· *The Nereids' Cave*

Collected by Chourmouzis in the Province of Pedias in the department of Herakleion, Crete, about 1825, and printed by him in *Kretika*, pp. 69–70. Reprinted in Polites, *Paradoseis*, no. 775, and in Schmidt, *Das Volksleben der Neugriechen*, pp. 115–17.

"Christianity," says Martin Nilsson, "easily swept away the great gods, but the minor daemons of popular belief offered a stubborn resistance. They were nearer the living rock. The Greek peasant of today still believes in the nymphs, though he gives them all the old name of the sea nymphs, *Neraïds*. They haunt the same places, they have the same appearance and the same occupations, and the same tales are told of them" (Nilsson, *Greek Popular Religion*, pp 16–17). Indeed, this tale, told by an old Cretan peasant at the beginning of the twentieth century, presents an amazing similarity to the myths of Peleus and Thetis (*Apollodorus*, 3: 13, 5). As Schmidt observes, in the Troilus of Sophocles the marriage of Peleus with Thetis is called a "wordless marriage": according to Schmidt, this allusion may be explained only if we admit that the myth, which was followed by the poet, refers to Thetis' keeping silent at her wedding to Peleus, like the Nereid's silence in this Cretan legend.

In other modern Greek myths, brave men succeed in seizing the Nereid's vest while she bathes in the waters of the lake or river, and so oblige her to follow them and become their wife. But, as Thetis did, every Nereid soon leaves her husband's house and goes back to the natural element where she belongs. (See Hahn, *Märchen*, no. 83; no. 34; and Schmidt, *Sagen*, no. 5.)

·77· *Kaemene Island*

This tale from Kardamyla, Chios, was published in Polites, *Paradoseis*, no. 930. The beliefs of Greeks of more recent times regarding the dead and Hades are of extraneous descent, from Christian and pagan tenets and traditions. According to popular belief, man continues into the other, lower world, to live another life, except that he severs all contact with the world, which he entirely forgets, once he has drunk of the spring of forgetfulness in Hades.

Martin Nilsson, the renowned expert on ancient Greek religions, tells us that the present-day Greek version of Hades is the subterranean world of Homer, without life or consolation, even though Christian teaching on Paradise and Hell is widespread. It is surprising how deeply the Homeric world of the dead impressed itself on the mind of the people, to the point that neither mythology nor Christianity was able to uproot it (Chantepie de la Saussaye, *Lehrbuch der Religionsgeschichte,* 2: 417; see also Nilsson, *Greek Popular Religion,* p. 115). According to Christian belief, the souls of the dead go either to Paradise or to Hell. The Chiote religion, however, considers that there may be hell on earth, in wildernesses or on mountains, where the souls of sinners, in the forms of various animals, endure their punishment.

Glossary

arapis From the Ancient Greek *Araps,* an Arab; any man of dark complexion, a Negro, in popular acceptance hailing from the African shores of the Mediterranean; in folktales a huge blackamoor, sometimes an evil demon.

Bashi-Bazouk A soldier, member of an irregular, ill-disciplined auxiliary of the Ottoman Empire (from Turkish).

bobota Bread or cake made of Indian corn (Modern Greek).

bougatsa A flaky pastry which may be filled with cheese, custard, etc. (Modern Greek). Known in Byzantine times as *fokatsia.*

bourikia Dialectical modern Greek, exact meaning unknown, probably of Turkish origin signifying a small cone shaped pan used for making coffee.

caîque Light skiff used on the Bosporus. Influenced by French *caïque* from the Turkish *kayik.*

cantari, kantari (pl. *cantaria, kantaria*) A measure of weight, the equivalent of one quintal or hundredwight (Modern Greek).

Charos Death personified (Modern Greek), from *Charon,* the ferryman of the ancient Greek Styx.

chotzas Muslim priest (Turkish).

doma The flat roof of a peasant's dwelling (Modern Greek).

drakos (pl. *drakoe*) An ogre of immense size and strength in human form, who lives in mountains in bands of forty brothers (Modern Greek).

drakaena (pl. *drakaenas*) An ogress, the feminine of *drakos,* who robs men and abducts maidens.

gelati From the Turkish *cellâd,* a headsman or executioner. A term used during the Turkish occupation of Greece, but not in contemporary Modern Greek.

giaour Turkish *gâvur* from the Persian *gawr* or *gabr*. One outside the Muslim faith. An infidel or unbeliever.

Giousel Dougnia Turkish for Maiden of the World, a homonym for the Modern Greek *Omorphe tou Kosmou,* meaning Beauty of the World.

ghello (*yello*) Witch in Modern Greek. In Ancient Greek, a kind of vampire or goblin, supposed to carry off young children. See Dem. B. Oeconomides, "Yello dans les traditions des peuples helléniques et roumains," *IV International Congress for Folk-Narrative Research* (Athens, 1965), pp. 328–34.

gorgona In Modern Greek a mermaid, or sea demon, representations of which are traditionally used, in Greece and elsewhere, as a ship's figure-head. Probably a development of the ancient Greek mythological figure of the Gorgon, whom Hesiod describes as descended from the sea god Phorcys. Hideously ugly in its first representations, the Gorgon is in later classical art shown to be coldly beautiful. Both ancient Greek and modern Greek figures are characterized by their power of striking with death whoever approaches them. Further, the Gorgon's head (severed by Perseus in ancient Greek mythology) was held to be a protection against the evil eye, which may explain the use of the modern Greek Gorgona as a ship's figure-head.

kantela Church lamp, usually placed before ikons (Modern Greek).

karagghiozi-faced lamb A black-faced white lamb. Karandjiozis is the chief figure in the traditional Greek shadow theater, therefore he may be associated with black or dark phenomena.

katevatos North Wind, literally "the descender" (Modern Greek). Compare the term "catebatic" used to describe types of wind in meteorology.

kollyva Portions of boiled wheat and dried fruit offered to the mourners at memorial services (Modern Greek); small cakes (Ancient Greek).

lamia A flesh-eating ogress with a predilection for children, figuring in modern Greek superstition as well as in ancient

Greek mythology, where she was said to be the daughter of Poseidon, a queen from whom the town of Lamia took its name, or a woman of Libya whose children were slain by Hera for having been fathered by Zeus and who, in revenge, set herself to kill any children who came her way. The name is said to come from Greek *lamos, laimos,* and to refer to her habit of catching her victim by the *throat.*

lepton A unit of value in Modern Greek equal to ¹⁄₁₀₀ of a drachma. A coin of that value.

Liakoura Popular local name for Mount Parnassus (Modern Greek).

Moerae Personification of the Fates in Modern Greek. From Ancient Greek *Moera,* the Goddess of Fate.

Neraîda (pl. *Neraîdes*) A water nymph or water fairy (Modern Greek). The *Nereids* of ancient Greece.

oka (*okades*) In Modern Greece and Turkey, a unit of weight varying around 2.8 pounds.

Omorphe tou Kosmou The Beauty of the World in Modern Greek, sometimes translated as Beauty of the Country. Compare the Turkish *Giousel Dougnia.*

pata-kioutou! Turkish *patkut:* the noise of repeated blows; something like "bam-wham!" "slap bang!" in Modern Greek.

pechys (pl. *pecheis*) Unit of measure in Modern Greek, equivalent to one ell (45 inches), an obsolete English measure.

stiphadha A dish of rabbit stewed with onions (Modern Greek). Compare Spanish *estufada,* and French *à l'étuve,* referring to a method of cooking in steam.

stoecheio (pl. *stoecheia*) In both Ancient and Modern Greek an element, thus, a being which stems from some great force of nature; a spirit.

tagari A peasant's woolen bag carried over the shoulder (Modern Greek). It is related to the Ancient Greek *tage,* rations, thus, a bag intended to hold the food and drink consumed by a peasant during the working day.

thirtyleaves and roses. A poetic expression composed of Modern Greek, *triantaphylla,* literally "thirtyleaves," and Ancient Greek, *rhoda,* roses.

tsarouchi (pl. *tsarouchia*) Clog-like shoe of hardened leather, traditional peasant footwear (Modern Greek). From the Turkish, *çarik,* sandal of raw hide.

Tyche Chance, Fortune, Providence, here used in the personified sense (Modern Greek).

Zwanziger In German, literally a piece of twenty. The spelling is transliterated in Modern Greek as *zvanzika.* An Austrian coin in circulation under the Kapodistrian government in Greece (1827–31), with a value of 20 groschen.

Bibliography

WORKS IN GREEK.

AMARIOTOU, MARIA. *Histories tes Manoulas mou* ("My mother's tales"). Athens, 1948.

Archeion Pontou (Pontine Archives). 1–34 (1929–64), Athens.

Archeion tou Thrakikou Laographikou kai Glosse Thesaurou ("Archives of the Thracian Treasure of Folklore and Language"). 1–25 (1934–63), Athens.

Athens. Serial of newspaper *Athine*. Athens, vol. 1, 1908, vol 2, 1909.

CHADZIOANNOU, KYRIAKOS C. *Kypriakoe Mythoe* ("Cypriot tales"). Nicosa, 1948.

CHOURMOUZIS, MICHAEL K. *Kretika*. Athens, 1842.

Deltion Historikis Ethnologikis Hetaerias ("Bulletin of the Historical Ethnological Society"). Athens, 1893–1956.

Hebdomas. Athens. 1884–92.

KORAES, ADAMANTIOS. *Mython Aesopeion Synagoge*. Paris, 1810.

Kypriaka Chronika (Cypriot chronicles). Larnaca, 1923–37.

Kypriake Spoudae ("Cypriot studies"). Publication of the Society of Cypriot Studies, Nicosia.

KYRIAZES, N. G. *Cypriot Proverbs*. Larnaca, 1940.

Laographia. Deltion tes Hellenikes Laographikes Hetaerias ("Folklore. Bulletin of the Greek Folklore Society"). Athens, 1909.

LIOUDAKI, MARIA. *Stou Pappou ta Gonata* ("At grandpa's knee"). Athens, 1941.

LOUKATOS, DEMETRIOS S. *Neohellenika Laographika Keimena* ("Modern Greek folklore topics"). Athens, 1957.

Makedonicon Hemerologion. Annual of the Makedonen, vol. 1. Athens, 1908.

MEGAS, GEORGIOS A. *Hellenika Paramythia* ("Greek folktales"). First Series, 3d ed. Athens, 1962.

———. *Hellenika Paramythia* ("Greek folktales"). Second Series. Athens, 1963.

MICHAELIDES-NOUAROS, MICHAEL G. *Laographika Symmeikta Karpathou* ("Carpathian folklore miscellany"). Vol. 1, Athens, 1932.

Nea Hellas. Athens, 1894–96.

Neohellenika Analecta ("Modern Greek selections"). Publication of The Parnassos Society. Athens, 1870–74.

O en Konstantinoupoli Hellenikos Philologikos Syllogos ("The Greek Philological Society in Constantinople"). Constantinople, 1875—.

Pandora. Athens, 1851–72.

Parnassos. Publication of the Parnassos Society. Athens, 1870–74.

PERDIKA, NIKI. *Skyros.* Athens, 1943.

POLITES, NIKOLAOS G. *Laographia Symmeikta* ("Folklore miscellany"). Vols. 1–3. Athens. 1920, 1921, 1931.

———. *Paradoseis* ("Traditions"). Vols. 1–2 (1904), Athens.

———. *Paroemiae* ("Proverbs"). Vols. 1–4 (1901–04), Athens.

———. Unpublished collection in Athens Folklore Archives.

STAMOULI-SARANTI, ELPINIKE. *Apo ten Anatolike Thrake* ("From eastern Thrace). Athens, 1958.

TARSOULI, GEORGIA. *Mia Phora Ki'enan Kaero* ("Once upon a time"). Athens, 1925.

Thrakika. Athens, 1928–53.

Zographios Agon. Publications of the Constantinople Greek Literary Society. Vol. 1, 1891; vol. 2, 1896.

MANUSCRIPT COLLECTIONS IN GREEK.

Folklore Archives, Academy of Athens.

Folklore Seminar, University of Athens (Professor Georgios A. Megas).

WORKS IN OTHER LANGUAGES.

AARNE, ANTTI. *Estnische Märchen- und Sagenvarianten.* Folklore Fellows Communications, no. 25. Hamina, 1918–19.

———. *Der reiche Mann und sein Schwiergersohn.* Folklore Fellows Communications No. 23. Helsinki, 1916.

Apollodorus: The Library. With an English translation by Sir James G. Frazer. 2 vols., London, New York, 1921.

ARGENTI, PHILIP PANDELY, and ROSE, H. J. *The Folklore of Chios*. 2 vols., Cambridge, England, 1949.

BOLTE, JOHANNES, and POLÍVKA, GEORG. *Anmerkungen zu den Kinder- und Hausmärchen der Brüder Grimm*. 5 vols. Leipzig, 1913–1931.

BOULANGER, JACQUES. *Les contes de ma cuisinière*. 2nd ed., Paris, 1935.

BRIGGS, KATHARINE M., and TONGUE, RUTH L. *Folktales of England*. Folktales of the World. Chicago, 1965.

BRUNNER-TRAUT, EMMA. *Altägyptische Märchen*. Düsseldorf, 1963.

CARNOY, EMILY HENRY, and NICOLAÏDÈS, JEAN. *Traditions populaires de l'Asie Mineure*. Paris, 1889.

CHAMBRY, ÉMILE. *Aesopus. Fables*. Paris, 1927.

CHANTEPIE DE LA SAUSSAYE, PIERRE DANIEL. *Lehrbuch der Religionsgeschichte*. 2 vols. Tübingen, 1925.

CHAUVIN, VICTOR CHARLES. *Bibliographie des ouvrages arabes ou relatifs aux Arabes oubliés dans l'Europe chrétienne de 1810 à 1885*. Liège, 1892.

CHRISTIANSEN, REIDAR TH. *Folktales of Norway*. Folktales of the World. Chicago, 1964.

COSQUIN, EMMANUEL GEORGES. *Les contes indiens et l'Occident*. Paris, 1922.

CRUSIUS, OTTO. ed. *Babrii Fabulae Aesopeae*. Leipzig, 1897.

DAWKINS, RICHARD MCGILLIVRAY. *Forty-five Stories from the Dodecanese*. Cambridge, England, 1950.

———. *Modern Greek in Asia Minor*. Cambridge, England, 1916.

———. *Modern Greek Folktales*. Oxford, 1953.

———. *More Greek Folktales*. Oxford, 1955.

DÉGH, LINDA. *Folktales of Hungary*. Folktales of the World. Chicago, 1965.

DIETERICH, KARL. *Sprache und Volksüberlieferung der südlichen Sporaden*. Wien, 1908.

DIEHL, ERNST. *Supplementum Lyricum, neue Bruchstücke von Archilochus, etc*. Bonn, 1917.

DIRR, ADOLF. *Kaukasische Märchen*. Jena, 1920.

DORSON, RICHARD M. *American Negro Folktales.* New York, 1967.

———. *Buying the Wind.* Chicago, 1964.

EBERHARD, WOLFRAM. *Folktales of China.* Folktales of the World. Chicago, 1967.

———, and BORATAV, PERTEV-NAILI. *Typen Turkisher Volksmärchen.* Wiesbaden, 1953.

Folk-lore. London, 1890—

GARNETT, LUCY MARY JANE. *The Women of Turkey and their Folk-lore.* London, 1890–91.

GELDART, EDMUND MARTIN, tr. *The Folk-lore of Modern Greece.* London, 1884.

GEORGEAKIS, G., and PINEAU, LÉON. *Le Folk-lore de Lesbos.* Paris, 1894.

GIESE, FRIEDRICH. *Türkische Märchen.* Jena, 1925.

GONZENBACH, LAURA. *Sicilianische Märchen.* Leipzig, 1870.

GRIMM, JAKOB and WILHELM. *Die Kinder- und Hausmärchen der Brüder Grimm.* Wiesbaden, 1933.

GRIMM, JAKOB. *Reinhart Fuchs.* Berlin, 1834.

HAAVIO, MARTTI. *Kettenmärchen.* Folklore Fellows Communications, no. 88. Helsinki, 1929.

HAHN, JOHANN GEORG VON. *Griechische und Albanische Märchen.* Leipzig, 1864. New ed., Munich, 1918.

HALLGARTEN, PAUL. *Rhodos.* Frankfurt am Main, 1928.

HALM, CARL FELIX. *Fabulae Aesopi collectae e recognitione C. Halmii.* Lipsiae, 1852.

HAUSRATH, AUGUSTUS. *Corpus fabularum Aesopicarum.* Leipzig, 1946.

HERTEL, JOHANNES. *Indische Märchen.* Jena. 1919.

HØEG, CARSTEN. *Les Saracatsans: une tribu nomade grecque.* 2 vols. Paris, 1916. New ed., Copenhagen, 1925–26.

Humaniora: Essays in Literature, Folklore, Honoring Archer Taylor, ed. Wayland D. Hand and Gustave O. Arlt. New York, 1960.

JOHANNES DE CAPUA. *Directorium Humane Vite Alias Parabole Antiquoru Sapientu.* Berlin, 1960.

KLAAR, MARIANNE. *Klephtenkrieg, neugriechische Volkslieder.* Athens, 1938.

KOUTRAS. *Ninety Mourabades or Stupidities and Clevernesses of the Old.* Athens, 1899.

KRETSCHMER, PAUL. *Der heutige lesbische Dialekt.* Vienna, 1905.

———. *Neugriechische Märchen.* Jena, 1919.

KRUMBACHER, KARL. *Die Moskauer Sammlung mittelgriechischer Sprichwörter.* Münich, 1900.

LEGRAND, LOUIS JEAN. *Recueil de contes populaires grecs.* Paris, 1881.

VON DER LEYEN, FRIEDRICH. *Das deutsche Märchen und die Brüder Grimm.* Düsseldorf, 1964.

———. *Persische Märchen.* Düsseldorf and Cologne, 1958.

———. *Die Welt der Märchen,* 2 vols. Düsseldorf and Cologne, 1953–54.

LIUNGMAN, WALDEMAR. *Die schwedischen Volksmärchen, Herkunft und Geschichte.* Berlin, 1961.

LO NIGRO, SEBASTIANO. *Racconti populari Siciliani.* Florence, 1958.

MARX, AUGUST. *Griechische Märchen.* Stuttgart, 1889.

MASSIGNON, GENEVIÈVE. *Folktales of France.* Folktales of the World. Chicago, 1968.

MEGAS, GEORGIOS A. *Begegnung der Völker im Märchen.* Vol. 3, *Griechenland-Deutschland.* Gesellschaft zur Pflege des Märchengutes der europäischen Völker. Collected and edited by Georgios A. Megas. Aschendorff-Münster, 1968.

———. *Der Bartlose in neugriechischen Märchen.* Folklore Fellows Communications, no. 157. Helsinki, 1955.

———. ed. *Festschrift für Friedrich von der Leyen.* Munich, 1963.

———. *Griechische Volksmärchen.* Tr. Inez Diller. Düsseldorf and Cologne, 1965.

Mélanges offerts à Octave et Melpo Merlier à l'occasion du 25e anniversaire de leur arrivée en Grèce. Athens, 1956–57.

MILIOPOULOS, PARASKEWAS, and VONDERLAGE, BERNARD. *Mazedonische Bauernstuben: Mazedonische Legenden, Fabeln und Märchen.* Hamburg, 1955.

MITSOTAKIS, JOHANNES. *Ausgewählte griechische Volksmärchen.* Berlin, 1882.

MORASI, G. *Studi sui dialetti greci della Terra d'Otranti.* Leece, 1870.

MOSER-RATH, ELFRIEDE. *Predigtmärlein der Barockzeit.* Berlin, 1964.

NICOLAÏDÈS, JEAN. *Contes licencieux de Constantinople et de l'Asie Mineure.* Paris, 1906.

NILSSON, MARTIN. *Greek Popular Religion.* New York, 1940. Reissued as *Greek Folk Religion.* New York, 1961.

NOY, DOV. *Folktales of Israel.* Folktales of the World. Chicago, 1963.

PERNOT, HUBERT OCTAVE. *Études de linguistique néohellénique. Vol. 1, Phonétique des parlers de Chio.* Paris, 1907.

PERRY, BEN EDWIN. *Aesopica.* Vol. 1, *Greek and Latin Texts.* Urbana, Illinois, 1952.

PINO-SAAVEDRA, YOLANDO. *Folktales of Chile.* Folktales of the World. Chicago, 1967.

PIO, JEAN. *Contes populaires grecs.* Copenhagen, 1879.

RANKE, KURT. *Folktales of Germany.* Folktales of the World. Chicago, 1966.

———. *Die Zwei Brüder.* Folklore Fellows Communications, no. 114. Helsinki, 1934.

ROBERTS, WARREN E. *The Tale of the Kind and Unkind Girls and Related Tales. Aarne-Thompson Type 480.* Berlin, 1958.

Le Roman de Libestros et Rhodamné. Amsterdam, 1935.

ROSCHER, WILHELM HEINRICH. *Neue Omphalosstudien.* Leipzig, 1915.

———. *Omphalos.* Leipzig, 1913.

———. *Der Omphalosgedanke bei verschiedenen Völkern.* Leipzig, 1918.

ROSSI, GIUSEPPE TAIBBI, and CARACAUSI, GIROLAMO. *Testi neogreci de Calabria.* Palermo, 1959.

ROUSSEL, LOUIS. *Contes de Mycono.* Léopold, 1929.

SCHMIDT, BERNHARD. *Griechische Märchen, Sagen und Volkslieder.* Leipzig, 1877.

———. *Das Volksleben der Neugriechen.* Leipzig, 1871.

SEKI, KEIGO. *Folktales of Japan.* Folktales of the World. Chicago, 1963.

BIBLIOGRAPHY 263

STEINHÖWEL, HEINRICH. *Aesop*. ed. Hermann Oesterley. Tübingen, 1873.

SWAHN, JAN ÖJVIND. *The Tale of Cupid and Psyche*. Lund, 1955.

THUMB, ALBERT. *Handbuch der neugriechischen Volkssprache*. Strassburg, 1910.

Von Prinzen, Trollen und Herrn Fro. Gesellschaft zur Pflege des Märchengutes der europäischen Völker. Rheine im Westfalen, 1960–61.

WAGNER, WILHELM. *Carmina Graeca Medii Aevi*. Leipzig, 1873.

WESSELSKI, ALBERT. *Märchen des Mittelalters*. Berlin. 1925.

WOSSIDLO, RICHARD, and HENSSEN, GOTTFRIED. *Mecklenburger erzählen*. Berlin, 1957.

Index of Motifs

(Motif numbers are from Stith Thompson, *Motif-Index of Folk-Literature*
[6 vols.; Copenhagen and Bloomington, Ind., 1955–58].)

B. ANIMALS

D. MAGIC

E. THE DEAD

F. MARVELS

H. TESTS

J. The Wise and the Foolish

Index of Tale Types

(Type numbers are from Antti Aarne and Stith Thompson, *The Types of the Folktale* [Helsinki, 1961]. Those numbers preceded by asterisks are unique Greek types catalogued by Georgios A. Megas.)

I ANIMALS TALES (1–299)

II ORDINARY FOLKTALES

A. Tales of Magic (300–749)

IV CUMULATIVE TALES

General Index

Trickery (*continued*)
elder brothers, 33; of serving maid against princess, 72; of skylark against vixen, 5; of rooster against fox, 8; of vixen against pigeon, 4; of vixen against rooster, 4; man loses boots and horse to thief, 183; man takes clothing for woman's dead son, 182; peddlar takes all goods from woman, 182

Truth: experiencing bad times, 133; refuses life of falsehood, 134

Turk. *See* Emir

Turtle: cleans fisherman's house, 74–75; turns into maiden, 75

Turtle shell: broken to keep maiden, 75

Twain, Mark (American author), xxxi

Twelve months. *See* Months

Twin brother: advised by old woman, 38; discovers brother's whereabouts, 41; marries Beauty of the World, 42; marries princess, 40; mistaken for brother, 41; performs tasks to win princess, 38–40; recognizes stone as brother, 41; rescues brother, 41; rescues princess, 40; transformed into marble, 41

Twins: born because of golden fish, 37. *See also* Brother

Veil: best embroidered will determine king's wife, 75

Vinegrower: beats churchman picking his grapes, 165–66

Virgil, xxix

Vixen: outsmarted by cub, 9; pretends distant fire warms her, 8; pretends to hear confessions, 4–5; pretends to join nunnery, 4; tricked by skylark, 5

Vonderlage, Bernard (German scholar), 211, 224, 231, 233, 235

von der Leyen, Friedrich (German folklorist), xliv, liii, 207, 208, 212, 214, 221, 222, 223, 224, 226, 227, 228, 229, 231, 233, 235, 239, 240, 242, 243, 245

von Sydow, Carl Wilhelm (Swedish folklorist), lii

von Wilamowitz-Möllendorff, Ulrich (German folklorist), xlviii–xlix

Wagner, Wilhelm, 212

Walnut. *See* Magic nuts

Wand. *See* Magic wand

Watches: taken by prince as remembrance, 31

Water: life-giving, 201; restores life, 72

Wedding feast: lasts forty days, 99; lasts forty days and nights, 46, 70; for prince and frog princess, 54

Well: entrance to sleeping kingdom, 71; trap for king's godchild, 85; trap for prince, 33

Wesselski, Albert (Polish folklorist), 213, 236

Weston, Jesse (English literary scholar), xx

Widow: feeds children with dough from her unwashed hands, 123; finds no fault with twelve months, 124–25; given magic jar by twelve months, 125; has five children, 123; visits twelve months, 124–25

Wife: assures husband of his identity, 177; bears child of sun, 60; chosen for king from best embroidered veil, 75; encourages husband to become a